BEST IN CLASS

A Novel

George W. Hess

D1714788

iUniverse, Inc.

New York Bloomington Shanghai

Best In Class

iUniverse books may be ordered through booksellers or by contacting:

iUniverse
1663 Liberty Drive
Bloomington, IN 47403
www.iuniverse.com
1-800-Authors (1-800-288-4677)

Because of the dynamic nature of the Internet, any Web addresses
or links contained in this book may have changed
since publication and may no longer be valid.

This is a work of fiction. All of the characters, names, incidents, organizations, and
dialogue in this novel are either the products of the author's imagination or are used
fictitiously.

Cover Design
by Jean Sault Birdsall,
co-creator with her husband, Bob Birdsall, of
Seasons of the Pines and *People of the Pines*

ISBN: 978-0-595-45756-4 (pbk)
ISBN: 978-0-595-90058-9 (ebk)

Printed in the United States of America

For Madeline Eve Moskal, my Magpie, my newest pride and joy.

For Mary Berndt Hess, the answer to my son's prayers.

And for

Pop Riordan,
Barb Riordan,
Mary Bodkin,
Bob Fletcher,
and Nice Guy Tom Ossman,

friends whose voices, wit, and wisdom still dance in my sorrowed mind.

"Man's destructive hand spares nothing that lives; he kills to feed himself, he kills to clothe himself, he kills to adorn himself, he kills to attack, he kills to defend himself, he kills to instruct himself, he kills to amuse himself, he kills for the sake of killing."

~ *Joseph de Maistre*

Acknowledgements

My Thanks

To Dennis O'Connell, author of *Black Vortex*: Thanks for being a fabulous story editor and a constant source of encouragement.

To Ken O'Brien, my very own personal technical encyclopedia.

To Pete Lowney, whose amazing memory of all things New York was a great help.

To Pistol-Packing Paul Moskal for his teaching me about the interesting world of firearms.

To Stan and Lynne Lewicki for their insight on Charm City—Baltimore, Maryland.

To my editors, Mary Alexion and my wife Florence Hess: Ladies, your patience is an angelic gift.

To the iUniverse Publishing team who made the book come alive.

And to all of my friends whose own lives helped me create my characters, without whom there is no story. Especially those who purchased and applauded my first work, *Class Reunion*.

And, as always, a thank you to the original Nana Flo Riordan and my mother Grandma Kay Hess for being such shining examples of grandparenthood.

And, finally, to Mr. Fowler, who told it like it still is:

"Writing is easy. All you do is sit staring at a blank sheet of paper until the drops of blood form on your forehead."

~ Gene Fowler

Prologue

The driver of the new, deep red Chevy Trailblazer had no clue as to how many locals or vacationers, in a single day, passed the little, green-and-tan sign that announced that this particular Florida locale was "A Little Bit of Heaven on 707." He guessed that most who passed it would easily miss the placard that boasted so highly of the small town of Rio, just outside of Jensen Beach. He was pretty sure that even those who noticed it would scoff at the hyperbolic claim. The buildings were old, the view unspectacular, and five-star gourmet dining was not happening in this part of heaven. But, for this motorist, the winding road led straight to paradise—a paradise once found and lost, hopefully to be found again. He drove with a calm that would soon be shattered by fear.

PART I

▼

THESE GUYS

"It takes a certain courage and a certain greatness to be truly base."

~ Jean Anouilh

CHAPTER 1

▼

TUESDAY, MAY 31, 2005

"Have a good day, honey. I'll see you tonight. We'll have the leftover filet and some of those fried potatoes that aren't any good for you. Love ya." As his wife of thirteen years, Regan, leaned in to kiss him goodbye, she whispered, "And a late dessert served á la carte and au naturel." Regan's "honey" left with a smile on his face and a vision of her soft, thirty-five-year-old body, with its still-shapely curves, stirring in his mind. Maybe she would do that thing with her long, strawberry blond hair tonight—that thing that stirred much more than his mind. He hoped that was the dessert his Regan had in mind.

It was the Tuesday after the Memorial Day holiday, and, as usual, Lieutenant Jeremiah Edmund Davies reported to work early. Work for the lieutenant meant the Hollywood Community Police Station of the Los Angeles Police Department's West Bureau. The weather was much like the previous day's with early temperatures in the low sixties, expected to reach into the seventies, with clear skies and not a drop of rain in the forecast.

The day before, his wife had held her annual, family Memorial Day barbecue. It was past midnight by the time the last of the "outlaws" had left his home and he had cleaned up the usual aftermath. Thirty minutes later, after his wife had finished romantically rewarding him for all his hard work, Jed finally got to sleep. Luckily their two kids, eleven and eight, had one more day off before the school bell would ring.

Using his initials, Lieutenant Davies had adopted the nickname Jed. He never cared much for his given name, Jeremiah. It might have worked fine for his grandfather, but Jed was happy to shed the name, which ranked somewhere in the 300s on the "most popular names" list for boys.

He was dog-tired from the previous day's and night's chores and pleasures. Catering to his bride's family and her late-night, amorous itch were efforts he enjoyed, but they had left him dragging. As he settled into his chair of four years, now molded to his slender, six-foot frame, all Jed was hoping for was a quiet day. He could easily live with an early quit and a long, afternoon nap in front of his new 50-inch Mitsubishi TV. It was a gift his well-to-do in-laws had so generously given his family last Christmas.

He arrived at work a few minutes after 6:00 AM dressed in one of his five suits bought from JC Penny at the Glendale Galleria—today's choice being a dark gray, complemented by a light blue tie that matched his eyes. Jed was halfway through his first cup of coffee when the phone rang. It was a patrol officer, a friend of Jed's from the station.

Jed would not get to finish his coffee, and his hands would not be caressing the Mitsubishi's remote anytime soon. His early-morning, front-door smile and hopes for a quiet dinner, followed by the promised, special dessert, vanished.

CHAPTER 2

▼

Officer Travis Thompson and his new partner had enjoyed a relatively quiet night on their Hollywood beat. Ever since he had been paired with the newbie the two had been labeled Mutt and Jeff. Travis was a tall, well-built black man with a stony visage and enough strength in his hands to break bones with ease. The female rookie barely made the height requirement for the force. The rest of her attributes—a shapely figure, green-flecked, dark eyes and a smile that beamed from her light tan, sculptured face—were in sharp contrast to her mentor's.

The California sun started to peak through the muted haze a little after 6:00 AM. It was a signal to Travis that he would soon be off patrol and on his way home to whatever to-do list his bride Tamara had for him today.

The Hollywood Community Police Station is one of eighteen in the city. Its men and women are responsible for a part of LA that includes 17 square miles of land and over three hundred thousand residents. There are seven "Basic Car Areas" in the community. Travis "owned" Basic Car Area 6A15 that bordered Griffith Park.

Travis liked his work and Hollywood. As he had done many times before, he began his final drive-by in the area. It was one that would give him a view of the famous Hollywood sign. The landmark was atop Mount Lee, within the boundaries of the 4,000-acre Griffith Park. He liked to remind himself that he was the keeper of the peace in this famous piece of real estate.

The smile on his tired face and his black and white Crown Victoria both came to an abrupt halt when he took his second look up at the sign. Travis's partner, Rosita Ortiz, a newly graduated probationary officer, was snapped forward by the sudden stop, and the seat belt bit into the space between her ample breasts. She turned to Travis and screeched, "What the hell …"

Travis's only response was, "Exactly!"

He pointed up to the sign and put the patrol car back in motion. He sped up the steep road to get them and their vehicle as close to the sign as possible.

In front of and at the middle point of the left upright of the white H was something that looked like a dark cross. As the car rushed up North Beachwood Drive and closed in on the famous landmark, Travis blurted out, "Jesus H. Christ!"

As Officer Ortiz took in the sight, the irony of Travis's exclamation was lost in her own shock.

Travis had seen enough in an instant to know he had to call it in. He figured the coordinator sergeant of his Basic Car District would not be in yet, but guessed that his buddy Jed would be.

"Lieutenant Davies here. What's up?"

"Jed, it's me, Travis. I don't have a code for what I'm looking at. There's a dead man up here in front of the Hollywood sign."

Most cops who had worked the community were familiar with the curious history of the sign and Griffith Park. Jed was not all that excited.

"So?"

"So, he's hanging from a goddamned cross, right the hell in front of the H. A big goddamned cross, and he's bare-ass naked except for some kind of sheet wrapped around his privates."

"What?" More of an evenly spoken query than an exclamation.

"You heard me. It's the whole deal. He's got big spikes through his hands and feet, ropes tied around his wrists holding him up, and a big wound in his side. Looks like his chest and face have been whipped bloody, and he has a, well, a crown of thorns on his head."

"*What?*" This time loud and very exclamatory. Now to himself, *Calm down, Jed. Breathe, breathe.*

A calmer Jed asked, "Anything else up there, Travis?"

"Don't know yet."

"How the hell did he or anyone else get close to the sign?"

"No idea on that either. With all the barricades and monitors and alarms to keep people out, someone gets a man on a cross right smack in front of the H. Just get the hell up here. Please."

"Okay, hang in there. I'll call the crime scene boys, and I'll be there in a few minutes. Don't touch anything and try and keep the gawkers out of there. It's getting light." As a last thought, he asked, "How's Ortiz doing?"

Travis looked over at his partner who was throwing up on the side of the road and lied. "She seems to be doing okay, Jed. Just hurry up with the cavalry. This place is gonna be crazy real quick."

"On our way. Jesus H …"

"Don't say it, Jed. I already got that covered. Just get here."

Jed was not the hurrying kind. It was especially true when a homicide was called in. The dead bodies didn't bother him much. He just figured they would still be dead when he got to the scene. No need to rush. This time was different. Travis's voice and Jed's own curiosity had the detective moving quickly.

Jed took Wilcox Avenue north to Hollywood Boulevard to the freeway and was climbing North Beachwood Drive within five minutes. He thought he would wait to see the crime scene himself before getting the watch commander and the rest of the police brass out of bed. He knew he would have to call the LA Park Rangers who covered Griffith and let them know they had a "situation."

He thought about the long Starline bus tour he took when he first came to the city. It included a stop to view the Hollywood sign and a bus driver's version of its history. He made a mental note to have someone call them before their 9:30 AM tour bus took off and let them know the sign that spoke of LA's glamour would not be one of their stops today.

By the time Jed was making his way, Travis had had the alarm systems shut down and the security fence opened. Jed drove up to Travis Thompson's car and jumped out. His suit was still well pressed, and the fashionable tie was still knotted smartly, but the usual calm demeanor had turned into frozen horror. His right hand flew up, his long, bony fingers grabbing and messing his normally well-groomed, sandy hair. The scar on his right cheek, a red badge of stupidity he had earned as a rookie responding to a domestic violence call, reddened. The lids of his bright blue eyes narrowed to focus on the unthinkable. Thompson and Ortiz, farther up the path to the sign, barely turned to acknowledge him. They just stared up at the 30-foot-wide, 45-foot-tall, white H. Without speaking, Jed joined them. The two seasoned, male cops had seen their share of the various kinds of gruesome harm one human could inflict upon another but never this. Jed noticed the smell of vomit on Ortiz, and could not blame her.

Jed's only words were a simple question. "What the hell are we dealing with here?" No answers came.

Jed's heavy, resisting feet slowly moved as close as he could get to the battered body of "Jesus." He felt like his mind had been shattered into jagged-edged sections. His eyes processed the coarse branches weaved into the crown of thorns. The detective then focused on a single one-inch-long thorn that appeared to have been beaten down into the scalp of this man, just above his closed right eye. Crusted blood surrounded the small, hard, imbedded spine. His eyes zoomed out and captured the fact that all the thorns he could see had been driven home—bloody, brutal, and swollen piercings. His memory leaked into his sensory absorption of the victim's gory head wounds, and he tried to summon up his own worst head injury. He remembered a childhood scene where the speeding five ounces of a Wilson baseball, lined off the bat of his best friend Johnny Dabkowski, traveled the forty-six feet back to the pitcher's mound, and slammed full-force into his forehead. The seams of the ball left a mark just above his right eye, and the impact shattered part of his frontal bone. Jed, age seven, thought nothing in the world could hurt more than this. He knew now how wrong he had been.

As Jed's eyes moved along the other bloody and bruised parts of Jesus, he had more thoughts of human pain. Memories of sights and sounds and feelings bounced from one parcel of his brain to the next. He felt them rebounding off the walls of his consciousness, like the vaulting ping-pong balls captured in the Lotto air mix machine. Memories of the tears and screams that came with his son's broken arm, a result of a misstep from the local tree fort, dashed through and pressed images in his mind's mirrors.

Jed's mind flashed back to his frustrating feeling of helplessness in the labor room, years ago. He was an up-close and personal witness to his wife's pain, her screaming, and the accompanying verbal assaults during those ten hours. The LA cop from New York City had been duly impressed with his California girl's command of obscene expletives. The best he could do back then was offer ice chips and a feeble attempt at telling Regan to "breathe."

Now, as Jed stared closely at each lurid violation of *this* body hanging limply on the cross, he knew that nothing he had ever felt or witnessed came close to this inhuman horror.

The cop remembered the Palm Sunday readings of Christ's Passion. How the minister, his helper, and the congregation—each playing different roles—droned out the words of one of the Gospel writers. The verbal reenactment never had any real impact on Jed. This wordless scene he was gaping at now hit him with a visceral slam.

This was not the cleansed and polished, sculptured, silver crucifix that had hung in his parents' bedroom for forty years. These were not the sanitized renditions of an artist's brush, with small drops of blood at the sites of the thorns and the spikes. Maybe it was more like the scenes in the Mel Gibson movie he had chosen to avoid. But, here and now it was a vision of shredded flesh, blood and madness. Jed winced and clenched his own fists as his eyes homed in on the six-inch, eleven-ounce spikes. The heads of the rusted metal implants stared back from the pulverized centers of the hands and feet. Jed stepped back ten paces, still processing the gore in the silence. Neither Officer Thompson nor Officer Ortiz had said a word since Jed had fallen into his apparent trance. To Jed it looked as if buckets of blood had been thrown at the body to cover the hideous scourging and indignities.

Jed, still in a silent, lugubrious state of disbelief at the human capacity for evil, finally turned and walked away. *Who was this man's Judas? Who was this man's Pilate?* When he reached the patrol officers, no one stopped him when he stared into their faces and spoke in a measured voice. "Jesus H. Christ!"

Ortiz—a bottled water lover—as she had done for herself earlier, had retrieved a chilled bottle of Dasani from her private cooler in the back seat of the patrol car. She was happy she had iced up at Mel's drive-in on North Highland halfway through her shift. She offered the bottle to Jed.

"Thanks, Ortiz. Wow! Nice and cold. What's your first name again?"

"Rosita, sir."

"Nice name. From now on, please call me Jed. Thanks for the water. I need it."

"No problem, sir ..., uh, Jed."

"Okay. Let's just wait for the technicians to show."

Jed uncapped the water and walked back to his car. He leaned against the door farthest away from the two officers. He took a small sip of the Dasani. It roiled the remains of his morning dose of caffeine. Not more than three feet away from where Rosita had vomited earlier, Jed's water, coffee and bile spewed forth with a violent projection. The tears that gathered on his cheeks were a mixture of the consequence of Jed's act of retching and a deep sadness.

As predicted by the weathergirl, it was a cool morning with a promise of the temperature climbing only into the low seventies. The lieutenant knew that the pressure to deliver answers on this mess would heat up much more dramatically. Jed gathered himself and cleaned up. He got in his car and radioed Los Angeles'

West Bureau headquarters. By the time he was finished convincing the commanding officer on duty that he wasn't kidding or crazy, the crime scene crew that he had alerted earlier, had arrived. Jed pressed forward with the West Bureau officer and asked for an ambulance, a fire truck, and whatever it would take to get a police barricade at the foot of North Beachwood and shut down the nearby hiking trails. The famous nine letters that spelled out HOLLYWOOD, sitting 1,800 feet above sea level atop Mount Lee, would be off limits for a few days.

He knew it wouldn't take long for the escalation to snake its way up to commander, to deputy chief, to assistant chief and finally to the big man with the full headdress of feathers, the old chief himself.

Shit, he thought, as the acid still rumbled around in his stomach. *No goddamned nap today.* Little did he know how sleep deprived he would be over the next few days. He looked down at the crotch of his suit pants, tried to muster up a small attempt at comic relief, and whispered to the seam, "No dessert for you tonight, my little friend."

CHAPTER 3

▼

The cross-country call lasted only thirty seconds.

The woman sitting on the bench in MacArthur Park was outfitted in a pair of Levi's and a well-tailored, Austin Reed, blue-and-white-striped blouse with the sleeves rolled up. Her dark hair was streaming out of the back of a pink New York Yankees cap with the dark logo in the center. Her dark eyes were shielded by a pair of pink-and-gray, polarized Oakleys. Her right leg was crossed on top of the left, showing off the bottom of a well-worn pair of Nikes, and she was reading a copy of *Black Vortex*, a new novel by some author named Dennis O'Connell. The same person who was about to dial her cell had loaned her the book for her trip, and told her that the author was a friend of his. The woman on the bench checked her Anne Klein watch, whose pink strap and face matched her hat just beautifully. She had just crushed out her second cigarette of the morning, was sipping a cup of coffee and picking at a cinnamon-raisin bagel when her cell phone chirped a simple ringtone—right on schedule.

She had arrived at the location named after General Douglas MacArthur a few minutes after 11:00 AM—the hour the park opened. She had made her way to the lake side of the park, just off Wilshire Boulevard. The young lady had not even been born when Jimmy Webb wrote and Richard Harris sang the seven-minute-long hit song about this piece of land built up from swampland in the 1880s. She did have some vague memory of Donna Summer's 1978 disco version of the song. Sitting a little more than six miles from the chaos that was taking place at the site of the crucifixion, she had dismissed any memories of the song. The woman in the pink cap had alternated between devouring the pages of her book and calmly taking in the beauty of the tall palm trees and the impressive view of downtown LA—waiting for his call.

When it came, the deep voice on the other end spoke slowly. "I hear you had a good day. How we doing?"

The woman answered, "Fine, just fine."

"Were all our 'employees' at the Griffith taken care of?"

"Yeah, yeah, they were convinced they were being well paid off for a simple college prank. Now they're, like, probably so damn scared they won't say a word. Plus we are layers removed from any transaction."

"Excellent." End of conversation. Time to move on.

The woman said to no one but the park, "Sorry, General. *I* shall *not* return."

CHAPTER 4

▼

JUNE 2, 2005

Two days later, Jed, finally in a fresh set of clothes, and a small task force of law enforcement types were crammed into one of the rooms in the Hollywood Community Police Station. It was 8:00 AM. Jed had stopped at Winchell's on North Vine to pick up one of their 14-donut-dozen specials and fresh coffee for the crew. Each attendee had a notebook with identical contents.

Section one provided a brief background on the victim:

NAME: Jesus Heraldo Cruz
SEX: male
HEIGHT: 5'4"
WEIGHT: 125 lbs.
EYES: brown
HAIR: black
OTHER NOTABLES: full beard, no old tattoos
AGE: 33
DOB: 01/20/1972
ADDRESS: 14th Ave., Miami, Florida
OCCUPATION: construction worker/carpenter
FAMILY: mother: Maria, age: 55; address: same as victim; father: José;
DOB: 06/25/1944; deceased 09/12/1999
REPORTED MISSING: Sunday, May 29, 2005—11:00 PM by mother—
last known communication was with mother via phone at 3:00 PM Sunday

His prints were in the system from a two-year tour of duty in the army. The litany went on for four pages. The narrative revealed a thirty-three-year-old, single man, second generation Puerto Rican, who worked as a carpenter for Jordan Construction in Florida. No wife, no ex-wife, no kids, no known enemies, a hard worker who never complained. A kind, religious man. A skilled craftsman who lived with his mother. The man had a few close friends. He had no known vices, no debts. And this roomful of professionals did not have a blessed clue as to why Jesus ended up on the cross.

Section two provided the details of the cross. The upright beam was ten feet long. The crossbeam was six feet long. Both pieces of wood were approximately four inches wide and four inches thick. One of the geeks from the lab guessed that the wood was cedar and included the tidbit that some scholars speculate that it was Cedar of Lebanon wood that the *other* Jesus was nailed to 2,005 years ago. The beams were cleanly milled. There was a two-inch notch in each of the pieces where they were connected by six 4-inch brass screws. The wooden chock that supported the feet of Jesus was of the same wood and secured by the same kind of screws. It was verified that the crown of thorns was indeed made from the bush botanically known as *Zizyphus Spina Christi*, more popularly, the jujube tree. The plant, believed to be the source of the original crown, grows to a height of fifteen or twenty feet and is still found thriving quite well around Jerusalem. The cloth around Jesus's loins was a common cotton cloth, probably just cut from a bolt. It was forty-five inches wide and just over five feet long. It was knotted just to the left side of the groin area. The three spikes that Officer Thompson had told Jed about appeared to be fashioned out of old railroad spikes. The rope around his wrists was common three-strand. The same efficient geek let them know that the brand of the rope was Samson, one and five-eighths inches in diameter, five inches in circumference. The two pieces were twenty-four inches long, weighed approximately eleven pounds, and had been wrapped twice around the wrists of the poor carpenter from Miami. Way more than needed to hold up a 125-pound man. Samson rope was available in at least five stores in LA alone. God knew how many more across the country. And, of course, the product was available to anyone with Internet access and a credit card. Jed had gone over this section twice earlier and concluded that they might as well be pissing up a Samson rope. This data would lead them nowhere fast. He would let the friendly geeks try and piece together anything meaningful from this mess of data.

Section three laid out the forensics and photos of the strange and sanguine crime scene. There was a huge, white canvas and lightweight, aluminum framing found flat on the ground, a few yards in front of the cross. The task force had concluded that whoever did the deed had used the framing and canvas to conceal their efforts. The white canvas matched the color of the H almost perfectly. There were no lights near the Hollywood sign like the old days. The night of the crucifixion sported a half-moon and a cloudy sky. Any late-night, early-morning passerby who looked up would assume they were seeing the normal darkened H. They would be unaware of whatever was transpiring behind the canvas. Behind the H was small, wooden scaffolding that probably aided in the raising of the cross.

The cross itself was suspended from the H. Two industrial-strength eyehooks were embedded in the horizontal beam of the cross. Heavy gauge, braided, nylon ropes were tied to the eyehooks and pulled over the top of the left upright of the H. The ropes were secured in the ground, 45 feet below. They were attached to a 3-foot stake with an eye opening at the top. All commercial materials easily obtainable and impossible to trace. The cross was prevented from swaying by a single rope looped through a smaller eyehook in the back center of the cross and wrapped around the upright. The ropes and the H, made of Australian steel and supported from behind by metal framing, had no problem handling Jesus and his cross's weight.

Conclusions were easily made that the perpetrators had brought a 40-foot aluminum ladder to make their way up to the maintenance ladder fixed to the back of the left upright of the H. The weight of the crucifix and body were enough to keep the ropes that were looped over the top of the H in place.

The ground below the scene was the recipient of the blood of Jesus. The carpenter had bled out there while hanging from the cross. The scene had yielded close to nothing else. The grounds had been raked clean of any clear footprints or vehicle tracks. No fingerprints and no fibers or hairs were found. No impressions on the ground, other than a few that looked like they were left by feet wearing the kind of booties doctors wear. No candy wrappers. Nothing but an empty, crushed Salem pack and two spent cigarette butts had been found. Maybe, just maybe, something. They would trace all that was left behind but it wasn't looking all that good.

The autopsy turned up only one body mark other than the obvious. The needle mark along with a toxicology screen indicated a large, merciful amount of a morphine-based drug in the victim's system. Jed wasn't sure if this was in fact mercy or just insurance that the hanging man didn't make a fuss or scream.

The task force members were already sick of looking at the pictures of the crucified man and the up-close shots of his wounds. Jesus's mother had only been shown a cleaned-up headshot to identify her son. She had also given the Miami police a number of her son's grooming tools for a positive DNA match. She confessed that her filing system for his medical records was sorely lacking, in fact was non-existent. Jesus had no insurance from his employer and, therefore, they had no medical or dental data for the victim.

The new picture that they were all given this morning was of the artful tattoo that had been inked into the victim's back. The dye in the flesh of Jesus, from the top of his shoulders to the top of his waist, delivered six lines of a message:

Jesus
was innocent!
So was
Alberto Antobelli!
Free
Maria Calabrese!

The first two lines were penned in a deep red. The next two in a dark blue, and the last two in black. The font was easily recognized and documented by the geeks as Caesar. In addition to the lettering, there were two colorful crosses tattooed horizontally, in opposite directions. The longer parts of the two crosses framed the top and bottom of the words. One section of the shorter pieces of the crucifixes bordered about one-third of the sides of the words. The crosses could not be matched to any known historical symbol or design. The techs concluded that they were likely original creations.

Jed was standing in front of the room and had the attention of the task force as he prepared to tell the stories of Alberto and Maria to those gathered.

Included in the grouping were two detectives from the Homicide Special Section of the Robbery-Homicide Division of the LAPD. Their division was located on the third floor of what was originally called the Police Administrative Building, now named the Parker Center after former LAPD Chief William H. Parker. Neither the nine-story building nor the division was a stranger to the famous and the infamous. The building, completed in 1955, was seen in a number of episodes of the TV show *Dragnet*. The division, RHD for short, had been intimately involved in the investigation of the Charles Manson case, the Robert Kennedy assassination, and the O.J. Simpson happening. Thus, a crucifixion in front of the Hollywood sign was naturally of interest to the RHD. The two detectives, a woman previously of the Van Nuys station and a man from the Wilshire Area station, were working with Jed to try and make sense of the death of Jesus.

Jed half expected the FBI to try and horn in on the spectacle, since a kidnapping and transport across the country seemed to be obvious, but, so far, only a phone call asking to be kept abreast. He actually thought about calling his friend Chris Lee, a big player in the FBI and a superstar in profiling.

The long hours of the days before this one had been spent grasping some of the obvious points. The crucifixion of a *Jesus*, whose last name *Cruz* and its meaning, "the cross of the crucifixion," taking place in front of one of the world's most famous landmarks, was news.

Surprise, surprise—someone had leaked the man's profession and the coincidences of his age and parents' names. The *LA Times* and national papers were competing for the cleverest headlines and digging for any bit of information the cops had. The national news hung onto the story for two days, then moved on to the next series of bad-news headlines. Speculation on motive ranged from racism to psychosis with a flair for the dramatic. As much as the Los Angeles police had tried to keep people and cameras away, they lost their battle to technology. The powerful lenses of the citizenry's telescopes generated man-on-the-street interviews with those reporting their up-close and personal views of the scene. The media's high-tech digital cameras spewed out graphic pictures and videotapes of Tinsel Town's only known crucifixion in history. The vision of the long-haired Jesus hanging on the cross with his head hung low on his right shoulder was riveting and haunting.

The brass was banging on RHD, Jed, and his supervisors for answers. The one press conference they held was ugly and brief. The big shots would much rather hold a press conference to award a medal to one of their own for bravery in the face of violence than one about a hideous crime in the heart of Hollywood. Even Governor Arnold was avoiding the cameras.

For a number of reasons, once Jed and the crime scene team discovered the statement and the demand on the back of Jesus, the body was covered and tightly guarded. So far, the press had gotten no wind of the tattoo. The other piece of concealed data was a subtle carving down the back of the upright beam of the cross. "FATHER, FORGIVE THEM." Once the crime scene crew discovered it, Jed moved quickly to get it wrapped.

Jed wanted to keep the information about the tattoo and the carving restricted. Shared only with those on the task force and, of course, with the bosses who had a need to know.

So far, the crime scene had yielded a lot of useless evidence. The speculation as to how it was accomplished, who committed the horrible act and why, had only led to frustration. Investigations into the organizations and the people in charge of security for the park and its sign got tangled and accusatory and only left them with more questions. All they knew about the *who* was that they were clever, daring, and, obviously, dangerous.

The first day of the task force had led to too many jokes and turns of phrases for Jed's taste, and he let the people in the station know it. Later on that first night, he rethought his position. So today, the room housed four whiteboards on easels, and he let the boys and girls have at it. Two boards were reserved for the "F" questions, as in, "What the f ...", "Who the f ...", and so on. The other two were set up to capture the crew's quick-witted comments in the shaky hope that one or two of them might lead to something meaningful. The murderers were clever. Maybe the clever folks hunting them would come up with a clue through their jocular musings. Before anyone had arrived in the room, Jed christened each of the four boards at the very top with JESUS, MARY, AND JOSEPH to dispense with the most common observation. Other than Jed's headline, the boards were to be cleared daily and the comments transcribed into a computer, printed for Jed, encrypted, and e-mailed to those working the case.

By day two, the search for data about the two names perversely inscribed on the back of Jesus was a bit more fruitful than the other evidence collected. And so, this morning, Jed was going to focus the task force on Alberto and Maria. He decided to open with the best technical statement he could muster up. "What we have here, ladies and gentlemen ..." The detective paused, took a deep breath, wrung his large hands and continued. "What we have here is one, big, fat mess. Supply the adjectival expletive of your choice. Now, let me expand on that. We have a big, fat, complicated mess that makes no sense. But, let me at least tell you what we do know about the two people whose names were expertly inscribed on the back of our victim."

Jed walked through everything they had gathered on Alberto and Maria. The facts had a certain sense of clarity to them, but no one, except for a few *not* in this room, knew the whole story. Those *in* the room were muttering about the chief of police wanting an answer within days. Jed's internalized response was, *Yeah, right, and I want a full body rub from Heidi Klum.*

Jed decided to get a copy of the trial transcripts for Alberto Antobelli and Maria Calabrese and whatever other public documents were available that were related to the trials. If he remembered correctly, they would be obtained through the county clerk's office in White Plains, New York. Luckily for Jed, he still had a number of "Christmas-card friends" scattered throughout the New York State law enforcement agencies. With a few calls and brief but enjoyable chats about the good old days, the transcripts would be shipped and in his hands within a day. Jed would have to give up his nightly habit of falling asleep to the latest, best-selling murder mystery for the mostly tedious reality of a criminal trial. Unfortunately for Jed, he did not have any other hole to dig. *Let's get a look at these two characters who made someone think it was a good idea to put poor old Jesus up on that cross.*

CHAPTER 5

▼

SEPTEMBER 1988

In the fall of 1988, the botched hit on Carmine Antobelli, Alberto's father, was enough to convince the mob chieftain that it was time to move away from the city. Dying in the Bronx on Jerome Avenue at the hands of some young punk was not the kind of transition into retirement that Carm had in mind. He would never find out if it was the blacks, the Hispanics, the Asians or the Russians that had tried to spill his fifty-three-year-old blood on the sidewalk. He had decided it didn't much matter. It was time to take his retired father's advice.

He mused over Papa Salvatore's *eloquent* words of wisdom spoken years ago and oft repeated. "It's getting too dangerous, Carm. The fucking niggers, spics, gooks, and commies all want a piece of what we got. We've gotta find a better way to make a living."

Papa Sal's prescient—albeit shamefully and racially tainted—view of their world had caused him to make a very wise and very quiet move seventeen years before someone had tried to make his son Carmine a screaming headline in the *Daily News*. In 1971, at the age of sixty, Sal had called in a few favors and arranged to buy thirty-five acres of property just thirty miles north of the Bronx city line. If the Feds could have gotten close enough to the serpentine series of transactions that the balding, heavyset, dark-eyed Italian and a few of his lieutenants had pulled off, money laundering would have been one of many charges leveled against one of their lifelong targets. But Sal had some of the best lawyers that money and fear could buy.

Sal's property was not far off the narrow and winding Taconic State Parkway in Westchester County, New York. The land rose from the valley that the main, local road ran through and up into the lush hills of Yorktown, New York. It just so happened that the backside of the property bordered a large, commercial complex with security that was almost as tight as what Sal had planned for his development, Nuovo Citta Estates.

It would be five years before Sal would get serious about leaving his Yonkers home and begin building his dream. He was busy stashing away dirty money to finance his upcoming adventure. Westchester property values did not disappoint old Sal. His investment was doing better than well. The plan was to severely limit who got to build on Sal's gated, green acres. The discriminating approach would only help fetch a higher price for an acre of property in the burbs. He decided he would allow a few minorities in just to stay out of the papers and out of court. Sal would be an equal-opportunity-housing land baron.

In the spring of 1976, before one stick of wood had been hauled onto the property for residential construction, an impressive eight-hundred-foot-long, stone and iron barrier was built across the frontage of the land. It stood fifty feet back from the road. The aged collection of maples, oaks, and pines that lined the road were left undisturbed and kept the massive barricade out of view.

Sal's fingers were in every detail of the plan. He had only been to Washington, D.C., once in his life, but one of the images that impressed him the most and never left him was the White House gate. He liked the strength and power that the white, concrete pillars and black, iron posts conveyed. Every time he would see the barrier in the movies or on the news he would think it would be nice to live that protected.

The only interruption in Sal's uniform barrier was a fifty-foot-long series of spiked, wrought-iron gates on either side of the twenty-foot-by-twenty-foot guardhouse. The guardhouse was constructed of matching stone. The gates were designed to allow automatic release and opening of the smaller sections closest to the guardhouse. The opening of the automated gates presented a break large enough to allow a small truck through. For construction purposes, the adjoining, wider gates had to be manually pulled back to their full expanse to allow for the entry of larger vehicles.

Sal was having fun. He had pretty much turned over the old "business" to his son and his lieutenants. Part of Sal's old business was construction and paving, but he was usually too busy staying one step ahead of the law and two steps in front of his competition to enjoy the finer points of the industry. Now he had the time and the desire to play architect and designer for Nuovo Citta. And a few lunches with the town's powers-that-be made for smooth legal sailing for his project.

When the gates were first completed, he made the ride up from Yonkers to check them out. He arrived in his new Caddy with three bottles of high-end Ruffino Chianti. His nephew Michael, who was in charge of his construction adventure in the hills of Yorktown, met him at four in the afternoon. With the broadest smile Michael had ever seen on his uncle, Sal raised one of the bottles and crashed it against the cornerstone of the guardhouse. Mounted on the stone were the words Nuovo Citta, spelled out in shiny, brass, two-foot-high, fancy lettering. Lettering that Sal had picked out himself. As the dark red wine colored the white stone, Sal yelled, "Salute, salute" and then told Michael to make sure one of the workers bleached out the wine from the stone the next day. Sal played with his new gates for a few minutes and smiled at the symbolic start of his little dream.

He and Michael sat on the steps of the guardhouse with the second bottle of Chianti and two of his Don Tomás cigars. Sal had been introduced to the mild cigar only a few years before by a fellow aficionado. He liked the smell and the taste of the rolled tobacco. The smokes crafted in Danli, Honduras, had quickly become the choice for Sal's habit. Michael, familiar with his uncle's wonts, always had a small corkscrew hanging from his large key chain. He opened the wine and they discussed the construction schedule. Sal's involvement in the details delighted Michael. He had great respect for the don, as well as a strong attachment to the paycheck he received weekly and the unreported cash that made its way into his pockets. They drank slowly and talked quickly. When the wine was finished, Sal told his nephew to leave the other bottle in the guardhouse for the workers.

Still smiling, he gave polite directions to his nephew. "Mickey, my paisano, you drive my car. We'll have an early dinner at Peter's. I'm in the mood to celebrate and I'm thinking about some steamed mussels, lots of white wine, and some cheesecake."

Peter Pratt's Inn, a converted, old colonial home, was only a short ride down Route 118 to Croton Heights Road. With a few sharp twists and turns on the local road, the two arrived at the large white structure and parked easily. The establishment that Sal favored for its savory cuisine had only opened a few minutes before. By the time they would leave, it would be chock-full of Upper Westchester County residents looking to spend their money on the fine food and drink. This was, for Sal, the official, celebratory beginning of his Nuovo Citta Estates.

By the time the Bronx bullet had just missed his son Carmine and his forty-three-year-old bodyguard everyone knew as Tank, Sal's Nuovo Citta was home to twenty-eight, well-to-do residents. Carm's house had been built a number of years before. The red-brick, white-shuttered, four-bedroom home had been used mostly for the holidays. That would change real soon. It was time for Carm to get out of the Dodge of the East.

CHAPTER 6

▼

THE ANTOBELLIS

Carmine would never be picked out of a lineup as the oldest son of Salvatore Antobelli. He was six inches taller and much thinner. He carried just a little bit of a paunch, not like the big one his father always patted after a good meal. His full head of graying hair was combed back over his head with no visible part. His bushy eyebrows, still with a lingering smack of black in them, were a perfect topping for his wide, often smiling, eyes. Carmine, because of similar looks and usually being dressed in a stylish suit and tie, was often accused of being the brother of John Gotti, the Dapper Don. Although Carm had acquired his father's taste in choice of occupation, the sporting of Guinea T's, baggy wool pants, and shirts best fitted for a bowling alley, was a choice he shunned.

On the almost-fatal day in September of 1988, Carmine's eyes were not smiling and his brain was in a high, proactive gear.

His exit from Yonkers was swift. The day after the attempt on his life, he met with his lawyers and told them to sell the house, and make sure he made a significant profit. He had one of his minions arrange with his cousin Mike to ship the selected, valued pieces of furniture to his Yorktown house. He met with his lieutenants at a local restaurant, which he had helped another of his cousins purchase, and gave instructions.

Although Carmine's looks had the air of a New York City Mafia don, his fifty-one-year-old wife Sophia bore no resemblance to the heavyset, pasta-cooking, kitchen-bound, silent and servile spouse often portrayed in the movies. Her slim and well-exercised body still turned heads. She had traded in the longhair look years ago for a more stylish, just-above-the-shoulders look. The color was not quite black. A little, light, professional streaking and the wispy texture of her hair allowed her to style it in a number of different crisp and attractive fashions. She was almost as tall as her husband, and, if she stood on her tiptoes, her eyes, dark with flecks of sparkling green, could look straight into his—a tactic she used sparingly when she wanted the honest-to-God truth.

Carmine adored her, and she had never left him in need of another woman's charms. Unless the evening demanded something different, her choice of clothes was simple and tasteful. Raising the children had kept her dressed most often in her uniform of blue jeans and T-shirts. Carm never complained. He always said she would look sexy wearing a gunnysack with holes cut out for the head and arms. Sophia appreciated the compliment, but the thought of burlap chafing her nipples made her wince.

She was not blind to how the money came into the household. She had been at first, but not now. And her tiptoe move, accompanied by a plea for Carm to exit the illegal side of the business only months before, had exacted a promise. The Jerome Avenue Remington .380 projectile that just missed Carm was cause for him to vigorously expedite the execution of the promise.

Although Sophia would have regrets about leaving her familiar Yonkers surroundings and friends, the move would put her much closer to her two sons, Alberto and Vincent. The much younger, seven-year-old daughter, Carlotta, would not be happy about moving, but Sophia could handle that with promises of a bigger bedroom, new furniture, and a dog all her own. Sophia was also looking forward to *really* decorating the newer five-bedroom, three-and-a-half-bath brick home. She knew exactly where she wanted to put the vegetable garden in the big backyard, and next spring she would try her hand at upgrading the landscaping, maybe even grow enough fresh flowers to brighten up the house inside and out. She would not mind leaving behind the bumpy roads of her Yonkers neighborhood for Papa Sal's newer and smoother streets. *Ah, and the trees, the beautiful trees. And the fresh air. It will be nice*, she thought.

Alberto, the older of the two sons, had been put in charge of Carmine's trucking enterprise. Vinnie, the younger, had attended Manhattan College and was content to work at his job in White Plains as a computer programmer. Vinnie was married to his college sweetheart and had one baby girl. Alberto was single. The handsome young man with Stallone-like looks enjoyed the life of a bachelor too much to think about ever giving it up—or so he thought.

Both sons were residents of Grandfather Sal's Nuovo Citta. Now Mama would be in the same neighborhood as her boys. She could revel in the beauty of her young granddaughter Emily and maybe, just maybe, be the down-the-street Nonna she always wanted to be. Vinnie was such a peaceful, loving boy, and Sophia got along fabulously with his wife Mary Kate—an Irish girl, but, hey, that was okay with Sophia and Carmine. She was good for Vinnie, such a good son, never any trouble.

CHAPTER 7

▼

TAKE ME OUT TO THE BALLPARK

As Sophia mused, she sighed. *Ah. And then there is Alberto. In nomine Patris, et Filii, et Spiritus Sancti. Amen.* The sign of the cross had never been enough to keep her eldest son out of trouble in his youth. He was brash, short-fused, and hotheaded. In those days, novenas and holy hours of adoration and countless rosaries were supplications that went unanswered and apparently ended up in God's wastebasket.

Being married to Carmine, Sophia had seen enough wiseguys in her time. She felt like her Alberto was the perfect understudy, a bad seed getting badder as he got older. She had caught him with a Marlboro at age eleven—probably not his first. The beer and whiskey came a year later. She had worn out a path from home to the grade school principal's office to retrieve her bully son with the smart mouth. Sophia had hidden much from her husband for fear of the anger that would lead to a beating of her misguided boy.

At the age of fifteen, the police had given the handsome, longhaired, tall-for-his-age child a ride home in one of their blue and whites. Carmine, who liked to keep his business under the radar of the New York City and Yonkers law enforcement crowd, thanked officers Bobby Reilly and Nick Leggio from the Bronx's 50th precinct for returning the bloodied Alberto. They would keep his knife and file it in their Kingsbridge Avenue station. The scene at Carm's two-story brick home on a usually quiet side street that ran between Riverdale Avenue and South Broadway, just north of the Bronx city line, was not pretty. As Sophia had predicted, Carmine let Alberto have it with both barrels and both hands. The welts would show up later, but, at that moment, the red-faced teenager was on his knees crying out his story.

"That prick Guido Saracini started it, Dad. I swear I was just standing there talking to some guys."

"Standing there with a knife in your hand? The only reason you're not sitting in the Kingsbridge jail is because those guys owe me a few favors. This family does not need to draw any attention from the police, and your mother and I don't need to hear your smart mouth."

The yelling lasted only ten minutes, but, for Sophia, it seemed like forever.

Carmine called Guido's old man and apologized for Alberto's behavior. He asked if Guido was okay. He was. Carmine knew the Saracini kid and liked him. They would come to do some business together a number of years down the road. Carmine's next call was to his close friend and bodyguard, Tank. That may have been the visible end of the incident for Sophia but not for Carmine.

He asked Rich Tomasello, aka Tank, to vet his son's character. Within two weeks the bodyguard and "*professionista* of many trades" reported back. His findings included a half-full pack of Marlboros in the back of Alberto's dresser drawer, another of Phillip Morris's red, white, and black cardboard packs with three joints in place of the smokes, betting slips stuck in with the joints, a rather impressive collection of Playboy magazines hidden in the basement, and a few knives stashed in various parts of the garage. And the big prize, a .25 automatic pistol. It fell into the category of "Saturday night special," a small, short-barreled "junk gun." The pistol and a box of .25 caliber bullets were stored in the heating return duct in his room, behind his headboard.

Tank told Carm he would have a serious talk with the boy. Carm trusted Tank with his life, and now he was handing over his son to him with complete faith in the man's *talking* abilities—thinking that sometimes they listen better to someone other than an angry parent.

"Hey, Alberto, come in."

"What's up, Mr. Tomasello?"

It was an unprecedented invitation for Alberto to meet his father's helper at his home. The walk was only a few blocks from Carmine's home. Alberto, in his Converse sneakers, faded blue jeans, and his black-and-red AC/DC T-shirt, had climbed the six front steps with only mild trepidation. He had underestimated his immediate future. Tank, standing almost half a foot taller than Alberto, was wearing his brown deck shoes, a newer-looking pair of jeans, and a pinstriped Yankees shirt with a number 7 on the back. After letting Alberto in the front door, Tank guided him into the playroom in the basement. At the edge of the toy farm that occupied the space was a small card table. On the table was a modest, neat display of Tank Tomasello's findings. Alberto's face gave away his guilt. After a brief conversation, soliciting verbal admission from the boy, Tank simply said, "Let's go."

Alberto waited until they were in Tank's 1974 black Chevy K-5 Blazer to ask where they were headed. "To the ballpark." A confused teenager shut up and just let his captor drive. The first stop was thirty minutes later.

"This is first base, son." They were on a side street, south of Fordham Road and just off Third Avenue. In front of the dilapidated structure that used to be an apartment building there were several youths hanging out. Within minutes the two in the Chevy truck witnessed a few high fives and a few low handoffs, an obvious drug buy.

Second base was a halfway house run by a friend of Tank's. The dreary place was loaded with strungout junkies trying to sip down cups of soup without spilling the broth down the front of their shirts. They were of both sexes with an age range of twelve to thirty.

Third base was a short ride down the Grand Concourse, across 161st Street and down River Avenue, for a brief stop at the Bronx House of Detention for Men. From the cracked sidewalk, Alberto could see the prisoners of all colors standing in the open air space of an outer corridor, a few stories up from street level. Their command of adjectival profanity and slang-based appellations for other human beings on this warm July day was impressive, and scary. Neither of the riders said a word to each other.

A quick drive took them to the Grand Concourse and the impressive structure that was known as the Bronx County Courthouse. "Now—sorry, I almost forgot about and skipped this place, Alberto—this is the shortstop position between second and third. You usually make a brief stop here before heading to third—prison. Let's see if we can make it to home plate."

Home plate was a sharp contrast to the large courthouse building and the noisy shouting of the incarcerated men. Alberto was led around to the back entrance of the funeral home on Morris Avenue. Tank rang the bell and was greeted by a smiling, old man with balding, gray hair and a classic, matching gray mustache. A wrinkled hand made its way out of the sleeve of the well-tailored black suit and shook Tank's hand vigorously. "So, Richard, my friend, what brings you all the way down to hell today?"

"Well, Uncle Frankie, I just wanted to show my young friend here one of your clients. Got anything interesting?" Tank knew he did. Last night's phone call had set up the meet.

"Well, today's special is a sixteen-year-old Irish kid. I don't get many of these anymore. But his daddy and mother still own the deli up the road and they have been hanging on in this old neighborhood."

"Cause?"

"Well, you can have a look for yourself. He just came in last night. I haven't prettied him up yet. Come on, son." Uncle Frankie led a resistant Alberto into the basement.

The coroner's Y incision and stitches on the young boy's chest were clearly visible. The pale body was laid out on a stainless steel table. The room's smell caused vomit to rise in Alberto's throat. The smell and the scene were too much, and he looked desperately for a place to dispel the choking fluids. Uncle Frankie pointed him to a sink against the wall. Alberto's vomit joined a gooey mess of discarded intestinal tissue. Once Alberto got back under some modicum of control, he stared at Tank with a pleading look.

"Not yet, Alberto. Come here. You see this little, gaping hole here? Now let's see how this boy's back looks. Wow, look at the size of *that* hole. Died quick, I bet. What was it, Frankie?"

"A semi-jacketed hollow point from a .357 magnum. As you can see, the shooter had pretty good aim. Entered just to the left of the heart, and the hollow point expanded fast and just did its nasty deed. Boy was full of smack; maybe enough to kill him, but the .357 got him first. Probably another drug deal gone bad. We get a lot of that in this neighborhood nowadays."

"Okay. Well, thanks again, Uncle Frankie. I think my young friend here would like to leave."

Frankie offered his hand to Alberto and shook the boy's hand with a surprising strength. "Hope we meet again, son, under better circumstances, of course. Take care, Richard. Say hello to Carm and Sophia and your mom."

The last stop before home was the Pinewood Bar on Broadway, just north of 242nd Street. It was at the last stop on the 7th Avenue local subway, home to a number of bars, pizza parlors, and delicatessens. Tank ended the quiet ride by parking his car just outside the White Castle restaurant. He picked up a few of the square hamburgers and then walked down to the Pinewood.

"Hey, Tank, what's up?"

"Not much, Jimmy. Can we get a couple of Cokes? I need to sit in the back and have a little chat with my friend here."

"You got it. With ice, right?"

Tank retrieved the drinks, dropped a ten on the worn, wooden bar, and guided Alberto to the last booth on the left, only a few steps from the men's room.

"Open those burgers, will ya, Alberto?"

After eating, Tank's words were slow and deliberate. "Kid, you are now officially *my* project. You probably don't know this but your father saved my life. He pulled me off one of those streets like you saw today. He has known my mom since they were kids. When my father, a cop in the 28th took one in the chest down in Harlem, not far from the Apollo Theater, it was your father who helped her out. Helped pay the rent; got her a good job as a bookkeeper up at Westchester County Medical Center in Valhalla. I took to the streets, bad habits like you, maybe worse. My mother called your father when I got a ride home from one of New York's finest. Your father took me for a tour of a "ballpark", just like we did today. I guess things were a little different back then. Because, well, your father kicked the shit out of me and told me if I ever got another ride home from the cops, there had better be an ambulance right behind them. Now relax. I don't plan to kick the shit out of you, *this time.*

"Every friend of mine, like Uncle Frankie, and there are lots of them, is on notice to keep their eyes out for you. Do not screw up on my watch, Alberto."

They finished their drinks and burgers and headed home. The squeeze of Tank's handshake and the pressure applied to Alberto's right shoulder brought the large man's message home in a very physical way.

"Not on my watch, Alberto. Got it? Consider yourself grounded for the next three years. Do not bring any more trouble to your mother and father's doorstep. And maybe, just maybe, we can go out to a real ballpark next year when they finish renovating the stadium and the damn Yankees get their butts back to the Bronx. I just can't bring myself to go to Shea to see the Yanks. It's not natural. You understand, kid?"

"I understand everything, Mr. Tomasello. Can I ask you a question?"

"Sure, but make it quick. We gotta go."

"Have you ever killed anyone?"

"Yeah, a couple of Asian guys in the swamps of a land and time far away. You would be my first stateside killing. Let's go."

Alberto's wiseguy attitude and habits disappeared like a doomed ship in the Bermuda Triangle. He found that he could immerse himself in the details of putting together the parts of Revell model cars. Other options included enjoying the mindless viewing of "Happy Days," "The Six-Million-Dollar Man," and the like on the new RCA color TV set in his room. When it suited him, he would actually pick up a schoolbook and take a stab at homework, always with the pop songs of Stevie Wonder, Paul McCartney and Wings, and others playing in the background on his hot-shit RCA 8-track stereo system. He would only play his Led Zeppelin, Black Sabbath, and AC/DC when he was home alone. It had to be played loud and loud did not sell in the Yonkers home.

As an ace card, if he ever needed one, he called and apologized to Guido Saracini.

In June of 1979, at the age of nineteen with five years of high school under his belt, Alberto was allowed to graduate. The principal and a number of his teachers had collaborated and created a modified course schedule for Alberto to insure his fifth year was his last. They knew the kid was not dumb, just always looking for trouble, and schoolwork got in the way of his search.

One of the few things Alberto was good at was working on cars and trucks, and Carmine had a whole fleet of trucks that distributed automobile parts across the five boroughs, Long Island, Westchester, and Northern New Jersey. At graduation Alberto was given a new black Pontiac Trans Am from the dealership on Tremont Avenue in the East Bronx. As was always the case, Carmine bought the car from someone who owed him a favor and was happy to court his kindness. With the keys in his hand, he warned his impulsive son, "One wrong move, Alberto, and this car finds its way to the used-car lot, and you get to learn the public transportation system routes. One. That's all and you're a pedestrian. Got it, son?" The other "gift" was a forty-hour-a-week job as a mechanic at Carmine's C&S Trucking terminal. Alberto was given a promise of promotions and very good money if he kept his nose clean and did as he was told. The second father-to-son promise was, that if he screwed up, Carmine just might have him beaten up so badly he'd be eating through a straw.

The young, impetuous high school graduate grabbed at the keys of the Firebird with a promise to do his dad proud. He did as he promised, and by the time Carmine moved to Yorktown, Alberto was running the whole trucking operation. Carm grew to be impressed with and proud of his oldest son—at least for a while.

Carm was happy that his friend Tank had taken his son out to the ballpark.

CHAPTER 8

▼

QUESTIONS

Jed would find only snippets of this part of the Antobelli history in the trial transcripts he was about to read.

He felt like Zero from the Beetle Bailey comic strip, the uneducated, empty-minded, buck-toothed, blond country boy who roamed around Camp Swampy clueless. Jed's *crowded* mind, like good old Zero's, now roamed without direction.

Even if Jed knew all the detail of this early part of the Antobelli chronicles, it would not help him with the answers to the haunting questions that hung over him like a comic strip balloon full of words, a large one.

Who are these criminals? What do Alberto and Maria have to do with the hanging? Other than the single demand carved on the back of poor Jesus, what the hell do they want? Who is so hot to have the crazy broad freed from prison?

CHAPTER 9

▼

MARIA

The LAPD had an interesting pile of data on the two people whose names were portrayed and innocence proclaimed on the back of Jesus Cruz—statements assumed to be authored by his killer or killers. The LAPD's information was not nearly as interesting and detailed as Maria Calabrese's memory of the facts. At some point Jed would ask his Danbury, Connecticut, comrades to parody Jack Webb's rendition of "Just the facts, ma'am." He hoped that the Sergeant Friday who visited the Federal Correctional Institution in Danbury might provide some enlightenment to the mystery. His strategy of hope proved to be fruitless.

Maria's three years in the Danbury Correctional Institution, which began in March of 2002, had not been particularly pleasant. She had not been considered much of a hardened criminal, and was sent therefore to incarceration at Danbury, a low security prison, only twenty or so miles from her home. As far as she was concerned, minimum or not, it was prison. She was a petite woman. When she had met Alberto, she had a young Goldie Hawn-like body with an intriguing Debra Winger face, and long, silky, dark hair. When sentenced, her five-foot, five-inch frame weighed less than 110 pounds. Her body, her pride and joy, and all its seductive features, had endured a number of embarrassing and demeaning assaults. Although she still stood at a full sixty-five inches, she had lost fifteen pounds. She looked frail and impuissant.

Like a child with a chilling, recurring nightmare that would not go away, Maria relived in her mind the horrible and the wonderful events that put her here. Every night, after the lights went out, she sought escape within the prison-issued sheets. But as she placed her head on the flimsy pillow, the movie that was a combination of her impassioned promiscuity and deadly fear played and played in her head with unnerving clarity.

When Maria's war-widowed mother told her in 1988 that they needed to move out of the Bronx, the newly turned seventeen-year-old expressed her objections with screams and loud, maledictory verbiage. Unfortunately for Maria, her mother was the only option she had, if she chose to live somewhere other than on the street. As much as she screeched about changing schools and leaving her friends behind, Mom would not, and could not, budge. Mr. Carmine was moving to Northern Westchester, and she cared for Mr. Carmine and Ms. Sophia's home. And they paid her twice as much as any of her friends who had the same occupation. And Mr. Carmine was going to build her and her daughter a cottage home on the acre of land that was his. Until then, they could stay in Mr. Carmine's house in his finished basement.

For a week after the horrible news was delivered, the seventeen-year-old Maria moped and whined about leaving her friends. She was about to start her senior year of high school. How was she supposed to fit in with some snooty Northern Westchester crowd? What she did not explain to her mother was that she was currently having serious sex with three different boys at her high school. She also failed to throw in her experimental fling with the taut-muscled, blond twenty-year-old named Carrie, a worker in the school cafeteria. The young woman had a *cool* one-bedroom, two streets over from the school, and she let Maria and her boys use it for their adventures. She even gave Maria her own set of sheets to put on and take off the bed before and after she and her boy-of-the-day tried to satiate each other. Maria did not recoil when Carrie suggested an afternoon of just the two of *them* on Carrie's sheets. *Hell,* Maria thought, *why not? And this creature even washes my sheets once a week.* Maria was almost as upset about having to leave Carrie and her bedroom and her sheets behind as she was about leaving her Yonkers stud muffins.

Each new sexual discovery for Maria was like a favorite Christmas toy. Once the package was opened, she could not get enough of it, thought about it constantly, and dreamt about it at night. If the young girl took the "Are you a sex addict?" quiz, she would have passed with flying colors.

A week passed and the whining stopped. It stopped because the conniving, crafty, and just a bit-twisted mind of a sex-addicted teenager thought of new conquests awaiting just a short drive up the parkway—a new school, new partners. New flavors for an insatiable consumer of tastes and smells. *Maybe even a new Carrie lurked in the wings of the pending transition. Bring it on.*

The new high school and new neighborhood did not disappoint. Word got out quickly that there was a new girl in town, Maria Calabrese—free and easy Maria. Free and easy were two of the best words the local horny teenagers liked to hear.

It took Maria a couple of months to find a new Carrie. She had grown to like the feel of her body against another woman's, and she missed it. The new Carrie was a Sheila Robinson, who worked in the same restaurant where Maria worked part time. Her mother had insisted that Maria find a part-time job to support her voracious appetite for clothes and makeup. Like Cafeteria Carrie, Sheila was a few years older and blond. Unlike Carrie, she was petite and fragile. Maria liked the change. In this relationship she felt—even as the younger partner—in charge of the sex. Her demands and curiosity for different experiences drove what happened in the little apartment that sat in the middle of town. Sheila's place was on the first floor of a two-story complex that was surrounded by a small park. The park was home to an old train station that was part of a public play area. Yorktown Heights had been a stop on the old Putnam Division of the New York Central Railroad that took passengers from the Bronx all the way up to Brewster in Putnam County. The service was discontinued in 1958, but the station still stood, and was now a stop on Westchester's North County Trailway traveled by adventurous bikers and a backdrop for the two female lovers traveling on their own sweet journey. In Sheila's place, their own private play area, Maria realized that she was turned on by the contrast of her olive skin and dark hair against the angel-white skin and naturally blond hair—all of it—of her new friend. Another accepted but disappointing difference was that Sheila did not offer her apartment for any of Maria's male frolics.

After a few visits, things changed for the pair of female lovers. Work was over, and it was late on a Friday night.

"No school tomorrow, huh, Maria? Wanna stop for a drink?"

"Come on, Sheila. You know there's no school, *and* you know I'm not old enough to buy a damn beer."

"Oh, that's right," Sheila laughed out. "Well, how about my place then? Call your mom and tell her you're gonna stay over. I promise you won't regret it."

The ride in Sheila's Ford Taurus took less than five minutes. Sheila retrieved two cans of Budweiser from her kitchen, and the two girls sat and drank on the small park bench. The gentleness of the fall night and the starry sky were a perfect backdrop for the two tired waitresses. Beers done, Sheila took Maria's hand, and they made their way over to Sheila's. Once in the apartment, Maria started to go into high gear, taking charge, and practically tearing off Sheila's white blouse and black pants.

"Stop, Maria. Let me lead tonight."

Hmm, Maria thought, *why not? Change is good, right?* She stepped back and spread out her right arm in a motion that invited her friend to go ahead.

"Good. Sit. Drinks first. Vodka?"

"Sure," Maria said as she pulled a joint out of her purse and lit it up.

They sat together on the small, plaid, polyester couch in the living area with only the bathroom light for illumination. In between sips of the cheap vodka and tokes, Maria let Sheila stroke her hair and tease her neck and ears with her tongue. The stroking moved down to the white material of Maria's blouse, where her nipples had already hardened, and then down to tight black jeans, up one thigh and then the other. By the time Sheila's hand moved between Maria's legs, the younger girl thought she would scream from impatience and desire. They finished the drinks and the weed, and Maria tried to move in on Sheila. Sheila pushed her arms away and said, "Not yet, sweetie." The vodka and weed had mellowed Maria just enough to summon up a patience she did not think she had. The rest of the night included a slow strip by Sheila as she danced to Sting's "Bring on the Night" and an invitation for Maria to do the same as Shelia watched. Then the two danced to the next cut, "Consider Me Gone." It was the first time Maria had ever danced naked with anyone, boy or girl. They danced slowly, held each other, and explored with their hands. Sheila would stop Maria once in a while and force her to look her in the eye. She led her to a kiss, first lips-to-lips, and then escalated to a gentle tongue probing. Maria could smell the faint remnants of Sheila's perfume and it calmed her. It was all sensuous and comforting. After the dance and the first round of mutual orgasmic satisfaction, Sheila drew a hot bubble bath for both. Maria wasn't sure she wanted the smell of her lover washed off, but she agreed to the cleansing. They shared the water, the bubbles, and the most intimate parts of each other. Some of the touching included another first for the younger girl. The night finally ended with Maria's back spooned into Sheila's chest. Sheila had her right arm around her new student and gently held on to Maria's tiny right breast. Sleep came. Maria would never be the same. Sheila had given her a new set of weapons in her search for satisfaction. Sheila's earlier words in the evening would always be with her. "Sex doesn't always have to be a race to the finish line, sweetie. Sometimes it's better to be the turtle in the race."

In the fall of 1989, after high school, Maria moved on to Westchester Community College and a new set of boyfriends. For the thirty-minute commute down the narrow Taconic Parkway to Route 100 and onto the Valhalla Campus on Grasslands Road, her mother helped her finance a five-year-old Honda. The car was purchased at a deep discount from a Brewster, New York, car dealer who was, of course, now a new friend of Carmine's. Maria, to her mother's surprise and delight, liked school. She did well and did even better moving on to new and a larger choice of boyfriends. She still worked some at the restaurant and still enjoyed the color contrast of Sheila's naked body against hers on the red-sheeted double bed in the apartment in the park.

Maria still preferred the sensations a male could bring with the ultimate act, but the variety was fabulous fodder for her nighttime cerebral fantasies. The kaleidoscope of different naked images in different positions played colorfully in her mind. The playing often urged her on to the touch of her own soft hands across her small breasts and down to her center. The girl loved it all—her lovers, their deeds, and the pleasures of her own hands.

She was now in charge of all, well, almost all, of her sexual relationships. The boys who begged for her favors were rewarded only if they were good-looking. And, Sheila allowed Maria to stage whatever play she wished, wherever she wished, and however she wished in the tiny rooms of her sparsely furnished, rented chambers, as long as she mixed it up once in a while with Sheila's slower dance of passion. It was like a wish granted to young Maria.

Now, a little more than a decade later, she lay in her prison bed, no longer in charge of anything. And given her physical stature, without a prayer of being in charge of any of the sex that was being forced on her, she woefully remembered her mother's frequent use of the warning, "Be careful what you wish for, my dear. Things in life come in all different forms."

CHAPTER 10

▼

ALBERTO AND MARIA

Jed's files and transcripts touched on the history of the two convicted felons and their crimes. No words on paper anywhere were available to him that would tell the whole story.

"Hey, there," Maria yelled across the street to the handsome man mowing his lawn. She knew that he was about ten years older than she was. In fact, on this hot August day in 1991, on the streets of Nuovo Citta Estates, Alberto had already turned thirty-one and Maria was days away from moving out of her teens.

Maria and her mother had moved into the cottage a while ago, and Maria had seen less of the Antobelli family since the move. The cottage was adjacent to Carmine and Sophia's home, a perfectly groomed lawn between the two. Sophia had indeed done her planting and landscaping, and its beauty showed on this summer day. Even Maria took the time to notice the large, ripe tomatoes on the vines of the ten staked, green plants. The yellow blooms on the squash and the pretty purple flowers wanting to be eggplant decorated the front edge of the plot. The edges of the two homes were lined with nicely mulched beds full of trimmed shrubs. They were joined by hostas of different shades of green and white, and patches of begonias, day lilies, and impatiens colored the beds. The three large maples were surrounded by rich green pachysandra.

A few blocks away, near where Maria and her car now stood, the sight of the bare-chested, well-trimmed body of the man behind the Toro gave her an unexpected tingle. She knew who he was. She had periodically seen him at the house her mother tended in Yonkers. But back then he was way too old for her to have much more than a remote crush on him. Screwing boys her own age was safe. The older boy might be a different story. Now that she was almost all of twenty years old, she was less fearful, more curious.

The man in the grass-stained sneakers and baggy, jacquard New York Giants shorts shut down the Toro, took off his dark gray Ray-Bans, moved closer, and spoke back. "Hi. Maria, is it? My name is Alberto. I remember you from the old house." He did not offer his sweaty, meaty hand. Alberto had always known the girl from the Yonkers days and had seen her around once in a while up here in Yorktown, after she and her mother moved up. Alberto's father and mother and this girl lived a few blocks away, but now she was on his street, Palermo Way. The skimpy, white tank top and cutoff denim shorts that hugged her backside made him take notice, and he walked to where she was standing.

With a flirty smile and a subtle wink of her dark brown eyes, Maria asked, "Alberto, do you think you can help me?"

"Maybe. What's the problem?"

"Well, I let my girlfriend borrow my car last night, and when she brought it back this morning, it was almost empty. We're just trying to get to the Shell station in town down on Commerce Street, but it ran out of gas."

Alberto had not noticed the petite blond who was in the passenger's seat of the Honda. He walked over to the car, trying to subtly flex his muscular frame with every step.

"Sure, I can help. I think I have at least a gallon left in the gas can I use for the mower."

Pointing to Sheila, he said, "Is that the naughty girlfriend that left you dry?"

Two notions jumped into Maria's bright but sexually dominated mind. *Sheila has* never *left me dry. If this hunk only knew.* "Yep. That's the bad girl. I plan to give her a good spanking later." She paused and got back to business.

"That would be great, if you could lend me the gas. I would replace it."

Alberto, trying to shoo away the thoughts of these two nymphs naked, one spanking the other, responded, "Ahem, no need, Maria."

"I insist." Maria wasn't sure if the morals and politeness her mother tried to pound into her or the tingle that was still working its way across her body parts made her say that, but it just came out.

"Well, okay. Let me get the gas."

Alberto got the gas can and an idea at the same time. "If you insist on replenishing the gas, why don't you bring it over later today, and I'll make us a nice lunch. We can share old Yonkers stories."

"Well, great. Can I bring my friend, Sheila?"

"Sure. I'll pick some fresh vegetables from my garden and throw on a few burgers. No problem. How does two o'clock sound?"

As the morning's hot Yorktown sun beat down on the unlikely twosome, each took a second or two to observe the sweat slowly easing down the center of the other's olive-skinned chest—his down his naked torso resting on the hair just above his navel, hers working its way down between the minor cleavage clamped in the halter.

CHAPTER 11

▼

DUE MALIGNITA SEMENTI

It probably would not help Jed's case to know the details of that fateful morning or what transpired at lunch, but it would have been interesting.

Sheila declined the invitation to lunch. She was a bit wary of the sweating hunk. Maria, on the other hand, was interested and tempted by the thought of an older man. *A well-built, good-looking, single goombah. Bring it on.*

Maria dropped her girlfriend off at 10:00 AM and turned around to drive one block to the Shell station. If Sheila was feeling the least bit jealous of Maria's lunch date, she did not show it. Maria's female lover only warned, "Be careful. See you tonight."

It was a Saturday and Maria's mother was down in Manhattan with the Widow and Widower group from Saint Patrick's Church. Her group had gone into the city to see the hit Broadway show *Lost In Yonkers*. This meant Maria did not have to explain her date with Alberto and hear the protests about the wisdom of having lunch with an older man—the son of the man who wrote her mother's paycheck every week, always with an extra twenty in cash as a tip. Just to muck things up a little more, Maria's mother was also a church buddy of Alberto's mother. *But, hey, it was only lunch,* the young college girl thought.

Maria sat in her kitchen and looked at the round, wood-framed kitchen clock with the proud rooster standing in the middle. The hands were sticking out of his fat belly, moving slowly around the face of the timepiece. She was thinking that, like the crocodile in Peter Pan, the cock had swallowed an alarm clock with a loud, annoying tick. She swore she could hear the miserable seconds ticking away—ticking way too sluggishly for her liking. She was anxious about lunch. She had already showered and dressed for her date, and the bird on the wall only read noon. She had re-dressed several times, switching between khaki shorts and a simple, red T-shirt, to the beige, cotton A-line skirt and a sleeveless, lace-trimmed, white blouse, and finally to the short-sleeved denim dress and sandals. The underwear always remained the same. The matching black, satin-like panties with the lacy trim and the push up bra trying its best to make what little she had up top appear appealing.

The son of a bitch of a rooster finally worked the clock's hands on up to five minutes before two o'clock. The hands had seemed to move a little faster after she put Bonnie Raitt's *Nick of Time* into the tape player. The album had won the Grammy two years before, and Maria had locked onto the bluesy "Real Man" cut as a favorite. She had only smoked one joint as the album and its eleven songs, including "Nobody's Girl", another favorite, played through twice. Now mellow and bonding a little better with the blasted rooster, she made her way to the bathroom to brush her teeth and check her curb appeal one more time. Satisfied, she left and made the five-minute walk over to Alberto's two-story, redbrick colonial with the green shutters and doors. Halfway there she realized the red gas can was still in her car. "Oh well. Guess I'll just have to come back soon some other time," she said to herself with a smirk.

She did not have to ring the doorbell. Alberto was sitting out on the deck that hung off the back of the house and saw her approaching. He was dressed in his dark blue Wranglers and a cream-colored, blue-collared golf shirt. He had gotten the Ashworth at the 1986 U.S. Open at the Shinnecock Hills Golf Club in Southampton, New York. He had been rooting for Trevino, who finished three shots back of the forty-three-year-old Raymond Floyd, but he still considered the shirt his favorite. Old as it was, it still looked good. Maria waved when she saw Alberto, and he waved her up the steps to the deck. She had called earlier to tell him Sheila would not be coming. He was not all that disappointed. Maria had wondered whether or not he had one of those blasted rooster clocks in his kitchen and whether or not he had felt the same anxiety she had. No rooster clock for Alberto, but a black-rimmed cat clock with twelve different varieties representing the hours was hanging on the back of the house.

As the two shook hands, the clock began to make a purring sound, announcing it was exactly two o'clock. Before the afternoon was over, the clock's hands would work their way through five different breeds and the accompanying, contented variety of purrs.

"Nice clock. My mother has a rooster clock but it doesn't crow."

"Thanks. I like it, but I came close to shooting the little critters at twelve and one because it took too long for them to purr—too long for two o'clock and you to come along."

Maria laughed. "Well, Mom's rooster was also in serious danger. Patience is not my best virtue." Another nervous laugh and, "Nice shirt. I like the Indian with the colorful headdress."

"Thanks again. I bought it … Well, actually, my friend Joe Rayner, who's a member at this club, bought it for me when he and I went to the 1986 U.S. Open together. Hey, what can I get you to drink?"

"Well, my mother might not approve, but it would not be the first beer I've had in my life. If you have one, that would be my first choice. It's hot."

"Oh damn. I forgot your gas can."

"No problem. I can get it later."

A meal of cut and grilled garden veggies was ready at two-thirty. The zucchini, yellow squash, cherry tomatoes and sweet red peppers were joined by a mix of sliced red onion, chopped fresh basil, a little olive oil and vinegar with a touch of oregano. A sprinkling of salt and pepper was added to finish the dish off. To complete the vegetarian's dream meal was freshly picked eggplant, lightly breaded and fried to perfection. Maria drank her Heineken and followed Alberto around as he coordinated the lunch preparation. Ten seconds after the veggies were on their plates, a timer rang followed quickly by a plate of hot, equally coordinated rolls.

"Hope you like veggies."

"Love 'em." She had the marijuana munchies bad. She did like veggies, but she would have snacked on horsemeat if it were all he had.

"Another beer? Or would you like to join me in a bottle of white zinfandel?"

The afternoon went on in a very different way from any afternoon or "date" either of the two deck mates had ever had. The tension each began with had dissipated. The conversation was on a personal level. It was funny, then serious, then biographical. All of it executed with a surprising, unexpected level of comfort and openness.

Most surprising and unexpected was the fact that the day ended with a quick drive to town in Alberto's twelve-year-old Firebird and a stop at Friendly's on Commerce Street. His shiny, black beauty with the charcoal-colored interior was still in cherry condition and now only came out on special occasions. Alberto drove an equally black Chevy El Camino Super Sport V8 with a white pinstripe and slick chrome wheels for his every day activities. The uniformed, young blond, name-tagged Doreen, served up a smile, a chocolate cone for Maria, a sundae in a cup for Alberto, and a "Thank you for coming to Friendly's." Alberto, trying to behave, still could not resist, as he opened the door for Maria, sneaking a look back at the cute Doreen with the well-endowed bosom pushing out toward the fabric of her red polo shirt. What he got instead was a clear rear view of the slim waist and equally pleasing posterior housed in the black pants of their server.

The twosome, born over a decade apart, took the short walk over to the park with the old train station. They settled into one of the park's wooden-slatted and steel-framed benches in front of the station. Maria was glad they did not enter the interior of his pristine car with the goods. Her fear of dripping would have overwhelmed her eager desire for the first bite of the sweet, silky ice cream.

Ironically, Sheila was only yards away in her apartment wondering if she would hear from the playful Maria that night. She never did.

That night the unlikely couple did the unlikely thing. They sincerely enjoyed each other's company—their feelings, their thoughts, their smiles and laughter. But not each other's bodies. For both, the perfect end to the evening was a quiet ride home, a peck from Alberto on Maria's flushed cheek. Two bad seeds behaving. If both mothers could have witnessed the day and evening of their usually wanting-to-be-wild and passionate offspring, they would have sworn that some angelic creature had sifted through God's wastebasket, retrieved their prayers for the redemption of their children, and placed them on the very top of the Almighty's in-basket.

"I really had a good time tonight, Maria. Can we do it again, like, maybe tomorrow?"

"You pick the time. I need to go to morning Mass with my mother. She insists it may be my only chance at salvation."

"I know the feeling. How does an afternoon picnic on my boat sound? It's docked down at the Tarrytown Boat Club."

"I know this sounds foolish, but I actually think I need to clear it with my mom first."

"Great. Call me in the morning. Tell your mom what a good boy I have been today, and let's hope for the best. And I'll get that gas can tomorrow, either way."

CHAPTER 12

▼

ALBERTO AND MARIA—
WHAT DO YOU THINK?

Maria's mother was not happy with the idea of a day on Alberto's boat.

Alberto's mother was more emphatic. "Are you out of your mind, my *figlio*? She's an *infante*, a baby. How old is she? Eighteen?"

"Come on, Ma. She's twenty. It's just a date."

"You're thirty-one for goodness sake. Jesus, save me from this."

"I'll be a good boy, Ma. I promise."

The two mothers talked. "What do you think?"

"I don't know what to think, Sophia. She swears Alberto was the perfect gentleman on their secret, little date yesterday."

"Well, I have to admit, he has been behaving and doing well with Carm's trucking business. Let me read him the riot act and let's see what happens. Okay?"

"I guess, Sophia. Is Mr. Antobelli aware of this second date?"

"Yeah, but he's too busy with his wheeling and dealing to give it his time. He left it up to me. The usual 'whatever you think, Soph.'"

The Hudson River was placid and the boat ride went smoothly, as did, surprisingly, the next two years of courtship. Two weeks after graduating with honors, with a B.A. in history, from Manhattanville College in Purchase, New York, in May of 1993, Maria walked down the aisle of their old Yonkers Catholic church in a layered, chiffon wedding dress. Alberto, smartly dressed in an Oleg Cassini, two-button tux with a gray vest and knotted, black tie, greeted the bride. Watching the loving couple walk back down the aisle, hand in hand and smiling sincerely, Sophia hoped someday to meet that wonderful angel that had taken the time to rescue her unanswered prayers for Alberto from God's large, round file.

If the two newlyweds could have wiped their sexual slates clean on the hot summer day in August of 1991, their consummation in the executive suite of the Crowne Plaza Hotel at the United Nations on East Forty-second Street would have been virginal. The two transformed bad seeds had shared dreams and patience waiting for the wedding.

The two mothers had watched and witnessed with hope over those two years. Their "What do *you* think?" had cautiously morphed into a frequent, "Well, what do you think about *that?*"

CHAPTER 13

▼

HONEYMOON

The midmorning United flight from LaGuardia to Aruba took them through Charlotte, North Carolina. The two bright-eyed and enamored flyers did not mind the layover. It just helped to build the thrill of the anticipation.

Their hotel was right on the clear waters of the Caribbean Sea. The unseasoned travelers reveled in the beauty and simple quiet of the seventy-four-square-mile island, just off the north coast of Venezuela, and the island's glorious beaches. They also reveled for seven days and six nights in the energy and intimacy each brought to the marriage bed, the marriage floor, and many other spots and surfaces on which the two hungrily devoured each other. At first both were uncharacteristically shy, afraid to unmask their inner predilections for any and all variations of coupling. The breakthrough came the second night after a dinner of steaks at El Gaucho, the first Argentinean restaurant to open on the island back in 1977. The steak and a bottle of Malbec wine had loosened the newlyweds up—enough to have Maria suggest they share dessert in their room at the resort.

Alberto was surprised and pleased with the new Maria. The door had hardly closed to the room before she had his colorful beach shirt with the fish and waves unbuttoned. She paused briefly to take in his muscular chest—with her eyes and then with her tongue. She impatiently moved down to his stomach, and then knelt on the plush carpet. The brown belt and tan khakis were gone with a swiftness that suggested to Alberto that this was not his new bride's first foray into the oral arts. He let out an audible, almost gleeful moan as his young wife dazzled him with her soft, quick tongue and the light touches of her magic fingers.

The night went on and on, and the thirty-three-year-old Alberto even surprised himself with his stamina. Somewhere along the way, as Maria was perching her lithe body on top of his in a position he had not ever thought of before, he thought, *God, she's an animal.*

At one point Alberto took over the initiative, and Maria was happy he did. She even weaved in the lessons she had learned on that warm, fall night in Sheila's apartment. She did the stripping to the music from the song, "From a Distance." It was a slow, enticing tune about God watching us, sung by Bette Midler. She let Alberto off the hook—no stripping to music required on his part—and helped him out of his clothes, and, for the first time, she danced naked with a man. Different body, body parts, and smells, but no less pleasurable.

By the time the well-spent couple boarded the plane for the return to New York, even the two bad seeds were calm and satiated. Alberto had spilled his at a record pace and Maria was an eager recipient. Alberto was truly hooked on the pleasures his young bride brought him.

The plane ride gave each reflective time. Maria's time was spent comparing the marathon, unshackled and shackled sex to her quickie rendezvous of her younger years. *Life is good. Sex is good. Now it can be almost anytime, anywhere, any way.* The soreness she felt from the roughest of the week was only an inconvenient, sweet reminder of the act.

Alberto's ruminations were part marvel at his wife's appetites, mixed with hope for their future. He knew he loved her and now he was learning to love the delectations that she brought. Just reliving some of their moments in Aruba made him hard. His thoughts moved on to the possibility of maybe having a couple of kids. They had talked about it, and both were in sync with the vision of the happy couple with a few little tykes carrying on the Antobelli name, being spoiled by their grandparents, and Sunday dinner at Carmine's house in Nuovo Citta Estates.

They agreed to wait a while. Maria would turn twenty-five in 1996. Alberto and she were in concert with the idea that for the next few years Maria could try her hand at making a living in the real world.

Maria bounced from job to job, never quite finding her niche. She grew unhappy and was thinking that pregnant and barefoot may be her best occupation after all. The one steady keel that kept the relationship between Alberto and Maria growing and close over those years was the incredibly, mutually satisfying romps. The voraciousness of Aruba had dimmed only slightly.

Other than a single late-night dalliance with Sheila, when Alberto was out of town on an extended business trip, a year after the wedding, Maria had been faithful. She blamed the night of the sweaty tangling of her small body with all of the body parts of sweet, blond Sheila on Alberto's being gone too long and the several glasses of Bella Sera pinot grigio she had consumed. She had enjoyed the *bella sera*, beautiful evening, with the blond nymph, but vowed to put it behind her. As enticing as the mix of Sheila's blondness with her own olive skin was, she was Alberto's girl and needed to behave that way. Maria knew Sheila had other partners, and guessed that the blond would be just fine without her.

Alberto's trucking enterprise was doing very well. Money was not an issue, and Maria decided it was time for the bambinos.

As Maria had insisted, they made their annual August evening visit to Friendly's and ordered the same as they had four years ago, on their first date. They made the same walk to the park and sat on the same bench.

"I'm ready, Alberto. It's time for babies. If you're ready, I am going to stop the pill."

He smiled. "Great. Can we start tonight?"

"Anytime you're ready."

He was ready. Alberto was ready for all this meant. Mama and Pop would be thrilled. No longer would his brother Vinnie be the only good guy in the family. Sophia's bad seed of a son was ready.

CHAPTER 14

▼

DEEP SCARS

What Alberto was not ready for was a wife whose numerous and youthful sexual encounters had rendered her infertile. Maria's pelvic inflammatory disease, PID, was brought on by a case of gonorrhea from one of her many teenage encounters. The bacteria from the tryst had made its way to her upper genital tract and caused her fallopian tubes to scar.

Back in 1986, Maria's clandestine trip to the clinic had cleared up the clap. The single, silver-bullet doses of the cephalosporin antibiotic brought relief from the annoying symptoms and a reentry to the world of promiscuity. She knew she was clap free. What she did not know was that the untreatable consequences of her frequent walks on the wild side had cruelly erased any chance of conceiving—ever.

After a year of trying, including watching calendars and giving it their lustful best, there was no result. This time the prayers of the two hopeful mothers for a grandchild had no chance of making their way to their deity's inbox.

A begrudging Alberto agreed to have his sperm tested. The doctor didn't think it was a good idea to have Maria help him in the little room. After he closed the door, with the sterile cup in hand, his first pick was the October 1994 Playboy. It promised a close-up, naked view of the Girls of the Southeastern Conference. A lot of the college girls were named Heather; there were a few Kellys; but one thing for sure, they were all pretty. Alberto thought the prettiest girls were from the University of Georgia and the University of Tennessee. As he went about his embarrassing business, he thought maybe he should have been a better student and gone to college and hooked up with a few coeds like these beauties. By the time he made it to the blond centerfold, named Victoria something, the end was in sight.

The small tape player that he and Maria had snuck into the doctor's office, playing moans and groans and pleas from their last sexual session in his earphones, helped the process along. Alberto and the cup were satisfied as the naked, thin, blond centerfold with the large bosom stared back at his closing eyelids.

The doctor gently walked the couple through the results, using words like volume, number and structure, sperm movement, and the fluid thickness, acidity and something else. Dr. Kevin Blumenthal began to move on with the detailed results. "And the numbers associated with …"

"Doc, you're killing me here. I just spent time in your bathroom, well, jerking off. Can you please get to the final answer?"

"Sorry, Alberto." The Doc nodded to Maria and continued. "Your sperm is fine, Alberto." His counts were so at the top of the ranges that the doctor was tempted to add, "You're healthy enough to impregnate a horse." But he held back.

The doctor turned to Maria and suggested she be tested. And she was.

The slippery slope formed quickly in front of the barren couple. Maria's problem was diagnosed, possible causes explained, and Alberto inflamed. The honeymoon magic that was still lingering and the visions of a *Father Knows Best, Leave It To Beaver* future dissolved like an ice chip spit out onto a hot city street.

For the sake of their families, the two bad seeds put up a good front. They even shared the same bed, and when inclined, Alberto made love to his ex-whoring wife. They explained their lack of a pregnancy as, "The doctors are still working on our issues. We're still hoping."

The pretense held up remarkably well for many years. Then the slopes, each now owning its own incline, got more slippery. Alberto's more quickly than Maria's.

Alberto was getting bored with the repetitive monotony of the trucking business. Maria was getting bored with a love life long turned monogamous. It was okay; it just wasn't enough.

Alberto's chosen cure was a return to the high and the rush that gambling had brought him many years before. His luck was not good. His debts led him into drugs—not doing, but transporting and distributing. The money was flowing. He resigned himself to a childless life and traded it in for the "good life." Divorce was not something he wanted; girlfriends would be too complicated. He decided that he and his wife would play the cards that God had dealt them. The couple stayed in Nouvo Citta Estates, but their home got a complete makeover. Their vacation destinations changed from Atlantic City and the Jersey Shore to Las Vegas and the Caribbean. His gambling luck did not change. So, with the help of an expert, he got into the other end of the bets. *Bookies never lost,* he thought.

Maria's travels down the incline were put on temporary hold as she grew used to the taste of money and the luxuries it afforded. She reveled in Alberto's new choice of lifestyle. She was not quite sure where all the money was coming from, and was not really caring. The change seemed to breathe newness into their relationship in and out of the bedroom. Alberto actually got kinder and gentler toward her. He was able to focus again on the sexual prowess of his barren bride and put the dreams of an Alberto Jr. lighting up their lives behind him. He was attentive, bordering on possessive—at least when he was around. The flurry of the pleasing activity that the money brought, and Alberto, the newly animated sex partner, willing to follow her lead to climax, ameliorated Maria's boredom for seven more years.

But then the soul-deep cravings came back with a searing vengeance. There was only one type of cure for Maria's addiction. Her first fix came with a reunion with Sheila. Sheila, still working at the restaurant in town. A little older, yet still very satisfying.

Then in the fall of 2001 the slope that had flatlined into a repetitive life pattern got precipitous. His name was Roberto Speck.

CHAPTER 15

▼

A FAVOR

"Hello, is Carmine in, please?" Sophia, working in the real estate office of C&S Homes, had picked up the call. Her husband had set up the office in 1998 on Route 118, right in the middle of downtown Yorktown Heights. Yorktown Heights is an unincorporated hamlet in the larger town of Yorktown, New York.

Sophia worked several mornings a week to help out. In the late 1990s Carmine Antobelli, Alberto's father, was deep into real estate. He had jumped on his *own* father's train with both feet.

Sal Antobelli's move back in the '70s had proved to be brilliant and lucrative. The Ruffino Chianti he had splashed back in 1976 in front of his Nuovo Citta Estates gates, accompanied by his shout for health and well being, brought exactly that and riches. Carm had expanded his ventures into Northern Westchester and Putnam counties in New York. Now, in the fall of 2001, he was in the throes of major developments across the state border in Fairfield County, Connecticut, with deals being made in the towns of Danbury and Bethel.

Carm's success did not go unnoticed by his former business associates from Yonkers and the city.

"Yes, he's in. May I ask who's calling?"

"Just tell him it's an old friend from his Yonkers days."

Sophia was tempted to hang up but instead said, "Please hold."

She motioned for her husband to pick up line two.

"Carmine, here. May I help you?"

A hearty and familiar voice spoke. "Carm, long time, no talk. I hear things are going real well up there in Yorktown. I need a favor. Can we do lunch some time?"

Sophia had watched her husband's usually pleasant and confident demeanor tense into a tightness of muscles and a pallid look that painted his grimacing face.

That phone call was the catalyst that introduced one Roberto Speck of Chappaqua, New York, to the Antobelli family. Speck was the son of one of the big city crime bosses—not by birth but by virtual adoption. The son the boss never had, Rob, as most called him, was his sister's son.

Teresa was a Sicilian blond who married a tall, light-haired man of Germanic descent. His name was Frederick, a professor at the City College of New York, CCNY. It was no surprise that their only son, Roberto—a name that Frederick conceded to his wife—sported an attractive mane of bright blond hair. It was also no surprise that he stood a trim, six feet tall. From birth, Rob was wrapped in love and learning. His mob uncle went to extremes to keep the beautiful boy away from the dark side of his business and yet close to him.

At the age of twenty-eight, Rob had a Master's degree in civil engineering from CCNY's Grove School of Engineering and a few years of experience as a junior-level engineer at the firm of Percopo Builders in Northern New Jersey. His uncle thought that his old friend Carm might be able to help Rob get on a faster track. After a quiet lunch with Rob and his uncle at a small Italian restaurant on the upper west side of Manhattan—owned by a friend of the uncle's—Carm offered Rob a position as the general contractor for all of his real estate development. Rob would incorporate his own company and set up an office in Yorktown Heights, not far from Carm and Sophia's place of business.

Carmine was surprised and relieved when the uncle made it clear that this was Rob's deal and that he would have no part in it other than to help his nephew set up shop. The deal fell under the cliché of an offer Carm could not refuse. The uncle was true to his word; his only participation was that of a cheerleader and, if asked, an advisor. Rob was bright and hard working, and the relationship between him and the Antobellis was symbiotic and fruitful—at least for a while.

CHAPTER 16

▼

BAD SEED BACK IN ACTION

"May I help you?"

"Yeah, I'm looking for Sophia," Maria responded as she took in the blond Adonis standing in the office. His blue jeans fit snugly against a muscular pair of legs and what she imagined was a delectable posterior. The brisk October day had called for one of Rob's L.L. Bean flannel shirts. Its kelp green material gave further accent to his well-tuned physique.

"Sorry. She and Carm just ran over to the A&P to pick up supplies for the office pantry. They were gonna pick up some sandwiches at Bella Luna to bring back here. They said they'd be back in an hour or so. My name is Rob. I work with, more accurately, for Carmine and Sophia. I'm their general contractor. I was in the office here doing some paper work and volunteered to hold down the fort while they ran out. My next appointment isn't until later this afternoon in Danbury. Is there anything I can do for you?"

Hmm, the bad angel resting on the thirty-year-old woman's left shoulder whispered into her consciousness.

"No, no. I'll just stop by later."

"Can I give them a message? Tell them you were here? Anything?"

Hmm. Go ahead. Take a shot. You know you've been itching. Look at him. He's as blond as Sheila and he's got a dick. Imagine your skin against his blondness.

"Nah. Unless Carmine and Sophia are bringing a sandwich back for you, I'm about to grab a bite for lunch over at the Coachlight. Care to join a lonely girl?"

And the rest, as they say, is history.

CHAPTER 17

▼

CONFESSION TIME

"God all-freaking-mighty, Maria. Are you nuts? You are married to Carmine and Sophia's *son*? If I had known."

By the time Maria felt she had to squab the legumes to Rob, they had met at a motor inn on Route 22 in Brewster, another in Peekskill and three more in Connecticut. She had cleverly deceived him by painting a false self-portrait filled with enough believable lies—including the big one about being single.

She did not want to rendezvous at his house on Highbrook Street because her mother, with whom she lived—another big, fat lie—was friendly with a couple on the street. Her mother was too tight with God to ever accept sex outside of marriage.

Daytime worked better than night. Her mother worked during the day and expected Maria to be home at night to help with dinner and chores.

She had the twenty-eight-year-old believing she was only twenty-four and not quite independent enough to piss off Mom. She also had him totally wrapped around her little finger and other body parts. She had him so deep in lust in their short time together that, after his incredulity over the depths of her deception subsided, he bowed to her desire to conspire and consort. She continued to meet him near his different work locations at least twice a week. She arranged the place. He paid the bill. An expensive lunch that would not be allowed on his expense report for tax purposes. *But, God almighty, she was hot and worth every cent.* He was hooked, addicted.

CHAPTER 18

▼

OOPS

"Damn, Joey. That looks like Alberto's wife. The hot little broad over there walking into the hotel."

"Shit. We can always use a little appreciation from the boss. We got time. Let's wait a while. It's hard to tell from here. She's got the big winter coat on and sunglasses."

"I'm telling you, that's her. Let's see if this place has a bar. We got time."

The sleek 2002, black Eldorado coupe made a u-turn on Tuckahoe Road and parked in the lot. In the hotel's small, dark bar the driver loaded up on a gin and tonic; the passenger settled for a bottle of Bud; and they both lit up a Marlboro, and waited.

From their van, the two FBI agents who had been following Alberto's wife for two weeks had seen the leather-clad twosome enter, and made a small note. They then pulled around back to get their remote listening devices closer to the action.

Carmine and his clan had been so clean for so long that the locals and the Feds stopped wasting any manpower on trailing, bugging, tapping, or observing. The only blip that had made it to the radar screen was Carmine's lunch with the still-active crime boss, the Little Don. And then, a month ago, one of the Feds, who was still dogging Carmine's lunch partner, Rob's uncle, picked up a conversation that involved Alberto, Carmine's son, and a hefty drug transaction. Although the post-9/11 frenzy had chewed up law enforcement resources in the

New York City region, the FBI had a long-standing bug up their ass for Rob's uncle.

James Acerno, one of the two agents keeping an eye on Alberto's wife, will never forget his boss's boss's directive. "If this bastard Alberto can get us to the Little Don, the next time he takes a shit, you plant a bug so far up his ass we'll know what he's thinking."

The suspicion was that Alberto was using his trucking business to facilitate transport of large quantities of the Little Don's drugs in New York and across state lines. By now, Alberto had grown the business to over one hundred trucks directly owned by his father and him. He also had a list of sub-contracts with friends of Carmine's to pick up any overload. Other than some paper issues and a monthly stipend that Alberto paid his father, Carmine had essentially turned over all aspects of the business to his son. A son who had morphed from bad boy to successful businessman and loving husband.

So far, the trumped-up traffic stops of Alberto's trucks that the local cops had executed on behalf of the Feds had come up empty. They had no cause for warrants, and the limited searches from the pullovers for failing to signal or a busted taillight were a total bust. Even the unwarranted, illegal, and clandestine searches of some of Alberto's vehicles yielded nada, zippo, and zilch.

Desperation led the FBI to a plot that involved Alberto's wife. Watch her. See if she has any bad habits. If yes, capture her dalliances on film. Get copious photos, recordings, and paper trails to threaten her, to turn her, to flip on her husband. Fortunately for them, Maria had recently met a certain Rob and returned to the dark and wild side. The two agents sitting in the white surveillance van in the lot next to the motel had a fantasy vision. It was one of the diminutive Maria being sweated out in an FBI interrogation room in one of her cute little outfits shortly after she had finished screwing the brains out of the pretty boy, Rob. When they found out who her precious Rob was—more importantly who his uncle was—the agents' personal surveillance tools and budget were considerably enhanced. They weren't sure if Maria and her beau tuned in the loud rock music that came from the hotel room's radio to enhance their orgasmic explorations or if they were being extra careful not to bring too much attention to their passionate utterances. They pretty much had enough data to bring Maria in and present her with options, especially the idea of working for them to get to Alberto and, hopefully, the Little Don.

Leo Tolstoy once wrote, "The two most powerful warriors are patience and time." And the FBI hoped that if they used enough of both, their surveillance of the two lovers, so close to the bureau's primary mob prey, would yield some valuable and incriminating evidence. So they followed and listened, and now, with a bigger budget, they watched.

The Feds were happy when the two stopped meeting all over several counties and two states. They felt they were in a position to secure enough quality video and audio to soon bring in the little nymph.

Rob had stumbled onto the fact that an old friend managed this Yonkers place. The arrangement was simple. Rob had a permanent key to room 113, and the manager got fifty bucks a visit, off the books. If for any reason the hotel got booked, the manager would let Rob know to stay away. For several weeks, this had not yet happened.

Maria was back home in a sense. "Rob, this is great. My old turf. We do have to be careful though. I know a lot of people here from the old days.

"Do we always get the same room?"

"Yep."

"You don't think the number 113 is unlucky?"

"No way. I think this is our new lucky number. Remind me to play it on the Pick 3 Lottery."

And for three weeks Maria followed the plan to pull around to the back of the hotel to avoid being seen by any of her old Yonkers pals or anyone else. This week Maria got lazy and was in need of one of those oversized Hershey Bars in the lobby's vending machine. Hence, the front entrance by Maria, and Alberto's troops making the sighting.

This was Thursday, January 3, 2002. The temperature was in the low thirties and the wind added just enough chill to force Maria to keep her clothes on in the room for minutes longer than she wished.

It had been a torturous holiday time for the twosome. They had had only three months since their chance, autumn meeting at Carmine's office to explore and satisfy each other—not enough time. Now, one post-holiday afternoon delight was not nearly enough to ease the burning of the flame. So, Friday, January 4, at noon it would be for their next adventure. No problem for Rob, who could be wherever, whenever most of the time. It was the nature of his job.

After Maria made her way out of the lobby and back to her car on that Thursday, Alberto's boys debated and then decided to call. "Rocco, shit, man. If we don't call and he finds out and finds out we knew, we are screwed big time."

"Okay, Joey, I'll do it." Rocco dialed his cell and got Alberto in his office at the garage.

"Hey, boss."

"Hey. What's up, Roc?"

"We weren't sure we should call, but Joey thought we should."

"Yeah."

"Well, we just saw your wife in a hotel on Tuckahoe Road."

"What? She's out shopping with her friend Sheila. She called a little while ago to tell me."

"Well, we're just saying maybe not. We're pretty sure it was Maria, even with the sunglasses on."

"What was she wearing?"

"One of those long winter coats, with a big fur collar."

"What color?"

"Coat was black, collar was like a light color, fox or something. And she was driving a silver Lexus, one of those sporty ones, a C300 or something, I think."

"An SC 300, silver, black leather interior. Goddamn that bitch."

The conversation went on for a few more minutes. The more Alberto's anger rose up in him, the more colorful his language got. Then he calmed down and slowly gave instructions.

"You got it, boss."

Rocco and Joey Abate, cousins and friends, finished their second drink and walked over to the manager's desk. Rocco was dressed in a pair of J. Crew black corduroys, black sneakers, and a dark green, long-sleeved Greg Norman mock turtleneck. He picked up his knee-length, black leather coat from the back of the bar chair and motioned for Joey to follow. Joey, always dressed like he was ready for a hot date, stood up in his black leather Florsheim dress boots and grabbed his tan leather coat. His pleated, black-and-white Donegal tweed trousers flowed sweetly with his steps, and the tight, dark pink V-neck sweater over his white dress shirt showed off his buffed torso and arms.

Rocco squinted his eyes and looked at the gold-colored nametag pinned onto the cheap black vest.

"Uh, James, how are you doing today?"

"Fine. May I help you?"

"I bet you can. Do you have an assistant?"

"She's out to lunch."

"Oh, do you have one of those 'Be back in five minutes' signs?"

"Uh, no. Why?"

"Too bad. I guess I'll have to be your assistant then for a few minutes while you talk to my friend Joey here."

"Excuse me?"

Rocco and Joey walked over to the side door that led to the space behind the desk and entered. James's protests were silenced with the appearance of Joey's Glock. The dark, four-and-a-half-inch barrel would win easily over any argument the manager might have. Joey took James into his office on the side of the desk area and Rocco manned the desk with a smile.

"Who was the chick with?"

"What chick?"

"Don't screw with me, James. The cutie with the Hollywood sunglasses who just walked out of your lobby."

After a number of threats, including the raping of all of James's family members and reaching down their throats to rip their hearts out—in front of James, of course—to be followed by a bullet to James's skull, the manager gave it all up. He wasn't sure who the woman was, but he gave up Rob's name, their deal for room 113, and the fact that the deal had been going on for three weeks, sometimes twice, sometimes only once, a week. James added, looking for favor and mercy, "He, well, he called from the room to see if tomorrow was okay for him. I told him it was. He said he'd see me then."

Rocco and Joey reported back to Alberto, who took a bottle of Grey Goose vodka, a footed, five-ounce rocks glass, and a pistol down to the basement. He retrieved three cubes of ice from the playroom refrigerator and began cleaning his gun. By the time Maria arrived home, the Grey Goose had mellowed Alberto just enough to incite his own devious deception.

"Hi, hon. I'm home."

"Hi. Did you and your friend have a good time at the Jefferson Valley Mall?"

"Oh, okay. A lot of looking. I just picked up a few things from Bath and Body Works."

Alberto did not bother to try and uncover her lie. He rightly assumed that the bitch kept a cadre of goodies in her trunk to support her alibis.

"I thought we'd order takeout from Miraggio's. I'm in the mood for some goombah food tonight *and* a taste of your cute little ass for dessert."

"Alberto, you sweet talker, you. Miraggio's sounds great. I'll take some of the stuffed shells. Hey, I'm gonna jump into the shower. Can we eat early? I'm kinda whipped."

"Sure. How's six?'

"Perfect."

Alberto drove to the Triangle Center and picked up Maria's shells and a veal dinner for himself. He drank almost a full bottle of Bellavista 1994 Solesine Lombardia. At dinner, the mix of 85 percent cabernet and 15 percent merlot given to them by his parents for Christmas did not stand a chance against Alberto on this night, and neither did Maria.

"I'm ready for dessert now, babe."

"So soon?"

"Yeah, the wine made me horny. Let's go."

Any hope Maria had had of going to sleep remembering the taste of Rob from today and the dreaming of the promise of tomorrow faded like dust in a hurricane. Her plan to use the "Sheila approach" to satisfy Alberto tonight, and save her already-weakened energy for her blond boy might as well have been filed with Lieutenant Colonel George Armstrong Custer's plan for Little Big Horn. Her first part of the Sheila act was tolerated. She was happy to see the smile on Alberto's face as she slowly undressed in front of his naked form lying on the bed. She knew he loved to watch her, and she was confident that she could dispose of his desires quickly. Wrong.

"Come here, now."

Maria tried to get on top. There would be none of that tonight.

He did not know if she was wet enough to take him or not, and he did not care. He was inside her and he rode her as hard as he could. When he had been cleaning his gun, he had decided that this was what tonight would be. It would not be one last time to make love. It would be one last time to screw her hard. She was screwing around on him, the barren, ungrateful piece of trash, and she would have to pay.

"Jesus, Alberto, you're hurting me." No response, just more of the same.

When he came, he wanted to whisper in her ear. "Don't worry, whore. It won't happen again." Instead he just rolled off, kissed her on the cheek, and walked into the bathroom to take a shower. Maria blamed it on the wine and just went to sleep, hoping to rest and recover for tomorrow's much gentler lovemaking. Alberto went back downstairs, manipulated his TiVo, and watched the whooping Miami was laying on Nebraska for the NCAA football championship. He played with cleaning his gun one more time. Alberto still made his weekly visit to the shooting range over on McLean Avenue in Yonkers, not far from his office. Although he had fired his pistol at paper targets thousands of times, he had never threatened a human being with the weapon. He looked down at the immaculate weapon. *You and me, big boy. You and me are gonna scare the shit out of the bitch and the numb nuts who thinks he can get away with screwing my wife.* To finish off the night Alberto poured himself a healthy dose of Grey Goose into his rocks glass and gently placed the secured pistol in the foam cushions that lined his hard-shelled, gun-carrying case.

For the next day, Maria would have to borrow a favor from an old girlfriend. Friday's excuse and cover would be lunch at Luciano's on Central Avenue and a movie at the Cross County Multiplex. The movie choice was *Monster's Ball* with Halle Berry and Billy Bob Thornton. Her girlfriend had been dying to see it since it was released the day after Christmas. She had heard so much about the sexy scene in the movie. She asked no questions and would fill Maria in on all the details of the film later that afternoon, just in case Alberto asked about the movie.

CHAPTER 19

▼

"Damn, Rob. You gotta leave the site again today? We were all gonna go over to Farruggio's up on Tuckahoe and grab some of those mini-sausage calzones or pizza and maybe a beer. You know, celebrate the holidays as a crew. Spend a little bit of that bonus money you threw at us at Christmas."

"Sorry, Johnny. I can't today."

"Jesus, Robby boy, are you busy banging some chick on these long lunch hours of yours or what?"

"I wish, Johnny. Tell you what. Let's do it Monday. Make a reservation for the whole crew and I'll pick up the tab."

"Shit, boss. Now that is an offer we can't refuse. Will you be back today?"

"Nah. I have to be in Fishkill by four for a potential project up in God's country. I'll see you Monday. Make the reservation late. Like for two, and then we can make an afternoon of it."

"You got it, boss. I'll tell the boys and the girl, Miss "Hot Hammer" Helena, to make sure they bring some clean clothes for the event."

Friday at noon the temperature was again an annoying thirty-three degrees and the wind had gotten gustier. Rob had arrived early enough to be already warmed by the room's heater that hummed in front of the green-curtained window. He was plopped on the floral, green-and-gold bedspread reading the sport's page. When Maria opened the door to room 113, he wasted no time in grabbing onto his addiction in her fur-collared down jacket. This time Maria had parked around back. And this time, not only did the two FBI audio voyeurs not have to strain to listen; they got to watch. They had counted on the creatures of adulterous habit to be in the same room. They were, and the two observers were in room

115, next door. Their hidden camera mounted in 113 and the enhanced audio system were quietly recording what might sell well as *Maria Romps Rob*.

One of the agents, an alum of Miami, insisted on having SportsCenter on. The ESPN noon broadcast could not get enough of last night's highlights of the undefeated Hurricanes crushing the Nebraska Huskers in the AT&T Rose Bowl to the tune of 37-14. It was their fifth championship in less than twenty years. The 39-yard run of Clinton Portis, just 27 seconds into the second quarter, got special attention. The alum watched with enthusiasm. He spoke softly but carried a big smile. "Bang, go. Bang. Get in. There you go, baby. Bang 'em hard."

When Maria entered room 113, the second agent, an alum of Virginia Tech—ergo a Hurricane hater—made the cheering agent shut up and turn the TV off.

"God, Rob. I did not sleep worth a shit last night, just dreaming of today. Warm me up quick, baby."

"I am at your command, Princess Maria." He took her in his arms and brushed his hands up and down her back, making sure to include and linger on her tight buttocks. Still clothed, Maria began to undress the already-warm Rob. As she kissed him with her tongue, hungry for his, the buttons on the ink blue flannel were expertly undone. He had no undershirt on, and offered his chest to her mouth. She knelt and undid the familiar Levi's 501's buttons with ease. She pulled down on everything. He stepped out. Naked, he watched Maria's mouth take all.

"Do you think that's enough film?"

"Are you nuts? You never know what she might say."

Agent Morrow, the Hurricane rooter, had asked and been answered by Agent Acerno.

A spent Rob bent down and put his hands under Maria's shoulders. She resisted. She still had him in her mouth and was making funny noises, almost laughing.

She looked up with a sheepish grin and finally let him help her up. Her mind, bent with the thoughts of her love for unbridled sex, was alive again. This blond beauty lifting her up to him had again given her the *taste*. The taste accompanied by a thirst and obsession. Their three months together had not diminished either's itch nor the heat with which they scratched it. The idea of multiple lovers, male or female, had been a taste she acquired early in her sexual awakenings. She was back where she belonged.

"My turn," she said. Today's performance would not include any of the Sheila lessons. There would be no slow stripping, no naked dancing, and no quiet music. Her only move was to jack up the heat on the room's heater.

"My pleasure."

The urgency meant no music, no noise to obstruct the Fed's audio feed. The flesh-filled, graphic video scenes meant the two agents had to pretend that they were not getting hard. *Hey, it's just work.*

Unbeknownst to the participants and onlookers, the scenes were ironically similar to the coupling and positioning, and the moaning and whisperings that were taking place on the big screen as Halle and Billy Bob did the nasty on the big screen just up the road.

Rob tore off the bedspread and almost tore off his little nymph's Lands' End charcoal pullover fleece. He tossed the soft garment on the chair beside the TV, and made easy work of the white blouse that was left. No bra impeded his hunger. He first took each breast in one of his hands. Tweaked her brown nipples and then brought his mouth to them and took turns. His mouth devoured the less-than-a-handful, just more-than-a-mouthful breasts. He knew that she loved the kissing and sucking he could perform on her tiny orbs.

Her moaning had heightened just before he placed her on the edge of the bed.

"God, Rob, why did you stop?"

"You know why."

Neither of the agents in the next room asked any questions. They just marveled with a sense of jealousy for the moment. Agent Acerno was partial to small-breasted women with perky, little nipples, and this one fit the bill.

Rob pushed Maria's back onto the bed. Her feet dangled just off the floor. Her brown leather boots with the high, thick heel put up a small quarrel against his pulling hands. The smooth, black, napa lamb leather pants and red panties came off without any resistance.

Soon Maria's moaning started to mix with exclamatory remarks, proclaiming Rob's skills and invoking a deity or two. After her third screech, Maria pushed herself up onto her elbows and retrieved Rob's head still buried between her legs. They both laughed and she coaxed him up onto the bed and rolled him over onto his back. She mounted him with ease, and repetitive, fragmented exclamations soon emanated from the big blond. He let her ride him hard. The headboard made an occasional bang against the wall.

"Ooh. Oh. Yes, yes. Oh, God. Don't stop." Rob was approaching his second explosive orgasm in less than thirty minutes, and in the spirit of the height of football season, he had planned to end this one with a triumphant, "Touch-down," as he raised his arms—but stop she did.

"What's wrong, baby? Do you want me to get on top?"

The cops in the other room were repeating Rob's first inquiry in their own minds. They did not have time to mull over the second.

No one except Maria, via a distorted reflection on the top, rounded rung of the cheap brass bed, saw Alberto enter the room. Her shock blocked out Alberto's voice and his first request.

"Get up.

"Get up. Get up now, you fucking whore." His words were cold and deliber-ate, and the venom with which they were laced dripped heaviest from the adjec-tive.

"Alberto, I'm sorry. I'm ..."

"I know exactly what your are, you slut."

Rob started to get up and yell, "What ...?"

"Now you, blondie—you do not make a single move. You are allowed to do two things: breathe, and, I suppose, allow that filthy pecker and disgusting balls of yours to shrink into oblivion."

Earlier, from his black Cadillac Escalade that he had parked in the back, Alberto had watched the two lovers enter the hotel, him first, then the bitch. He had let fifteen minutes go by, walked into the lobby, and had a brief conversation with Rob's manager friend. The manager's eyes moved from Alberto's face to the 4.3-inch barrel of a Beretta 92-Type M Inox. The 9mm was pointed at his gut, and he quickly turned over his extra key to room 113. Alberto took the key. He pushed the pistol's side-mounted safety on. Slowly and carefully, holding onto the black plastic grip, he placed the double-action semi-automatic and its eight rounds in his brown leather jacket's right pocket. The custom sound suppressor was in the left pocket.

No one had heard the door to room 113 open. The heated bodies on the dampened sheets had barely felt the cold air that was let in. The two agents had been frozen in ignorance. Their camera was focused on the bed and its immediate surroundings. They had no shot of the door.

Once Alberto was in the room, it went quickly. "Come here, now, Maria. Turn around." He pulled her naked back into his chest and put the gun in front of her face and aimed at the bed. The safety was now off, the slide had already been racked to load the first round into the firing chamber, and the custom-made silencer was in place He took her right hand and married it to the trigger, and placed his on top of hers. "Shoot him. Between the legs, preferably." She began a protest. As Alberto was helping Maria apply the twelve pounds of force required to pull the trigger which would cause the bullet to fly, the jacket to eject, and the next round to find its way into the chamber, Rob jerked himself up. Alberto squeezed, trying not to allow Maria's fright to cause the pistol's kick to take them off aim. A soft "bang" filled the room. The 124-gram Luger, full-metal-jacket projectile went higher than Alberto had hoped. The bullet, traveling at over 1,000 feet per second, caught the naked Rob on the right side of his jaw and traveled upward. *This* the agents saw.

The brass casing ejected from the side of the Beretta's chamber and landed silently on the rug.

The next bang, a booming one, came from agent Morrow's gun. The .40-caliber discharge slammed into the door just above and to the side of the lock. The door splintered. An anxious Morrow kicked the door. The key and chain locks gave way, and the door opened.

"FBI. Drop it, now."

Alberto swung around at the sound of the SIG pistol blasting at the lock of the door that he had just secured. Maria's naked body was still spooned into his and her finger still wed with his to the trigger.

The debate as to whose finger was ultimately responsible for the trigger being squeezed on Alberto's Beretta at that moment was an academic one. Another soft "bang" and the bullet raced toward the open entrance of 113, and then into the unprotected chest of Agent Morrow. Alberto's practice at the shooting range made it an easy shoot from such a short distance. The second round from Morrow's SIG went harmlessly into the ceiling as he flew back from the door.

The shock of seeing his partner of eight years blown back and crumbling on the concrete sidewalk slowed Agent Acerno down. Morrow, the tall, handsome, athletic, hero type had always been first at any door, always anxious to lead the way against the bad guys.

Acerno yelled, "FBI. You will not get out of that room alive. Drop the gun and slide it out the door."

CHAPTER 20

▼

BANG, BANG

The road to trial for the two FBI killers was a short one. The prosecutors expedited everything. If the defense tried to delay, they were run over by a team of government lawyers and judges who had been told to get these two to justice, and do it quickly.

The trials in the United States Courthouse of New York's Southern District, in the city of White Plains, did not take long. The focus was simple: a federal law enforcement official had been shot and killed, and the husband and wife from Yorktown, New York, did it. Life without parole, period, for Alberto. What came out at his trial were just the key facts, as the prosecutors knew them. That was enough—intent, gun, shootings. The crime of passion being pushed by Alberto's lawyers was not being bought.

What did *not* come out at the trial was Alberto's entire original plan. After Maria killed her lover, he would have her sweet, soft mouth and tongue service him one last time, with his pistol held to her pretty little head. The spilling of his bad seed into Maria's mouth was to be followed quickly by a single, deadly shot to her temple. He would wash her mouth out with the gin he had in a small bottle in his jacket to erase away traces of his semen and then wipe the pistol clean. He would reapply Maria's prints from her dead hand to the Beretta. Then he would call in Rocco and Joey Abate from the bar to help cleanse the room of any of his prints and be gone. This bit of information was not shared by Alberto and was not necessary for the jury to convict.

The jury was politely thanked and dismissed by Judge Barbara Brandenburg. Her red cherrywood mallet solidly slammed the matching sound block that was perched on her bench. The "bang" of the gavel and her words, "court adjourned," were purposeful and well heard.

Maria's trial had more pleading going on. "She was *only* guilty of adultery and forced into the rest." Apparently the jurors did not care for adulterers or Maria, and she was found guilty on the charge of second-degree murder. She would spend twenty-five years in prison. Same closing, different adjudicator. A judge's thanks to the jury, "bang" with the wooden gavel, and adjournment.

Just two months after the two bad seeds had spawned their evil in a Yonkers hotel room, they were found guilty as charged and sentenced.

For Agent Acerno, any investigation of Alberto's drug connections and activities was over. At the trial the testimony of the good-looking agent with the nasty scar down the right side of his face was as cold as his heart felt. He laid out the facts, as he knew them, omitting many of the details of the fateful *Maria Romps Rob* footage.

Any reprimands the FBI tried to dish out were met with more coldness and a large helping of indifference. He was forty-nine years old. He had put in more than his twenty years. The pension was not a lot, but where he planned to go would not take a lot. His partner had been long ago buried by his family. Agent Morrow's twelve-year-old son had been given the folded U.S. flag, and the son, the wife, and younger daughter, along with many others, saluted and said their silent goodbyes.

For Rob and his uncle, their shared dreams of Rob's successful career had literally gone up in the smoke of a 9mm pistol. Hopes for a cleaner, safer kind of business for the Little Don's family to build its future on were brutally dashed. Rob, the cornerstone, the building block on which his uncle had bet, was gone. Carmine had already brought in Guido Saracini, the kid from the neighborhood, now a master carpenter and owner of his own contracting business, to run the general contractor vacancy created by Alberto's bullet.

For Alberto and Maria, there would be no more annual trips to Friendly's to enjoy the anniversary ice cream treat. And Maria would be forced to trade in the gentleness of Sheila's light-haired body for a series of visits by some of Danbury's darkest and hardened veterans.

Carmine, Sophia, and Maria's mother were shattered and inconsolable and angry for the next few years. And then things only got worse.

In March of 2004, the high-security U.S. Penitentiary in Lewisburg, Pennsylvania, had a new vacancy. Alberto Antobelli was found dead in the men's shower with a shiv, believed to have been created from a metal bed slat, firmly planted in his throat.

CHAPTER 21

▼

FRIDAY, JUNE 3, 2005

Jed had taken notes from his nighttime readings. He conducted his morning briefing the next day and passed out a copy of his notes to the team members. Friday morning did not come with the usual anticipation of a "weekend" for most of those assembled in the task force room.

"I'm not sure there is much here that will help us, but it may trigger something in one of you. No pun intended. I see the whiteboards aren't lighting up with a plethora of new information. Let me summarize what I have gleaned from Alberto's and Maria's backgrounds and trials." And he did. He got some nods and questioning looks. The roomful of years of experience came up with the same verdict as the White Plains juries: Goddamned guilty as sin. If there was anything Alberto was innocent of, no one could come up with it. And why free this Maria Calabrese was a mystery to all.

One of the task force members, Michael O'Mara, on loan from LA's West Bureau, raised his hand to verbalize the thought. "Excuse my French, Jed. But what the hell is up with this innocent shit and *free* Maria? He brought the gun, and the slut of a wife got caught screwing a guy who worked for his father. Bang. The gun goes off, and they are both responsible. The only thing these two may be innocent of is having brains. Let the bitch rot."

"Thank you, Mike. Good question. I notice our New York liaison is hiding in the back of the room there. Got anything for us on the things I asked for, Roxie?"

Roseanne "Roxie" Amato was a recent New York transplant and still had friends back in the Big Apple metropolitan area. Her usual crisp, cute countenance had been noticeably injured by her twenty-two-hour days. Her dark hair, normally groomed to perfection, and the flawlessly made-up face had been the two to take the biggest hits. She would not give in to being less than stylishly dressed though—that took up the other two hours of her day.

"Well, Jed, you want the long or short version?"

"Short for the dead ends, long for the answers and clues that will close this case by two this afternoon."

"Sorry, boss. This *will* be short. Alberto's and Maria's mothers are *still* grieving, spending a lot of their time in church or in bed. Any approaches have been waved off. No big surprise.

"Carmine, Alberto's father, talked and would prefer to see Maria hanging in her prison cell rather than free. He clearly echoed Mike's sentiments on Maria. However, his language was a bit more colorful, significantly louder, and accompanied by more entertaining hand gestures. Carmine had pretty much gotten out of the 'business' and was doing pretty well at the real estate game. He was clueless about the affair, and when probed about his son's drug and gambling deals he seemed to plead a believable innocence. He blames them both for their stupidity. Insert any expletive you can think of into the report of any part of the conversation. Apparently, Carmine, his wife, and Maria's mother were all thrilled with the apparent success of the relationship—scared at first, given his past and her youth, but pleasantly surprised. Well, and then unpleasantly shocked at the tryst on Tuckahoe Road and the Beretta shoot-'em-up.

"Rob Speck's uncle talked one time with one of the New York City detectives. Just to brighten up your day, I'll quote a short excerpt.

"'Listen, Detective LaBarge, I had no bleeping idea that the little bleeping bitch was dragging my nephew Rob into a bleeping hell. And as for that stupid bleep, Alberto, I'm glad he's bleeping dead and hope he's burning in bleeping hell. So his mother-bleeping slut of a wife is screwing someone else? So what? He should've beat the shit out of her and him and ended it at that—the old fashioned way. He's gotta go and bleeping shoot poor Rob? And then an FBI agent?'

"The Little Don continues. 'And her. She bleeping sucked him in with her juicy bleep. Yeah, he made a mistake but, hey, don't we all think with our dicks sometimes, huh, Detective? Free her? Oh no. Let the bleeping bitch rot in prison, and lick on and suck up all the prison bleeps she wants. Better yet, send the shiv that iced Romeo up to Danbury and have one of her bleeping prison girlfriends stick it where the sun don't shine. Free her? No, bleep her.'

"It goes on a little longer but I think you get the gist of the Little Don's feelings.

"He is now pretty much staying out of sight. But another one of our New York City contacts said that the Little Don truly was clueless about the affair. Apparently his adjectival expressions relating to the whole thing, that seem to be mostly limited to some form of a single word that begins with the sixth letter of the alphabet, are sincere."

Jed said, "God, I bleeping love the way you talk, Roxie. But it sounds like we got less than equine excrement from your friends back east. Did any of your New York buddies bother to interview the folks at Lewisburg, where Alberto was terminated?"

"Well, yeah, briefly. They were told there was no information to be had as to the identity of the assassin, the reason for the killing, or any known outside connections to the event. They informed my friends that they had to get back to helping O.J. find the real killers, but if anything came up on Alberto, they'd be in touch. That's it from my end, boss.

"Wait, hang on. As for Maria, right after the Jesus thing, she was moved out of Danbury. Don't know where, but word is she is not talking to anyone. Maybe she knows something, maybe not. If I come up with anything that helps us solve this thing by 2:00 PM, I'll request more airtime with the gang here."

Roxie gave a polite and subtle bow and melted back into her chair in the rear of the room.

"Well, *great*. I'll come back to you soon, Roxie, on your other work. Then the only other item that I have been holding my breath about is the cigarette pack and the two butts that we found at the crime scene. Detective Fleming?"

The female detective from RHD, Ruby Fleming, was a thin, smart-looking brunette who had been smart enough to bring along the overworked, underpaid LAPD crime lab technician. She pointed to him. "Mr. Dempsey can fill you in, Jed."

Dempsey pushed his six-foot frame out of his chair and stood. "Well, Detective Davies, I assume that whatever I say in here stays in here."

"Yeah, just like Vegas," someone in the room mouthed.

"Go ahead, Mr. Dempsey," Jed said with a comforting smile.

"Well, the fingerprints and the DNA on the cigarette filters were easy to trace."

Jed's first reaction was to leap for joy. His second was, *why the hell have you been sitting on this for even a minute?* And then a sullen feeling took him to, *there's a "but" coming here somewhere.* Jed held his peace, and Dempsey moved on.

"Well, it's conclusive, beyond any doubt, that the prints and DNA belong to the wife of one of the lawyers who works for the Office of the City Attorney. She claims she has never been on the grounds—on foot, horseback, or in a space vehicle—of the Hollywood sign. And she and her husband took off two days before the incident for a weeklong trip to see their granddaughter in Seattle. Um, the woman is sixty-five years old and not too steady on her feet, according to the people we interviewed."

"Well, how the hell did the pack and butts get up there near the damn crucifixion scene?" Jed knew the answer to his own question. *These people are screwing with us. Wasting our time.*

"Sorry, Mr. Dempsey. It's not your fault.

"Back to you, Roxie."

"I've combined your west coast findings with mine. There has been no communication from the killers with any officials on either coast. LAPD, NYPD, FBI, DOJ, the judges, etc. have *squadouche*. Nothing with any governors or their offices, or the prisons. No demands. No proposals. We even probed a bit with the Sons of Italy and their response was like all the rest, *niente*." Roxie had given her best Italian accent for the word that meant "nothing."

"Thanks again, Roxie. Something has to break somewhere, soon. The whole scene seems to be a bit overdramatic for someone who just wants to publicly express a desire for Maria to walk free. And why the hell wait three years after she was put in prison? And why the hell here, in our backyard? Jesus, we have enough problems." Jed did not even realize his unintended pun, but he realized he was rambling on. "Okay, before we close down, I'll open up the floor for suggestions, ideas, anything."

The fruitlessness of the meeting went on for another hour. "Alright, then, we have set up shifts so you all can get some rest. I'll be in at eight tomorrow to brief the brass. If nothing breaks, I plan to leave at four and take anyone who is interested over to Miceli's for pizza and beer, and oh yeah, some vino for you *I*-talians in the group. Usually an invitation from any boss to the first pizza house established in Hollywood in 1949, now a famous, full-scale restaurant, would bring a round of applause and laughter. Although it did bring this crew a slight distraction from the emptiness of their investigation, deep frustration still followed the participants out of the room like a ghostly smoke clinging to their bent shoulders.

It had been three days since Officers Travis Thompson and Rosita Ortiz had discovered their little buddy, Jesus, nailed to the cross. Jed remembered the faint smell of vomit on Ortiz at the scene. Right about now, Jed's stomach was producing the same feeling of nausea and the urge to vomit. He had nothing new on the crime except some smart-ass criminal's plant of the by-products of a sixty-five-year-old woman's dirty habit. And now he had his own growing, bilious taste and disposition.

Jed actually left the office before 8:00 PM that night. He had endured the twice-daily ass chewing from the bosses, but, for now, there was nothing else he could think to do that would help. He needed sleep. He needed some real food. And he needed to see his family. Not quite sure of the last CDs he had put in his car stereo, he turned it on, hoping for distraction. Up till now, his rides home had been full of late-night cell phone calls and/or no desire to listen to any music. He was delighted when Roger Daltry's voice and Peter Townshend's guitar began to rhythmically proclaim, "Long Live Rock and Roll." As he approached home, the British group, originally formed in the 1960s, made it to the twelfth cut on the fourth disc of the *Thirty Years Of Maximum R&B* collection. When the stereo started to pour out the song, Jed actually smiled and laughed out loud for the first time since the day of the Memorial Day picnic. He turned into his driveway and listened for a minute while the four rockers pounded out the trademark work. The song pretty much summed up Jed's own ultimate question. "Who are you? Who, who, who, who? I really wanna know." He smirked as he thought of all the intricate crimes and clues that were so cleverly uncovered on *CSI*. Maybe he should give ole Gil Grissom a call.

His wife Regan heard the car pull in and was surprised when he did not come in immediately. She went out to witness her haggard husband drumming on the steering wheel and singing loudly and badly in his car.

Later that night, after a dinner of salad, lasagna, and garlic bread, washed down by two glasses of Louis M. Martini cabernet, Jed got a much-needed back rub. The front rub was also most welcome and enjoyable.

But, when all was said and done, with the lyrics of the Who's question still looping in his muddled mind, his last thought before falling off to sleep was a simple one. *Who are these damn people?*

CHAPTER 22

▼

JUANA—ONE OF THESE DAMN PEOPLE

It was the year 3 B.C.

June 2002, three years Before Crucifixion and the day Jesus Cruz met his maker in the hills of Hollywood.

The opening act of the young lady's evening followed its routine course. The early, gentle, June breeze pushed its way through the side openings in the room's large bay window. The music that floated into the ceiling speakers in the bathroom was classical and calming. Tonight's selection was Ravel's *Pavane for a Dead Infanta*. The sound of the warm, running bathwater slightly muted the rhythmic notes. The stale-smelling haze of the smoke from the rolled joint she was enjoying hung below the fluorescent glow of the room's ceiling fixture. The psychoactive tetrahydrocannabinol, THC, let her ease into the evening. A glass of *Allende 2000* sat on the corner of the vanity. The deep red of the Roja wine was a colorful companion to the stark-white granite that topped the cabinet. The fruit of the grape grown along Spain's Ebro River would play the role of liquid refreshment between the segments of tonight's performance. For now, it would relieve the dry mouth and throat that the weed brought on—later it would pleasantly enhance the calmness the drug delivered.

The first act always began with the full-length mirror that was mounted on the back of the heavy, oak door. Her first few moments of staring delivered a reflection that those in the outside world were used to seeing—a young woman of average height with raven, shoulder-length hair. An inch of the wavy, shiny hair hung down onto her forehead. Below her bangs were dark eyebrows and matching dark eyes. Her nose had a slight bump. Her cheeks were tan and slender, leading to full, dark pink lips, just above a rounded chin. Her body was trim and hard, shaped aesthetically in all the right places.

The clothing, as usual, was an expensive, heavy, silk blouse along with a pair of worn Levi's. She liked the contrast. She liked the look. She liked the soft feel of the silk on her upper body and the tightness of the denim on her legs. Today's blouse was snow-white and buttoned up the front. The buttons ended a few inches below her throat. She had already discarded the black Nikes and athletic socks in the bedroom.

She mussed her hair, which added to her allure, and unzipped the jeans. Slowly, watching her own movements in the mirror, she began the process of removal. The Levi's put up only a minor fight against her trim hips, revealing a pure white pair of lace panties. With a slight push, the jeans fell to the floor. She stepped out, right foot, then left, and took a brief assessment of her body from the feet up. Below her knees the legs were thin but strong. Where her legs widened above her knees the muscles were even more defined. She liked her legs and the strength she had worked into them. She briefly and softly caressed the smooth panties. Each hand moved along the material from her center in a semi-circular movement and met at and massaged the base of her spine.

Her hands then traveled to the top of the blouse and with measured movements, one-by-one, the buttons were loosed from their holes. Her arms slid out of the blouse, one at a time, and she let the top fall to the ground behind her. The black bra was in sharp contrast to the white of the panties. The tan of her skin played middleman in the color scheme she now studied.

In her dreams the next movement would reveal firm, flawless breasts with erect and inviting, dark-pink nipples.

But today, like every day since *him*, she would be greeted by the haunting images that had put her in a life of hell.

The young woman slowly turned away from the mirror and, with closed eyes and a deep breath, easily removed the dark bra. Now, with eyes open, she retrieved her glass of Roja wine, took a deep swallow, placed it on the tub's edge, and returned to the looking glass. Ravel's dampened, placid notes echoing down were in harsh contrast to the brutality that the young beauty's reflection testified to. The left breast was fronted by a circular scar the size of a 50-cent piece. The areola and nipple had been carved out of her and the hot ash of a cigarette had dotted the blood-colored landscape left behind. The right breast had an X whose crossbars were the exact same length as the diameter of the circle that shown on her hideously mutilated left. It looked like a madman had started an extremely perverse game of tic-tac-toe on her body.

She closed her eyes and let her hands caress her damaged breasts and flirted with the carnal dreams of what might have been.

Her hands left her breasts to further her nakedness. The only object that would be left on her body was a silver locket that hung from her neck on an eighteen-inch chain. The shed panties took their place on top of the discarded blouse, and she placed a thick, white, terry cloth towel lengthwise on the carpet in front of the mirror. She turned the bath water off and could now fully take in the gentleness of Ravel's notes. The focused young woman bent her knees, braced herself with her right hand and lowered her body into a sitting position in front of the mirror. With her arms folded across her chest, she recalled the time her mother took her to the ballet to hear the music and watch the beautiful *Infanta*, a Spanish princess, dance a mournful regret of the loss of childhood. As Maurice Ravel's exotic harmonics pressed on, the woman opened her eyes and slowly spread her legs. With her arms still crossed, her eyes focused on her perfect center. The most sensual and sexual part of her body was unflawed and still perfectly connected to her vascular and cutaneous nervous networks, still able to deliver pleasure.

The woman had given herself the sobriquet Juana.

Juana had accumulated a number of toys to help deliver relief to her tortured soul. But tonight, it would be a solo act. She dropped her hands and retrieved a second towel that she had placed on the floor. Juana draped the towel across her shoulders and arranged it to cover her breasts. She widened the space between her legs and with flat palms massaged her inner thighs and dark, curled hair. Her mind's eye conjured up images from the passionate love scene in *Desperado*, a movie released in 1995. Every time Juana replayed the sizzling scene in her mind, she enjoyed her resemblance to the beautiful Salma Hayek—and swallowed her jealousy of the actress's perfect nipples long enough to let the images of Antonio Banderas heat her own lust. The heat that the tub water had brought to the room had caused her bangs to cling to her forehead. The dampness felt warm and soothing. A different dampness, coating the hair at her center, caused by the touch of her rotating fingers, meant it was time to get up.

Juana turned away from the mirror and made her way to the tub. She dropped one towel at the base of the cast-iron rectangle. She folded and laid out the second across the back of the tub. The marred beauty, now calmer and warmer, retrieved the glass of wine and stepped into the warm water. As the first, deep sip of the liquid's blackberry and blueberry flavors warmed her throat and belly, Juana felt the water heat her skin and blood. She felt the bubbles of the Queen Helene bath therapy greet her tingling skin. All but one swallow of the wine was gone when it was time for the performance to continue. The last bit was saved for the end. With her head resting against the towel at the back of the tub, she lathered her skin with the body wash. The name of the wash, *SweetSpot*, had caught her eye in the beauty shop. The implications of the name made it too hard to resist, and she had purchased three bottles. The scent of the geranium and lavender soap hung just above the water. She was ready.

The orgasm came slowly. The stillness of the almost-empty house was finally interrupted by the piercing scream that signaled the first of Juana's releases. The second and third came only seconds later.

Ravel's masterpiece gently dropped piano chords into the room as the young woman came to the end of the night's sensual and sexual rite.

It wasn't the same every time, but she knew when her body was done. What was the same every time was the emptiness that would follow. Her body responded and loved her own touches, but it would never be as good as she knew it could have been—with the hands of another instead of her own.

If only her resemblance to the sexy Salma included the naked, unblemished breasts displayed in Juana's favorite freeze-frame of *Desperado*. She had memorized the exact spot in the DVD, chapter 19 of 28, one hour, eleven minutes and twenty-three seconds into the movie. A friend had given the DVD to her because of Juana's likeness to the seasoned actress born only twenty months after Juana. She often wondered if she was wearing out the track on the disc because of her playing the scene over and over.

CHAPTER 23

▼

The ritual, again, had been a cherished few moments of highly pleasurable liberation that distracted Juana from the pain, but it was not complete satisfaction.

Juana used the towels to dry and quickly drank the last gulp of wine. When she opened the door that led to her dressing area, the only other resident of the large home was waiting impatiently for her. The eight-pound, eight-inch-tall, snow white Maltese adored his mistress and enthusiastically licked the dampness from her toes. She named him Jeter when she picked him up at the rescue kennel. Her Yankees had just won four World Series in five years, and Juana adored the handsome shortstop who had been the heart of the pinstripers. Unlike Jeter, but like Juana, the little pup had physical issues. His back left leg was severely maimed—cause unknown—and he had to struggle to get around.

As the Maltese, a member of a breed known as "Ye Ancient Dogge of Malta," with a history that traces back at least twenty-eight centuries, expertly lapped her toes, Juana reflected on the fact that little Jeter's issues had not darkened his spirit. She wished the same was true for her, but it was not yet so.

Wrapped in a wine-colored, thick cotton bathrobe, which she had retrieved from the closet just off the bathroom, she stood on the lush, white carpet and let the bottom of her feet enjoy the softness. With her lightsome companion tucked into her right arm, Juana moved out of the dressing area, through the large bedroom and into the library. Her only stop was at a crucifix and a picture of her dead mother—long gone from a hideous case of breast cancer—her sister and her. The scene was from a sunny day in 1970. The three females were standing and smiling on the deck of an old Circle Line vessel with the Statue of Liberty in the background. The two items hung side by side at the far left of an empty, wood-paneled wall. She stared for a minute at the picture of a once-happy, smiling Elena. Juana shifted her eyes to the pure white ivory figurine hanging sadly from the cross made of cedar, then smiled and kissed the feet. She carried her smile to the snow white, silk sheets of her queen-size bed. Juana put Jeter down on the bed and threw the dark red robe on the empty side of the bed. The mix of color and cloth made her think of fresh blood spilled on virgin snow. She carried the thought into her slumber.

Jed may have known quite a bit about Alberto's and Maria's histories, but he knew as much about Juana as the Texas Rangers knew about winning the World Series.

This was the woman who would have the very brief cell phone chat with the Broker in MacArthur Park shortly after Hollywood happened. *This* was one of Jed's damn people.

CHAPTER 24

▼

JUANA'S STORY

This was the woman who had been christened Joanne Romano, after being born into wealth and depravity on the morning of January 20, 1964. Even what was predicted to be an easy, natural entry into the world turned out to be a twelve-hour struggle—suffered bravely by her mother, resented by her father. The life that followed had its moments of joy, but, by the age of six, the terror that was her father was felt by little Joanne, almost on a daily basis. The only respites came when Big Tommy Romano went away on business for days at a time. The father had insisted on an American name for his daughter, but Elena easily fell into the habit of calling her beautiful baby Juana—the Spanish equivalent and meaning "God is gracious." When Juana was three years old, a second daughter, one with her father's light hair and eyes of blue, was brought into the turmoil that her mother Elena continued to endure with a saintly patience and prayers of hope. The earlier good times for Juana's mother took a turn for the worse.

Big Tommy R. was good at making money. He could sell car parts to the Pennsylvania Amish and baby back pork ribs and a six-pack to the Muslims. And sell he did. He was the top salesman for years in a company that sold, installed, and monitored Teletherm automatic fire detection systems and Telewave automatic intrusion detection systems for homes and businesses. His bosses were never sure whether it was his six-foot-five frame that carried a buffed two hundred pounds that frightened his customers into buying the latest and greatest in store protection against theft and break-ins or an effective sales technique. They didn't really care, as long as Tom brought in the profits. If they took the time and effort to watch him in action, they would see that it was the latter. Tom was the consummate salesman, and he knew the hardware and telecommunication technologies cold. He knew when to push and knew when to back off. Knew when to talk, knew when to shut the hell up. An older salesman had once joked that to be really successful you have to make the customer—if male—feel like you'd be willing to suck his dick, if that's what it took. Well, young Tom took that advice to heart and he could project the willingness to do such with the very best of them.

At the age of twenty-four Tom had made a lot of money, and he liked the things it brought. His clothes were high-end. Brooks Brothers suits, Johnston & Murphy tailored shirts, and Hugo Boss silk ties. The shoes were fine Italian leather, always expertly burnished by the little guy named José in the lobby of his office building. He drove a 1961 white Alfa Romeo Spider hardtop with red leather interior. And he had season tickets to the Redskins—not easy to come by. Big Tom also had girls, lots of them. None who knocked him over, but plenty good enough to keep his strong urges for mild depravity under control. His money and his looks, including a well-groomed, light head of hair, deep green eyes, and a face that always appeared tanned and rugged, qualified the young man as chick-magnet material. And attract he did. And bored he would get. And move on he would.

Sometimes the girl would be the one to move on. It was usually when Tom could no longer bottle up his pent-up indignation at having to "suck all the damn dicks" to make his way in the business world. He knew he was better than this, but he wasn't quite sure what else he could do to make this kind of money. The anger never resulted in much more than a long session of verbal abuse, the occasional throwing of objects, and an infrequent punch or two. His women tended to frown on this part of the relationship.

It was an especially warm spring day in 1963. Tom had made his way from Fairfax City, Virginia, along Route 50 into Arlington to his office building. He checked his cordovan loafers with the fancy tassels that perfectly matched his belt and decided José had some work to do. As he turned the corner to José's stand, he saw a stunning young girl talking to the shoe buffer. Her silken skin was darker than his own. She was a few inches shorter than José, and, although José liked to wear his hair long, hers beat the length of his by more than six inches. It was pulled back into sets of carefully braided strands, each with a dark sheen. There was some strength to the bare arms and a stature that spoke of athletic familiarity. Intrigued, Tom strutted over to the stand. José looked up and said, "Mr. Tom, are you ready for a shine today?"

"Absolutely, my man. But I don't want to interrupt you."

"No problem, Mr. Tom. My sister was just getting ready to go to work. She works over at the C&P of Virginia building. We have some issues to deal with. Our mother is not doing well. We're just working out how to handle it. Right, Elena?"

With a demure look, Elena looked briefly at the big man and answered her brother. "Sure, Joe, it's all set. I'll talk to you tonight."

Her fleeting glance was like an invitation to mystery. Big Tom knew zero about the sister of the guy who shined his shoes, and yet after she walked away and out of sight, Tom looked at the empty space wishing she would refill it.

Tom carefully queried José, whom his sister called Joe, about the pretty young lady who had just walked away. Tom was Joe's biggest tipper, and when Tom asked if Joe thought it would be okay if he asked his sister out, Joe just nodded with a smile. The doubled tip the shoe man got made the smile even broader.

Tom's salesmanship quickly moved into high gear. This time his target was a woman for whom he would happily suck any body part. Within three days he and Elena were having lunch at West Potomac Park. It was a short cab ride from Arlington to the land west of 17th Street and south of Constitution Avenue NW, in Washington D.C.

The park was home to the Jefferson Memorial and the Lincoln Memorial as well as a number of athletic fields. Tom was prepared with a heavily quilted blanket on which to spread the picnic lunch he had prepared with the help of his local deli. As a good salesman's luck would have it, the shrimp salad, fresh croissants, pale green Muscat grapes, a mild and salty Queso Blanco cheese, and a chilled bottle of chardonnay-dominated Tattinger champagne were all greeted by a sunny, warm day. Just in case all this was not good enough, the thousands of cherry trees of twelve varieties—a glorious collection that began with a gift of over three thousand trees from Japan in 1912—were in full bloom.

Thanks to the then Mayor of Tokyo's gift, shipped from Yokohama on the S.S. Awa Maru, the view that Tommy and his date shared with many others along the West Potomac and East Potomac parks was magnificent and romantic.

Tom had never played the romantic card before with any of his female prey. This girl, he knew, was different, gentle, precious. Smitten was not in Tom's vocabulary, but that is what he was—with a capital s.

Joe's sister Elena talked about her lunch date for days. Even in her best lunch outfit though, she had felt underdressed for the elegance Tom presented her. They made a date for dinner the following Saturday, which sent the young girl scurrying for a new outfit.

That night, Tom whisked her across the Potomac in a limousine and they entered the lobby of the grandiose Willard InterContinental Washington Hotel. The stone and marble of the structure, the long, graceful draperies adorning the huge windows, the elegance of the carpeting, and the richness of the dark wood in the Willard Room made Elena giddy. Tom's date was happy that she had spent almost a week's salary on her black chiffon dress. It tied around her neck and barely brushed her knees with its slitted, wide-arrow-shaped hem. When Tommy gave her a "Wow" and a "Whew, look at you," she was very pleased with her choices. As she slowly sipped the glass of champagne that Tom had ordered, she prayed that her nerves would allow her to elegantly swallow the caviar he also ordered.

As much as the extravagance of the place and the food caused Elena to have to work hard to hold back the butterflies, her beauty and innocence had the consummate, cool, and confident marketing wizard equally noggin over heels.

Within weeks the couple became much more comfortable with each other. Tommy was still out there selling well and making the "big bucks," but most of his spare time was devoted to courting the young Hispanic beauty. Within months and with Joe's and her parents' blessing, they were wed at Saint Ann Catholic Church in Arlington. Joe was the best man. Both families were not large, so the reception was small but festive. It was held at the Key Bridge Marriott, overlooking D.C. The couple said goodbye to their guests at 11:00 PM, made their way to the top floor, drank more champagne, and enjoyed the views of the Potomac where their storybook romance had begun. They took a little time to take in the views of Georgetown and the rest of the Washington nighttime skyline before nervously making their way to the king-size bed that dominated the room. The hotel had provided two complimentary bottles of champagne and a bouquet of roses, and the bedspread had been turned down.

Unlike any other woman Tom had fallen for, he had been patient for her sexual favors. She just seemed so kind, so innocent, so angelic. Elena was all those things, but he found out later that night that she was also skilled in the intricacies and art of lovemaking—a mistress of motions and touches that surprised and thrilled him.

"My mother told me, Tom, that a wife needs to pay attention to her mate's needs in *every* way. And if you do it right, you will give him a reason to come home at night. This is my first audition for my new husband. Let me know how I'm doing at pleasing you. I made a mistake a while back, so I am not virginal." The fact was that Elena would never have asked her mother any advice about sex or men, but she liked the innocent white lie.

"That's okay, Elena. I understand mistakes, probably better than you."

"Good, did you bring any wedding night bedclothes for yourself?"

"Not a stitch."

"Good. Get rid of the monkey suit, gringo, and I'll be back in a minute."

By the time Tom had thrown his tuxedo on the desk chair in the suite, poured the bubbly, and sat down on the edge of the bed, his new wife emerged from the bathroom in a pellucid, red—the hottest of the warm colors—lace teddy. The two had passionately kissed and groped frequently prior to tonight's fashion display, but this stunning, dark-haired Latino in the sexy satin and the serious swelling, rising between Tommy's legs, were clear signals that the green starting flag had been waved. Elena took the first step and moved to him and kissed her new husband. She let her hands roam around his back and chest and gingerly between his muscled thighs and teasingly across his anxious center. As anxious as Tommy was to play Lewis and Clark on his new wife's body, he let her run the show. She gently sucked on his nipples, to his delight and intermittent moaning. Elena moved down to kneel in front of Tommy and removed his boxers. She touched, teased, licked, and mouthed him in every way even *he* could think of.

With his uncontrollable orgasmic release, now spent somewhere across Elena's chest, she pushed him onto the bed and straddled his large frame.

"Here, pick your head up a little and take a drink. Your mouth must be dry."

After quenching a second of Tom's thirsts, she took the small towel she had placed next to the bed and wiped herself free of his passionate deposit. Then she took her own long sip of the Moët.

"Now, Señor Romano, are you ready to finally make love to me?"

"Not yet, Señora Romano. I need a few minutes, please."

He lifted her off him. Made his way to the bathroom for a minute. Came out and refilled the champagne glasses. He took his bride in his arms and grabbed one of the glasses on the way over to the window that offered a view of where they had their first date, and contemplated what she had just done to him, for him—so open, so giving.

"Where in the name of the *Madre de Dios* did you learn all that?"

"I took an accelerated class from *mi madre*."

"Quite the teacher."

"I'm glad you think so."

"Your question implies that I get to make love to *you* now. That means two things, if it's okay with you."

"Tell me."

"Let me show you."

Tommy put her down on the soft gold carpet, took a swig of the drink and handed her glass to her. They both drained the liquid gold and she waited. Tommy moved behind Elena and slowly lifted the soft gown over her shoulders. He explored every part that had eluded him for months and some that hadn't. When he was ready, he gently lifted her onto the white sheets and let her bring him inside her for the first time. The couple was coupled and each believed that they were beginning a masterpiece of matrimony.

"Tom, what's the second thing?"

"Patience, my dear, patience."

An hour later, the conquering salesman with an ego was sitting in the faucet side of the warm tub. The bubbles rose above both of their chests. A second bottle of the bubbly had been opened, and their glasses were perched on the edge of the white tub. Tom massaged each foot, toe by toe, even dried a few off with the hand towel draped on the side of the tub, and licked and sucked on them with his eyes glued to the smile on his Latin lover's sultry, damp lips.

"*Mi* madre did not give me any advice, but I figured if I do this often enough, your pretty little feet won't stray far from home."

The next morning, after making love one more time and having a sumptuous breakfast—mimosas included—they made the short cab ride to National Airport for a week's honeymoon in Bermuda. The beautiful island and glowing couple joyously shared six days of the ongoing masterpiece.

When the couple returned home, which was Tom's four-bedroom colonial in Fairfax, Elena felt like a handsome angel had come down from heaven and given her a beautiful new world. Tom was even amazed at his own genteel behavior. For the first time he could remember, he felt like he actually loved someone more than he loved himself.

CHAPTER 25

▼

Things changed shortly before the arrival of his daughter Joanne in January of 1964.

Tom Romano, successful salesman, had never learned to like the mental image of having to think about tasting another man's privates to make a sale. It had always angered him, but money was money. And up until his wife's seventh month of pregnancy, he could release his intense ire by lying down on his back on their king-size, satin-sheeted Serta Perfect Sleeper and coaxing Elena into his evening's choice of sexual release.

The birth and care of this new child made his once-upon-a-time, dark-eyed, passionate and willing partner less available for his preferred anger management therapy.

Well before the birth of their second daughter three years later, Tommy Romano had discovered another comforting blanket to help him cool his burning jets. His color of choice was white, but in a pinch he would settle for the street brown. Either way, he was quick to learn the necessary and intense ritual. After he finished his long day of the degrading, "sure I'll suck any body part you want" selling, he would often stop off at a local Fairfax tavern. After two beers, he would decide if it would be a "horse" night or not.

A few months before, a fellow salesperson had introduced Tommy to the experience after he had screwed her brains out in her hotel room. It was a stay-over evening between a two-day sales trip to Philadelphia. He thinks her name was Tricia. He wasn't sure, but he *was* sure that "what's-her-name" was a hell of a lot better looking with her hair let down and her ample breasts no longer fettered by the crisp, navy business suit she wore earlier. The naked veteran, ten years older than he, was ready to teach her naked pupil.

"First, handsome, put everything in the proper order. Here, lay out the heroin, the "Mr. Happy", now the U-100 syringe with needle, the spoon, lighter, and cigarette filter. I've cleaned the spoon and needle with alcohol already. Now put the rubber belt on your lap and the citric acid and glass of water here. Put the "H" on the spoon. Add a little citric acid. Suck up enough water into the syringe to fill it about two-thirds. It's a one cc with the capacity for one hundred units. You only want fifty to seventy-five. The acid breaks down the white stuff so we can easily suck up the mix and take it home, sweet home. It's your first outing, so I'll hold the lighter under the spoon, but first let's get this belt around your arm. Good, you have excellent vein exposure. Okay, big guy, let's fire it up. Good, it's bubbling. Now take the cigarette filter, put it in the spoon and let it soak up the liquid "train ticket to heaven." Okay, since you're a beginner, let me help."

Tricia drew the concoction up into the syringe through the white fibers wrapped in the brown cylindrical paper sitting in the spoon to filter out impurities.

"Ready, Freddy?"

A nervous but adventurous Tom took a long sip of the glass of Dewars that sat on the hotel room's nightstand and said, "Ready."

"This spot here on the bend of your arm is the easiest place to get the needle into the vein right. Now we place the needle kinda flat on your skin so it doesn't get wiggled around too much. You still with me, Tommy?"

He nodded.

"Good. Now watch. The needle gets put in so it goes down the length of the vein and *not* across it. If you try to go across you can punch through the vein and lose the juice. We need to make sure we get the vein. If you feel it burning or see any blistering when it goes in, we missed. Do not inject till we're sure we're home. Still watching?"

Another apprehensive nod.

"Good. Now here's an important part. I'm gonna pull back a little on the needle's plunger, and if we see a little of your blood come back to join the "H," we're good. Sometimes we get a little air with the blood. It won't hurt you, and the more times you do it, the better you'll get at this part."

Tommy reached with his free arm for another sip of the blended scotch whiskey. His partner smiled and pushed his scotch arm away.

"Don't dilute the product. Just sit back and enjoy. Okay, ready. Do you want to do the honors?"

Tommy, the nervous rookie, gulped out a, "No. Just do it now, please."

Tricia—which actually was her name—gently pushed the mixture of the derivative of the Papaver somniferum plant, probably from Burma, cut with a bit of talc, flour, and cornstarch, into Tommy's vein. She watched as the opiate did its magic within seconds and extracted the needle.

She could imagine her pupil experiencing the dope crossing the blood-brain barrier and its conversion to morphine, binding quickly to his opioid receptors. She could sense the rush that came first with its surge of pleasurable sensations. His rush would be joined by a warm flushing of the skin, dry mouth, and a heavy feeling in his arms and legs.

She gently pushed her partner, now in a new euphoria, back onto the bed, waited fifteen minutes to make sure he was good, and then retrieved a new syringe and began working the ritual all over again. It was Tricia's turn.

CHAPTER 26

▼

ELENA'S TURN—1973

By the time Juana Romano turned nine—a very precious nine—and her younger sister, nicknamed Princess, was almost six, Tommy's wife Elena had witnessed, up close and personal, what the years of diacetylmorphine, called heroin, after the German word for heroic, had done to her husband, to her life.

The drug, originally introduced by Dr. Heinrich Dresser of the Bayer Company in 1898 as a cough suppressant and pain reliever, had dramatically suppressed any hint of the good qualities that had attracted Elena to the handsome and charming sales whiz and doting provider. The warmth *she* used to give to ameliorate his deep fears, anger, and insecurity had been replaced by a syringe full of white and water with a needle as the welcomed administer and comforter of choice.

Elena's feet had not left home, but neither had they been massaged once since she had become pregnant. The honeymoon apparently was long over. She still prayed for the sweet Tommy to return to the planet.

Tricia was long gone. He had made his own connections and was expert at dealing with the kit. Somehow he managed to still sell—just less, but enough to get by. If his wife even hinted at updating their twenty-year-old, 4-bedroom, brick colonial in Northern Virginia, the response was cold. She was buying her two young girls clothes at the discount stores, and the private Catholic education she had hoped for was out of the question. Elena had been working three nights a week at a local hospital as an aide. Now she had to be vigilant about what

Tommy was like *if* and when he came home at night. She had cut back to a tentative one night a week.

When Tommy came home on that Friday night in June, neither she nor the now-aware and frightened children could tell if Tommy was happy because he was just happy to be home or it was a drug-induced mood.

The answer came shortly after Tommy had changed into his hang-out-at-home jeans and his white Redskins shirt with a burgundy 9 on the front, back, and sleeves. Only the last name of the famous Christian Adolph, aka Sonny, Jurgensen III was lettered across the back of the jersey. Shortly after the man of the house was seated in his chair at the kitchen table, Elena had an ill feeling about the immediate future. Up until that summer night, Elena thought her biggest problem was that she still loved, really loved, this man.

It certainly wasn't the first evening that things got tense, but tonight the fierceness and hurtful words of her husband reached a terrorizing level. Tonight's meal started with a glass of merlot and shrimp cocktail for the two parents. Elena was still hoping there might be a latent trace of romance that could be coaxed out of her husband. She had made Shirley Temples for the girls and had coached them to "please be pleasant tonight." Tommy wasn't absorbing the desperate plea for normalcy and family harmony.

"Kids, leave the room. *Now.*"

The two moved their little feet with fearful obedience at their father's dispatch.

"Where the hell do you get off buying this shit, like we can afford it? I told you business was way down and we need to conserve every freaking penny I make for this family."

"I was able to put a little away over the last few months, Tommy. I thought we could have a nice dinner and maybe take the kids over to Burke Lake Park later. Like the old days, when you and I used to go. We could go to the picnic area by the lake and bring the apple pie I made for dessert. Maybe sneak in a small bottle of wine, and bring some sodas for the girls.

"For dinner I have some nice steaks and baked potatoes with the green beans you like so much. The kids keep asking when Daddy's gonna take us on the swings and slides."

Tommy finished the first glass of merlot and most of the shrimp.

"We'll see. Serve dinner and tell the kids to come back in."

"Could you grill the steaks, honey?"

"Sorry, I gotta make some calls. You do it."

Tommy made his calls. The youngest daughter screamed for Mom's help with a toilet issue. And the expensive steaks got overcooked.

Elena prayed that Tommy would just happily indulge. Her prayers went unanswered.

"What's wrong with the little girl? Can't she handle going to the bathroom without screaming for you. Damn, she's old enough."

"Sorry, Daddy," said the youngest from the hallway that led to the dining room.

"Sorry, honey. There's been a bit of a problem with their toilet," Elena intervened.

The family reconvened around the oval, oak kitchen table. Elena cringed as Tommy bit into the overdone T-bone. She had no idea where he was mentally—between the uppers, downers, and whatever else he was into now. Wherever he was, it generated a red rush of blood to his neck and head, and she waited. But not for long.

"What the hell is this? You spend money I don't have on a special 'let's feel good, happy meal' for the family and burn the goddamned meat. I bet the potatoes are undercooked and my *favorite* freaking beans are cold. You stupid bitch."

Tommy stood up slowly with his plate in hand and moved to the glass storm door that led to the deck. He didn't bother to open the door when he flung the plate out. The glass shattered out onto the deck and a few shards rained down and shattered into tiny pieces on the tiled kitchen floor. Any comfort his kids may have salvaged from their mother's promise of a domestically tranquil, maybe enjoyable, dinner were shattered with the glass, and they sat frozen and fearful in their chairs.

"Now get me another glass of merlot and fry me a damn hamburger. Surely you can't screw up a simple hamburger." He adjourned to the family room just off the kitchen.

"Sorry, honey. It'll just take a minute. Kids, eat what you feel like. Juana, maybe you can help your sister cut up her meat."

"Sure, Mom."

In the late 1890s the bearded Mr. Joseph Lodge of South Pittsburgh, Tennessee, could not have ever expected that some of his finest cooking vessels would become a number of American abused women's best friends. Elena proceeded to extract one of Lodge Manufacturing's fine products, the 9-inch, 6-pound, cast-iron frying pan she had received ten years ago as a wedding gift. Without hesitation, with the kids looking on, with Tommy sitting in his favorite chair waiting for his fried hamburger, and his back to the kitchen, Elena wound up and delivered a two-handed blow to the right side of her onetime Romeo's skull. The thud the pan made was accompanied by a subtle sound of crushed cranium, soon followed by a slow-flowing river of blood. Tommy's blond head just sagged down onto his left shoulder. The red flow made its way down to the white of the jersey and then melded into the burgundy and gold stripes on the right sleeve. The heavy jersey was the perfect material to imbibe the liquid.

Juana screamed, "Mom, stop! Don't!" Her younger sister just watched with shock and tears blurring what she was looking at. Elena made sure she had a strong grip on the heavy black handle with the hollow center and wound up for another blow to the slumped figure. The lithe nine-year-old jumped off the chair and grabbed her mother's arm in mid-swing.

"Let me be, Juana. I'm gonna end this, *now*, once and for all."

With her hands still trying to hold back the arm with the 6-pound weapon, Juana's softest voice spoke three serious, life-altering words. "I'll do it."

Elena's surprised face watched the next words out of the mouth of her young Juana. "There's a better way, Mom."

By the time the Fairfax County Police and the Fire and Rescue unit would respond, the hotshot salesman, father of two, Tommy Romano would be lying inanimate at the foot of the stairs.

Juana had coached her mother into wrapping the source of Tommy's bleeding in a towel. Together they dragged him up the stairs to the second floor and executed the better way. His last breath had been purchased by the administration of an overdose of heroin. His stash and works lay open in his oak nightstand. The sorry-looking bang on his head had the possibility of being the result of his fall. A fall that easily could have been precipitated by the overdose. The opiate that brought on the muscle spasticity and stopped his breathing would eventually be the official cause of death. Elena and her daughter vacuumed the carpet on the stairs to erase their struggle to hoist Tommy up the steps. They cleaned the broken glass from the deck and the kitchen floor, and finally the shards still sticking their sharp edges out from the frame. The vacuum sucked up the small splinters that had flown onto the floor. The fragments from Tom's dinner dish were added to the glass in a large, black, leaf bag. Juana then put the bag in the washing machine in the basement and covered it with dirty towels that she wetted in the slop sink. Elena and Juana cleared the dinner table and put the dirty dishes in the dishwasher.

"Hang on, Mom. Before you call, let's put out the dessert and let's take one last look around." They did. "Mom, where's the frying pan?" Elena grabbed it from the stove and scrubbed it hard with a Brillo pad, rinsed it, and put it away.

Juana breathed out the words, "Okay, now, call." As Juana's thirty-two-year-old mother picked up the phone, she was grateful for her precious nine-year-old daughter's penchant for mystery novels and TV shows. The nights she gave in and let her baby stay up late to watch *Colombo* and *McMillan and Wife* in her and Tommy's bed had paid off in an ironic way. A way Elena never would have wished for.

The altered scene did not give the police much else to suspect or believe other than the staged obvious. The mother was distraught over the death. The younger daughter had frozen herself to her bedcovers in a fetal-like posture. The older sister, who had delivered the lethal injection, sat next to her mother in the bedroom, her arm around Elena's waist. Juana, who had secretly observed with fascination and fear all the details of her father's opiate ritual, was proud of her ability to repeat the act so perfectly. Now under the policemen's watch, she put on her most doleful look. Her mind furtively holding on to relief and a sad sense of joy.

CHAPTER 27

▼

JUANA—A NEW LIFE

After the death of the salesman, Elena moved quickly. Tommy's life insurance policy, like most, had an exclusionary clause. Death by drug overdose voided the pay out. Bad news. But the good news was the bastard was dead, and she could make a handsome profit from the sale of the house. The better news was she was not in jail, and the best news was that the girls seemed happier. Staying one step ahead of the sheriff, so to speak, Elena and family relocated to the town of Shenandoah, Virginia. The small, rural town is nestled between the Blue Ridge Mountains and the Massanutten Ridge, along the banks of the Shenandoah River in Page County, Virginia. Elena's mother's sister, Aunt Eva, lived out there and had a management position at the Massanutten Resort. Eva was sure she could get her niece an administrative position. And so, Shenandoah it was. A two-story, older, but well-kept, three-bedroom home with a small family room was now home. The redbrick home sat close to the quiet street and had a patch of lawn large enough for a swing set and a small inflatable pool. The three Romano women had traded in their tormented past for rural tranquility. At least for a while.

CHAPTER 28

▼

JUANA—A NEW DADDY— 1976

Elena loved her job at the resort—new people, new friends, a challenge she could handle. It was less than a twenty-minute drive down U.S. Route 340 and across U.S. Route 33. The girls adjusted to their new school just fine.

She and the girls were living a rural, quiet, almost idyllic life. Their time together was purposeful and playful. Schoolwork was always done on time, and Elena made sure she made ample time for family. Picnics, visits with Elena's aunt and her family, ballgames, and fun hours spent around the kitchen table that served as host to an assortment of children's games brought smiles, laughter, and, best of all, peace in the home.

Elena had been asked out several times by men at work but always pleaded out. She was not ready. Things were just too good as they were. *Keep it simple. It's working.*

And then Conrad came along. Elena met him at the night class she was taking at James Madison University, only a half hour from home, even less from her office. Their course in elementary education was taught by a teacher with flair, who could turn instruction on the most boring of subjects into an hour of animated, classroom interaction. Conrad Jameson began arriving early for class to insure a seat close to the attractive Elena—the one he had seen talking to the other woman after class, showing off pictures of her family. It seemed like an easy opening.

"Hi, may name is Conrad. Are you enjoying Professor Berndt? They say he's the best."

A surprised Elena responded. "I sure am. I did not know school could be this much fun."

"Why are you taking the course?"

"I have high hopes of someday getting my degree and actually teaching. I like my job but I've always wanted to teach. I know it will take a long time this way, but I like the idea, and so far, I really like the classes.

"How about you, Conrad?"

"I'm doing some continuing education for my job. I teach at a school here in Harrisonburg, and I also teach a Sunday school class at a Baptist church in town."

The anti-Tommy, Elena thought.

Elena had thought any romantic relationship was out of the question for her—ever. But here she was again, the subject of a whirlwind of a man seeking her attention. Conrad was a man of average height and weight, and hair almost as dark as her own. He had deep brown eyes that spilled sincerity to accompany his gentle words. His clothes were simple, blue jeans or khaki slacks, golf shirts, and either a pair of Nikes or soft, tan leather shoes. The pleasant-looking man had some minor receding going on. He had a good-looking, gold-and-silver-banded Mickey Mouse watch on his wrist. The colorful mouse of many talents stood proudly in front of the champagne-colored dial, his hands like a double-jointed traffic cop ready to move around the numerals. There was a small gold cross hanging from a matching chain around Conrad's neck. It was nestled in between the lapels of his shirt. When asked, he told Elena that his mother had given him the cross for good luck when he was a boy.

None of the slick suits and accessories that her first husband had fussed over so.

Coffee after class led to dinner and roses, and shortly to steps down the aisle. It was a walk into the deep well she had thought she put behind her in Fairfax, forever. Marriage. But here she was again.

The girls had gotten used to seeing Conrad around and were happy to see a glow on their mother's face once again. The wedding was a simple ceremony at Shenandoah Baptist Church. Conrad moved into Elena's house. They thought it too upsetting to move the girls again so soon. Elena had a gentle, loving man sharing her first floor master bedroom, and the girls had a new daddy—a strong, protective man. The way it should be for little girls growing up.

Within six months, what wasn't the way it should be was Conrad's expansive love and adoration crossing the line with the eleven-year-old Juana. His touches graduated to his sexual, oral demands and eventually to invasion. The young girl was afraid to upset her mother, who seemed so happy. *God, how happy she was. Why is Conrad doing these things to me? Why can't he stay downstairs with Mommy and put his thing inside her mouth and inside her thing?* Juana couldn't spell pedophile if asked, but she could paint a very clear picture of one, and his name was Conrad. The schoolteacher, Mr. Sunday School Mentor, who liked kids a little too much. Not the Conrad Elena believed in.

Conrad was a name from the old German meaning brave, bold ruler, counsel. Juana knew *that*; Juana was a smart girl. After Conrad started coming around with a name she had never encountered before, she looked it up in the big library at James Madison University. Her mom took her there sometimes on the weekends to get more detective novels. On one Saturday she looked at a reference book of names and found it. Juana also knew that what he was doing to her was not brave. His rule over her fear was indeed bold, and counsel was not something the young girl would be seeking from this new daddy.

But sadly for Juana, Conrad also knew things. He knew the truth about what she had done to Tommy, her real father. Juana almost hated her mother for having told him. Her mother trusted this deviant. His threats to expose her and her mother kept Juana under his thumb and on top of his body—enduring a horrid punishment for her sin.

CHAPTER 29

▼

DADDY STOPS—1977

Juana was surprised and relieved when it seemed she no longer warranted the unwelcome attention of her stepfather.

The relief came when Conrad discovered that his twelve-year-old stepdaughter had begun menstruating. It happened one morning when her mother was out shopping with younger sister, Princess. Conrad had heard the shower running in Juana's bathroom. He waited until the water was no longer splashing against the tan, tiled walls. Soon her room was filled with the sounds of Barry Gibb and the twins, his brothers Robin and Maurice. They were singing the second cut from the *Saturday Night Fever* album, "How Deep Is Your Love." Conrad knew the song that had won the trio a Grammy. He knew it because Juana had begged her mother to take her to see the R-rated movie until she gave in out of desperation, and Elena had asked Conrad to join them. And he knew the song because his stepdaughter's cassette player seemed to be stuck on this album day and night.

Conrad gently knocked on her door. A semi-naked Juana cringed in anticipation of what usually followed that knock. She tried her best to ignore the tap, as if the music was blotting out the request for entry, and ran to retrieve a bra from her dresser. She got there too late. Conrad had made his way into her room before she had a chance at better modesty. How she wished her mother had not let him convince her that it was safer to change out the knobs on the doors. Where there was once a lock was now smooth, brass-coated metal.

He started as he always did by smoothing her dark, silky hair.

"I like it when it's wet, baby. Come on, let me comb it out." The back of Conrad's hand brushed against her budding left breast, and he felt the hardness he so craved. Juana had lost count of how many times her stepfather had violated her and had threatened to divulge "her murderous ways." It no longer hurt as much as it used to—physically that was. Today she had a surprise for him and a surprise for herself.

He liked her on top. He liked to look. He liked to fondle her youth. As Conrad came hard, spurting his semen into the unsmiling victim of his depravity, he moaned and held tightly onto Juana's fragile hips. He smirked, as he looked straight into her blank eyes. When he finally released her, Juana moved off him and let out a stifled scream. She had started her menarche while Conrad had been inside her. She only realized it as she came away and saw the blood on his wilting penis. Conrad opened his eyes and looked where Juana's eyes seemed to be glued.

"Aw shit, you dumb bitch. Why didn't you tell me?" Conrad's tirade went on for minutes as he got up and went to the bathroom to clean up. "Rip off the damn sheets and don't drip your mess anywhere. Wash the damn things before your mother gets home and clean yourself up, you stupid, bleeding bitch." His outburst went on and included words and phrases usually reserved for barroom brawls. They drove the still-naked, shaking, young girl to tears.

"I ... I didn't know till just now, Conrad. I'm sorry. I'll clean everything."

"You better." If your mother finds out, she'll be very goddamned mad at *you*, and there will be hell to pay around here. Get to it." She did not yet move.

He slowly walked over to his stepdaughter. He took in the sight of her lovely young body, drinking in the beginning of her fixed, young breasts, now with rigid, darkish nipples pushing out at him. He gazed down to the slightest start of the dark pubic hair and the blood that had caked on her thighs. He said, "I'm sorry, Juana. I didn't mean to yell like that. Let's just get everything cleaned up, and we'll have a nice dinner when Mom and your sister get home." His thoughts deviated from his words to the sick tune of, *God, I am gonna miss this young ...* As he finished his selfish thought of her youth lost to him and his need to sate his lust, he brushed back her dark hair, kissed her with an open mouth and left the room.

After the morning of shared blood, there were no more knocks, no more of Conrad sharing her bed. Juana was not sure if it was because she was now a fertile female and Conrad was scared, or if the sanguine incident had generated a permanent turnoff for the abuser. Either way, she was grateful for the comfort of his absence in her room.

CHAPTER 30

▼

UNLUCKY

Juana had a new sense of self—a damaged self—but she hoped one that was on the mend. A few months after Conrad had given her a new freedom, she was doing better with her schoolwork. She had gathered a number of new friends, mostly girls. And she started believing that normalcy was actually a possibility—until that Saturday night.

Her stepfather had played golf during the day and brought his foursome home for an early-afternoon poker game. He had slowly but surely introduced his fondness for certain vices into Elena's household. His tolerant wife silently hid her denial under the cover of "boys will be boys." Conrad decided his bad luck on the golf course this day, which had earned him a triple bogey on the last hole, could be changed before the first cards were dealt. His healing potion would be a double scotch on the rocks. He was wrong; and by 7:00 PM, he had added significantly to the ten dollars he forfeited on the links. He decided that his day could not end with two losses. That might just cause a bad-luck hangover.

The wife was out with her girlfriends for a game of Bunco, which meant she would not be home till about 11:00 PM. For Juana, it also meant that she could cheat a bit on her nine o'clock curfew. Conrad never noticed anymore, anyway. Tonight, he cared not at all about her curfew, especially when he had his expensive, eighteen-year-old, blue-capped product in his hand. The smooth, amber drink, which was carefully crafted from the spring water of a long and lonely glen in Scotland, could always douse any ember of caring. Conrad had finished half of the bottle of Glenlivet and made a hopeless attempt at sobriety by showering.

Juana snuck quietly in the side entrance just past nine-thirty. The last of the long, summer day's sunlight was giving up, and all was quiet. Juana let out a silent sigh and walked to her room. She was grateful that her room was the first in the series of rooms down the long hallway. Although she knew Conrad did not really pay much attention to her or her hours anymore, she was still not in the mood for any kind of confrontation.

Juana was undressing in her bedroom. She was mulling over the flirtation that had slipped in and out of the evening with her three girlfriends and the two boys who were over at Jenny's house for a game of Monopoly. She had only known the one boy, Mark, for a short while, but was sure now that he was sweet on her. His sweetness was on the other side of the emotional earth from the memories of Conrad, and, for that matter, the memories of her own father, Tommy. She was shaken out of her warm ruminations by an ugly and familiar sound coming from somewhere in the house. She quickly threw on a bathrobe and treaded lightly out of her room and into the hall. The ugly moaning was coming from down the hall. *Had Mom come home early and the drunken Conrad talked her into bed? No. That noise was coming from …*

Juana now knew at least one of the reasons why Conrad had so peacefully abandoned his abuse of her. Rage turned into deliberate action. *I've killed once before for reasons almost as bad as this.* The assemblage of wooden-handled knives in the kitchen that were stacked neatly in an angled, large wooden block, in ascending order of size, had always given Juana a kind of an eerie chill. At this moment the sight of them simply gave her choices. She did not debate for more than a second. It would be the largest one. With knife in hand, she made a stealth journey back down the hall to the door of her nine-year-old sister's room.

God, Princess is more than two years younger than when that bastard started on me. When did he start telling her *that that was how daddies loved their daughters and that's what daughters do to make Daddy happy? "Don't you wanna make Daddy happy? It will be our secret and you can't tell."*

I was eleven. How was I supposed to know anything? Just put your mouth here and your hands here. Later, "Just lie down here like this and spread your legs. It will only hurt a little at first, baby." What, like the dentist or the shot the nurse gave her?

Juana could not even see Princess, just the hairy back of the sitting Conrad on the far side of the bed, but she could hear the familiar sounds of a child's mouth moving and stifled tears. The warped stepfather had his bottle of scotch and glass set on Princess's nightstand, accompanied by one of his burning Marlboros. He was actually sipping and smoking and coaching as he watched the light hair on the top of his young victim's head. "That's good, Princess. Can you put your hand under here." He guided her hand and moaned, "Oh, yes, that's perfect."

Conrad had not heard Juana until she made her move across the bed. His turning took her target, his back, out of range. The slash of the knife only nicked Conrad's arm. With the bleeding arm he slammed the retreating Juana, and she flew off the bed and against her sister's dresser. She was stunned. The naked nine-year-old, still on her knees, was frozen in fear. The black-handled Henckel with its eight-inch blade was on the rug next to Juana. Conrad grabbed it. Still drunk and now in a fury, he grabbed Juana by one ankle and pulled her flat to the floor. He stood over her. She tried unsuccessfully to rally to her feet. Juana screamed. "Leave me alone, you goddamned pervert."

"Shut up, you little bitch." The noise of his hard slap and a whimper from the unbelieving younger Princess preceded Conrad's next words. "You think you're all grown up now, wearing a bra, bleeding between your skinny legs, hanging out with boys?"

Juana, though furious, decided that submission might be her best weapon.

"I'm sorry, Daddy." She choked on the last word but forced it out, hoping it would ring some kind of sensibility bell in the madman's head. No such luck— just the baddest kind of luck.

"Daddy. You're calling me Daddy, now? I'm not your fucking daddy. Don't you remember? You killed *your daddy*. You think I didn't know? Well, you ain't killing this daddy. And just so you know it, you little tramp, your little sister is much better at sex than you ever were. And you're all just lucky that I haven't turned you into the cops."

As Conrad slurred the vile words, he got down and pushed up the hem of Juana's robe over her slim hips. He straddled the twelve-year-old and forced himself inside her. He drove himself into the young girl with a violent, thrusting motion and moaned. Juana could tell he was about to come. Conrad, still pumping, still moaning, tore open the front of Juana's white terrycloth robe. He put his left hand on her throat. His blurred eyes were focused on the tan left nipple of his stepdaughter's breast. The rest went quickly, the cutting, the vicious cutting, the hot singe of the cigarette ash, the resisting, the screaming, and Conrad's final rape of Juana.

He laughed. "No man will touch you now. Your little tits …"

Before he could finish his sentence, Princess had thawed her body out of its fear-laced crouch at the other side of the bed. Her first swing was not unlike the underhand softball pitch she had been trying to perfect. Her stitched, white-cov-

ered Rawlings was replaced for this pitch with the remains of Daddy's eighteen-year-old scotch. The swing caught him under the right side of his jaw. The
bottle broke in half when it bounced out of her hands and smashed into the corner of her dresser. Daddy faltered. Before Conrad could regain his balance, the
up-and-coming softballer took one expert swing with her child-size, wooden
Louisville Slugger that she kept by her bed. Just as "Daddy" had taught her, she
kept her eye on the ball—his head—and took a step forward and swung hard. It
was her first home run. "Whap." The meat of the bat slammed against the top of
Conrad's skull with a crushing force. Conrad was silent, fallen, and lying on top
of the bloodied Juana.

Juana, with a maniacal rage and crimson scowl, pushed out from under her
attacker and told her sister to get out and go call the police. Twelve years old and
already a lifetime worth of hate filled every part of Juana. What came next was
not particularly cathartic as much as it felt like the right thing to do, natural and
necessary. With Princess out of the room, she rolled the still-naked, unconscious
Conrad over onto his back. She was the only one to hear her own words. "It's
over, you miserable bastard. I wish you were awake to watch, like I had to watch
all those times as your smelly sweat dripped on my body and you made me ..."

The bright red liquid from the mutilation of Juana's chest was still dripping
from the blade of the knife when she snatched it up.

The whetted tip of the Henckel knife, stamped with its unique trademark
showing two simplistically drawn people, joined at the shoulders, one's arm up,
the other's arm down, slammed almost to the hilt directly into Conrad's abdo-
men. The weapon with the happy, bonded, little stick-people cleanly separated
skin and tissue and then a few organs from their blood supply. As his blood was
alternately gushing and oozing out, the total castration went quickly. Juana
would never be sure why at that point she decided to jam his destructive anatom-
ical parts into his mouth, but she felt it was part of a fitting end to the demise of
old Conrad. She then ripped the gold chain and its tiny, polished cross from his
neck—the same cross that she had had to look at when he pulled on her hips to
jam himself into her. She tied the broken links together and draped it over the tip
of his thing, hanging out of his dead mouth—Conrad and his cross had run out
of good luck.

Juana spat out her next words with a hatred no twelve-year-old should ever
have to own.

"*This* is what stepdaughters do to make their little sisters being raped by their
stepfather happy. Our little secret. Don't tell anyone."

Juana mustered up whatever saliva she had left in her and deposited the spittle on his right eye. She picked up his smoldering cigarette and found a home for it in his umbilicus. She splayed his left arm out to his side, palm down and retrieved the youth-size Hank Aaron Slugger. The blow sent poor Mickey's body flying along with the broken crystal across the room. Juana never knew where the second hand ended up. She just knew she would never have to watch it moving so slowly again, while it sat on the edge of her nightstand, as her stepdaddy rammed himself inside her. Her final act of this most bizarre, yet cathartic, ritual was to hold onto the neck of the shattered Glenlivet bottle and scrape it back and forth over Conrad's right nipple and then forcefully implant the jagged edge of the top end of the broken bottle, blue cap and all, into the part of his naked chest where his previously beating heart was housed. Juana's portrait of her new daddy completed, she went to tend to Princess.

Juana, a simple name, a complex past. Two daddies down before the age of thirteen.

If there were a Bad Luck Hall of Fame, Juana and Princess and their twice-widowed mother would be voted in on the first ballot.

This was the young girl who would grow up to be one of Jed's "damn people," or perhaps she was just a damned person.

In June of 2005, Juana was a key piece of a violent puzzle that was not in Jed's baffling pile of data.

CHAPTER 31

▼

OTHER THINGS JED DID
NOT KNOW

Jerry Whalen was in a big hurry to be born. Unfortunately, he picked a bad evening. Hurricane Hazel had already wreaked its havoc on North Carolina, starting at the coastline near the South and North Carolina border and making its way north. By the late afternoon of October 15, 1954, it had whipped through Virginia and Pennsylvania.

Three days before, Mrs. Mary Whalen, Jerry's mother-to-be, had made the trip from her small home in Dunkirk, New York, to her sister's brand new home in Hamburg, New York. The ninety-minute trip up Route 5, along the shore of Lake Erie was a rainy one. When her husband protested about the trip because of her pregnant state—seven months and counting—and the pending, rainy forecast, her reply was simple. "Hey, we're from Western New York. A little rain can't hurt. We get snowstorms. Remember? And we Collins girls never deliver early." And so, a not-so-happy husband drove the family car and his wife to her sister's. Mr. Thomas Whalen tried to force a smile as his newly waxed Ford Crestline Victoria with its cream-colored body and deep red hardtop splashed its way up the lakeshore road. He tried not to think about what the new construction dirt flowing on the streets of the small Hamburg development would do to his fully chromed-out beauty, not to mention the full whitewalls he had recently spent an hour detailing to perfection. He could have worried less if he had known nature's carwash was on the way.

Three days later, Hazel slammed into Western New York with a windy and wet vengeance. Luckily, and thanks to Mary Whalen's babysitting of her sister's two toddlers, the move into the new home was pretty much complete. Unluckily, at the same time the rain and screeching winds broke the newly planted, small crimson maple in the front yard in half, the power went out—with a bang. The sun had set, candles were burning, children were crying, and Jerry Whalen wanted out. Making it to Our Lady of Victory hospital, only three miles way, was out of the question. So, Baby Jerry said hello to the world on the kitchen floor of a Hamburg, New York, home with one hell of a storm pounding the roof, windows, and walls of his aunt's new, home sweet home.

The Western New York native would grow to see his share of historic ice storms and the wonderful lake-effect snow that had an obscene habit of burying the people of the area in multiple feet of the paralyzing white precipitation. He did not particularly revel in any of it. *Hell,* he thought, *these crazy people even had T-shirts saying that they survived the blizzard or ice storm of this or that year.*

Almost fifty-one years after Jerry's run-in with Hazel, on the morning of Thursday, June 2, 2005, sitting in his office at One St. Andrew's Place in lower Manhattan, there was a gentle knock on his door that brought another storm of major proportions—a shit storm he could have lived without. He would soon wonder whether or not he would get a survival T-shirt.

Jerry was a member of the executive staff of the United States Attorney's Office for the Southern District of New York. Although he was fifty years old, he was viewed as a fast tracker in political terms. He had graduated summa cum laude from Canisius College in Buffalo, New York, and held a law degree from the State University of New York at Buffalo. After ten, very lucrative years at a big, downtown-Buffalo law firm and a nine-year stint with the Department of Justice as criminal attorney for the Western District of New York, he ran for and won a seat in the New York State Assembly. While still serving in Albany, representing a portion of the residents of Chautauqua County, he was tapped by an old friend from the Department of Justice. His time spent in the red-carpeted Assembly chamber and his work on the State-Federal Relations Committee got Mr. Jerry Whalen noticed.

In 2003 he accepted a special appointment in the executive staff for New York's Southern District. Now a bigger shot in the DOJ with more public exposure, Jerry had been told he was being groomed for higher office, as in New York

State Senator. The ambitious lawyer liked the idea. He always liked a challenge and considered himself a risk taker with a winning track record.

Today's challenge came in the form of a white, purple, and gold FedEx box about the size of a folded newspaper.

"Mr. Whalen, this came for the big boss. It's been scanned and appears harmless. It was sent from a FedEx facility in Herndon, Virginia, yesterday afternoon. It got to us just now with the 11:00 AM mail delivery. And as my position of head lackey, slash, mail-filter girl requires me to do, I opened it. In my other role, as executive assistant to the head executive assistant, I quickly made an executive decision and decided that this requires a true executive. And, that would be you."

Curious, but unalarmed, the handsome, even dashing, blond-trying-not-to-go-gray man spoke. "Thanks, Lea. I'll take care of it."

She handed him the package and made her exit. Before Jerry got to the package, he could not resist watching the sweet, young body of his assistant swish its way out of the room.

The top of the open box was in fact displaying a folded copy of yesterday's *Los Angeles Times*. The bottom half of the front page had a color photo of Jesus nailed to the cross in front of the H. The picture captured the scene, including the first three letters of the Hollywood sign. The half-inch headline read, "HORRIBLE CRUCIFIXION IN HOLLYWOOD HILLS." Jerry had read a similar article in the *New York Times* during his nineteen-mile commute from Scarsdale to Grand Central on the Harlem Line's 7:14 AM train. He also remembered one of the tabloids screaming out, "JESUS GOES HOLLYWOOD!" He pulled the *LA Times* out of the box. Below it was a standard piece of white copy paper with the words, "Only for the eyes of the United States Attorney of the Southern District of New York." The words were in red, read by Jerry, and ignored. Below the piece of copy paper was a small sea of annoying, pink packing peanuts. At least these were anti-static, Jerry thought. Buried in the formed chips of Styrofoam were two small packages sealed in bubble wrap.

"Lea!" Jerry's loud voice brought the sexy and bright aide to the office quickly.

"Can you please get me some evidence gloves? And come in and shut the door."

"Sure."

"Bring four pair, please."

A nod, a modest wink, and a quick swish of Lea's posterior out the door and then back in rendered a whole box of the hand condoms.

The first package retrieved from the box looked like a blood sample trapped in a small vial. The second was a 4-gigabyte Memorex thumb drive in a protective, plastic carrying case.

Jerry decided he would hold off on the blood vial until they had a look at the second package. He knew what he was looking at but wasn't sure exactly what to do with it. With an open right palm, he invited the lovely Lea to do her magic.

"Okay. Let's have a look-see here."

Lea opened the case and slid the drive out to expose the USB connector. She shooed Jerry out of his chair, sat down, and plugged the mini drive into the port on the front of Jerry's Dell desktop. Lea had already set up her boss's PC to default to Windows Media Player to play media files. Once Windows XP recognized the thumb drive, it automatically prompted Lea to open its content. The drive contained a single MPEG file. The acronym stood for Moving Picture Expert Group, the name of the set of standards used for coding audio-visual information in a digital, highly compressed, high-quality format.

Jerry was standing just to the right of Lea. Prior to the speakers coming to life, his gaze had alternated from Lea's fingers flying across the keyboard with a few simple strokes to the nineteen-inch flat-panel screen, and frequently rested on the hint of her left breast rising and falling inside the red, silk-chiffon, V-neck blouse.

The speakers began sending out the haunting opening of the overture of the musical *Jesus Christ Superstar*. Neither recognized the music until the familiar notes of Andrew Lloyd Webber played out what could be called the signature song of the play. It was only a few seconds into the overture when the computer screen was painted pure black. When the audio portion of this custom show switched to the familiar lyrics of Tim Rice questioning the character Jesus and his motives, Jerry and Lea were watching a wooden cross and the man hanging from it being slowly raised up the Hollywood sign's H. The camera work was close to professional quality. The brutality and eeriness of the scene on the screen froze both of the viewers' eyes to the images. It would be a minute before they had to remind themselves to take a breath. The music died away, and the video zoomed in on the crown of thorns and the blood that had dripped from its inflictions.

There was a transition from the horror on the H back to a blackened screen. Within seconds, with lyrics adapted from the Bible's book of Ecclesiastes by Pete Seeger and sung to his music, the Byrds began their classic rendition of the song, "Turn! Turn! Turn!" By the time the 1965 hit was winding up—telling the twosome glued to the screen that there is a time for every purpose under God's domain, including peace—the demands of the Jesus killers had been spelled out in detail.

The letters and words had glowed and rolled across the LCD monitor in some kind of horror-film, blood-dripping font. The text was bright red on the dark backdrop and terse.

Mr. U.S. Attorney, our demands are simple.
Free Maria Calabrese, now.
You will pay us FIVE MILLION DOLLARS to make up for your mistakes.

If you agree to these terms, post a new link on your Web page
(just to the left of that pretty little picture of your smiling face)
http://www.usdoj.gov/usao/nys/

Title the new link "Conviction Review".

Password protect it for my eyes only.
Use the letters "ESORWOLLEY". All caps please.

Place only two lines on the page.

"Site Under Construction.
Try again soon."

If you follow these instructions, I will present you with the compliance process by which we, together, can satisfy our demands.

If you don't believe we are serious, ask Jesus.
Oh, sorry, that's right—he's dead.
If you fail to respond as requested, more Innocents will perish.

RSVP no later than June 9, 2005—or else!

The Byrds music did a fadeout and the bloody, 14-point text somehow bled more heavily and then just bled away, leaving the black screen.

Jerry Whalen and Lea each let out a long, nervous sigh but were yanked back to the show by a loud, lurid series of piercing screams. Flashing images, jumping from one corner of the screen to the other, quickly accompanied the sounds. The first image was the left hand of a man with a large spike pounded through its middle. Then the right hand; then the two feet; then the bloody wound in the man's side. The images stopped flashing and fell off the screen, only to be replaced by the familiar image of the crown of thorns, and, finally, by a full image of the crucified man. The video panned out to a wider view of the brutal scene. And then stopped altogether.

The politician's usually plastic phiz cracked and sagged. The shaken man spoke with a halting voice. "Lea, can you play this back on the big screen you had installed over on that wall?"

"Sure, it's just a few cable connections and a couple of changes to the TV input. Why, boss?"

"Why? I'm not sure. I just need to see it again on the big screen. Try and get a sense of the music, the reality of the video. It was too much to take in so quickly."

"Uh, okay. And make a few backup copies of that freak show for safekeeping too. Take your time. I need a few minutes to gather my wits."

On the big screen it looked even more real, but Jerry did not want to admit it.

"Damn video could have been overlays and whatever else you techie-type people can do with computers. Pictures could be clips from Mel Gibson's damn movie. What's it called? *The Passion.* Shit. Who knows?"

"I don't know, boss. It all looked pretty damn real to me. And these guys, whoever they are, seem pretty serious. A bunch of nobodies can't pull off a crucifixion at the Hollywood sign."

"Yeah, but a bunch of wiseass teenagers who had nothing to do with it, screwing around on their nerdy PCs, could be just busting our chops. I ain't buying it yet. I don't wanna own LA's mess."

"Yeah, but, Jerry, no teenagers would have been invited to the raising of the cross. What are you gonna do?"

"First things first. What time is it?"

A surprised Lea looked up at the fancy LaCrosse clock on the wall. Inside its cherrywood frame, and just above the pendulum inside the glass casing, the hands of the clock could be read from anywhere in the room. But he asked her.

"Quarter to twelve, boss."

"Okay. I wanna see it one more time on the big screen. And then shut all this stuff down and lock it in the wall cabinet. Make sure the vial is still wrapped well. And then we're going to lunch."

"You want me to make reservations at P.J. Clarke's?"

"No. We're going undercover, over to Slainti's."

The showing on the big screen did not reveal any trickery, just a crisper, larger vision of butchery and a replay of the demanding, confusing instructions.

"Let's go, Lea. Tell the secretary we have a meeting uptown."

Lea knew Slainti's meant burgers, hand-cut cheese fries and a long afternoon of large Guinness drafts. She wasn't sure from the look on her boss's face whether or not he was anxious for the anonymity of the bar with the uncomfortable wooden booths or the cold bite of the Guinness.

Three Guinness drafts and a few bites of a tasty meal into the afternoon, Jerry Whalen took off his silver wire-rimmed glasses and put them on the scarred, dark wood table. "Here's what I need you to do, Lea. First, mention none of this to anyone. Call our FBI friends in LA. Get all the LAPD has on the crucifixion on the premise that we have a slight interest in this Maria bitch. If they ask how we know about her, just fake it. You know, FBI buzz and all that. Tell them we'd like a DNA readout on the blood from the scene, so we can do our own checking. Get it and see if it matches our vial. Give the LA Feds and the LAPD nothing back. Not a thing. For now, *we* sit and wait.

"I'll fill in the boss. I'm sure he'll agree that we won't react to this chicken-shit, amateur, terrorist crap. Damn, if we did any caving, every nutcase in the country would jump in with a new, crazy scheme. I don't want this thing putting my career at any risk. If it doesn't go away, I'll have to help solve it or take the heat. On the other hand, I could be a *hero* here. Well, let's wait and see."

There was no change to the Web site, not even a serious thought to giving in. Thursday, June 9, came and went without incident. When June 16 came and went a week later, Jerry declared to the lovely Lea that they would be visiting the pub at 304 Bowery the next day for a repeat of their fine cuisine. The DOJ attorney told his right-hand gal that he now believed that the bar, whose name in Gaelic means *cheers* or *to your health,* was his new lucky charm.

Hell, maybe he'd even make a trip to Atlantic City this weekend. And keep things rolling.

Jed, privy to none of the contents of the package delivered to the DOJ's Manhattan office, would continue to live the life of a cop mushroom—way too much in the dark, when it came to useful data.

CHAPTER 32

▼

FRIDAY—JUNE 3, 2005

"Hey, Johnny boy, how's that good-looking bride of yours treating you these days?"

"Damn, Ace, you ask me the same question every day we're together, and I answer it the same way. Nothing has changed since you asked me yesterday."

"Aw, I just like to hear you say it, Johnny. Humor an old cop."

"She's treating me better than I deserve. You obsessed with her or something?"

"Well, yes. You know I think Beth is one of the sexiest women on the planet and that she should be with me, not you."

"Well, tough shit, old man. She's mine and you can't have her. Why don't you go find yourself a woman?"

"Finding one's easy. Trying to convince the good-looking young ones that they could have a sex-filled future with a slightly overweight, underpaid officer of the law is significantly more laborious."

James Acerno, fifty-two-year-old ex-FBI agent, replayed this conversation that took place on a hotel stakeout in Yonkers, New York, January 4, 2002, every Friday morning in his head. That was when he made his weekly call to the widow of his ex-partner, Johnny Morrow. On this rainy, breezy morning, he had just hung up with the lovely Beth. The medium-height, brown-haired, handsome agent would touch the scar that ran down the right side of his face as he spoke to Johnny's wife. Their conversations usually lasted only five minutes and ended up with Acerno's asking Beth to give his best to her now-fifteen-year-old son. After

Johnny's burial, Ace danced around the question of Beth's financial health but never directly asked. Whenever he asked the generic, "How are things?" the answer always came back, "We're doing fine." He knew her father had some money. Ace guessed that between life insurance and Dad, she *was* doing okay. He would find out later that his guess was off the mark.

Birdsnest, Virginia, was not a very pleasant place to be when it rained. For James, nicknamed Ace, that meant no beach time, no reading on the new deck that faced the sunny south. And no way to jog off the sadness and images of his bulleted sidekick that the call brought. He wondered how long it would take for the piercing, painful memory of young Johnny's blood running red onto his cradling hands to soften. No time soon, he reckoned. He was about to realize how exact his guess was.

It took one additional day for the same kind of package that had made its way to the desk of Jerry Whalen to make it to Birdsnest, Virginia. The package and its identical contents, minus the vial of blood, arrived via FedEx at the outwardly modest home of fifty-two-year-old James Acerno shortly after he hung up with Beth Morrow. FedEx trucks were seen in the tiny hamlet of Birdsnest about as often as presidential parades. The young girl from the tiny, old, brick, one-door, one-window post office up at 9034 Birdsnest Drive who delivered Ace's mail had guided the driver to the small but meticulously maintained home. She was curious as to what would bring a special delivery to the quiet man's home. A barefoot James greeted them in his cutoff jeans, a maroon-and-orange Virginia Tech T-shirt, and an off-white golf cap with the Nike swoosh in the front. He signed for the package, thanked the mail carrier for her help, and went back inside. Her curiosity went unsatisfied; his was about to explode.

CHAPTER 33

▼

ACE

"Hey, Jimmy, are you ready for church yet?"

The feet pounding down the stairs, young Jimmy Acerno's response to his father's voice, brought knowing grins to both parents. It would have been nice for them to think that their twelve-year-old boy could barely wait to hear and take to heart the word of God. They knew better. Since the father-and-son Sunday ritual of church, chow, and carbines had been instituted two years prior, little Jimmy had his Sunday-go-to-meetin' garb on at least twenty minutes before roll call. First stop was the Holy Comforter Catholic Church in downtown Charlottesville for 11:00 AM services. Then the family Buick Sport Wagon would ramble up Emmet Street to the family-friendly Tavern restaurant for some sweet-potato pancakes and waffles with sides of bacon and sausage. Last stop before Jimmy's Holy Grail was Nana's home just off Rugby Avenue to drop off Mom.

As Dad drove down Route 29 toward Route 64, Jimmy was shucking off his Holy Comforter dress slacks and pants and trading them in for jeans and a T-shirt that labeled him as a fan of the University of Virginia Cavaliers. He loved the symbol of the crossed sabers. It emotionally prepared him for his next two hours of blazing weapons. Then the anxious lad brushed back his mop of dark hair and proudly put on his Baltimore Colts cap, completing his own personal, combative, defender-of-justice imagery. Only four miles south of the exit from Route 64, not far from the beautiful river named after Queen Anne of England, stood the Rivanna Rifle & Pistol Club. Dad made the boy take a few deep breaths before they made their way to purchase several rounds of various calibers for the handguns and rifles they had brought. This place, and the ritual followed there, was the birthplace of Jimmy Acerno's sobriquet, Ace. The fact that A-C-E were also the first three letters of his last name added glue to the sticking of the nickname. When James turned eighteen and traitor to the Charlottesville milieu by enrolling as a freshman at Virginia Polytechnic Institute, he tried to lose the somewhat pretentious handle. But when he proceeded to deliver an A in every course, his fellow Hokies revived the briefly hibernated hypocorism. Even when he struggled to escape with a B minus in his second-year physics course, Ace was still Ace, and so it would be for years to follow. The glue got stickier and stronger when James entered the FBI and was by far the best shooter in his class. Handguns, shotguns, carbines—it didn't matter—James was still Ace. They joked about renaming Hogan's Alley, the FBI's Practical Application Unit's realistic urban-situation training complex, Ace's Alley. Through his many assignments with the FBI, including a five-year stint with the Explosive Unit and Bomb Data Center, he was always Ace—until he found Birdsnest, Virginia.

James Acerno was sure that his new hometown did not qualify for city status. The government of North Hampton County ruled all things in Birdsnest. On the Internet, under towns in the county, good old Birdsnest did not make the cut.

The place with the avian moniker is pretty much smack dab in the middle of Virginia's part of the Delmarva Peninsula. The peninsula takes its name from the three states, Delaware, Maryland, and Virginia, which make up the 180-mile-long strip of land. Because of the fact that the Chesapeake and Delaware Canal cuts through the northern isthmus, it is not technically a peninsula but an island, but peninsula it is called. Virginia's strip of the Delmarva is seventy-five miles long and never more than twenty miles wide. Route 13 splits the parcel right down the middle, north to south. Birdsnest's bragging right in Web-based information is that it is one of the nicest places to stay lost. And that is exactly what ex-agent James "Ace" Acerno had in mind when he settled down in Birdsnest in the summer of 2003. The temperature in the little place usually stayed above forty degrees and heated up into the eighties and nineties in the summer, which suited his plans perfectly.

Up until the strange FedEx package made the sixty-minute, toilsome but peaceful trip up from Virginia Beach, Ace had managed to stay lost. Lost and satisfyingly stuck in a self-imposed strict regimen. Ace liked order, and in Birdsnest you made your own.

In the six months after purchasing the 1960s, pale yellow, clapboard, three-bedroom home, Ace spent all his time turning it into a highly functional, one-bedroom, bachelor domicile. The one bedroom, including a spacious and elegant master bathroom, took up a third of the footprint. The back wall of the bedroom was home to his small office area. The space was furnished with a wooden desk, a Dell laptop computer, a Sony shelf stereo system, and a Sony 32-inch, high-definition, flat-panel TV mounted above the desk. Next to the desk, prominently displayed and securely locked, was an impressive gun collection, long and short. Each rifle and handgun was expertly buffed and, happily for Ace, had found a new home in which to be regularly discharged. Ace had no intention of becoming a deuce. The new kitchen area, full of new, stainless-steel appliances and other gadgets, took up another third. The last of the space was dedicated to his voracious audio and video appetite. One wall was home to his 60-inch Sony Grand Wega and all the appropriate surround-sound audio accessories, including a Sony turntable for his vinyl collection. Between the kitchen and his great room was a full bath, a mudroom from the garage, and his laundry facilities. Both bathrooms were wired for full sound with speakers in the ceilings. James had never married and always saved and invested well. So, when it came time to get lost in Birdsnest, he figured he owed it to himself to get lost in style.

Ace's days were numbered, or at least labeled—just not in the usual impending death way. Monday was clean-and-wax day for his 1964 Caspian blue Mustang convertible. Ace loved driving his long-hooded, 289-cubic-inch, V8-powered baby. And he loved it to shine. Hence, a rigid maintenance schedule to keep it beaming. He had completely redone his one-car garage. The undressed, old, two-by-four wall studs were covered with waterproof sheet rock and then with white, tongue-and-groove, composite panels. Tools were hung in an orderly fashion along one wall. A wooden workbench and mounted pegboard held his hand tools. The painted floor was usually spotless, and a new garage door sealed out the elements. His small yard was sand and stone with a number of barberry shrubs, clumps of tiger lilies, and a single crabapple tree dotting the landscape.

Tuesday through Friday meant a three-mile morning run and a thirty-minute session with the free weights. Ace called his morning sprints his "God or no God" time. As he took in the beauty of the Eastern Shore and its many shorelines, he would debate "chance, or God's hand?" So far, God was running at a 95 percent win rate. Tuesday through Friday afternoons were reserved for his reading and writing. He was working on a novel based on a modern Monticello, the home of Thomas Jefferson just outside Charlottesville, Virginia. The re-creation would only be miles away from the original but centuries away in terms of the wizardry of the inventions that its new builder would include. Ace had no high hopes for the commercial success of his offbeat product, but he found the exercising of his imagination and the research fascinating. His nights, except for Friday, were never structured. He would pick one of the nights to do his grocery shopping and another to do what minimal housekeeping and laundering was required. His choice of meals was even less so.

Most nights, after a dinner of anything from a PB&J to a grilled rock lobster tail, he would watch the evening news and settle in for his choice of an unrealistic cop show with a tall glass of Grey Goose vodka being chilled by a handful of ice. As an ex-Feeb, he enjoyed the glamour on the screen that he somehow missed during his years of service in the real world. Other 'must-see TV' was either watched or recorded on his DVR. Major sporting events, anything NFL, and American Idol and Nashville Star were among the 'gotta-watch' productions.

Friday night, however, the eagle did indeed fly—along with the Goose and a few other things. Ace would make the twenty-mile drive up U.S. Route 13 and across State Route 180 to Wachapreague, Virginia, home of fabulous inshore and offshore fishing and the Island House Restaurant. But for Ace, most importantly, home of the sweet, forty-year-old Candice Kane.

CK, her chosen sobriquet to avoid the obvious, potential abuses, was an evening shift RN at Shore Memorial Hospital in Nassawadox, Virginia. The 143-bed facility was just north of Ace's home and sixteen miles south of CK's small beach house just outside Wachapreague.

CK, a native of the Eastern Shore, had been with child when she married at the age of seventeen. Her son, Richard, worked up in Norfolk, Virginia. Her abusive ex-husband of seventeen years had been among the missing even before the divorce. CK lived alone and, as did Ace, she liked it that way—except on Friday nights. The ritual of an opening cocktail of Grey Goose on the rocks, followed by the Steamed Seafood Sampler with clams, oysters, shrimp, and snow crab legs and a bottle of Mondavi chardonnay had begun shortly after Ace had moved to the area. It started with CK's dead battery in the Island House parking lot, easily jumped by a helpful Ace. After Ace registered the shocking fact that this woman looked strikingly like Beth Morrow, there were introductions, a brief exchange of bios, a "So, do you come here often?" line. And finally an agreement to meet the following Friday for dinner. It was only weeks after jumping the battery for the diminutive, mildly freckle-faced CK that an extraordinary dessert was served at CK's home, and Ace was jumping her bones and she his. He would always stay the night and make a hearty breakfast for the two of them. CK looked good to Ace anytime of the day. Her thin frame, broad smile, and sharp wit made for an inviting target for his affections. The morning would roll into a beach day—with the enticing CK in one of her many revealing two-piece suits—during the warm season, and a driving tour of the history of the surrounding area on the not-so-warm days.

Ace would make it home to Birdsnest no later than 8:00 PM, unless CK was inclined to entertain a goodbye bone jumping. Then he'd be home by nine. Sunday, for CK, was a day of sleep in preparation for her evening duties at Shore Memorial. For Ace, it was first the Lord's Day at the First Presbyterian Church in Cape Charles followed by whatever Ace wanted to do for the rest of the day. He needed to unwind before his upcoming, regimented week with all of its demands. Ace, now going by James, and CK were "pals with privileges," passionate, intimate privileges, and they both were happy with that relationship.

The last Friday of every month meant another pal-with-privileges adventure and satisfying a passion of a different nature. The pal who provided the privileges for Ace was a retired police detective from upstate New York and the beneficiary of his parents' good fortune. Michael Sheehan, a tall, stout, ball-cap-wearing fellow had inherited five acres of land in Machipongo, Virginia. The land came with a large four-bedroom home, a view of the inlet that came from the Chesapeake, and a three-hundred-foot-deep shooting range. Rain or shine, Ace would load up the trunk of the Mustang with a few weapons of his choice and a cooler of Killian's and make the six-mile, six-turn trip to lovely Machipongo, Virginia. James Acerno had met Michael early on in his Birdsnest days at the Great Machipongo Clam Shack on Route 13. They were both devouring plates of blue crabs and bottles of beer. After witnessing each other's shared predilections, Michael came over and introduced himself. They sat for hours discussing their pasts as law enforcers, lovers of guns, blue crabs, and beers. Ace's new friend and neighbor invited him over the following Friday for a session at his range. Ace fell in love with the property, the view, and the old house. Michael actually had two ranges side by side. One had targets mounted on bales of hay. The other had targets with little poles with flags on top sticking out of the ground at various distances and a tall mesh fence at the back of the range. A practice range for another of Michael's passions, a game that Ace could never master, even in a mediocre manner. Ace was a better marksman. Michael was clearly the better golfer. They agreed to mentor each other. And so, the last Friday of every month was range day. Both were protected somewhat from the elements by shed-like, salt-box roofing with closed-in ends, all supported by six-by-six posts and two-by-ten beams. Ace would pick up the crabs from the Shack on the way, and appetites would be sated. So the cowboy from Charlottesville, Virginia, found his way in the land of the Assateague Indians with his CK, crabs and beer, carbines and Berettas—a happy man. Who says, "You can't get no satisfaction?"

The first Friday of June 2005 delivered no such satisfaction for Ace. The arrival of the FedEx mystery disrupted Ace's routine in a way he did not welcome and did not understand. He listened to the same music and watched the same video that Jerry Whelan and his assistant Lea had viewed the day before. The Hollywood crucifixion had made the NBC evening news on channel 30, WAVY, but there was little detail given, other than the obvious.

Now on his computer screen, Ace watched the first showing in shock and wonderment. He watched the replay with his FBI-acquired focus and scrutinized the weird presentation in detail. The first thing he concluded was that whoever these people were, they had to be crazy, clever, card-carrying sickos on a wacko mission. His last reaction to the show, the demand to free Maria was verbal. "Innocent? That bitch should have shared Alberto's fate. Shit, I'd be happy to stick a shiv in that whore myself." Ace wasn't a big believer in hate, but for Alberto and Maria, his partner Johnny's killers, hate was not a strong enough word for what he felt. Before giving the delivered thumb drive another run on the PC, he checked the multiple-time-zone wall clock hanging to the left of his chair and saw that it was past five o'clock in London. And as any decent Alan Jackson fan would do, he accepted the fact that "It's Five O'clock Somewhere" and went to his side-by-side GE refrigerator to grab a cold bottle of Killian's Irish Red lager. He looked out the large bay window he had put in the front of his house, cursed the rain, took a long swallow from the bottle, and went back to the viewing.

Mr. George Killian Lett's lager creation was frosty cold; the crown of thorns close-up was even more chilling.

Why are they sending this to me? Who the hell are these people and why do they think what they think and want what they want? Ace picked up the casing from the bullet that had killed his partner from the small hutch on the top of his desk, squeezed it in his free hand and paced without answers. He exchanged the spent Irish brew for a new one and cursed the rain again. Whenever Ace found himself in a bad spell, which wasn't often, he would wind his way up the steps from his deck to the small, crow's nest-like platform. His sanctuary was ten feet above the lower decking and on a good day he could glimpse a view of the waters from the Chesapeake Bay that crept into the inlets on the west. For Ace, it didn't take much more than a good cup of hot coffee or a cold bottle of Killian's and thirty minutes in his own bird's nest to conclude that things were not all that bad in his life. Today's rain deprived the marksman of his healing refuge, and the image of the bloody thorns could not be washed away by a *case* of the rich, flavorful brew.

He made it to the Island House for dinner that night, but CK could tell her scar-faced lover was in no mood for dessert. The roads and decking were still soaked from the day's steady rains. There was almost no moon in the cloudy sky and the breeze made the temperature feel a chilly 60 degrees. But they braved a walk, a silent stroll past the Wachapreague Motel and Captain Zed's Bait and Tackle Marina to the southernmost inshore dock with a bottle of Williamsburg Governor's White wine dangling from Ace's hand. CK wondered why James had strayed from the preferred Mondavi chardonnay. She found out soon. James laid out his now-dry rain slicker on the wood and they sat on the edge of the pier. And for the first time, Ace told CK the story of his scar. Simply put, a mistake on his part in a botched drug raid in the Williamsburg section of Brooklyn. That was Ace's only mistake in all his years of precarious copping—until Johnny.

He hoped that the arrival of the thumb drive did not lead him to another scarring mistake—internal or external. The confident Birdsnest resident was uneasy.

His unknown partner in unease, Jed, did not even know what Ace knew. It would be a while before he did.

Like Whalen, Ace decided to do nothing. The last brief segment of Ace's version of the thumb drive presentation simply stated, "We'll be in touch, James. Sit tight." Based on the content, he assumed the thumb drive and its messages had been delivered to DOJ in New York City. *Let those FBI sonsabitches who gave me all the shit over Johnny's death handle it. I'm retired and lost and loving it in Birdsnest.*

Those guys whom Jed was losing sleep over, these guys who hung a Jesus on his Hollywood turf, were counting on this kind of reaction from the pissed-off, ex-FBI man. Turned out they had their numbers correct.

Ace did get on his high-speed satellite Internet connection and check the DOJ Web site. No new links were posted, no place to try out the strange ESORWOL-LEY password. The thumb drive's threatened June 9 deadline came and went. So, on Friday night, June 10, Ace put on a clean pair of jeans, had his Seafood Sampler, his Grey Goose, and the lovely, talented Candy Kane for dessert—licks and all.

CHAPTER 34

▼

MORE OF THESE GUYS

The distinct ring of his private phone brought Carmine to attention. Since he had left the "old life" behind—shortly after someone had tried to have him left behind for dead in the Bronx in 1988—this phone rarely rang. He knew the ties to his associates would not—could not—ever be truly broken. He owed too much to his loyal fellow businessmen who had had his and his family's backs for so many years. And he felt it wise to treat himself to having a very private number, no matter where he lived. A number only a few close friends possessed.

But damn, he and his smart lawyers thought they could safely put this kind of call in the past and still make sure the faithful minions were well rewarded and pretty much on their own.

But now, in the year 1 B.C., 2004, the private line with the distinctive ring on his Verizon landline was eerily chirping. At least the late, Friday-evening call was from Del, the lieutenant whom Carm considered the brightest and most cautious. Carm recognized the voice immediately. Of course the call came from a pay phone. This one happened to be at the corner of Riverdale Avenue and 262nd Street, not far from one of Tony Dellacamera's restaurants and a block away from the College of Mount Saint Vincent, where Carmine's youngest daughter had attended school. Carm's Carlotta had often treated herself to "Uncle Del's" to-die-for sausage and mushroom pizza during her stay with the Sisters of Charity.

The code Del used was the same as it had been years before. Even though the phones should be clean, they were both always overly cautious. "Sorry to bother you, sir. I'm calling on behalf of the New York Police and Firemen's Fund. Our goal this year is to *try*," followed by a noticeable pause, "and raise 10 percent more than last year."

"Sorry, I am very busy right now. Could you call me back at another time?"

"Sure, sir. Would tomorrow evening be okay?"

"Uh, no. How about the day after? Later in the afternoon. I should be around."

"Thanks so much, sir. We really appreciate your support. This is an especially important year for the fund."

Carm hung up the phone gently and began a not-so-gentle, verbal litany that began with "son-of-a-bitch" and escalated from there.

He and his family had just had a peaceful, enjoyable Easter Sunday. The weather on Sunday, April 11, 2004, had been mild and rain free. Carm, though not deeply religious, felt good about the idea of resurrection and a new begin-ning. His real estate ventures in Westchester County and Connecticut were doing very well. A year before, he had partnered with a developer in Northern Virginia, and their timing could not have been better. The only thing—prior to this Friday night call—that caused him a bit of unease was how highly leveraged his business finances had become. His move from well-funded, conservative real estate ventures into the thus-far-lucrative world of high finance and risk had reaped significant reward. His tolerance for more risk came slowly at first. But the more he made the more he accepted the jeopardy. But now, with his latest set of complicated deals, he felt as if his own greed that had fueled the flames of fortune had also raised the risk that came with it—maybe just a tad too much. But this was the last set of big deals for Carm, and he wanted to go out big. He would turn seventy next March. If all went well, by the fall of 2005, he would sell the business, pay his debtors, and walk away with more money than he could spend, even if he lived to be 100—and in his mind that was what he planned to do.

He had worked hard on the details through the rainy week after Easter. All signs were looking up, and this helped to boost his confidence and soothe the worry. On Friday Carm was happy to finally see the sun and even happier to hear the news of better-than-projected construction schedules. So, on this Friday night, he took his Sophia for a short ride past the Croton Reservoir, down Route 100, into the eastern part of Ossining, to the white colonial with red shutters. The Traveler's Rest and its grand food had been around since the 1800s. Its fireplaces, gardens, and stream and waterfall were fitting backdrops to the exquisite cuisine. The place with its fabulous lights and decorations was an annual Christmastime must for the Antobellis. Tonight Carm went for the roast Long Island duckling, and Sophia, her favorite, the veal scaloppini. Carm's bourbon Manhattan, light on the vermouth, was made to perfection. Sophia dared to have one of those fancy cosmopolitans. They both loved this spot and the tranquility it offered. Even at their age it was a place that made them want to hold hands and dream of post-dining romance.

The charm of the evening ended minutes after they made it hand in hand to the bedroom. The unexpected ring of the second line deadened Carm's mood. An unwelcome intrusion.

CHAPTER 35

▼

LOW ON A HIGH HILL

Del's emphasis on the word *try* meant Fort Tryon Park, one of a number of code words representing places for an important, clandestine meet. And forget about two days from now. Carmine and Tank would join the chorus of Cloisters visitors at 9:30 AM sharp the following morning when the park opened. He knew Del would be there. He did not know who else or why.

The sixty-seven acres of high ground that is Fort Tryon Park sits in the northwest end of Manhattan, bordered by Broadway on the east, the Henry Hudson Parkway on the west, Riverside Drive on the north, and West 190th street on the south. John D. Rockefeller donated the land to New York City in 1931. That same year it was declared parkland. Four acres of the large park that offers spectacular views of the Hudson River and the Palisades on the New Jersey side are occupied by the Cloisters, also a creation of old John D. The museum, made of stone, a branch of the New York Metropolitan Museum of Art, is a replica of a medieval monastery. It rises from the towering cliffs of Fort Tryon Park in the Washington Heights section of Manhattan. The Cloisters has a dominating tower that stands above the other sections of the castle-like structure. The city landmark incorporates parts of actual Romanesque and Gothic cloisters. The eclectic edifice contains building materials salvaged from five medieval European monasteries, a Romanesque chapel, and a twelfth-century Spanish apse. The name of this complex that houses an immense collection of medieval art denotes a site dedicated to religious reclusiveness and worship. Such a male enclave would be called a monastery, the female a convent or nunnery. Within the Cloisters are also a number of covered walkways and courtyards. The impressive buildings guarded by the park's unspoiled landscape belie the surrounding bustle and noise of Manhattan Island. The whole experience gives a feeling of having been dropped out of a time machine back into the times of knights, nuns, merchants, and peasants. Richard the Lion-Hearted, Joan of Arc, and Queen Isabella would have found comfort in this setting. The same would not be true for Carmine Antobelli and his friends today.

Carm's mother used to take him to the Cloisters when he was a child, and he loved everything about it. He had proposed to Sophia in its Fuentiduena Chapel, under the large crucifix hanging from the ceiling in front of the altar. Carm, in later years, marveled at the generosity of Mr. Rockefeller and his foresight to insure his city would have pockets of beauty like Fort Tryon. On a much smaller scale, Carm insured his own developments contained public common areas of unspoiled land. Most of his furtive business meetings on these grounds were serious and fruitful. Never catastrophic, never life threatening. He was anxious to see what cause had summoned him back here today.

The Saturday-morning, thirty-five-mile drive for Carmine and Tank Tomasello was uneventful. As they exited the Taconic Parkway to jump on the Saw Mill River Parkway, the radio show hosts and callers on WFAN were blasting A-Rod, the 25-million-dollar man with the .189 season average, for taking the collar one more time. The fans' venom extended to the entire Yankee team for dropping one in Fenway to the detestable BoSox.

"Tank, can you turn that shit off, please? I'm not in the greatest of moods to start with. Watching the game last night did not help my temperament, and I don't need to relive that pitiful performance."

"What would you like, boss?"

"Anything but that and the damn news stations. Put on that oldies station and drive faster. What do you think we're walking into Tank?"

"Don't know, Carm. My guess is that it's not good. You know Del does not call unless something serious is going down or there's a family party he wants to invite you to—and then he would use the regular line."

CBS-FM was into the fifties that morning, and Johnny Mathis was warbling out "Chances Are" when Tank made the U-turn off the Henry Hudson Parkway to head north to the entrance to Fort Tryon. They parked and walked past the gate and took the path on the right to get to the café, open only on Fridays and Saturdays at this time of day.

"Nice job the city has done on this place, huh?"

"Yeah, boss. Cleaned out all the overgrown junk, cleared all the paths, and sent the drug dealers packing."

"Okay. I need to take a piss, and I want a cup of black coffee."

"It's almost sixty-five out there already. You sure you want coffee?"

"Yeah, I need a wake-me-up. Del's probably there already."

CHAPTER 36

▼

DEL'S DELIVERY

Anthony Dellacamera was in fact there, sitting at a square table. A large cup of coffee sat on the linen tablecloth, joined by an apple Danish. He was known by most as the gateway to the retired crime boss, living up in Yorktown. He was known to his mother as Anthony, to his wife as Ant, and to his high school friends as Tone. When he entered Carm's world thirty years before, he asked that all call him Del, one and only one nickname, please. He was a multi-talented man. His skills ranged from running a first-class restaurant operation to running a genuine Italian, buffalo-horn-handled stiletto up from a man's gut to the dagger-shaped cartilage that is the beginning of the sternum. He preferred doing the former but, unfortunately, had found the latter to be a necessity at times. The last, after a couple of hopped-up junkies in Queens raped his niece and her boyfriend, both in the same fashion.

Carm, his bladder relieved, and Tank, with two cups of coffee, walked to the table. The warm day had all three men in comfortable chinos. Tank wore only a short-sleeved Ralph Lauren. Carm had on one of his many Arrow button-downs. And Del wore what looked like a Tony Soprano special with the long, pointed collar. The dark blue color gave Del a look of serious business. The medium-height, medium-weight, dark-haired Del stood to greet his friends. In public, the handsome Del knew better than to be giving the usual hug and kiss that was their way. A handshake and an exchange of pleasantries and family news were all that would take place in the café. On the walk inside the Cloisters, the discussion would be different.

The trio made the short trek over to the Cloisters. Tank paid the entry fees, $15 for Del and him, $10 for the senior citizen, Carm. They made their way to one of the walkways and reached a point where they were alone.

"What's going on, Del?"

"Noto's goomba came to see me early yesterday morning before I helped open up the new deli on Route 9 in Briarcliff. He didn't say much except there's big trouble brewing and there would be a package for us to pick up at the gift shop here. It would have my name on it. He said the package was from the Little Don and that we should pick it up. He also said Noto wants to meet with you privately. The Don is in Sicily right now, but he'll be back in a few weeks. He wants to meet the first week in May."

"Shit. I'm gonna be in Florida. I'm taking Carlotta and little Sal to Disney for his fourth birthday. We've had this planned for a year."

"Well, I'll relay that message and see what happens. Let's get Noto's package first."

"Okay. But I don't need this shit. I'm too old for the old games. What the hell does the little man want from me, for Christ's sake?"

Del was the only one who went into the gift shop. He went past the postcards, reproductions, and other mementos and straight to the counter. With his classic, heart-warming smile, he asked if Linda was in. She was. The clerk pointed to a young lady rearranging a shelf full of books.

"Linda?"

"Yes, may I help you, sir?"

"Yes. Someone left a package for me here. My name is Anthony Dellacamera."

A smile accompanied Linda's, "Oh yes. I have it in the back, sir. I'll get it for you."

She returned with a museum gift box the size of phone book, neatly taped around the edges. She handed the box that weighed a few pounds to Del with another smile. Del tried to tip her a five. She blushed and explained that she could not accept it, but that if he wanted to make a donation, she could surely accommodate that. He smiled back, gave her the five, thanked her, and vainly wondered what the lovely Linda was doing later tonight.

When he handed the box to Carm, he shook it. No noise.

The threesome exited the building and made their way down the trail. After making a right onto another path, they landed in a section of the park with tiers and rows of white park benches. They knew the area from previous encounters, and they knew it was lightly traveled. Luck was with them and the place was void of any humans.

Carm sat with the box. Tank and Del stood in front of him to block him from any possible visitors. Tank leaned down and sliced the seals with his high-end, pricey, Swiss Army knife made of black, polished metal with the red shield and white cross emblem mounted on the top. The digital readout embedded in the middle of the knife told him it was exactly 10:30 AM. What it did not tell him was that what was in the package would signal an unwanted and drastic change in his life and that of his friend, Carmine.

Carm opened the box gently. Under the Styrofoam peanuts was a smaller package in another gift box. Inside that box Carm looked with surprise at a Christmas ornament. There was a white, enamel dove mounted on a pewter, sun-shaped base with a white ribbon attached for hanging. All three were thinking, *peace offering?* Carm put the dove aside and lifted the smaller box onto his lap. There was a fitted piece of cardboard that was beneath the ornament, and the box still maintained weightiness.

The three gasped as Carm unpackaged the hidden object.

Perfectly sealed in a rectangular glass paperweight was a pasty, severed finger. The glass enclosure looked like something that IBM or AT&T or whoever might give out to their customers at Christmas to remind them who their friendly vendors were by putting their logo inside the heavy glass.

To Carm and the others, the lifeless finger looked like it could belong to any man. The ring on the drab digit told a frighteningly different story. A gold band held a beautiful, square, black onyx stone. It was polished, with rounded edges and a small diamond mounted in the middle. If Carmine could have gotten the finger and ring out of its glass tomb, he was sure the inscription inside would read SCA—Salvatore Carmine Antobelli, Carm's father and the grandfather of the dead man whose finger the ring had adorned, Alberto.

Old Sal had willed the ring to his oldest grandson and the wayward man never took it off. After Alberto shot the Little Don's nephew, Carm pressed the authorities in and out of prison as to where the ring ended up. The answer always came back the same. "No clue."

"Here, Tank. Put this back together, and let's get the hell outta here. I need a shot of something, now."

"Okay, boss, but give me a second here."

Tank placed the big box on the bench, replaced the paperweight and ornament in the smaller one, and put that next to the other. He fished through the packing and to Carm's surprise came out with a glossy, eight-by-ten print enclosed in a plastic sleeve.

"What the ..."

"Easy, Carm. Let's get a look."

Tank looked around and they were alone. He sat next to Carm and Del moved around to the back of the bench. The three looked at an artistic rendition of a family tree—Carm's, or at least part of his relations and bloodline. The bare branches of the tree were a deep tan against a stark white background. They had names written in a black, thin, script font hanging in ancestral order from them. Below the branch, near the top that had Carmine and Sophia as the progenitors, hung their three children, linked to their respective spouses and followed by their children.

The trio eyed Alberto's name. A dark red X had been scribed through it.

"So goddamned what, you little son of a bitch? Tell me something I don't know, Frankie Noto. What the hell is this guy trying to do or say here?"

From behind Carm and Tank, Del squeaked out, "Trying to get your attention, Carm. Why? I don't know."

The patient Tank turned over the document, causing another set of gasps followed by a muttering of some of the world's foulest strings of profanities. The printed, red line on the back of the piece of glossy paper read, "Only the beginning, my friend."

All thoughts of peace that the dove had elicited flitted away like a frightened sparrow.

CHAPTER 37

▼

WELCOME TO DISNEY WORLD

"That travel agent did a pretty darn good job, don't you think, Sal?"

"Yeah, Papa Carm. I can't believe we're at the pool already. Can I go in, Papa?"

"In a few minutes. You just had lunch a little while ago, and your mom will be down in a few minutes. You know how those women are. They need their beauty time."

"Yep. Too bad Dad couldn't make it."

"Yep, but you got me, Sally boy. And I bet I can spoil you better than your dad."

"Hey, look, here comes Mom. Hey, Mom, can I go in the pool, please?"

"In a minute, Salvatore."

The flight in first class on the United Airbus from LaGuardia went beautifully. All the screaming and kicking banshees were back in coach, and Carm had sipped down two, mid-morning, nerve-calming, mini bottles of vodka on the rocks to go with his smuggled bag of pistachios. The limo driver had them across the 528 toll road and down I-4 and in the park in less than a half-hour. Sixty minutes later, they were unpacked in their villa at the Disney World Boardwalk Inn Resort. And now, in the hot afternoon sun, he watched his beautiful twenty-three-year-old baby girl smiling at her own offspring.

It was a damn good thing for the older Doctor Boccardi, Carlotta's husband, that Carmine liked him. Carm mused briefly on how his fury over Carlotta's unplanned pregnancy at the young age of nineteen grew into a beautiful grandson—life without whom was now unimaginable. The doctor, then still in medical school, did the honorable thing. Sophia cared for baby Sal in order to allow Carlotta to go back and finish her college degree. Carm got over his fury and went on to become very fond of his new son-in-law, the gentle doctor.

This afternoon's visions of the dark-haired daughter with the trim and fit body and sweet, glowing smile reminded old Carm of his early days with Sophia. *Ah, those days at Jones Beach and Sherwood Island Park with Sophia in her bathing suit—much less revealing, but still enticing.* He looked away from his bonnie babies and glanced at the gray hairs on his slightly protruding paunch. *Ah, but those days are gone for you, Carm. It's the next generation's turn. Let's just take the hand God so often deals. We all get older. It's been a pretty damn good hand so far, except for Alberto. Ah, except for Alberto. What wrath has the boy dug up for me today with the Little Don?*

A sprinkle of warm pool water broke Carm's reverie. He jumped up and announced, "Okay. Let's hit the water, wiseguy."

The next Orlando day, May 2, 2004, came with the same hot sun and the usual 3:00 PM, teeming sun shower that lasted all of two minutes. Little Sal with the unruly dark hair and illegal smile wore Papa Carm and Mom out by five. Then it was a noisy dinner at the ESPN Club and an early retreat back to the bright and spacious, two-bedroom villa for showers and quiet time. As Carlotta and Salvatore settled in for another reading of "Blueberries for Sal" before TV time, Carm and his double Manhattan on the rocks made their way to the window in his bedroom that looked out on the pools.

The forecast for Monday, May 3, was for much lower temperatures and plenty of rain. The forecasters got a gold star. Carlotta and her four-year-old son had made an early exit for Epcot. The rains came soon after. And at 11:00 AM, as arranged by Del, so did Frankie Noto, the Little Don.

CHAPTER 38

▼

A CLOUDY DAY

"Come in outta that shit, Frankie. Come on. Give me your umbrella. Need a towel or anything?"

"No, Carm. Let me just shake this wet stuff off a bit and show me the way to the men's room, if you could."

"Yeah, right down here, Frankie. Let me take your hat. You believe this Sunshine State crap falling from the skies?"

The fifty-nine-year-old Frankie made his way back from the bathroom and greeted Carm with a prolonged hug. Frankie Noto, aka the Little Don, measured all of five-four. He was trim and still sported a full head of bushy dark hair with a few strands of silver adding salt to the pepper. He had a pleasant face, with a broad grin and a hint of a bump below the bridge of his nose. Today he wore his signature Gucci loafers. Florida called for the white leather ones with the light gold trim in place of a penny strap. Colder weather or more formal occasions would bring out an identical pair of black loafers. His pants were tan khakis and above the white leather belt was an Alfred Dunhill, brushed-cotton, taupe, long-sleeved shirt.

As he looked at his stainless-steel Gucci timepiece, he said, "Well, I guess I made it on schedule. Thanks for taking the time out of your vacation. How are Carlotta and her boy? And how are you, Carm?"

Carm was dressed in a dark blue pair of Lucky brand jeans, sandals, and a deep green Lacoste polo. Three vacations and six years ago Carlotta had dragged him mildly kicking and screaming into Lord and Taylor, telling him that she had to get him into the twentieth century before it was too late. She flattered him by telling him how hip and young the jeans made him look. He acquiesced and quickly became used to and comfortable with a style that he had eschewed all these years.

"Carlotta and little Sal are fine; having a blast so far. I'm doing just fine, Frankie. Busy as hell with all this construction I got going on, but we're doing okay. Can I get you something before we sit? I had some cappuccino and cornetti sent over from Tony's bakery just outside the Disney campus."

"Yeah, great, Carm. Thanks."

As Carm fetched the coffee and pastries, he inquired about Frankie's health.

"Shit, Carm, I'm doing okay. It's just these damn blood pressure pills the doctor makes me take. Lasix, what kind of name is that? They should call it PLAR-Hix. You know for 'Piss Like A Race Horse.' Cause that's all I seem to do these days."

"Well, sorry to hear that. I'm glad we could meet here. This has been planned for little Sal for a year."

"No big deal, Carm. I'm actually on my way to Siesta Key to visit my sister. It's only a two-hour shot across 4 and down 75. Well, maybe two-and-a-half hours including pit stops for my bleeping bladder."

"Okay. Well, let me clean up and we can sit and talk."

Coffee and cake were over and so was the small talk. Frankie took another trip to the head muttering his opinion of Lasix, returned, and sat at the faux-pine table in the dining area. Carmine set small bottles of campari, amaretto, and anisette in the middle of the table along with a bottle of Chivas Regal and an ice bucket. Frankie folded his hands, intertwining his fingers. He raised his right index finger to point at the Chivas and then motioned his digit down to the white, wooden chair on the opposite side of the table. Carm poured the Chivas, straight up for Frankie and one on the rocks for himself, both into Tervis Tumblers with butterfly fish imbedded, and sat as Frankie's finger had requested.

"I'd like to say I apologize for the theatrics at the Cloisters but I *won't*. I needed your attention."

"But, Alberto's finger, my father's ring? How?"

"Friends in low places, Carm. Not important. I let Del weasel a few extra days for you and Carlotta and the boy before I came, but now I am here." Frank Noto took a sip of the smooth malt and calmly stated, "I need *you* to get *me* six million dollars in liquid currency."

CHAPTER 39

▼

EPCOT

At the same exact moment of the Little Don's surprising request, Carlotta was startled by her Nextel phone playing its version of Patsy Cline's "Crazy." Her crazy husband had set up the special ringtone for her to recognize that it was he who was calling.

"How's the girl I'm crazy for doing today, and how's the cutest four-year-old with her doing?"

"Well, Doctor Boccardi, both of your patients are just fine, just a tad dizzy at the moment. We took a ride in the clamobile and said hi to Nemo and his turtle friend. Then I let your little charmer, who is just over the forty-inch restriction, take us on Test Track. Whoever's in charge of that death machine drives almost as fast and as badly as you do; but we survived. We're gonna grab an early lunch with M-I-C-K-E-Y at the Garden Grill. Then Salvatore wants to go to the Italy Pavilion and see the gondolas."

"Sounds great, hon. Wish I could be there."

"Me too, but I know you're busy. Anyway, Papa Carm is taking good care of us."

"Good. He's doing okay?"

"Yeah. He had some business to take care of today, but he seems just fine."

True, perhaps, if FINE stands for Freaked-out, Insecure, Neurotic, and Emotional.

CHAPTER 40

▼

"FINE?"

"Six million dollars? First, I don't have it. Second, what the hell for, and third, why me?"

The tonicity of Frankie's words shifted from cordial to menacing. "Let me start with door number two, the what for, Carm. Then I'll work into number three, and then I'll finish up with what the consequences will be if you don't have and can't get it."

The warm Disney mystique of the pristine complex that was modeled after the best parts of Atlantic City turned cold, bone-chilling cold. Carm's shiny new villa lost all its comfort and charm. For Carm, it now felt like the greasy backroom of the 242nd Street pizza parlor where Tommy Delmonte had beat the bejesus out of him for talking to Tommy's girlfriend.

"We go way back, Carm, back to the days when this business was much simpler. When muscle meant money, and better weapons; a stronger army put the fear of God into the people who we took or made the money from. Things are much different now. Can't bribe our way as easily as we used to through the layers of laws and stay outta trouble. And the money—much bigger, much more serious, much more deadly games for the dollars.

"You know, Carm, how much I envied the way you and your father got out of the business. And at the right time. These young punks today forgot how to respect their elders. Always looking to put one over on us old guys. Steal a little here; steal a little there.

"I was giving the *getting out* a try. You know that, Carm. Hoping you could get my nephew Rob into a safer business, show him the ropes. Help us build new fortunes and a way for the family to live a peaceful life. Just like your Papa Sal did with his nephew. But I didn't make the move out when I should have, like you. I had no sons to help get me out and now it's too late. Rob is gone. Your Alberto and his slut of a wife shot him. But I digress. Let me get back to door number two, the what for.

"After he blew away my Rob, I decided, 'Screw this legit stuff. Maybe it's just not meant to be.' I got called to Sicily a year after the hotel mess. Did you know that there's a Noto, Sicily? That's where the family name comes from. Aw, shit, I told you this before, Carm. I guess I'm just reminding you of my ties. Last year the bosses over there told me that they were getting into a new line of business, one that would take a lot of up-front money, and did I want in?

"Jesus, Carm, this thing is brilliant. They even got a whole bunch of PhDs who put together this business plan. I don't wanna get too deep here, Carm. But these guys are putting together an organization that will change the whole way we deal with the dope. We're gonna go upscale, high-end, a boutique kind of service for the rich and famous. Let the Latinos and blacks deal with all that street shit and the risk. Let them kill each other over a couple of thousand bucks. These college guys got charts and graphs and shit showing how the raw materials flow from places like Afghanistan and Southeast Asia into the processing end of the business. Their plans take it all the way down to the delivery and collection processes. They talked about random-generated firewalls along each step of the game. Like something computers do. I don't understand the computer part, but in the business it means they change all the players after every big move. Change them, rotate them, whatever. But there are no constants. No easy trails. Damn, it's impressive, Carm. So, sure, you bet I want in, big time. All I needed was ten million. So, I figured finish up a number of big deals, stop the cash outflow, and redirect. Hit my rainy day millions and I'm in."

Carm was silent, waiting for some kind of punch line that might make sense of all his questions—especially, the "why him?"

"Now, onto your why, Carm."

The next thirty minutes of punch line for Carmine Antobelli felt like a series of major bombs dropping, all followed by a series of staccato revelations.

Boom. "Your son and my shit-for-brains son-in-law Steve, my accountant, thought they could put one over on me and make a bundle for themselves. Well, they did put one over on me. But they screwed up big time. They cost me five million."

Bang. "First, there's the three million worth of dope your son was transporting in your trucks that is among the missing. When he died, *his* loyal workers took off with *my* goods. Alberto was gonna cut it once more before delivery, dilute my product, screw my loyal customers. And he and Steve were gonna get rich. Dope's gone now. Customers don't pay without product. I'm out three; count with me, one, two, three freaking million, Carm. When I was looking for all the cash my books showed, it was all fairy dust, cooked by the recently deceased Steve."

Bang. "Then there's another two million. My late son-in-law and your son looked and saw how much I made on the gambling business. Decided to get in the game. Became their own bookies. They left one million in bad debt out there. When Alberto died, his debtors and my money were in the wind. The other million was the result of Alberto's personal predilections and losses to my bookies. Rule number one. If you're gonna be a bookie, don't bet. As in, don't shit where you eat."

"Jesus, Frankie. I had no idea he was booking and betting."

At this point, Frankie, the veins in his temples bulging blue, stood up and slammed the empty, twelve-ounce Tervis cup.

"Bet?" Almost a screamed response from Frankie. "He was way out of control, Carm. Never cut out for this business. I let him in to help me out as a favor to our friendship. Shit, Sophia told my wife how proud she was of Alberto and his new ways. So, I figured, keep it in the 'family.' Help out my buddy Carm's son.

"Bet? Shee-it. He loved the ponies. Christ, he loved the ponies, the Orioles, the Bears, the Colts, and every other damn kind of animal he could bet and lose on. He was laying bets all over M-E-T-R-O-politan New York—and losing big. There's another million in the miscellaneous column, but I don't have the patience. Your son thought he was playing with house money. But it don't work that way too long. I need the losers' money to pay the winners and collect the juice. I caught up with him and poor Stevie who was hiding Alberto's problems. It took me quite a while, but when I went looking for my treasure chest, numb-nuts Stevie could hide no more. And *I* was already on the promise with Sicily."

The Little Don walked around to Carmine's side of the table and stood behind his old friend. He squeezed Carm's shoulders and put his mouth to his right ear. "I want six from you. I need six from you."

Frankie walked away, heading for the men's room again. Carm refilled the glasses with scotch and caught his breath. When Noto returned, he sat and opened his palms to Carmine.

"I don't have it, Frankie." It took Carm fifteen minutes to lay out the high-lights of his leverage problem. His voice even squeaked a little when he explained that, against the strong-willed Nancy Simonetti's accounting advice, he had even tapped all of his retirement investments to make the next deal work. And there was no liquid cash coming back to the tune of six million, or even close, for at least two years. "I got almost nothing to sell, Frankie. For now, all I got is debt and a shitload of lots with poured basements and open-air housing. The profit all comes on the sell. If I sell now, all I get to do is pay off my creditors and come up empty."

Frankie cut him short. "That's your problem, Carm. I need my money by next fall to get in on the deal. And because of my stupid Steve, I already owe Sicily a couple of mil. That's where I was last month. Begging the boys in Italy to give me some time. I gave them Stevie on a slab as a token of my sincerity and commit-ment. They put up the ten million for me as a favor, and now I gotta pay it off on a schedule. I gave them a promise, and they take their promises much more seri-ous than any bank you ever dealt with. Their version of foreclosure involves pain, suffering, and funeral homes. And I'm partial to living. I go way back with these people in Italy. They gave me my start, and I've been a *big earner* for them ever since. And with the Noto Commission, once you're in, you either deliver or the only way out ..." Frankie pointed his right index finger and a raised thumb at Carm's forehead.

"'The Tractor', Bernardo Provenzano, is involved in this one, Carm. And you do not disappoint 'the boss of bosses.'" The mention of the man whose nickname referred to his personal ability to mow people down gave new gravity to Noto's problems. Provenzano was even bigger than his own legend. The native of Corle-one, Sicily, had been an enforcer in the Luciano Leggio family. When Leggio became the new godfather, after an internal Mafia bloodbath, Provenzano moved up in rank. In the early 1960s when things got dangerously hot for the Tractor, he went underground and became the unseen comptroller, treasurer, and CFO for the mob. After another series of government and Mafia wars in Italy, Proven-zano rose to the head of the Sicilian Mafia and operated undetected by the gov-ernment. If this man was involved in Noto's new game and it was his money in the pot, any threat would not be an idle one.

A sip of Chivas and a pleading, "But I don't have it, Frankie."

Frankie got up and walked over to the briefcase he had brought and set on the side of the couch. He carried it to the table and placed it to his left and opened it.

Still standing, he leaned in toward Carm. "You remember the nice family tree you got at the Cloisters?"

Carm nodded.

"I did a little research of my own on your business, Carm. I knew some about your problems. I was hoping you had your own rainy-day cash squirreled away somewhere, but I guess not. And, with all my heart, I don't want it to come to this, Carm. But the boys in Noto, Sicily, want the money I owe them or my own family tree gets seriously pruned. And I want in on their new deal. I own some of my own mess because of Steve, and I'll find a way to work on some of that, but I need your six mil."

Before Carm spoke, Frankie held up his left hand and dropped a thick, for-mal-looking, envelope-size package on the table in front of Carm.

"You don't need a family history lesson about who I am connected to in Noto, Sicily. Just know they are more ruthless, less caring, and more deadly serious than anyone you have ever met. I need my first million by September 2005 as a sign of good faith. And you're gonna get it for me or that insurance policy in front of you, for your sister, will unfortunately be redeemed. By the way, you are benefi-ciary."

Noto pulled out five more packets, all in the same type of heavy-paper sleeve, with five more names on them—including his wife Sophia.

"I chose your sister to go first, well, because she's been a little ill lately. If you don't have the rest by the end of next fall, the other five will have to go all at once to avoid any serious suspicion. Some kind of nasty accident. You know the kind. All the money will go to you. And then it will all come to me. And you get to live.

"You see, Carm, that's the consequence I promised I would speak about. Plain and simple. My other son-in-law, the one *with* brains, is in the insurance busi-ness, and all this shit gets done on that wonderful Internet. Online, I think they call it. Once they die, and my coroner signs off on the cause, the money will move very quickly without much question. Accidents happen all the time, and you, my friend, are the beneficiary or second in line and executor and all that. Yeah, I took care of that too between my lawyer and yours—with just a bit of persuasion. Oh, and there are doctors with real credentials, friends of mine, who vouched for the health of your family in order to secure the policies.

"Well, I was gonna bring this up later, but we were able to get a $250,000 pol-icy on Alberto prior to his demise. Had to. It was an appeasement to keep the dogs away.

"Now, back to the living. There's no other way, Carm, unless you can get real creative and come up with the price of life. You can't call out the Zamboni of bad debt and make it all go away. Oh, and in case you have a heart attack or anything before then, we have a few policies on you. The others will still have to go. We'll just have to adjust the paperwork to get the money to the right place.

"Now, in case your mind is racing to other outs, like call the authorities, maybe kill me, or whatever, I have them all covered. Forget Federal Witness Protection. Forget everything. You have nothing but today's meeting to tell anyone about. I'll be taking those policies with me, and it's your word against mine.

"Now I gotta take one more piss and then I gotta go. Oh, almost forgot. Here are the names of a couple of Alberto's delinquent debtors. Maybe you can get something from them. And here's an envelope with a few photos of the kind of work that the Notos of Sicily are famous for. I suggest you view them on an empty stomach."

Carmine Antobelli watched his old friend walk to the bathroom, and, without looking, pushed the papers aside and grabbed at his tumbler, finished its remains, and replenished the glass with the pointy-nosed creature of the sea looking back at him.

Frankie, the Little Don, returned with a resolute, but softened, visage. Carm stood up and Frankie walked right up to face him.

"Listen, Carm." As Frankie started to speak, the room, for Carmine, took on a different kind of chill. It held a familiar sense of shared sadness. Like the sweet-smelling waiting room of a funeral parlor, where friends try to comfort a family member. Like a hospital room with its myriad of antiseptic and bodily scents and visitors trying to convince the damaged patient that time will heal all.

"Carm, I've already done what I can. I've made my daughter a widow. I've begged with the bosses to keep the capos away until I have time to make good on the promise. I've kept you and your family, except for Alberto, out of it until now. It cost me, but I did it."

Frankie rolled up the right sleeve of his Albert Dunhill.

"Each of these burns bought me three months of time. I can't give any more than I have."

Carm winced at the grotesquely scarred epidermis that ran from just above Frankie's wrist to the crook of the elbow.

With his sleeve still revealing the five branded and charred six-point stars—part of the Noto family crest—Frankie moved in and hugged Carmine.

He pulled Carm's head down to his shoulder and, with a tone of hope and armorless weakness, whispered in his ear.

"Find a way, Carm. Find a way."

These were this day's final words between the congress of two that eventually begot Jesus of Hollywood.

Well, I eventually did get to have Tommy's girl, Sophia. And poor old Tommy Delmonte is still in Attica. Maybe I can find a way. Carm left this thought and picked up the papers.

CHAPTER 41

▼

THE BROKER

On July 22, 1977, in the Kingsbridge section of the Bronx, it was a Johnny Carson, "How hot was it?" day. Although the temperatures only made it into the middle eighties, there was not a lick of a breeze to be found, and most of the natives were getting restless. Air conditioning was not a household staple, and the concrete and brick absorbed and echoed back the sun's heat. Heat didn't bother Richard Charles Huse, and the shirtless, seventeen-year-old redhead was in his familiar spot. The tennis ball hit the concrete wall with a thwack and came racing back to Rick with a series of sharp bounces. Rick gave a slight tip of his Mets hat, quickly licked the first two fingers of his right hand, and scooped the ball into his well-worn Rawlings fielder's glove with the grace of Derrel McKinley Harrelson, aka Bud, the longtime Mets shortstop. With a quick turn of his hips and torso and an extension of the strong right arm, the battered yellow orb would be sent back to the square marked on the concrete with borrowed, white spray paint. Rick guessed he had simulated two ballgames' worth of outs—if all the balls were hit to short—when the "boys" started on him.

"Hey, R.C. Think you can beat out Louie Iozzino for the shortstop position on the American Legion team? Huh? You gonna be a big leaguer and play for the Mets? I heard Joe Torre doesn't like redheaded faggots."

One of the things Rick hated more than being called R.C., after the damn cola, was Patrick Shawn O'Keefe and his band of smart-asses. With another hurl of the ball, he ignored them; then the glass bottle, full of Royal Crown, slammed its way onto the pavement in front of him.

Rick's mother always warned him that his temper would someday get him in trouble. When the third bottle of Royal Crown landed, Rick, who enjoyed peaceful times and never a provoker, had had enough. Not because this was the third bottle to smash near him, but because this was the fifth incident of the summer with Patrick the Prick. His next move would have been a surprise to his cautioning mother. He turned his back and walked away from his laughing tormentors who were sitting on the street steps above his makeshift infield.

Two nights later, Patrick Shawn O'Keefe was floating in the depths of Spuyten Duyvil Creek that separated Northern Manhattan from the Bronx. One day after his unfortunate fall, he was found, washed up on the rocks, on his way to the East River—with his neck, and his face, void of any grins, nearly separated from the rest of his lifeless, bloated body.

That week, Richard Charles Huse did not meet with any more local harassment. It was this experience that taught Rick to be patient. A good plan is better than irrational violence, if you want to achieve your goal. This was the first, but not the last, time Rick would kill. But as he aged and wised, he preferred less violent means to an end. He favored brokering his deals or the deals of others in order to make his way in the world, and make it in a monetarily rewarding fashion.

By the time Frankie Noto was finished with Carm in Disney, Rick, at age fifty, now known widely as the Broker, was semi-retired. Many years before cutting back on his workload, he gave up the killing business. Carm knew this, but the Broker, a friend who owed him, was one of the first calls he made after returning to Yorktown, New York.

CHAPTER 42

▼

THESE GUYS

These were some of "these guys" who begat the Jesus Cruz happening. Now dubbed simply by LAPD, Jesus H.

These guys. So many. Some good, some evil, and some desperate.

Some that Jed knew of.

Some that he did not—not yet.

PART II

▼

THE CLASS

"Be slow to fall into friendship; but when thou art in, continue firm and constant."

~ *Socrates*

CHAPTER 43

▼

END OF JUNE 2005

The sharp, stinging pain racked every part of his body; the visceral screams went unheard in his own ears. He was surprised that through the agony his lips and tongue could register the taste of blood. Blood that dripped like rivulets from a forehead that burned with throbbing pangs. Sweat, mixed with the red trilling from his wounds, lathered his entire body. He stretched his arms against the leather tethers that held him tight to the wooden wall. He could not reach the piercing thorns that invaded his forehead and his temples, nor any part of the crown encircling all.

A light from above burst into the room and revealed his nakedness to all looking on. A distorting mirror hung from the opposite wall by two wooden supports, not unlike the way he hung. He could see himself, the sizes and shapes of his mutilated form darting in and out of the evil, magical looking glass.

He could see the laughter of the mob looking on. He saw the spit, hurled from their lips, land on his blazing skin and sensed it steam off with a silent hiss.

"It is time. It is time." He spoke the words spinning around in his head. Then screamed them with the loudest scream any man could offer. His arms were released from the tethers, and he fell, and fell, and fell through darkness toward an inviting light.

"Jesus, Jed, are you all right? You were tossing and screaming, and look, you're soaking wet."

Jed saw his wife Regan sitting up in bed with the light on her nightstand shining too brightly.

"Yeah, yeah. Just a dream I guess. Was I saying anything?"

"Yeah. You were saying, *and screaming and yelling*, over and over again, 'It is time. It is time.'"

"Sorry. I'll be okay. I guess it must be time to get away from this Jesus thing.

"Go back to sleep. I'll be fine. Sorry, Regan."

CHAPTER 44

▼

FORE

It had been a little less than a month since the discovery of Jesus on the cross in Jed's Hollywood territory—long days and weeks of dead-end leads, frustration, and pressure. For Jed, the annual golf outing to Pipestem State Park in West Virginia with his three buddies from his college years could not come soon enough. And after three weeks of no forward progress on the Jesus H. case, his boss let Jed take the time for the *sacred rite of the Fearless Foursome.*

Three of the self-named Fearless Foursome had become close friends at the John Jay College of Criminal Justice, a part of the City University of New York. The college, named after the first Chief Justice of the Supreme Court and founded in 1964, is made up of four separate buildings located on Manhattan's West Side. For the three John Jay Bloodhounds who graduated fourteen years ago, Jed, Grady O'Connor, and Chris Lee, it had been four great years of shared classes, shared interests, tedious commutes, and hard work—and just a little shared mischief along the way.

Chris Lee's roommate from those days, Drew Birdsall, who back then was attending Manhattan College, rounded out the quartet. Chris and Drew were friends and immigrants from Lexington, Virginia. Drew's college, founded in 1853 by the Christian Brothers religious order, was so named because of its original location then known as Manhattanville, a section of New York City at 131st Street and Broadway. In 1922 Drew's college outgrew its space and moved to a mildly hilly piece of property in the northwest Bronx. It was *this* part of New

York City that was the scene of a number of firsts for the four college boys—some mischievous, some not. The most important being their first hacking adventure together at Van Cortland Park Golf Course. The 6,122-yard-long course, located only a few miles from Chris and Drew's apartment, is the oldest public course in the country and was the venue of the inaugural, life-altering gathering of the Fearless Foursome.

His preparations for their annual golf trip had become a kind of ritual for Jed. As he cleaned his clubs, packed a couple dozen of the Titleists he always received for Christmas, and decided what this year's wardrobe would consist of, he would begin to recall the memories that bonded these lionhearted duffers so tightly and so sincerely. Bonded them beyond the shared, endless quest for the right clubs, the perfect golf ball, the smooth and level swing, the tempo, the temperament, and a personal magic number that would validate their tiring pursuit of the game.

Although they did not talk all that often now, each knew he could pick up the phone and be in touch with a friend instantly, as if they had not spent a single day apart. Jed was happy about that fact. He was also proud to be a part of a coalition that was fearless when it came to teeing up a passive, white sphere that weighed 1.62 ounces with a diameter no less than 1.68 inches. More important for Jed was the comfort with which they shared their deepest thoughts and parts of their souls. Life had taught Jed that those kinds of friends were not easy to come by.

As announced by Chris Lee's annual letter describing the details of the upcoming junket, this year's outing would be the twelfth annual gathering of the tetrad since they left college. As usual, they would gather at Chris's place in Lexington, Virginia, and wend their way to the course in West Virginia. They were a bit of a multifarious group that had grown to love each other, love each other's families, and voluntarily submitted themselves to the abuse so generously offered by the sport.

Another part of Jed's ritual, after packing, was to take his wife and kids out to dinner as a kind of peace offering before abandoning them for the better part of a week. The next day's 6:00 AM flight from LAX to Dulles would get him into Virginia by 3:30 PM local time; so, it would be an early night for Jed after their meal.

At 5:30 AM, June 21, 2005, two days after an enjoyable Father's Day, Jed finally made his way through all of the pleasures of checking in at LAX and took a comfortable seat in first class. Jed had been disappointed in Tiger's failure to win the U.S. Open the previous Sunday. But, he had to give kudos to the New Zealander, Michael Campbell, for topping Tiger by two strokes at Pinehurst.

And today for Jed, it was, *Good luck next time out, Tiger; bring on West Virginia for me. And see you later, Jesus.*

Jed's previous cross-country trips on United Airlines for the golf outing had earned him a goodly pile of frequent-flyer miles and the luxury seating. As he settled in, his mind registered one more time the gnawing reality that LAPD's Chief of Police did not get the Hollywood sign crime solved in a week—and neither did Jed get his desiderative body massage from Miss Heidi Klum. *So, Friendly Skies, take me onward and eastward to happier times.*

While it had been easy for Jed to forget most plane trips, he would never forget his first LA to Washington flight for one simple reason—Rhonda. It was his first golf outing since moving to LA in June of 1995. It was a late-evening red-eye. Back then first class was something Jed only got a peek at when he boarded the plane. What *was* first class was the flight attendant assigned to coach. To say the young lady with the silver Rhonda nametag was attractive was like saying the Titanic had a minor buoyancy issue. Even more impressive than her shiny dark hair and deep hazel eyes, and all the other things that made you look, was the sweetest sense of care and comfort that emanated from her soothing Southern "How can I help you this evening, sir?"

When things were slow, the two had snippets of conversation about their professions and their families. Jed noticed Rhonda's eyes light up when she talked about her little girl, Whitney, and her youngest, a cute, sweet whirl of boundless energy named Chase. She even brought Jed a free beer, and they exchanged displays of wallet photos of their families. Jed confessed to her that he was nervous about taking this golf trip when his wife was alone at home and a few months pregnant. Rhonda smiled a mildly wry smile and said, "Trust me. Women are a lot stronger than you men give us credit for"—words that Jed would have cause to remember very soon. On every flight since then, Jed had been looking for the "angel of the airlines." And, as on all of his subsequent flights, he would not find her today. But her memory would make the flight smoother and shorter, and for that he would always be grateful.

And, he learned quickly, when his wife breathed her way through the birth of their first child, how right Rhonda had been about the tenacity of the female species.

The twin-engine, 155-foot-long Boeing 757-200 jet took off on time. About thirty minutes after the huge aircraft reached its cruising speed of 467 mph, Jed was able to stop thinking about the nagging mystery that was Jesus Cruz. He had fast forwarded his way through all the details of the case and finished up with remembering the emptiness of his efforts. He thought about the cold white-boards in the task force room filled with words that led them nowhere and the patience his wife had summoned up in order to put up with his obsession.

The movie on the plane provided no inviting distraction, so Jed decided to move on to his usual air-trip ruminations and to keep an eye out for Rhonda. The mental travels through his history with the threesome he was about to join for four days began with retrieving a faded picture of the four of them. They were standing on Van Courtland Park's first tee—many hooks, slices, three putts, and beers ago. Their late-1980s outfits and their looks were different than today. So were so many other things for the foursome.

Jed decided to mix things up on this plane ride and start with Grady, and see where that took him. He usually started with Chris because Chris's story was always on his mind. But this time, he would save that till the end of the flight. And Chris would be the first of the three whom he would see.

The details of the Fearless Foursome's lives did not need to be grease penned on a whiteboard for Jed. They were etched in his brain with the same clarity with which his friend Drew Birdsall could recall, after a round of golf, every shot he made.

CHAPTER 45

▼

GRADY

Jed's plane continued its trek east and he began musing about his friend Grady. A quote he had encountered in his research for one of his many college term papers and never forgot came to mind. The author of the simple quote was Frank McKinney Hubbard, born September 1, 1868, in Bellefontaine, Ohio. He was an American cartoonist, humorist, and journalist better known by his pen name "Kin" Hubbard.

Will Rogers declared Kin to be "America's greatest humorist." Kin left the world many insightful thoughts. This was Jed's favorite. "Boys will be boys, and so will a lot of middle-aged men." And when it came to living up to Mr. Hubbard's observation, Grady was the leader of the pack.

To understand Grady O'Connor's passion you only needed to know two words, "NYPD Blue." His grandfather, father, and two uncles were all City cops. Grandpa Ted was retired from "the job"; his sons were all detectives in different Manhattan precincts.

From an early age, living in the Bay Ridge section of Brooklyn, all the talk Grady heard at holiday parties was about "the job." By the time he was ten, Grady felt like he already had blue blood running through his young veins.

Bay Ridge, with its boundaries being 61st Street to the north, 86th Street to the south, Gowanus Expressway to the east and the Belt Parkway to the west, was home to the Brooklyn end of the Verrazano-Narrows Bridge. The bridge that connected Brooklyn to Staten Island was named after Giovanni da Verrazano, who, in 1524, was the first European explorer to sail into New York Harbor. The bridge's 693-foot-high towers, each weighing 27,000 tons, defined a good part of the Bay Ridge skyline. The bridge shared the spotlight in Bay Ridge's history with the fact that John Travola danced his way to stardom in *Saturday Night Fever*, filmed in this part of Brooklyn. This was the Brooklyn that fathered the O'Connor clan.

Grady loved his hometown with its Skatepark in Owl's Head Park, its festivals, its great restaurants that they got to go to on special days, and the friendly cops of the 68th precinct. He even tolerated his Our Lady of Angels grade school uniform and the subsequent hazing he got when he went on to Fort Hamilton High School. With his bright red hair, the most obnoxious students constantly teased him that he should streak his hair with black stripes and play the school's mascot, a tiger. All of those days were only a prelude as far as he was concerned until he joined the force. His mother imposed one more on poor Grady.

At his mother's insistence he would be the first O'Connor to attend John Jay. "If you still wanna be a cop when you finish your degree, Grady, fine. But degree first." With his dad, Shawn, arms folded across his chest, standing behind his mother, the seventeen-year-old Grady could only respond, "Yes, Mother."

One year later, now in college, to his own surprise, he easily transferred his eagerness to become one of New York's finest to the classroom. Although it did not come as easily to him as it did to most of his classmates, he put in the hard work to ensure he made the grade. He would make sure that Mom and Detectives O'Connor would not be disappointed.

At John Jay, his new buddies encouraged him to work on his appearance with the same fervor with which he labored at his schoolwork. As much as Mom tried to tidy Grady up before heading to the subway, he always seemed to be mussed up by the time he made it to Midtown. His unruly, bright red hair that topped his five-foot-ten frame defied any attempts at an orderly arrangement. After lunch, you could take a pretty good guess at what he had eaten. But Grady had an energy and air of confidence that attracted people and a smile that his mother told him would get him into trouble with the ladies. Unfortunately for Grady, his mother's prophecy turned out to be true, just not as she had envisioned it.

Grady was simply a loveable character on a mission. There were no dramatic story lines to date in Grady's biography. He made it through John Jay, spent some time at the police academy, and started on patrol—exactly where he wanted to be. He married a nice Italian girl from the neighborhood who had an artsy degree from the Pratt Institute. They eventually bought a small two-bedroom co-op on Shore Road, not far from the family. Grady progressed through the ranks and made detective, made two babies along the way, but still had the worst, lunging golf swing that Jed had ever been privileged to witness.

Grady always had two things at their golf trips: the highest scores and the most fun. The redhead invariably came to the golf course and the poker table with a soul full of great expectations. He almost always left both with another layer of humility trying to weigh down his indefatigable optimism. As Jed thought of his redheaded friend, he thought, if you can't love Grady, you can't love *any-damn-body.* He wondered more than a little bit, though, how much Grady loved himself. The redhead's need for chemical assistance to maintain his emotional balance was not a well-kept secret.

Grady was now a detective in the Manhattan South precinct. Jed thought Grady might have some insights into the mysterious hanging on the hill in LA. *God knows—no pun intended, Lord—I need some.*

As Jed was wrapping up his thoughts about the detective who worked in the heart of "the city that never sleeps," there were several people, including another redhead, a few miles and a short train ride north of Grady's precinct, working on the details of their own game.

These people were some of *those guys* responsible for Jed's Jesus H. that he so desperately wanted to find.

CHAPTER 46

▼

JED

Jed moved on with his thought and pondered how *he* was very different from Grady. Friendly enough, but less outgoing. His family had no NYPD Blue in their history. When asked why John Jay, he would calmly tell the story that was his epiphany.

Jed's older sister Fran had pretty much been his self-appointed guardian from as far back as he could remember. She was the oldest. He was the youngest of four. It was a warm August evening and the Queens Valley playground was loaded with kids escaping the confines of their apartments in Kew Gardens Hills. Even at the age of eleven, Jed knew his oldest sister was just too pretty not to look at. He had watched his eighteen-year-old hero get ready for her senior prom back in May and was mesmerized by her elegance—dreaming that some day a girl that pretty might have feelings for him. That August day, even without the fancy dress and funny hairdo, Fran, in her tan shorts, red St. John's University T-shirt, and worn sneakers, was just as pretty to look at.

Unfortunately, two of the older boys playing three-on-three basketball agreed with Jed's assessment. Jed was playing a pick-up game of stickball. The other team called "last inning" because it was getting dark. Jed knew Fran was waiting over by the swings for him to finish his game. Jed's buddy struck out to end the game, and he was disappointed by the one-run loss. But, hey, tomorrow's another day. With his Yankee hat turned backwards on his head and his personal, wooden, stickball bat in his hand, he turned to meet up with Fran. At the age of eleven, he harbored some minor resentment about his mother's insistence that his older sister watch over him this night, but Fran was the best at watching over while appearing to do otherwise.

He searched the swing area and saw nothing but a few older kids smoking cigarettes and sipping something from a brown paper bag. After doing a 360-degree search, Jed, with some trepidity, approached the older kids and asked if they had seen anyone who looked like his sister. They shrugged him off and went back to their Mensa-like conversation. For Fran not to be there was a first-time, scary experience. The panic would set in five minutes later when she was truly nowhere to be found. Grady had seen cops in the neighborhood many times over his youthful years but never actually talked to one. To him they were always about someone else's life, not his, not his family's, and certainly not his hero-sister's. At the age of eleven, the sight of a blue-and-white cruiser on the street was intimidating. Even though his school had the smiling policeman or woman in once a year to convince the kids that they were their friends, he hoped he would never have a reason to deal with the men in blue.

Now he prayed for one to come by. Jed's home was three blocks away, and he was torn between running home to tell, and scare the hell out of his mom and dad, and staying put, hoping Fran would show. Although his parents dragged him and his siblings to church every Sunday morning, Jed was never very big on praying. With a sweating forehead and a rumbling stomach, he worked on the best prayer he could. The words "Jesus" and "help us" were oft repeated. The blue-and-white sedan that turned the corner by the playground looked like the friendliest car he had ever seen. Risking getting run over, Jed darted across the street and jumped in front of the NYPD vehicle. He struggled to get out his words, but the friendly cops calmed him down and quickly got the message.

When Jed tells and retells the story, he skips through his fear and jumps quickly to the three cop cars that came screeching and blaring into the neighborhood and the eclectic group of short, tall, thin, fat policemen running in different directions. It was the longest five minutes of Jed's life. Two of the cops emerged from the back of one of the apartment buildings with Fran. She was being supported by one of the cops; the other was on his radio. Two more cops came out with two of the boys Jed had seen playing basketball. Their hands were cuffed behind their backs, and one had only his boxers covering him from the waist down.

Jed looked back and forth at the players in this horrible scene but settled his focus on his sister. His precious sister was held up by the cop. The ever cool, calm, and collected Fran was crying uncontrollably. Her torn St. John's shirt covered her shoulders and chest. The cop not holding her up had given her his shirt to cover her from the waist down to her knees. The bruise on her cheek did not look pretty, but the look that Fran gave to Jed, which included a slight smile and shake of her head from right to left, somehow told him that his hero was okay.

And she was. The cops had gotten there in time. Their rapid response had been based on reports of a series of rapes in the area. Their response had saved Fran from a horribly damaging violation. Jed's flagging down the police car had triggered the response.

At that moment Jed was his beautiful, older sister's hero and she would never let him forget it.

Case closed for the young Jed. "Mom, Dad, I'm gonna be a cop just like the ones that saved my sister today." Seven years later, Jed was taking the E Line of the Queens IND train to midtown Manhattan and John Jay College.

And now, in June of 2005, he had a woman as pretty as Fran who had feelings for him, and a proud member of the LAPD he was.

The cop would have been a lot prouder at this moment, if he had made any progress on Jesus H. and finding *these guys*.

CHAPTER 47

▼

DREW

Jed figured the Boeing and its 124 feet of wingspan and 200 passengers were making their way over the last of the western states when it was time to make his way to the lavatory. Being in first class made that an easy trip. Being in first class also made him think about having his maiden can of Budweiser for this year's FF outing soon. His plan was to have a few, take a long nap, and be ready and fresh for the three-hour drive to Lexington, Virginia.

As he settled back into one of the twelve first-class seats, he tried to think of any quote that might put a convenient label on his old friend, Drew Birdsall. Jed resigned himself to the fact that it might take an in-depth medical and sociological research effort to capture all the things that made up the Birdman.

He was the biological product of Mr. & Mrs. James Birdsall. Mr. B. was a graduate of the Rutgers School of Law. Once James, aka Jimmy, finished his degree and passed his bar exam, he took a pass on an offer from a local firm in Newark and migrated from the Garden State to the Old Dominion State. He had been solicited by one of his father's friends who had a local practice in Lexington and was looking for a partner for a few years before he moved on to retirement. An offer that included the opportunity to take over the firm upon the older lawyer's stepping down. On his first visit to the charming little city, Jimmy noticed a number of things. First, there seemed to be more gardens in Lexington than he had ever seen in Newark. Second, the traffic was significantly less hellish. There was more—including the air quality, the history, and the beauty. The most defining beauty he would notice was the twenty-two-year-old paralegal who greeted him when he entered the law office of Jonathan Gordon. The bright blond behind the desk in the outer office was the youngest daughter of his potential employer.

Jimmy's decision was not difficult. It was a month before he moved down to start work. To his surprise, just with his signing bonus, he had enough to put a down payment on a small three-bedroom in the heart of the city. "A house, a damn house. And my own driveway to park my car. Hot damn!" Jimmy wasted little time honing his skills in the real world of small town lawyering. If he spent an eighty-hour week at the profession, like most of his fellow graduates were currently doing, it was only because he chose to do so. He wanted to own the art and skill of being a good lawyer. And he wanted to end up owning this practice. He did not want to disappoint. Jimmy also wasted little time wooing young Allison Gordon. The Adonis-like Drew was the first born of the handsome blond couple.

The depth of Jed's friendship with Drew developed slowly. They went to different colleges and academically shared little of the same interests. Most of their initial time together was on the weekends when the Fearless Foursome all sacked out in Chris and Drew's place, renamed the Hotel Ree Ree. The Birdman may have been the prettiest-looking teenager that Jed ever met. During their first encounters he assumed the perfectly curled, long, blond locks that hung off his head and rested on his shoulders required serious maintenance. Jed also figured that the crispness of his golf apparel was the result of a focused effort.

As Jed decided to signal the flight attendant for a particular can of the beer that was the *child* of Eberhard Anheuser and Adolphus Busch born in the mid-1860s, he thought to himself, *Boy, was I wrong about this kid Drew.* In Drew and Chris's basement lodgings on Irwin Avenue there was no choice but for most things to be up close and personal when the four would stay over for a Van Courtland Park golf outing—including hygiene and dressing. Jed always had to work some at getting his hair under control and was careful to make sure his clothes were properly folded and hung after his visits to the laundromat in the basement of his parents' apartment building.

In some awe, Jed would watch Drew come out of the small, steel shower stark naked, grab a towel, and walk into the bedroom. After he dried his body, he would simply make a rough pass at the beautiful blond locks with the towel and that was it. His clothes usually never made it out of the wash basket, but when he threw them on his Greek god-of-nature-like body, the look was impressive. To add to those advantages, Drew had a Don Johnson-like, gravelly voice. When he reached the legal drinking age in the spring of 1990, the other three, already legal, took Drew to Peter Lowney's Happy Shamrock Tavern. The golden boy threw on his dark brown leather jacket and walked the few blocks. Minutes after he hit the smoky establishment, he became an instant chick magnet. The mix of college and local girls that the other three would have to work their lungs out to make headway with were ready to buy the Birdman a drink. And Drew never seemed to even notice the effect he had on these poor women. And he never got real serious with any of the willing many.

Drew did have one major, social issue, though. He was annoyingly encyclopedic. In a heartbeat, he could go from a normal college kid hanging out with the crowd talking about what college kids talk about to Mr. World Book. In contrast, his most redeeming social value was the unique ability to accept a nudge, soft or hard, or a harsh or gentle "shut the hell up, please," and recede back into normal mode. Drew would always smile when Jed told him, "Damn, Birdman, you are just too damn pretty to be that smart. Can't you just stand there and look darling, and keep the Jeopardy questions to yourself?"

Jed grew to enjoy Drew's company and his ways. Graduation in 1991 caused them to part their ways, but that crazy four-letter word, golf, would bring them together for years to come. And with the golf came the Birdman and his Britannica brain.

CHAPTER 48

▼

DINNER WITH UNCLE MIKEY—1993

In addition to being a wealth of knowledge—some of value, a lot of little—the Birdman could tell a story with a quality that would capture his audience with the same rapture of a Girl Scout leader telling a ghost story to a circle of eleven-year-old girls around a campfire in a dark campground. Jed was halfway through his beer when his memory bank took him back to one of Drew Birdsall's classics, "Dinner with Uncle Mikey."

If you let him, the Birdman would tell and retell the Uncle Mikey tale. Jed and the others never grew tired of it, because each time it was told, more details were revealed.

Drew, in the fall term of his second year at Fordham Law, was still living in the basement apartment of Aunt Ree Ree and Uncle Mikey's house on Irwin Avenue in the North Bronx. A few years ago, the young man of numerous neurons had secured the mildly interesting fact that he was living on a street named after William E. Irwin, one of the few World War I servicemen to have an avenue named in his honor. Poor Will had died in the Argonne Forest of Northern France in the service of his country. William's family had lived in the neighborhood, and so the street was so named.

As usual, when Drew was around on one of the Saturdays that he was not at the law library, Aunt Ree Ree would listen for his noises that traveled up the old hall stairway to her kitchen door and call to him down the stairs. If it was Saturday, Drew guessed it would be an invitation to Sunday dinner. It was, and, for the first time, he asked if he might bring a friend.

"Sure, honey. We're not having anything fancy, just some of that roasted chicken that your uncle likes so much, and I thought I'd serve some kind of potatoes and that canned corn you like."

"That's great, Aunt Ree Ree; it'll be perfect."

"Okay. How does six-thirty sound? The Giants game's on early and the Jets have a bye week, so dinner won't interfere with Mikey's *second* religious service of the day."

Drew had never had anything but delightful times with his aunt, the hard working Xerox salesperson, and her husband, the still-working ConEdison manager, who much preferred water, boats, and fishing poles to power plants.

Drew drove his old clunker of a Chevy a few miles to pick up his friend. The bumpy roads reminded him that he needed shocks that he could not afford and was too proud to ask his dad to pay for. After the usual quest for a parking space on Irwin, he and his friend made it up the concrete stairs to the front door of Mikey and Marie Reardon's home. Drew decided to make a formal entrance instead of through the side door and the shared hall that led to his apartment and his aunt's place. He knocked and waited.

When Uncle Mikey opened the door, the aroma of his Sail tobacco burning in the Dunhill pipe—that Aunt Ree Ree had asked him not to smoke with a guest coming to dinner—drifted out on to the landing.

When Drew introduced Uncle Mikey to his friend, it was the first time in years that he had ever seen his uncle cough with a pipe in his hand. Drew took a deep breath and spoke.

"Can we come in, Uncle Mikey?"

The Mick made a quick recovery from the fact that Drew's *friend* was a female, and had skin that was a light shade of brown—certainly not one of the many Irish girls who roamed these parts.

"Sorry, come in. Come in."

By this time, Ree Ree was in the living room observing the entrance scene. At the sight of the young girl, she almost dropped the plate of vegetables she was about to serve as a before-dinner snack. Not because the girl was black, but because she was knockout gorgeous and standing next to her nephew, a perfect complement to his own beauty. Introductions were made, and everyone, except Aunt Ree Ree, took a seat in the large living room with magnificent, stained woodwork that bordered a tasteful, rose-patterned Waverly wallcovering. Mikey turned off the TV and settled back in to his tan La-Z-Boy. Drew and his friend made their way to the inviting and matching sofa.

Ree Ree's simple solution to breaking the ice was offering a drink.

"Anything in particular you guys want?"

"No. Anything is fine," Drew's friend, Karen Sanford, answered, and the other two nodded in agreement.

Given free rein, Ree Ree returned with four cocktail glasses and a metal cobbler shaker full of Cosmopolitans.

Cocktails gave way to dinner served with a choice of a glass of chilled Hess Select chardonnay or a cold glass of Budweiser. The boys opted for the beer. Karen opted for water and explained that she would have a glass of the wine after dinner. Ree Ree poured herself an ample dose of the wine.

As Drew had predicted, Uncle Mikey led the inquisition. He had already learned that Karen was a year ahead of Drew at Fordham Law and lived close by. Drew jumped in to short circuit a lot of questions and explained how they had met. Both had been leaving Fordham's Manhattan Campus at West 62nd street on their way to the 59th Street subway station at Columbus Circle. The hub station served a number of subway lines. The Birdman and Karen were taking the same line and shared a thirty-plus-minute, jostling ride on the Number 1 line, the Broadway—7th Avenue Local.

"And, well, Uncle Mikey, we just became instant friends and have been ever since."

"So, Karen, what does your Dad do?"

As previously discussed, Drew, who knew the questions would come, forbade Karen to give the answers she so wanted to.

Well, Mr. Reardon, my father, Fred Sanford, and my brother, Lamont, run a junkyard in the South Bronx.

"He works for the city, sir."

And no, not as a sanitation engineer.

After a few more bites of dinner, the Mick moved on. "Yeah, so, what does he do for the city?"

"Actually, he's a member of the city council representing the 11th District in the Bronx. He was a state senator for a lot of years, but he got tired of being away from home so much."

"Oh, so you live here in the Bronx?"

"Yeah, not too far from here. And my mom teaches school up at the Riverdale Country School."

"So, what are your plans after law school? Do you have any idea yet?"

"Yes, sir, I hope to get a spot in the Bronx or Manhattan D.A.'s office."

Eventually the coffee and homemade cheesecake came and the conversation slowed down a bit. The four sated folks retired back to the living room with a coffee refill and a bottle of Kahlua. Uncle Mikey took both and reloaded his Dunhill.

Karen asked if she could look around the room filled with so many pictures in wood, metal, and precious Lenox frames. She stopped at a five-by-seven, worn frame with a picture of a younger Uncle Mikey in a seventies tuxedo set in front of two volumes of Penn State yearbooks. He was on the right side of the groom and Aunt Ree Ree was on the left side of the bride. All their smiles were brilliantly captured in the old photo. For Karen, the most noticeable impact of the image was the black couple in between Drew's aunt and uncle.

"Allan and Emma were our best friends in college, and they were in our wedding as well. Some night when you have more time we can bore you to death with our wedding album and all the crazy stories that go with it."

Karen turned around to Uncle Mikey and said, "I would really enjoy doing that. Maybe next weekend I could come over and help your beautiful wife cook an early dinner on Saturday, so that we don't interfere with the Giants game. And then you could tell me your fascinating tales of the good old days."

"It's a date."

The night got much more serious after that—Courvoisier, the cognac of Napoleon—serious.

"Uncle Mikey, Aunt Ree Ree, I've asked Karen to marry me."

The last time Marie ever suspected that a tear was forming in her husband's ducts was when the Baltimore Ravens stomped all over his G-Men, 34-7, in Tampa, in Super Bowl XXXV. Somehow this young girl had charmed the crusty fisherman in record time. He managed to choke out a, "Did she say yes?"

"Yes, I did, sir."

"Okay, then, no more "sir" for you, young lady. From now on it's Uncle Mikey. Okay?"

"Got it, Uncle Mikey."

"Drew, have you told your mom and dad yet?"

"No. We thought we'd see how it played here in New York before we took the show on the road. How do you think it will play in the land of Stonewall Jackson?"

The Mick, a history buff, was tempted to educate the two young people about the icon of the Confederacy and tell them that Jackson, before the war, had actually practiced civil disobedience by creating an organized Sunday school class to teach black children to read. Uncle Mikey didn't.

"I think it'll play just fine."

Two weeks later, it did. Eighteen months later, the wedding in the main chapel of the College of Mount Saint Vincent, Karen's alma mater, and the sumptuous reception at the New York Athletic Club on Central Park South in Manhattan played splendidly. Uncle Mikey had complained about the long trip from the chapel to the reception but surrendered his complaints when he saw the piles of fresh shrimp cocktail and the open bar with cocktails of another kind.

Karen would indeed go on to be a prosecutor in the Bronx DA's office. Drew lasted only three years as a Wall Street lawyer. He decided to start his own business. All Jed knew about it was that it had something to do with software and security, and money, lots of it. It was apparently high-tech stuff and high-end clients. They had a beautiful, brick colonial home in Fieldston, a private community with over two hundred homes and estates on a 140-acre tract. It was only a few blocks from Karen's parents' Fieldston stone-and-stucco Tudor and within walking distance of Uncle Mikey and Aunt Ree Ree's house. The main campus of Manhattan College and significant economic status separated the two neighborhoods. None of that stood in the way of the Reardons and the Sanfords becoming close friends, bonded by a true enjoyment of each other's company and further bonded by Karen and Drew's three beautiful children.

Jed often wondered what it would be like to have a black woman as a partner for life in every way. He was glad that Drew did not spend a lot of time wondering. Jed felt that *because* of Karen, Drew was the happiest of the class.

Jed smiled at Drew's success and the pleasure of having him as a friend. Maybe a friend who could help him with his Jesus problem—maybe not.

CHAPTER 49

▼

THE BIRDMAN AND THE BLACK GIRL

The Early Years—Untold Stories

"S'up with you two lovers here?" B.C. Barrows said to Drew and Karen as the subway made its way north out of the Dyckman Street stop on the Seventh Avenue local.

B.C. stood for Box Cutter, and he was standing in front of and close to the two seated passengers. Drew started to stand, but Karen grabbed his left arm with her right hand and forced him to stay down.

"Nothing, sir, we're just heading up to the 242nd Street stop. We're on our way back from school in the city. We're just classmates at Fordham Law. We were talking about our class in tax law."

"S'matter? No black boys in your class to have that talk wit?"

"Well, yeah, but they don't live up here in the Bronx. Drew and I just share a train ride when we get out of this class, our last of the day."

Karen still had a grip on Drew's arm as she stared into the bloodshot eyes of B.C. He was dressed in red sneakers, a baggy pair of blue jeans, and a black T-shirt with some kind of white dragon spewing red fire on the front. To complete the look, he wore both a bandana and an unzipped, light gray, hooded sweatshirt. The hood framed the face of a black kid in his late teens and probably a brain broiled by a lifetime of misery.

In his best Ebonics and gangsta slouch, he went on. He moved his face to within inches of Karen's face. "You ain't sucking on this here white boy's dick are you, bitch? Your sweet-looking black ass should belong to a brother. You know, a brother, like, maybe, old B.C. here."

The train slowed as it approached the 215th Street stop. Karen's grip was not enough to hold Drew back now. Drew knew he was bigger than this punk, and he had had enough. What he didn't have was an answer for B.C.'s steel gray Stanley box cutter. As Drew jumped up and prepared to reach out and grab this prick, the cutter, which Karen had been observing the black man twirl around in his right hand, but out of Drew's view, came across Drew's right forearm. It easily cut through the cotton of his light blue, long-sleeved shirt. The two-inch line of blood, halfway between his wrist and elbow, started slowly, and then quickly drenched the cotton. Drew screamed. Karen screamed louder, jumped up and planted her size-seven, mocha Rockport boot squarely into B.C.'s groin. He yelled and cursed. He yelled some more when she brought the heavy, black heel of the boot down on his left foot. Karen grabbed Drew's good arm and pulled him out the open doors of the train. The few passengers who had been on their car followed them out. Old B.C. was clutching his bruised manhood and looking down at the throbbing foot.

A friendly passenger called 911 from a phone booth. An ambulance was dispatched within a few minutes.

Drew would live—a few unwanted stitches and a seething anger, but he would live. Karen feared the effects of this bastard's attack on their relationship. Her fear was unwarranted. It only brought the courting pair closer together. It was just a story he did not want to tell, to relive, to share.

CHAPTER 50

▼

NO GRAY

There was one other part of the Drew-Karen saga that the detailed Birdman did not share with the rest of the FF club. It was the night that the encyclopedic, chatty Adonis was told for the millionth time to shut up, *please*—this time by the girl he had fallen in love with. The details were conveniently omitted whenever Drew told his story of their fairy-tale romance. It was the summer before "dinner with Uncle Mikey." Drew's landlords were on vacation in the Poconos, and Karen had suggested that she come over, help the klutz clean his place, and make him dinner. This would be their tenth date, if you didn't count the many train rides they shared to and from Fordham Law.

"Shit, Sanford, works for me."

"I said 'help clean,' Birdman. So, you be prepared to help."

Stripped sheets, cotton bedspread, and all discarded clothing were loaded into a large basket, and Karen sent her Birdman off to the local laundromat for hours. She removed several CDs from her purse and took out the Travis Tritt *Country Club* album from the combination boom box. She replaced Travis with Stevie Wonder's *For Once In My Life*. She then proceeded to remove dust that might have been around for years from various places in the apartment. Karen cleaned and rearranged the kitchen storage units and scrubbed the bathroom with enough chemicals to put her on the potential terrorist list. By the time Drew made it back, she was almost finished and the Steveland CD had been replaced by Natalie Cole's Grammy-winning *Unforgettable*. Natalie's song and album, with the help of good old and interred Nat, had walked away with five of the shiny, gold awards. If asked, the Birdman could tell you that the Grammy was a replica of the machine that was invented in 1887 by the German, Emile Berliner.

With her long black hair pulled back and grime on different parts of her body, Karen restacked the last of the freshly cleaned dishes.

"Just put the laundry basket on the bed on the right."

"Sure, boss. Wow! The place looks great. Smells a little toxic though."

Karen grabbed the can of Glade off the counter and said that she was about to take care of that.

"Check your girlfriend out, Birdman. What do you think of the look?"

"Um. I guess I see a beautiful woman in a dirty white Manhattan College Jasper T-shirt."

Karen took a minute to walk around the apartment and spray the pine-scented air freshener and then came back to Drew.

"Don't bullshit me, Birdman. I look like I've been rode hard and put away wet."

"I'd still be more than happy to give you a big, fat, wet and sloppy kiss, Champion."

When she gave him a quizzical look, he added, "Gene Autry's horse. Sorry, just another piece of useless trivia."

"Well, come on then, Gene. Slobber away."

The kiss lasted longer than any before. When they came up for breath, Drew started to say something, but Karen stopped him. She walked into the small bathroom and turned on the water in the steel shower stall and came back to her helpless prey. She pulled a three-pack of Trojan condoms out of her back jeans pocket and threw them on the kitchen table.

"I found these on your nightstand under your constitutional law book. Tell me, handsome, exactly how many women have you slept with?"

"Uh, three that I remember."

"Three? You philandering bastard. When did these events take place and who were the hussies? I want details, and I want them right now. I wanna know who I'll be measured against. *If* I ever let you violate *me*."

"Okay. Well, the first was my mom, when I had nightmares. Then, there was my sister, in the back seat of our station wagon on a trip to Disney World. And, oh yeah, I fell asleep once on my grandmother's lap when she was babysitting us. Oh, sorry, it was actually four. Not too long ago, I made love to Miss March 1990. I think her name was Deborah something, a California gal, nice-looking brunette. If you wanna meet her, I think she's in the second dresser drawer over there under my sweatshirts. *And,* I think the condoms were probably left here by my old roommate, Chris."

"Wow, that's pretty tough competition. And, sorry, pardner; the born-on date is not that old on these balloons."

"Well, maybe I did pick them up on a hopeful whim. Guilty as charged, char-woman."

"Okay, since we're speaking of guilty, before this relationship goes any further, I need to make sure you know the rules."

"The rules?"

"Yeah, with a capital 'R.' I just happen to have a copy in my purse. Hang on."

Karen handed Drew a piece of yellow legal paper with a list of fourteen items. They started with "The female ALWAYS makes the rules," and worked their way up from there. Drew tried to hold in his laugh, as he took in what appeared to be a life sentence of submission to the female and the Rules. Karen grabbed the paper back and told Drew he could memorize them later. Drew bowed toward her and spoke.

"You got it, kid."

"Kid. Did you just call me kid? You did, didn't you?"

A confused Drew just shrugged and apologized.

"Okay, Birdman, listen up to the supplemental set of Karen's rules. You will never call me kid, doll, toots, or anything that starts with sweet, like sweetie, sweetie pie. Wait. Let me amend that. You can call me sweet cheeks, if you like. In addition, any of the following wordage is strictly prohibited. 'You go, girl' is never to be uttered in my presence, and that goes for 's'up, dawg,' and a few others I can't think of right now. You got it so far?"

"I think so, General Sanford. Can I call you general?"

"Yeah. But you have to salute at the same time."

They both laughed as Drew came to attention and gave his best stiff-arm and hand salutation.

"Okay, soldier, now get your clothes off, you filthy, no-good, law-yer-wanna-be. And throw them in the new hamper I bought your sorry, sloppy ass."

She watched with fascination as he did. *Damn. This sometimes motor-mouth man looks like a Greek statue.*

"Now what, boss lady?"

"Just wait and watch a minute."

The first thing that changed was the rapid removal of whatever was holding her hair up. The second was the soiled T-shirt. She had been braless. The sneakers, socks, and jeans were next. All that was left was a red thong that hugged her slim hips. Karen walked over to the hamper and threw her discarded apparel in with his.

"The water's hot by now, Drew. Pull some clean towels out of the laundry basket. We need to wash up." She looked down at the rising taking place between his taut legs, and, with a false confidence, said, "Keep that thought. I'll be sure to take care of it soon."

She adjusted the temperature of the water, and they both stepped into the stall. Drew was surprised when Karen went in with her thong still on.

"What's a matter?"

He pointed to the thong.

"I expect you to take *some* damn initiative. I can't do all the work."

He did not have to be told twice, and the now naked twosome washed each other with gentle passion and amazing patience. Karen turned off the water and reached out for the two towels. In the cramped stall they slowly dried each other. Karen grabbed a third towel and led Drew into the bedroom area. She retrieved a sheet from the clean laundry pile and threw it on the bed and then placed the towel in the middle of the sheet.

Drew looked up at the two windows that looked out on the driveway.

"What the hell are they?"

"They're called curtains, dufus. You don't expect me to make love to you in a room with dingy white shades do you?"

She turned and grabbed his hand and led them over in front of the mirror that sat atop the oak dresser. She pushed him behind her so that his head stood above her left shoulder.

"What do you see, Drew?"

"Well, I see a silky grouping of the protein keratin, joined by certain fats, small amounts of vitamins, and traces of zinc with a black melanin and water. Then there's these two clavicles here, in your case about four- or five-inches long, attached over here to the acromion of the scapula at the acromioclavicular joint. And moving down we have a very attractive pair of auburn-colored areola surronding two very inviting papillae, all perfectly mounted on a dyad of—oh, let's take a guess here—size 34B bosoms. Ah, and here we appear to have a small nevus, likely congenital, residing between these two beautiful orbs that are a tribute to God's creative talent. That is the only flaw detected so far on an otherwise perfect body. And now I have a problem. We're about to run out of mirror here before I get to the other interesting parts."

"Do you own a gun?"

"Of course, I'm from Virginia, am I not?"

"Is it registered here in New York?"

"Of course, I'm in law school. I know the rules."

"Good, can I have it?"

"Now?"

"Yeah."

"Why?"

"Because I'm going to shoot you, smart-ass. And then I'm gonna call my father's friends in the 50th precinct and claim it was self defense against a life-threatening assault of useless babble."

"Sorry. Can I try again?"

"Quickly, please."

"I see the girl I want to marry. Can we skip the ceremony and move on straight to the honeymoon part?" He saw the scowl come across her face. "Okay, let me try again. I see a beautiful couple. The guy's a bit pale compared to the flawless caramel-colored girl. Does my paleness bother you? Is that what this is about?"

"Listen, Drew. Remember the kid on the subway with the box cutter?"

"Yeah. He was seriously doped up and an insecure bigot, sorely lacking in education, and social skills. What about him?"

"The world will always see us as a white man with a black woman, and they will stare some, talk some, and wonder a lot what it might be like to be us. Some people won't like us being together. The kid with the cutter was just bold enough to express his bias. Others will feel the same way, maybe not as viscerally, but, just the same, they will feel it. They'll just be too educated and socially skilled not to vocalize it to us. There will be subtle stares, and they probably will talk to others about it. And, some of these people we will consider friends. We'll just never know what they are truly thinking or feeling. Can you handle that?"

"Hang on a second. What if the kid had been a white skinhead with a knife and said he sure hoped I wasn't screwing the nigger chick and diluting the one, true race?"

"Well, I would have kicked him in the nuts twice instead of once, and I would have slammed my foot on both of his, to start. So, I guess the question still stands. Do you think *we* can handle that?"

"Well, your parents have for over thirty years. We'll just ask them how they do it. Can we talk about this after you ravage me, so I can stop wondering what it might be like to be an us?"

"Sure. Leave the condoms in the package, please."

"Why here? Why now, Karen?" It's not the most romantic of settings."

"Because it's time. It's our time, and this space is all ours. You're all I need for the setting."

Karen let Drew lead her over to the sheeted bed.

"Oh, oh. Hang on. Don't go anywhere." He returned from the kitchen with two cold bottles of Heineken and retrieved a cassette tape from his underwear drawer. Drew gave Natalie and her dad the boot and placed his special compilation full of Garth, Travis, Vince, Reba, and other folks in the tape deck of the box. As Kenny Rogers began "Lady", he handed Karen her beer and said, "I was kind of dreaming this might be an extra special day for us, so I spared no expense." She laughed. They toasted and each took a long sip of Mr. Gerard Adrian H.'s brew whose first born-on date was December 1863 in Amsterdam.

Drew took the beers and put them on the floor. He guided her slowly down on to the sheet and towel she had scattered on the small bed. And, with a *lot* of kissing, she eventually guided him gently between her open legs. She hoped he would be tender, and he was. On his first thrust she winced, whimpered and worried, but it was over quickly, and a virgin no more, Karen relaxed and waited for the explosive discharge of neuromuscular tensions that she had only read about or witnessed in the movies. As her pleasure rose, she opened her eyes to look at her white Adonis. To her surprise, Drew was watching her. They started with a shared smile and then a mild chuckle and then some feelings and sounds and words they had never shared before.

This was a tale never told to Jed by Drew, the story spinner, but it would not have surprised him. His thoughts of Drew on this airplane ended on a seriously less passionate note. His mind once again wandered back to the crucifixion in Hollywood. Maybe Drew, Mr. Security Man, and his D.A. wife would have some ideas on how the bad guys pulled it off—or maybe they wouldn't.

CHAPTER 51

▼

At that point of his journey in the clear skies Jed felt a serious call of nature. The forceful whoosh of the blue toilet water put an exclamation point to Jed's relief. Steps away from his first-class seat he was abruptly thrown forward in the cabin. He tried to grab onto the back of his seat but only crashed onto the cabin floor as the Boeing's battle with severe turbulence went on. The dramatic drop in the 757's altitude pushed Jed's stomach into his throat. The hardcover copy of James Patterson's *The Big Bad Wolf* flew from his seat and slapped his left cheek. Glasses, empty and full, and other occupants of the tray tables were chaotically tossed about in the air. Jed's ungraceful landing was accompanied by a loud, involuntary "holy shit!" As his mind raced to lock onto the words of the "Act of Contrition," his own expletive was followed by a cacophonous choir of common and colorful phrases of surprise, fear and outright terror.

By the time Jed had caught enough breath to say the words, "Oh my God, I am heartily sorry ..." the atmospheric pressure and the big jet were once again in harmony. The items that had pitched and flung about were slowly retrieved by the attendants. Jed regained his balance and his seat. He felt a slight pain in his cheek and a colossal sense of relief—much outweighing that of his toilet trip. Thoughts of his family flashed through his mind's eye. The captain explained the unexpected, and apologized and assured. Jed decided to put Patterson's hero's efforts to make Washington, D.C., a safer place on hold. He would be over-whelmingly grateful just to kiss the ground at Washington's Dulles terminal.

Ten minutes later, a flight attendant whom he had not yet seen on this flight came out of the galley behind the first-class cabin. She was holding glasses and a bottle of champagne, and without a word spoken, poured. All but one of his fellow cabinmates eagerly accepted. The bad news was that Jed had been scared out of his wits. The good news, the plane was still flying. Even better news, the flying plane now came equipped with an angel named Daniela pouring bubbly. After all the flights of not seeing his Rhonda, here stood another dark-haired beauty with sparkling eyes that bested the champagne she served. Her beauty was one thing, surely pleasing to Jed's eye. But it was her *eyes* that were the most striking. When she looked at Jed, he felt like he was the only person in her world. Killer eyes, with kindness and intensity blended to perfection. A slight aftershock of turbulence bounced the jet just enough to cause Jed's new angel of the airways to grab onto the empty seat across from his. She made a safe landing onto the seat's cushion, still holding the bottle.

Daniela smiled and held up the saved wine. "Didn't spill a drop."

Jed laughed and raised his glass in a toast of congratulations. The lovely looker winked, clinked his glass, put the champagne to her lips. "You won't tell, will you?"

"Not a chance."

CHAPTER 52

▼

CHRIS

By the time all things had settled down in the rattled jet, there was only an hour or so left of Jed's journey.

With a cold beer in his hand, his thoughts moved on to the one that he believed was the most complex of the foursome.

Chris Lee was as American as apple pie, and Sony—with its four U.S. R&D and engineering facilities and its five major U.S. manufacturing sites. And, at the age of thirty-six, he owned a 45-inch flat-panel, high-definition TV just to prove his support for the American industrial complex. He was red, white, and blue, through and through. He just looked Japanese.

His non-Japanese-looking father, Edward R. Lee, always joked about his son possibly being the only Asian-looking descendent of Robert E. Lee, the famous Civil War hero who was on the losing side. Chris's father had been born into a wealthy Lexington, Virginia, farming and cattle family. He was a well-built, plain-looking Southerner and as white-bread, right-wing conservative as they come—most of the time.

Young Chris got his good looks from his mother, Gin Sato, also American-born but to Japanese parents who had immigrated to the States before the start of World War II.

Chris's parents met in 1966 at a party at Gin's sorority house. They were both in their third year at the University of Virginia, in Charlottesville. Gin was a member of one of UVA's sisterhoods that was hosting the affair at their brick house just off campus. As a third-year student and a sister, Gin held the office of secretary, and made it her personal duty to ensure that the male visitors to their house felt welcome.

The young Wahoo from Lexington was there because, for social purposes, Edward preferred the relative sanity of the sorority get-togethers versus their male correlates. Growing up in the 1950s in Rockbridge County did not present much opportunity for Edward to meet Asian boys or girls. As Ed walked down Rugby Road, he was hoping for a pleasant evening. When Gin greeted him on the porch of the house on that Saturday night in October, his hopes escalated. He was struck speechless with her unique beauty. The ease of her smile and the brightness in her eyes had him stammering a weak "Ahem," followed by a squeaky "Nice to meet you, Gin. I'm Edward Lee."

Chris Lee grew up hearing the story of that first encounter many times. Edward, always the amateur jokester, liked to recall how "She had him at 'hello'—or was it at 'ah so.'"

Nineteen months later, two days after commencement ceremonies at the university, Ed and Gin were married in the seventy-eight-year-old, Gothic-style UVA chapel. They had both experienced serious trepidation about introducing the other to their respective parents, but all waters remained calm, and the in-laws came to become close friends. Graduation and marriage meant a j-o-b for both. It was back to Lexington for the newlyweds. Ed joined his father in the farming and cattle world. Gin chose a less earthy profession and accepted a job teaching at a local elementary school. Her career was a brief one. The woman with the pure complexion and long, dark, glistening hair gave birth to the first of three on President's Day, February 1969. In her mind Gin had chosen a boy's name long before becoming pregnant. It would be Christopher, strangely enough in honor of the Italian who had discovered her great country almost five hundred years ago. Ed wanted to name the boy Robert Edward but ran into a difference of opinion from Gin. And because Ed was smart enough to score over 1300 on his college boards, he realized that "if she ain't happy, he ain't happy." So, Chris Sato Lee it was. Gin Lee wanted her son to discover life in as wondrous a way as Columbus had discovered America.

The five Lees—including Chris and his two sisters—lived close to the idyllic life that Ed and Gin had talked about in their college years at UVA. After the wedding, with their parents' help, they had put enough money together to build a four-bedroom home on land that Edward's father had owned and gifted to them. The family of five was at ease and focused. They confidently took advan-

tage of the excellent education opportunities Lexington had to offer and the natural pleasures that their fifteen acres of land proffered. They enjoyed the normally
pleasant climate on a property dressed with ancient maples and oaks. Gentle
streams, small fishing ponds and a string of pets, large and small, ran through the
Lees' homestead. All that and a view that went on for miles made for grand times
at the Lee residence on the windy path that was Jacktown Road.

The Lees' Lexington harmony experienced its first signs of discord in the winter of 1985 when Chris was a junior at the old Lexington High School. With a
resolved courage, he requested a meeting with Mom and Dad in the business-like
confines of Dad's home office. At the age of seventeen, Chris was approaching
the six-foot mark. He was an impressive and handsome blend of his father's athletic physique and his mother's Asian beauty. He had her dark eyes and straight,
jet black hair that just seemed to fall perfectly in place. His looks and his natural
grace, which he never paid much heed to, commanded your attention.

Edward, with a stone face, and Gin, with a maternal rumbling of fear in her
stomach, listened to their precious firstborn.

"Dad, Mom, I have decided I want to go away to school when I graduate."

So far, an okay opening statement for Dad and Mom to handle, but that
changed quickly.

"I want to go to New York and get a degree at John Jay College."

Two mild blows, but still manageable—maybe.

"And, in my heart, I know I want to be a police officer or maybe FBI, and
John Jay is the best there is. And I want to know life in a big city before I make
up my mind on where I choose to spend the rest of mine."

The usually garrulous Edward struggled to form a cogent series of words to
express his mind's instinctive response. Words that would hopefully steer his
young, handsome, growing, seventeen-year-old son in a different direction.
Edward's political vision always had *someone else's children* protecting the state.
But before he could gather himself, Chris went on.

"And after I get my degree, I want to join the Marines." After the
not-so-funny punch line neither parent saw coming, Chris sat down in silence,
nervously hoping for a chance of acceptance of his plan.

Other than acquaintances who went there—some to die there—Edward never
had to deal militarily with the draft or Vietnam. But like the rest of his and Gin's
generation, the television and newspapers brought the horror of war and its bat-
tles into the dorms and homes of America in living color. They were all too famil-

iar with the college protests of the sixties and seventies and the emotion and reasons behind them.

Edward's thought process went calmly into overdrive. And he and Gin controllably expressed their serious misgivings about their son's educational choice and career path.

In 1985, the U.S. armed forces were not engaged in any major, public wars, but both parents knew how quickly that might change. The constant conflict in the Middle East and the fears of Syria's terrorist activities did not make the local Lexington news very often, but for those locals whose sons and daughters were in the service, worry was something they lived with every day.

When it was apparent that Chris was sensitive to their concerns but not wavering in his resolve, Edward decided he would try to divide the issues. The one—college—was imminent. The other—the armed forces—was too far out in time for all of them to logically discuss in any real detail. Dad started the delicate inquisition. "Chris, how much do you really know about John Jay?" Chris responded as if he had prepared for an oral Ph.D. dissertation. He recited much of the information that was outlined in the college's brochures, including the parts about its being the largest college of criminal justice in the United States and a part of the City University of New York system. When Chris began to give a curriculum vitae of the man for whom the college was named, Gin thought he was showing off. Edward was impressed. Impressed with the detail of his son's knowledge and especially impressed to learn about the American born in 1745. Johnny boy had served in the Continental Congress as president, co-wrote the Federalist Papers, was ambassador to Spain and France, and served as the first and youngest chief justice of the United States, and, in later years, as governor of New York. Edward let loose with a little smile and an "ah" when Chris finished his discourse with the tidbit that Mr. Jay retired to the life of a country farmer near the town of Bedford, New York.

Gin, still not smiling, steered the conversation back to more current issues. "Have you chosen a major?"

"I think so, Mom. I think a Bachelor of Science in Criminal Justice will give me the best shot at having a number of different job choices after I get out of the Marines."

Gin grimaced at the last part of the statement—not the job part, but the Marine part. She did some more steering. "Let's stick with next year for now, okay? Do you know what the high school grade average and SAT requirements are for John Jay?"

"Come on, Mom, you know my grades are almost straight As, and my SAT's are way up there. But, yes, I do, and my counselor at school and I don't think there will be any problem getting in."

"Okay, Mr. Smarty Pants, what's it gonna cost? Do you know that?"

"Yeah, Mom, the tuition, even for out-of-state students, is comparable to our Virginia universities."

Edward decided that things were going all Chris's way too easily and decided it was time to trip up the son he was so proud of and maybe a little too protective of. "Do you know what the dorms are like there, Chris?" Edward knew a few things about John Jay from one of his buddies at the Lexington Golf and Country Club who had attended the college years before. Things that included the fact that John Jay had no dormitories.

"Well, Dad, actually there are no dorms at the college."

It was clear that Chris truly had done all his homework and then some.

"Actually, there's another boy at the club, who I play with in some of the junior events and hook up with sometimes, who is planning to attend college in the Bronx. His father went there. And his Aunt still lives up there and has a house with a furnished basement apartment that she plans to let him use. When I talked about going to John Jay, he asked if I would like to room with him. It would be real cheap, close to the subway, and there's a golf course nearby. And it's in a pretty nice part of the Bronx, close to the college he's gonna go to."

Edward's trump card of a trick question had been crushed and crumbled by his son's knack for getting all his web-footed, short-necked, short-legged, broad-billed anatidae in a row.

Before he let Chris go on with a description of his well-developed set of plans, he moved to the small refrigerator behind his desk and retrieved two cold, yellow cans containing a smooth twelve ounces of beer from Colorado. Gin, even though her name would make most think of a colorless alcoholic beverage made from distilled, neutral grain spirits flavored with juniper berries and aromatics, rarely drank. And even more rarely drank beer. But she accepted her husband's offer without hesitation. Chris got a Pepsi handed to him along with an interesting smirk.

After another hour's worth of discussion, accompanied by slow sips on the cold Coors, the parents conceded to let Chris apply to John Jay, and, if accepted, attend. After that they, as a family, would take things one step at a time.

And so, one day in the late summer of 1987, at 6:00 AM, Chris and his father took the family's new, white Jeep Cherokee, loaded with trunks of clothes and supplies, a 13-inch TV, and boxes of stuff Mom had packed for her Chris, to

New York City. They, along with Gin, had made a visit last fall to John Jay and the home of Aunt Marie—affectionately known for years by her nieces and nephews as Aunt Ree Ree. The seven-hour route and ride were no longer a mystery to the two passengers. The mysteries that awaited Chris as a fulltime resident of the Big Apple were a different issue. There was only a little conversation in between the consumption of the turkey sandwiches and soda that Gin had packed for her boys. Chris was too excited to talk much. Dad was suffering from too much disquietude.

Their first trip had taken them through the Lincoln Tunnel to Midtown to see the college. This trip would be straight to Aunt Ree Ree's. So, this time, Dad and son enjoyed an aerial view of the Hudson River as they crossed the George Washington Bridge. As he was doing so, Edward couldn't help but think how much easier things would be for *him and Gin* if they were driving their son to Washington and Lee in Lexington, but that discussion was long over. Other than the horns-a-plenty that blared at them for the ten minutes that they had to double park on a narrow Irwin Avenue, the unload went smoothly. Chris's friend from the club, Drew Birdsall, had arrived a few days before and was already well settled in the narrow but deep, three-story, brick house. Dressed in a pair of cutoff jeans and a new white T-shirt with the words "Go Jaspers" in green, he helped carry Chris's stuff down the small side alley that lead to the basement apartment door and down the two steps into the kitchen. They maneuvered through the roomy eat-in kitchen into a large living and sleeping area. Edward was okay with the place and the neighborhood. It was just too far away from home. He was more than okay with the well-built, blond boy named Drew, whom he also knew some from the club. He knew his father well enough to know that he would not put his or Edward's son in an unsafe environment, but it was still New York.

As they were moving in, Edward couldn't quite figure out what the two old, heavy, pine doors leaning against the wall were all about. But he kept his mouth shut. He took notice of the décor. The cream-colored walls had been accented with a tasteful green-and-white wallpaper border since his earlier visit. The old, twelve-inch-square, rock-hard, black-and-red linoleum floor tiles had been covered by a nicely cushioned, light tan sheet of linoleum. It appeared that Aunt Ree Ree worked diligently on this old brick home—which Ed guessed was significantly older than he—to keep up her reigning title as "Favorite Aunt." After all the stuff was in, Chris quickly loaded his clothes into the large closet behind the kitchen and in the bottom two drawers of the single dresser between the two small, twin beds.

Chris looked settled in and Edward was ready to get on the road. He motioned for Chris to grab the two trunks, assuming they would only be in the way.

"No, Dad, we need them here."

"Why?"

With the question asked, Drew went into a small storage room in the front of the apartment and retrieved a similar trunk. The two boys turned the three trunks on their ends, quickly picked up the two pine doors, and fashioned two adjacent desks out of the parts. Drew then retrieved two small desk chairs from the same storage area and placed them under the two makeshift desks.

"A housewarming gift from my Aunt Ree Ree. What do you think, Mr. Lee?"

"I think I am no longer needed here. I wish you guys the best of luck. Chris, don't forget to call your mother. You've got our 800 number. We'll pick you up at Thanksgiving. Be good, son. I'm proud of you. And you, Mr. Birdsall, take care of my only boy. And, by the way, what the hell *is* a Japser?" Edward's smile let Drew know he knew exactly what a Jasper was. He turned to go and stopped at the door that led to the two-step exit. "I've been there, son. So I know the familiar, 'send money, please' routine. Call me. Oh, by the way, you didn't completely unpack."

Chris gave him a curious stare and then slapped himself on his forehead. The short walk out to the car gave Edward a moment to put his arm around his son and squeeze his shoulder, a physical connection that sent a stronger message of love and hope than any words might convey. Chris reached in to the last foot of the cargo area and retrieved the new set of Ping irons he had received as a graduation present from his parents. They were accompanied by his older MacGregor persimmon woods. The clubs were housed in a new Burton bag of dark green cloth and tan leather. When he turned away with the bag on his shoulder, his father handed him two dozen Titleists and said his last words. "Keep your head down at *almost all* times, Chris. Down, as in study hard, as well as when you and Drew are swinging from your heels. Just remember to keep your head up as you roam through this city that never sleeps." The hug was quick but fierce. The two men did not bother to say goodbye.

By the time Chris and Drew were chowing down on the first of many meals courtesy of Aunt Ree Ree, Edward was already pushing his way back across the GW Bridge. He had a pile of dollar bills on the passenger's seat to pay tolls—tolls he was not used to in southwest Virginia—and tears in his eyes that he had become used to.

Chris was the primordial, living statement of the fierce love that existed between him and Gin. Edward knew that "letting go" was a natural part of being a parent. But before Chris called for his watershed family meeting, Edward's vision of letting go did not mean being so far apart. Did not mean his son purposely choosing to put himself in harm's way. As Ed made his way to the New Jersey Turnpike, the tears and the traffic slowed, but his visceral apprehension stayed with him all the way down the hundred-plus miles of the less-than-botanical views of the Garden State. His acceptance of the situation and pride in his son's courage grew slowly, as Ed made his way across the bridges and tunnels that would eventually take him home to Gin and his girls.

Edward was not excited about having to spend fourteen hours of his sixteen-hour day in the Jeep, but he wanted to get home. He never considered spending the night alone in some motel along the highway. Leaving Chris behind left him empty enough. He needed some comfort and that was only going to be available on Jacktown Road in the form of the family still living with him and a stiff shot of Virginia Gentleman bourbon.

CHAPTER 53

▼

CHRIS AND SARAH—JUNE 1990

For Chris Lee, the summer of 1990 was not much different than the previous two long breaks from his studies at John Jay College. The god-sent privilege of living with Drew at his Aunt Ree Ree's Bronx home allowed him to leave a lot of his belongings at the Bronx apartment over the summer. So, for three summers, he packed up his golf clubs and the appropriate spring/summer wardrobe and made his way home. Summer vacation meant working at his father's business and making enough cash to support his social and sporting activities during his time in New York. It was also a time for hooking up with old friends from his high school days. And a refreshing change from the big city. Having turned the magic age of twenty-one earlier that year meant hooking up *and* having an occasional beer—an acquired taste he had cultivated during his college experience. That was *one* of the things that were different for Chris this summer. The second was his father's surprising intervention with the chief of police, a long time friend, to secure a volunteer position in the department for Chris. The job wasn't much more than ten hours a week of clerical work, but the fact that his father initiated the opportunity meant a lot to Chris.

Like a lot of father-son conversations, theirs was brief. "Dad, I am really surprised and excited, but ..."

"Chris, if your but is, 'Is this a ploy to make me want to be a Lexington cop after graduation and not a Marine,' it's not. You're old enough to decide what you want to be. I just thought it would be a part of your educational process that you would enjoy. Just leave the guns at work."

The exchange ended with a shared laugh and a sincere hug that reminded Chris of the one his dad and he had shared in Aunt Ree Ree's driveway a few years before.

His beers with his friends, his berth in the small Lexington police force, and his father's business duties filled up most of his time—or so he thought until the end of June.

Chris usually worked a few afternoon hours Monday through Friday at the station. Most nights that he did not need to get home early, he would change at the station into his gray Manhattan College running shorts, a Christmas gift from Drew, and his raggedy, blue-and-gold John Jay Bulldogs T-shirt. His outfit wasn't exactly an impressive fashion statement, but today's run from the Washington Street station up South Main, through the residential part of downtown and back, would normally end with a ten-minute ride home, a quick shower and nicer apparel.

On Thursday, June 28, 1990, for Christopher Sato Lee, the most significantly different thing about this summer occurred at the southwest corner of Nelson and Main. Chris had three or four different, 3-mile running routes through downtown Lexington. Routes that would take him through the campuses of Washington and Lee University, the Virginia Military Institute, and many of the historic residential areas of the city named after the Revolutionary War site of Lexington, Massachusetts, the last stop on Paul Revere's famous ride in April 1775.

In June 1990, after running through Virginia's version of Lexington, first settled in 1777, Chris experienced a screech heard only by a few close by, but one that would change his world. As Chris was coming near the end of his run, he slowed to cross Nelson Street to head back to the station on East Washington. He had one Adidas-clad foot planted on the pavement when the shiny, black Ford F-150 that he was expecting to stop almost didn't. Luckily for him, he had pulled his leg back as the truck's front tires squealed to a stop a few feet past the stop light. Chris, a New Yorker for most of the year, was no stranger to crazy traffic, but *this was Lexington, for crying out loud*. He was also familiar with the kind of verbiage that accompanied New York traffic.

He waited till his heart stopped pounding to begin formulating a classic string of adjectival expletives that would start with "you" and end with "idiot." But before he could begin his commentary on the idiot who almost ended his running days and maybe a lot more, a petite angel came running across the front of the big truck with tears in her eyes.

At first glimpse, noticing it was a female, the word "bitch" was trying to sneak its way into and rekindle Chris's suspended diatribe. At second glimpse, as he was standing at the curb, sweat staining his "classy" outfit and still dripping off his forehead, he froze. He could not find the will to take his eyes off the young girl's teary-eyed face. The best disparaging utterance he could muster was, "Damn, lady, did you think that red light at the top of this pole was just a suggestion?"

"I am so sorry, sir. I guess I'm still not used to these stoplights being on these poles on the side of the streets. I am so, so sorry. Are you okay? Did I hit you?"

When the grungy Chris, with a light five o'clock shadow, failed to answer, the perfectly groomed blond girl, in a crisp pair of Levi's and a soft yellow Ralph Lauren polo, came closer and took his hands and asked again. With her touch, the tall, handsome boy with the glistening sable hair felt a strange tingle.

"I think I'm okay. Just a little shook up. I guess we both need to be a little more careful at these intersections. Are you okay?" Chris couldn't believe that in a few short seconds he went from a strong desire to strangle the idiot who almost maimed him for life to hoping he had a chance to carry on a conversation with his would-be mutilator.

His unnamed angel responded that she was shook up as well but okay.

Chris would have to tell his parents later that night about the encounter, since some law-abiding, do-gooder witness had quickly brought the local police into the incident. Once Chris and his now-named angel, Sarah, convinced the policeman, who knew Chris, that all was well, they agreed to exchange names and addresses and phone numbers. And, as they say, for the serendipitous couple, the rest was history. And history began with an agreement to meet later that evening at the Palms restaurant, only a few blocks from the intersection where the two strangers had crossed each other's paths.

CHAPTER 54

▼

DINNER IS SERVED

Chris put his still-slightly trembling body into his Jeep and made the drive out of town, out Route 60 West to Jacktown Road. He wasn't sure how much of the trembling was from almost being struck down by a half-ton truck or almost being seriously wounded by the mythical Cupid's arrow. After explaining his recent close call with deadly peril to his parents, he shaved and showered with atypical attention to detail. He could not remember the nature of Sarah's outfit, so, he decided to go with a safe pair of tan Dockers. The soft pants, introduced only a few years before by Chris's favorite jeans maker, Levi Strauss, had become his customary response to occasions that fell between jeans and the one suit he owned. The July night was still warm, and Chris topped off the khakis with a dark blue polo shirt with a small insignia representing the Lexington police department sewn onto the right short sleeve. With a minor brushing, his dark hair layered into place. He checked the mirror and worked on his smile.

He remembered to call his buddies and let them know that he would not be available for their usual Thursday night basketball-and-beers pickup game, and said a quick good-bye to his inquisitive parents and gawking sisters. Their *date* was for 7:30 PM and Chris wanted to be early. As he drove out of the farm and to the Palms, he recalled how Drew could easily recite the history of the building that housed the eatery. It was built in 1836 for use as a local debating club and library. Chris knew the rest of the story by heart, including the transfer of the club and library to Washington and Lee University, its subsequent sale in 1909 to private hands, the unfortunate burning of the structure in 1915, and its restoration for use as a feed and grain store and ice cream parlor until 1975. That year the first floor of the building became what it is today—a warm, down-home place to eat and drink. Chris did not want to turn into his encyclopedic buddy Drew, but thought he might use his knowledge of the colorful history later to impress this Sarah girl.

Chris and his Jeep luckily found a parking space close to the 101 West Nelson Street restaurant at 7:20 PM. To his surprise, Sarah was already standing outside the restaurant, dressed in a shiny black blouse with buttons up the front and a modest, cream colored, pleated skirt that hung just above her knees. She was holding a single yellow rose in her hand. Chris tried to remain cool and walked slowly to the unexpected vision. When she saw him, she smiled and waited. When he reached her, she gently handed him the rose and said, "Yellow can mean a lot of things. One is 'welcome back.' I'm glad you decided not to leave me standing here waiting. I would not have blamed you. More importantly, it also stands for 'a promise of a new beginning.' Our first beginning was, well, less than rosy."

"Sarah, thanks. I think you have just made yellow my new favorite color. I'm, ah, a little embarrassed I didn't bring anything."

"You brought yourself in one piece. That's more than enough. Can I buy you dinner?"

"Sure, but I'd be happy to pay."

"How about this, Chris? If, after tonight, you decide there should be a next time, you can treat then. If you hadn't been so quick on your feet, my insurance premiums would have gone up way more than what tonight will cost me. But can we get to the new beginning part and leave the tire marks behind us?"

"After you, Sarah."

The new twosome entered the green door under the colorful awning of green, yellow, red and white stripes. Sarah, a detail person, sensed the age of the brick that framed the old, green, wood doors. She stopped to notice the cute sign on the outside wall that had palm trees planted between the letters of its moniker as part of its logo. She guessed that the promise of fine food and beverage on the sign would come in the form of casual fare. And that suited her mood just perfectly. The devilish part of the law student did not fail to notice the reflection of the large church steeple in the door's window. She smiled at the mirrored image that dominated the vista of downtown and thought, *um, might be a nice place for a wedding.*

Chris was blind to the characteristics of the establishment and could only absorb the attributes of his female companion.

College was out for the summer, but the Palms still had enough customers to generate the usual noise. After being trumped by the yellow rose, Chris decided to take charge, use his influence with the staff, and guided his date to one of the booths. The left section of the dining establishment offered a choice of dark teal booths with oak-edged tables or freestanding tables. The larger part, the right side, was filled with a massive bar and more tables and booths. The ceiling was high and metal, colored somewhere between orange and rust. Although Chris and his buddies usually preferred the oak-trimmed, tile-surface bar, a booth it would be tonight. The warm welcome given Chris by the young, blond, and pretty hostess named Julia indicated his familiarity with the place and the staff. Sarah, five minutes into their first date, already felt an impulsive tinge of jealousy. The bartender, a few of the wait staff, and the regulars at the bar gave the familiar patron, now a nervous man, a few high eyebrows.

Chris calmed down enough to offer Sarah a place on one side of the booth. He took the other. The seats were uncushioned wood, but the two were wound a bit too tight to notice.

Sarah, apparently not a shy one, started the conversation.

"Chris, I know all about me—I think. And, since I started this precarious relationship by trying to run you over, why don't you start tonight by telling me all about you?"

"Why don't we start by getting a drink?"

"Beer's good for me; pick one."

By the time their first Michelobs were finished, Chris felt he had pretty much met his biographical obligations, but Sarah tried not to let him off so easy. She started asking some innocent, touchy-feely questions about past and current loves and future hopes.

"No more questions for now, please, counselor. I enjoy watching *LA Law*, not being part of it. Let's get something to eat. And when we're done, you get to do the talking."

They made their way through another beer as they quietly ate. Chris went for "The Stonewall", a turkey, ham, Swiss, and lettuce on a Kaiser roll. Sarah opted for the hot, veggie pita with melted provolone on a toasted pita. When the deep-dish apple pie that they agreed to share was served, Chris asked to be excused for a trip to the men's room.

He thought the confined and chemically malodorous space a very unlikely setting for the sweetness of his current reflections.

God almighty. What would Fonzie do? The Fonz could always slam a jukebox and solve any problem. Okay, take it easy here, Chris. It's just a girl. Damn, you've lived with the likes of them all your life. But, hell, a girl who brought you *a rose. All right, smart guy, Mr. A Student, what do we have here? We've got a girl about five-six, wearing a light-colored skirt just above the knees and a black-as-night silky blouse. Her blond hair is nice and long but kind of frizzed out at the ends. Her eyes, well, her eyes are deadly blue and she does not show an ounce of fear to look directly into mine. The nose is a bit pinched, and the ears stick out just a bit too much to meet the Playboy perfection of pulchritude standards. And there are no noticeable chest restraints making her breasts look as small as they seem. Nice legs, though, and quite a smile. Is she smarter than I am? That could be a problem. Come on, Fonzie, help me out here.* No help came.

After washing his hands twice, Chris gently slammed the towel dispenser and took a long look in the mirror. Quietly and stubbornly he whispered to himself, "My momma warned me there would be a day like this. Just like the day she met my dad."

As he exited the restroom, he made a firm decision to order another beer to go with the apple pie and get himself and her under control. Time for him to take charge.

One look at the whipped cream and two cherries that Sarah had decided to add to the pie and the devilish look on her face removed all of Chris's resolve. He let her pummel him for another half-hour and revealed more about himself than he ever had before to another human being. Chris felt like Sarah was a skillful surgeon, who had anesthetized him with her sprightly charm, and then masterfully dissected his heart and mind. He sensed that he had finally arrived at the end of her third degree when he fessed up to never having a serious girlfriend since high school. She performed the entire operation without generating any noticeable pain or worry for her patient.

"Can you handle another beer, Bronx boy? Or do you have to go? In any case I need to visit the ladies room. You decide. I'll be back soon."

To this point, Chris, always teased as the Best of Class or Best in Class, felt like he'd be lucky just to get the chore of erasing the blackboard when this date was over. He decided to make a bold move and see what happened. While Sarah was gone, he arranged to pay the bill and overtipped, got two take-out cups of coffee, and took a step outside. He was glad he had never taken up smoking because this moment sure felt like one of those that called for the wrapped tobacco. Instead, he just took a few deep breaths and waited. When Sarah exited the restroom and saw the empty booth, she looked to their server, who shrugged his shoulders and just pointed toward the exit. When she found him, Chris was leaning against the brick building with a paper bag and his bright rose in his right hand.

Looking a little flushed, she asked if everything was okay.

"Everything is just fine, Sarah. I just felt the need to get out of the witness chair."

"I'm sorry, Chris. Maybe it's a defense mechanism I have grown to perfect when meeting new people—especially someone as handsome as you, someone as nice as you. Perhaps we should just call it a night and try again when I can maybe feel comfortable operating in a lower gear. And I told you dinner was on me, sneaky boy."

"Maybe next time, but what do you say you let me *drive* for a while tonight? It may not be low gear but I promise you won't experience any whiplash."

"I guess that's the least I can do since I've been trying to run you over all day."

"Good. I'd like to hold your hand as we walk these big city streets, if you don't mind."

"Well, only if you let me kiss you on that beautiful right cheek I've been longing to peck all night."

"Okay, but make it quick. We have places to go." *Don't give up control, Chris.*

He led his date about a half-mile southeast down Nelson Street, and, as they walked, shared a little of the Palms rich history to keep things comfortable. Sarah listened in polite silence. As they crossed Main, West Nelson became East Nelson, home of the local state liquor store. Without hesitation Chris led her in, nodded to the manager Karl Carlson, a friend of his dad's whom he had known for years, and moved to the shelf that held the Grand Marnier. He selected a small bottle, paid, and led Sarah out. Her silence signaled a shift and a comfort that Chris was anxious to explore. He led again, now with his left hand holding the paper bag and rose, his right softly draped over Sarah's shoulder, and the French brandy liqueur stuffed safely in her purse. He directed her by touch to take a left onto Main Street, heading south, and within a short walk the twosome ended up at the Stonewall Jackson Memorial Cemetery. It was past dusk. The historic cemetery was officially closed. So, Chris chose a spot on the long, gray, appropriate stone wall that ran the length of the cemetery grounds on Main. He hoisted his posterior up onto the chest-high blocks and invited the pushy blond to have a seat next to him. He opened the bag with the two coffees, requested the liqueur from Sarah's purse, and mixed a drink he had only sampled in his parents' home.

"So, Miss Sarah, what do you know about one of our local heroes, Mr. Thomas Jonathan 'Stonewall' Jackson?"

"Not much, Mr. Chris. Are you gonna educate me?"

"No. We'll save that if we decide to have a second date, and I'll be happy to let *you* pay next time. Now, if you have any hopes of pushing me past being half-in-love with you on second sight, it's your turn to talk."

"What do you want to know?"

"Talk, pretty lady, please, just talk. But your last name would be a good start."

CHAPTER 55

▼

SARAH

"Jones—believe it or not. You're sitting here with Miss Sarah Jones. My real parents have been dead as long as I can remember. Please don't ask me any details. I'd prefer to leave them behind me. I was kind of adopted by a wonderful set of new parents in Pennsylvania when I was only thirteen. Jeff and his wife Lorraine did not hesitate to take me in, a forlorn little orphan. In need of love and support."

Other than pausing for a sip of her delicious coffee, Sarah went on for an hour, non-stop. She gave a cloudy view of that time and the series of difficulties she remembered. She chose to omit a number of forgettable times. She was effusive with praise for the way Jeff and Lorraine helped her break the chain. Good times, good schools, good friends, and assurances that they would find ways to get her through college and beyond. All precious gifts that were part of the healing process.

Sarah was in Lexington as a first-year law student at Washington and Lee University—moved in early to an apartment to get her bearings. She had graduated with honors from the University of Virginia and had been accepted at the W&L School of Law, one of the smallest, yet highest-ranking, law schools in the nation, whose roots went all the way back to 1849. Chris knew quite a bit of Lexington history, and he knew you had to be very bright to even think about attending the same law school whose alumni included Supreme Court Justice Lewis F. Powell,

Jr. Sarah, the aspiring barrister, explained that she had a number of options, but really liked the idea of small city life.

Sarah Jones, the young lady who had caught the attention of and mesmerized the young Chris Lee on the historic streets of Lexington, finished the last of her laced coffee and eased off the wall. She stood directly in front of the still-seated, cutest man she had ever met.

"Listen, I'm out of story-telling energy. As tall, dark, and handsome as you are, Chris, and as short, pale, and blond as I am, tell me, is there any chance for a second date?"

"Well, if you're gonna spend three years here, someone has to educate you about 'Stonewall' and Robert E. Lee and all the rest. I think I can manage that, even with me being out of town so much. What do you think, Miss Jones? It's only the end of June. I don't leave till the end of August."

"Agreed, but—see, I'm trying to get back in control here, big boy—you have to walk me home. And there are a few things I need you to do."

"Yeah?"

"Do you even know how to kiss a girl?"

"Yeah."

"Kiss real good?"

"Well, I've never asked for ratings on a scale from one to ten."

"Well, this judge has yet to have the opportunity to render a score. Think you can make it from here to my apartment?"

"I know this town, lady. You're on my turf. Where are we headed?"

"Over there." Sarah pointed to a house just across Main Street.

"Smart-ass."

To Sarah's surprise, Chris moved forward, gave her the rose, stuffed the bottle back in her purse, and threw her 110 pounds over his right shoulder. He had one hand firmly on her skinny butt and the other securing her athletic legs across his chest. She made him put her down when they reached the other side of the street, and they made the twenty-five-step trip to the rear of the house with his arm around her shoulder and her hands squeezing the taut muscles above his hip.

The entrance to her apartment was at the back of a well-maintained brick home on South Main Street. There was a flight of steps that led up to her place.

They stood for a moment in the muted glow of the small light that had come to life with their movements. She retrieved the brandy from her purse and took a long swallow. Sarah handed the bottle to Chris and he did the same. She took the bottle back, put it in her purse, and placed it down on the old brick walk beneath them.

"Quiet for a moment, Chris. Don't move."

He tried to ask why, but she put her delicate fingers to his open lips. So, he just stood trying to find his breath. He looked into her smooth-skinned face adorned with those damn eyes, haunting and blue. During the four minutes that it took for the motion-activated 100-watt bulb, encased in its begrimed, moth-laden glass to lose its spark, she made him stare directly into her eyes. The silence and the staring made the young man more nervous than standing over a four-foot putt for a bogey when the match was on the line. At minute three, his nervousness escaped into a small giggle. Sarah had not flinched. At the 210-second point she smiled a smile that only lit up her eyes even more. And, finally able to breathe with some ease, Chris beamed back.

Never, in his limited dating experience had he ever experienced anything close to this whirlwind of emotion and warmth and sheer visceral fear. Little did he know that Sarah was also in uncharted territory. Her apparent calm and cool was the biggest acting job she had pulled off in her short life. She had no idea where her current performance came from. It just came.

When the last glimmer above them found its way into the dark night, Chris moved forward, hoping to taste Sarah's lips. And to savor the mouth that had been filling the air around them with the enticing aroma of the brandy. She gently stopped him by putting her hands on his chest. She let her hands linger for a few moments and then turned him around slowly so that his back was against the railing of the steps. Sarah turned and backed into the taller man's body. She took the shaky hands that were at his side and placed them in a crisscross motion inside the silky, black blouse that she had somehow—without Chris noticing—unfastened. She helped him work the simple restraint on the soft, cotton, snap-front bra and replaced the two sets of hands on her bare breasts. She could feel the roughness of his fingers brush across her welcoming nipples. Sarah was not sure what drove the impulse for this kind of intimacy so quickly, but she knew that was what she wanted at the moment. She also knew—a knowing accompanied by serious dread—that she would have to have a long conversation with Chris about her real past, before this relationship raced along any more quickly than it already had. Well, at least, before he took her as his bride in that church on Main Street with the tall, white steeple pointing to heaven.

Chris let Sarah's hands lead this sensual dance. They were gentle and moved very slowly. What he could not relinquish control of was the instinctive arousal between his legs. Suddenly her hands stopped moving. She felt his reaction pressing against the small of her back.

"Chris, I'm sorry. I probably have been unfair. I am not a virgin but it has been a very long time for me. I'm not ready to make love. But, if you forgive my teasing, I would love a second date. I just need some time to absorb tonight. I guess that's the bad news."

Chris let out a deep sigh. "Sarah, so far everything about tonight has been great news. It's a little too fast for me too. It's okay. Does tomorrow night sound good for you?"

She laughed. "Let me give you the good news before I answer that. A close friend once told me that before you get too committed to a relationship, 'You gotta do the breast test first.'" She explained that it was a simple and tried and true test. "Until tonight I have never tried it, but I believe you passed with flying colors."

"Okay, the suspense and your friend's secret set of rules are killing me and driving my curiosity crazy."

"Sorry. If the man lets you guide his hands and control the speed, he probably cares more about you than the sex. If the man tries to take over, the opposite is likely true. You want the first guy. So, 'first guy,' what time tomorrow night? I'll make dinner. That way you can't pick up the check without me looking."

Sarah released Chris's hands and turned to face him.

"Now, how about showing me if you can pass the midterm?"

She reached up and pulled his head and lips down to hers. A shaky Chris wasn't sure what the criteria for success was, so, he just started slowly. Their closed lips met. The scent of the coffee and cognac with its orange flavor eased its way to both of their inhalations. Sarah moved closer into Chris's body and moved her hands from his neck to his back and held on tight. The kiss lasted a full minute. Chris wished it would last forever.

Sarah pulled away and released her newfound friend and let out a breath and a "whew."

"Well, it seems you aced the multiple-choice part of the exam. There's only one more part left. It's called creative kissing."

Sarah tried to continue talking when Chris moved her to the first step of the staircase leading to her apartment. He lifted her up by the hips, and placed her on it. The motion-triggered light did its thing, and Chris looked into her inviting eyes.

"How long does this portion of the exam take?"

Sarah laughed and replied, "You're limited to five minutes."

"Humph. Well, I'll give it my best try."

Sarah was surprised when Chris moved to her right, pushed the hair away from the nape of her neck and lightly kissed it. His lips, with his tongue massaging her soft skin, moved to the side of her neck, tickled her ear for a few seconds, and then finally found Sarah's open lips. Chris took his full five minutes. Sarah's eyes were closed, and her body heated when a smiling Chris broke away.

"See you tomorrow night, Sarah Jones. I'll bring the wine and you have the rest of the Grand Marnier. Drive *carefully* in my town, young lady. I'll expect my grades to be posted in your kitchen when I get here. I'll be here at seven sharp." He turned to go but stopped at the sound of her voice.

"Hey, Chris." With a deft set of moves, Sarah removed her tan bra and gave the poor boy a flash of her perky little breasts. She threw the bra at him and closed her blouse, put the index finger of her left hand inside her slightly opened lips, and tilted her head down, and lifted her bright blue eyes up.

"In case you decide not to come back, there's something to remember tonight by."

He wasn't sure if she meant the small cotton garment or the brief glimpse of her ivory breasts. He picked up the bra and decided he would try to be entertaining.

"I'll be back, and, by the way, I prefer my women in black undergarments."

Then he turned and walked away for good this time—until tomorrow night. Chris had actually been with very few women while clothed in their undergarments—whatever color they may have been—but he was pleased with his cleverness.

By the time Chris made it back to his car, he wasn't sure if he had just met the girl of his dreams or the craziest—yet prettiest—nutcase in the county of Rockbridge. He mused and muttered to himself, "Maybe both." He drove home slowly and distractedly. Sarah had reminded him of someone throughout the course of the most interesting evening. As he made his way up Jacktown Road, it hit him. That crazy blond who faked the orgasm in the movie his sisters made him take them to. He talked to himself as he strode up the driveway to the side door of the house.

"That's *it*. All those different looks. From serious to laughing without a second's notice. From someone who seemed to be hiding something deep inside to the clowning quiz-giver and wonderful kisser."

Chris gently knocked on his eldest sister's door. The rhythmic, mellow sounds of Bonnie Raitt's "Nick of Time" were wafting into the hall. The title cut had earned her the best pop female vocal performance of the year award and the collection the album of the year. Chris heard some rustling as Bonnie was wrapping up her moving confession of a baby boomer's anxieties about everything from death to fleeting love.

"Yeah."

"Katie, it's me, Chris."

Katie's door opened to a spacious bedroom, meticulously kept. No clothes on the floor, all music, books, and trophies neatly arranged. *Probably alphabetized, if I know Katie,* Chris thought. Older brother was pretty good at organization and maintenance, but the dark-haired girl with her mother's looks was black-belt neat. She was wearing gray Virginia Tech sweatpants and a white Manhattan College T-shirt with green lettering that he had given her last Christmas. The soon-to-be sophomore Hokie had a paperback copy of John Sanford's *Rules Of Prey* in her hand as she opened the door. Reading mysteries, movies, and movie stars were Katie's guilty pleasures, and, with a 3.9 grade point average, no one complained.

"Still reading the serial-killer novels, huh?"

"Yeah, smart-ass. This one's about a guy named Maddog who offs an unsuspecting college junior, named Chris, with a Remington and a copper-jacketed hunting bullet."

"Great. But I got a pressing question. Remember that nutty movie you dragged me to last year in Roanoke 'cause you needed a ride? The one with the blond who causes a stir in a diner with her moaning?"

"Yeah. *When Harry Met Sally.* Next question?"

"What was the name of the actress, the blond who had chameleon tendencies?"

As Katie looked up to the taller brother, she offered her palm. "Information is power, buddy boy. Five bucks."

Chris handed over the five.

"Meg Ryan, born Margaret Mary Emily Anne Hyra, November 1961, in Connecticut. Was Bethel High School's homecoming queen. Did some film in the early eighties, did a stint on *As The World Turns* for a couple of years. Old Betsy Stewart Montgomery was married to or related to or slept with half the characters on that show and …"

"Okay, okay, I give up. Meg Ryan, huh? You don't happen to have any pictures of her in your library here, do you?"

Katie walked over to her bookshelf. It was loaded with everything from calculus texts to celebrity tabloids. Next to the magazines was a dark green koozie. Chris had bought it for her in New York. When he had seen the words on the foam can holder, "I don't need the encyclopedia, my wife knows everything", he scarfed it up, paid the two bucks, and covered "wife" with a piece of bright white tape, and inked in the word "sister." Katie scanned her collection and pulled out a magazine called *Celebrity Sleuth*, marked the spot by positioning the one below it at a right angle, and handed it to Chris.

"Now, what the hell is this about this late at night?"

"Well, I just came back from a fascinating date with a girl who I think looks like this Meg Ryan, and I couldn't remember the actress's name. So, thanks, Sis."

"Whoa, college boy. You don't get off that easy."

Katie pushed for details, and as close as the two were, most of Chris's answers to the sisterly interrogation consisted of, "I'm not really sure."

Pointing to the picture of the naturally blond, blue-eyed Meg, Katie ended the conversation with, "Well, if she looks like this, you're halfway there. Hopefully, she's not a serial killer luring you in for one of her satisfying executions. Good night. Let me know how things work out. I'll be happy to clue you in on how screwed up we females can be when we put our demented minds to it." She kissed his cheek. He moved away with a "Thanks". She couldn't resist. "And, oh, by the way, her name is an anagram for a European country."

Chris turned back with a, "Huh?" but Katie had already closed her three-panel, oak door. He'd think about the anagram later. Right now he was focused on this amalgamation of joy and fear he had never known before tonight. He guessed that this kind of emotional confusion is fairly common among the male species. Then he guessed it just might be time for a cold nightcap and a mindless observation of the local mountains and stars that hung brightly above them in a dark, country sky. He would look at the magazine tonight, maybe even read some of it—tomorrow.

CHAPTER 56

▼

GOLF IN THE MOUNTAIN STATE—APRIL 1990

Jed remembered Chris's telling of the near rundown at the hands of Sarah's car and the emotional hit and run that was their first date. He also remembered young Chris's conquest of the Pipestem golf course way back when—before Sarah.

It was the spring break before the summer that Chris discovered the wonders of Sarah that the four courageous college boys took on the "field of battle" known as Pipestem Resort State Park golf course. The Geoffrey Cornish-designed, tree-lined and well-trapped golf track, featuring views of the Bluestone Canyon, was a long way from New York, but the game it presented did not differ much. It was still one of man's best and worst inventions. It was an unlikely place for four young men attending college in the Big Apple, but the Pipestem in West Virginia it was. The praise or blame for the choice could be squarely placed on one Chris Lee and shared with the impulsiveness and no-fear attitude of all four, twenty-one-year-old collegians.

The Fearless Foursome consisted of Jed, a native of Queens, New York; Grady, born and bred in Brooklyn; and Chris and Drew, the two transplants from Virginia. The closest either of the two New Yorkers had ever been to the Commonwealth of Virginia was a high-school class trip to Washington, D.C.

West Virginia might as well have been a foreign country for all Jed and Grady knew about it.

Today, *netstate.com* would inform the unknowing and inquiring, and warmly greet the Web visitors.

"Welcome all to West Virginia, land of rugged mountains. The "Mountain State," with the highest mean altitude east of the Mississippi River, is also the state with the largest single natural scenic and outdoor recreational area in the eastern United States; the Allegheny Highlands. Eighty percent of the state is forested with over 110,000 square miles of hardwood forest, wind-swept mountains and photo-perfect valley landscapes. All of this can be found within a day's drive of 20 major eastern cities."

Back in 1990, Drew, the Birdman, Birdsall was all the others needed to provide the travel dialogue about their destination. Encyclopedia Boy had done his usual research. And on the ride down south, he shared. He gave a *netstate.com* equivalent and then moved on to the history of WVA coal mining, beginning in the early 1800s. It was a narrative that held the interest of the other three for ten minutes. When they started moaning halfway through his didactic monologue, he decided to hold off on the rest of his infomercial. He would have to pick his moment to impart the interesting fact that until 1861 West Virginia was part of Virginia. He'd be sure to let them know later that the great Commonwealth of Virginia was so named to honor Queen Elizabeth of England, often referred to as the "Virgin Queen."

The beautiful, yet distant, site of their first trip had been home to an annual Lee family summer vacation for many years. Chris challenged the other three college boys to make the spring road trip to play on a course that actually had some fresh, unpolluted air, and was surrounded by mountains, not concrete and high-rise buildings. Chris's close-to-straight As for two years and his father's tiring of the long trip had resulted in a 1986 White Jeep Cherokee becoming a vehicle available to Chris on a fulltime basis. The four-door, 2.8 liter V6 with a manual five-speed was a challenge to park and drive in the crowded city, but, for a college boy, "Wheels were wheels." And whenever Aunt Ree Ree's husband, Uncle Mikey, was out on one of his fishing trips, Chris's Jeep got the privilege of sharing the small parking area behind the house with Ree Ree's red 190 Mercedes. And, for sure, Chris's relatively new wheels would serve well as the transport for the first trip of the FF crew to the beautiful Mountain State.

Edward R. and Gin Lee were thrilled with the idea of Chris bringing his college and golfing buddies to their home as the first leg of their excursion. Gin politely explained to her husband that the boys were on a tight schedule and only had a night and a day before heading off to golf. So, they would have to forego, at least on this trip, Ed's classic tour of his historic hometown of Lexington. Gin loved this time of year. Her expansive gardens started to come to life, the streams that flowed through their property seemed to regain energy, and she could guilt-lessly let the furry critters, which normally roamed in their home, outside for most of the day. And, now, her boy was coming home with his friends. Life in Lexington was good, and Gin would make sure that their guests from New York would leave with fond memories. In support of that intention, Gin also made sure that the local grocery stores and Omaha Steaks would see a noticeable spike in their April sales.

It was a night and day of sumptuous meals, including a myriad of Gin's home-baked goodies. Drew's parents joined them for dinner and a country breakfast of fresh fruit, sausage, bacon, ham, and Edward's famous brown-tainted scrambled eggs the next morning. Gin did not forget what it was like to come home from college and the appreciation of *real* food. The boys did not disap-point. They had, indeed, brought their appetites for home cooking along with the eagerness to play.

At two in the afternoon, while the Fearless Foursome was whacking shag balls with nine irons down the hill on the side yard to a flag Ed had planted just in front of the white pines, his bride waved the flag planter in.

"We're out of beer, Ed."

"No way."

"Way. Take Chris into town with you and load up. Talk to him. See how he's really doing. We haven't had any time alone. He seems fine, but work your charm and put me at ease that he's okay."

Father and son loaded up, with a few extra cases on the old man's tab for the golf trip, and they had their talk. Chris was fine, happy with school and his friends. Still thinking about the Marines. Neither had any prescience of what would happen the following August when the mechanized infantry, armor, and tank units of the Iraqi Republican Guard would invade Kuwait and seize control of that country.

For now, all was well with the Lee clan. More food, more beer, and more boasting among the anxious golfers filled the night. Chris's sisters thought they had never had so much fun, or had seen the serious Christopher in such a light-hearted mood.

The resilient group of four, fortified by Ed's killer breakfast, was repacked and ready to roll at 7:00 AM in the trusty Jeep. Clubs, suitcases, and Ed's contributory Budweiser were piled high in the back, and they were on their way.

The two-and-a-half-hour drive across U.S. 64 and down West Virginia's Route 20 started out quietly, as the boys were a bit tired and sated. Thirty minutes into the trip the ever-educating Drew started into his spiel about the history of the small West Virginia towns that all seemed to have two names. Thirty minutes later, Chris jammed George Strait's *Ocean Front Property* album into the tape player and adjusted the volume of "All My Ex's Live in Texas"—to the delight of two of his three passengers—to a level that effectively closed down the Britannica.

Thus far on the trip, the two New Yorkers drank in the beauty of the two Virginia states with the same vigor that Chris and Drew had reveled in their discovery of the glories of the Big Apple.

They teed off at 11:00 AM. Chris and Jed, as usual, were down the middle of the fairway of the 359-yard hole. Drew's patented power fade had him in the right rough. Grady had made a heroic, first lunge at his Top Flite that resulted in him being the first to take a trip into the timberland. The course was home to some of the forests that made up 80 percent of the state's land. Before the day was out, Grady had seriously bonded with a number of parcels of West Virginia's 110,000 square miles of woodland in pursuit of an errant, spherical flight path. The weather was perfect and the golf was fun as usual. The sun was warm and the beer was cold. And the bond among the four only grew stronger in this pleasant setting. Chris and Jed tied at 87. Drew was in the low nineties and Grady broke the three-digit barrier once again—on the wrong side. But by the time the tetrad had devoured the cheeseburgers and fries in the Mulligans Sports Lounge at the clubhouse, the only numbers that mattered were the price of the meal and the size of the tip—except for Grady, still not a member of the magic, double-digit club.

They stopped at the lodge and picked up the key to one of the twenty-six cabins—theirs being a four-bedroom. Chris had been here before, so, the incongruence of the seriously rustic outside and the comfortable inside was no surprise. For the others who approached the structure with some trepidity, it *was* a pleasant surprise when the wooden door opened up to a quaint, good-sized room with clean, pinewood floor and walls. Chris had not shared any of the details of the accommodations with the others, other than to say it's fine. So, the appearance of a 25-inch TV—with cable—and amenities that included appliances for cooking and refrigerating brought a collective sigh of relief. The large fireplace framed in stone and a stack of wood further delighted the new visitors. The furniture was noticeably low to the ground and a bit vintage. The bathroom was functional— and inside. All in all, it looked like the kind of place where four college boys could live well and play hard. And they did.

Chris caught fire on the course and followed his 87 with a 79, leaving the others far behind in their inaugural contest. The next day Chris eagled number 13, a short par five, and rolled in an eighteen-footer for birdie on the 399-yard eighteenth for a 78.

Nighttimes were filled with pizza or burgers, always with beer, and the recounting of memorable shots. When the poker game ended on night number three, they adjourned to the TV and surfed channels.

It was by chance that they stumbled upon a replay of a dog show held in the New Jersey Garden State Exhibit Center. Drew, in charge of the remote, paused long enough to see the presentation of the Best in Class prize to the owner of a Japanese Akita. The announcer described the dog as pinto in color, meaning mostly white with brown and black patches around the face and neck. He went on to compliment the breed and this particular dog, weighing ninety-eight pounds, standing twenty-seven inches tall, as a wonderful combination of dignity and good nature, along with alert courage and docility. And, to the delight of three of the foursome, this Best in Class canine, a member of the brave breed favored by the Japanese Samurai warriors and emperors, was named Mr. Lee. The owner, a Margie Arenzi, accepted the trophy, and acknowledged and thanked the late Helen Keller, the first to bring an Akita to America. She blushed and expressed her pride in Mr. Lee, named after the brave and graceful actor Bruce Lee. Margie gushed that her extraordinary pooch was truly deserving of the title of Best in Class, this event's equivalent of Best In Show.

Grady was the first to apply the glue to the nickname and adhere it firmly to his friend Christopher Sato Lee. "You heard it, baby! Mr. Lee, you are now and forever christened 'Best in Class.' Bruce Lee was Chinese, you're Japanese, and the dog is Japanese, so, close enough, huh?" Grady stood and bowed at the waist with arms outstretched toward Chris. Jed and Drew quickly followed and joined in the show of honor and respect. All three shifted into a full kowtow, knees on the ground, arms outstretched, and heads bowed to touch the ground to their personal Buddha.

The title usually stood on its own but frequently took on its acronymic form of BIC. It quickly worked its way—as phrases often do with college cliques—into their lexicon. If the four boys won a pickup ballgame or polished off two large pizzas and a case of beer in one night, it was commonplace to hear, "B-I-C, baby; that's us."

On the last night in the cabin, pokered-out, almost golfed-out, and nursing the last beer of the night, they agreed that *this was the place*. If this Fearless Foursome was to maintain a connection over the years to come, there was no better way than this. They swore an oath that they would regroup here at Pipestem two years from now and every year thereafter. They all agreed that they would need a year after graduation to get established, but that was it. After that it wasn't "if they could make it;" it was "when they would make it." Jed recalled the unique and deep sense of bonding that was happening on that first WVA trip. He was more impressed at its unwavering strength many years later—so much more than just a golf-centered tie.

Their final morning was cloudy with a threat of thunderstorms. The mildly hungover warriors trudged their way to the first tee. Drew decided that this was a good time to try and educate the clouded minds of the others about the origin of the word golf. "Did you guys know that many people incorrectly believe that the word "golf" originated as an acronym for "gentlemen only, ladies forbidden?" Well, that's just bush bosh."

His audience was busy selecting which golf balls to hit and/or lose, but Drew pressed on with vigor.

"Well, they're wrong. The answer is that, like most modern words, the word "golf" derives from older languages. The languages involved with this word are medieval Dutch and old Scots. The old Dutch word 'kolf' or 'kolve' meant 'club.' It is believed that word passed to the Scots, whose old Scots dialect transformed the word into 'golve,' 'gowl' or 'gouf.' And by the sixteenth century, the word "golf" had emerged."

Before Drew could go on to expound on the fact that luge and polo are the only other two sports that he knew of that were four-letter words, a trio of golf balls were flung at his feet, accompanied by a chorus of other colorful four-letter expressions. The surprised Drew hinted that his golfing buddies might try and keep an open mind to the many bits of valuable information he could impart to them. The three hinted back very strongly that he should consider shoving his six iron up his behind and shut up. Drew quickly did the latter and teed up. His ball would find its way into what was usually "Grady territory." Game on.

The thunderstorms held off. Grady managed to find the fairway on the first hole, and the foursome shot their best rounds of the four days. In fact, the lifetime, elusive, two-digit round finally came Grady's way—in a fashion. On that day he had turned in his Grizzly Adams buckskin outfit and fondness for the wilderness for some fairways and greens. The silence leading to Grady's approach shot on 18 was tense. The hacker, a long way from his Bay Ridge, Brooklyn, home, only needed a two putt from twenty feet to reach his Holy Grail of 99. Jed and Drew stood behind the redhead and watched his three practice strokes. Chris, with his ball marked just a foot away from the hole, was tending the flag. The first fifteen feet were uphill. Grady O'Connor glided his Wilson flat blade smoothly through the ball and sent it steadily rolling toward Chris and the flagstick. The sound of the Top Flite tapping the metal below Chris's feet brought cheers and a perilous fling of Grady's putter. "Never mind 99, baby. That's a 98!" Drew and Jed's cheers echoed through the valley. When the celebratory threesome cleared the slight rise of the green, they saw that Chris, after Grady had walked back to the ball after his final scouting, had moved the flag three feet to the left of the actual hole.

With the flag back in its rightful place and the ball returned to its original spot, Grady failed to come close in his next three tries. The others conceded his 98. Chris slapped him on the back. "Great round, Grady. Come on, I'll buy you a beer." A silent, very disgruntled Grady walked off and told Chris where he could shove his beer.

The thunderstorms never did come that day. But they were not far behind for one of the tightly forged foursome.

CHAPTER 57

▼

DINNER AT SARAH'S—
JUNE 1990

On his first amazing Lexington date with Miss Sarah, Chris, under the probing interrogation of the blond beauty, recalled his recent trickery at Pipestem. He offered it as the one thing he most regretted in his young life. He had the sense that the incident went deep with Grady. Chris's guilt would not resurface on the second date.

Chris had been surprised at the events of the night before with the mesmeric Sarah. He had been unprepared then, but enjoyed reliving every minute as he tried to sleep afterwards with her brassiere clutched in his right hand. He was not sure how to mentally or emotionally prepare for the impending second date, so, he just threw himself into his work and other chores. He dressed pretty much the same as the night before, and, with the sounds of Garth Brooks warbling about "The Dance," made his way down Jacktown Road and into town. He paid little attention to the street signs announcing his slalom-like passing of Cornstalk and Windsong Roads. He was used to the aged and large trees jutting out from the hill on the right side of the road and the pastoral view on the left. The green pastures were home to the cattle of many colors that dotted the idyllic landscape. Chris, for sure, did not pay much attention to the words about the good and bad of Garth's experience. Just blanked out his brain to make it to his destination in one piece. Once he hit West Midland Trail, aka U.S. 60, it would be a short, flat ride. U.S. 60 became Nelson. A right onto the one-way Jefferson, left onto White, and another left onto Main put him at the scene of last night's visit to Mr. Jackson's cemetery. He parked on the street and did a last-second beauty check in the rearview mirror. He got out and stopped when he reached the black, steel, gated entrance to the gravesites. With a stiff salute to the tall statue of Stonewall that was mounted high on a tiered set of stone platforms in the middle of the cemetery, Chris half-mockingly whispered, "Wish me luck, General." He took a few deep breaths and made his way to the rear of the brick home, painted red with white trim. The sun was doing its last dance of the day on the black, tin roof that protected the back of the house. Chris shakily climbed the back stairs of the house on South Main, glad that it was still light out. There was no doorbell to ring, so, he gently knocked. When the door opened, he was glad he had not wasted any time on preparation. When Sarah opened the door and smiled, the scene behind her looked like something out of a movie set—and the star in the scene took his breath away. There was too much to take in to notice any one thing first; she was all he could look at.

Her blond hair had been fashioned and swept onto the top of her head. Her makeup was glamorous and sparkly. The light in her blue eyes slowed him down from taking in the rest of the scene. He noticed the modestly styled dress of calico cloth with a pattern of light yellow roses winding its way through the white background. The three-quarter-length sleeves left only a brief view of her tanned arms, joined at their end by cotton-gloved hands. The nine buttons down the front ended in a v-shaped wedge below her waist. The seams of the wedge and the trimmed hipline gave way to a full and full-length skirt. Chris felt like he missed the part of the invite concerning dress code—felt like he was wearing his Nike high tops to a wedding. Sarah gave him a peck on the cheek and invited him in. Chris's senses were in complete overload and jumped from the beauty in front of him to the rich, antique furnishings of the living room, to its freshly painted and decorated walls and windows, to the perfectly sanded and varnished oak hardwood floor trimmed out with eight-inch, stained molding, and ceiling trimmed out in matching crown molding, and finally to the wall of electronics. The sun's rays streamed through the three skylights in the room and danced across a collage of plant life, including freshly cut, colorful zinnias and carnations. It was a varied collection that looked like the fruits of a successful heist from the Mountain View Farm Greenhouse. Somewhere in the intricate shelving Conway Twitty was singing Chris's all-time favorite song, "The Rose." There were only two people that knew that this song was his favorite, Chris and his mother. They shared the same passion for the depth of the words and the richness of old Conway's voice.

The apartment's looks belied the century-old brick home and its stairs in need of repair. Her beauty was no mystery but the scene was.

Sarah exchanged his bottle of Inglenook vin rosé, clutched in his strong right hand, for a glass of Thomas Jefferson cabernet franc that she had already poured for him from her own stock. She then pulled her stunned, new friend over the threshold. She was tempted to regale the boy with her own Drew-like recitation about Mr. Jefferson's belief that, "We could, in the United States, make as great a variety of wines as are made in Europe, not exactly of the same kinds, but doubtless as good." And add the fact that T.J.'s vineyards over in Monticello only made that hope come true in the last few years. But obviously his attention was otherwise occupied, and she still wanted him to feel the superior Virginian.

"Wow. Wow! Sarah, you like Conway?"

This time she couldn't resist the regaling. "You mean the sexy crooner born Harold Jenkins on September 1, 1933, in the small town of Friars Point, Mississippi? The kid who was taught his first guitar chords by his riverboat pilot of a father and went on to win a Grammy for his duet with Loretta Lynn in 1971 for 'After the Fire Is Gone?' Yeah, well, I guess he's okay."

She paused to mark his surprise and went on. "I just picked up the cassette today. I've been playing it for quite a while."

"Why?"

"Because your mother told me it was your favorite. It wasn't easy to find the *Number 1s* album, but I didn't quit until I did. It was my first trip to Roanoke. The locals I checked with here said if Henry at Roanoke's Record Room ain't got it, nobody does. The only problem was that Henry only does mail order—that is unless you sweet-talk him into granting a personal visit. Henry was quite helpful, and they were right. Henry pretty much has it all, and if he doesn't have it, he will find it. I was very happy to make a new friend."

"You called my *mother*?"

"Yeah, we had a real nice chat. I can't wait to meet her."

"You went to Henry's house in *Roanoke*?"

"It's a short trip. Nice little town. Henry's a doll. I told him over the phone I had a special evening planned. He had old Conway waiting for me."

She did not go on to mention that Henry gave her the bio info on Mr. Twitty.

The conversation rated another "Wow" from the somewhat astounded Chris.

Chris took a healthy sip of the bright ruby-colored wine as Sarah closed the door. He slowly spun around to take in the details of the grandeur and high-tech equipment housed strangely in the upper flat of the old, brick Lexington dwelling. To add to the eclectic surroundings, Sarah had placed green and white balloons in a string over the small fireplace.

"This place is fabulous and crazy, and you're crazy too. 'Splain it all to me, Lucy."

"Later, Desi—except for the balloons. Did you go to any of your high school proms?"

"What?"

"You heard me. I could have asked your mother, but I figured I'd wait for your answer."

"Well, yeah, my senior prom at Lexington High."

"Who was your date? Was she special to you?"

"Can I please sit down, or am I not allowed to sit on one of these classic antique chairs?"

"Tonight, you can sit wherever you want. Now talk."

Chris chose the button-back Victorian chair and its soft red upholstery. He figured if his shaky right hand spilled the wine this would be the best choice of possible landing zones. Sarah chose an early-twentieth century French settee, whose flowered pattern had swirls of red on a light background that matched Chris's perch. To Chris, the contrast of the red- and yellow-rose patterns surrounding his prom date's body was riveting. Sarah, sitting there, looked like a perfect candidate for a classic portrait by Mary Reilly, the famous artist from Manassas, who had done a stunning Lee family portrait not too long ago.

After another deep sip and a deeper breath, Chris spoke. He put his glass down on a doily-covered, Victorian, walnut end table that matched the chair's wood framing. "Funny. Her name was Sara too. Sara Stockton. Was she special? Absolutely. She was about your size. Her hair was darker, and she was a beauty with a sweet smile and a soothing voice, *and* smart. Was she special to me? No. To be honest, I had to call in a favor from a cousin in Chantilly, Virginia. My ego told me I needed to go to the prom, but I was not dating anyone, and I was too embarrassed to beg one of my classmates or one of my *sisters*. And, of course, I wanted to go with a girl who would turn heads. That ego thing again, you know. I have always been close to my cousin, Stacy, and she came through. When the others at the prom quizzed me, well, I fibbed that the sexy Sara on my arm had been a well-hidden sweetheart. Luckily, Stacy and Sara were close and she actually enjoyed the ploy, and we both had a great time."

"How great?"

"Stop it, J. Edgar. We danced a lot, spent a little time with a bootlegged bottle of Gallo afterwards."

She ignored his request to abate her inquisition and pressed on, feeling comfortable and devilish at the same time. "Afterwards? Where was this 'afterwards,' Mr. Romance?"

He told her about their brief trip to a hill overlooking Buffalo Creek. Friends of his parents owned a home not far from Lexington that overlooked the narrow creek and provided beautiful views of the Blue Ridge Mountains. He knew his parents' friends were not in town and would not mind his enjoying the views. He explained that it was pleasant, but not much else to report on.

"Yeah, we changed into jeans, but there was no peeking going on, and that's it. Okay? You're wearing me out. Jeez."

"Sorry."

Conway just finished the sad lyrics of the "Somebody's Needin' Somebody" cut and moved onto the sexy, suggestive "Slow Hand."

Sarah's "sorry" lasted only a brief moment. "So, did you and this hussy watch the sun come up?"

"We did, and with all our clothes still in place, and with only a bit of minor closeness. We later made our way down the private drive to Buffalo Bend Road and joined some others for breakfast. It was at some greasy spoon I can't remember the name of. I drove Sara home after she napped at my folks' house, and that was it. Done, over, finished, kaput. *No más.*"

Chris gulped the rest of his wine, got up, and took Sarah in his arms and kissed her and stepped back.

"Now, how about your story, Miss Prom Queen?"

"Never went. I had shyness issues."

"Well, looks like some elixir has cured those ills."

"No, I think it's you, and I think it's time—finally—to live."

"Good. Can you start by relaxing and explaining all the fancy dress and decorations?"

"Sure. The dress was the only thing I ever kept that was my mother's. She used to wear it to church dances. It's been well preserved, and I was saving it for a special occasion. And, well, tonight's the night. The balloons make this room the proms I never went to, and you are the prom king to my prom queen. A little underdressed, but I'll live with it. Anything else you want to know?"

"Yeah. This room looks like a fancy antique store. How come?"

"One of my few passions. I have the money, and this is how I like to spend it. It has helped a pretty empty soul imagine that it is sharing space and time with those that lived large. It is pretty much my only serious vice, besides you, as of now."

The wine was refilled and Sarah delivered brief highlights of the "from wheres" and "when builts" about the dark, rich, wooden furniture that filled the small space she now called home.

Enough time had passed that Conway's 1988 recording had made its way past all the various pleas, emotions, and thoughts related to love and lament, and landed on the final cut, "The Clown." As was true for "The Rose", Chris knew every word of *this* slow song with the soft guitar, blended piano notes, and swishing drum sounds. The cadential lyrics spoke of the clown's lover who instilled a high-wire kind of fear in the doting, enamored jester. What Chris did not know was that Sarah had listened to "The Rose" and "The Clown" enough times to have the same words emblazoned in her own complex system of electrochemical processes in the brain reserved for memory. What he did know was that when Sarah took the wineglass out of his right hand, placed it on the doily, hit a few buttons to recapture the fifth track of the album, and took him in her arms to dance the first dance of their unique prom, he had found a treasure and a mystery he had never taken the liberty to dream of.

Sarah had found a magic she never possessed until this "prom night." The steady confidence with which she brought Chris into her arms and comfortably cradled her head into his chest were things she had only watched others do—mostly in the movies. Her hands gently moved around his taller neck, and their bodies warmly fused into a smooth set of movements across the soft Persian rug that softened the hardwood oak floor that had become their stage.

By the time the music was telling the world that a seed beneath a cold snow was but the beginning of a sun-coached, brightly blossoming flower, Sarah had lost all her haunting memories. Those cold daggers of violation that blocked out any hope of "warm and tender" were nowhere in sight. Just Chris and this moment.

And, Chris had lost his resolve to make sure this relationship—at least on a sexual level—did not move too fast. Sarah's slow moving hands across his neck and then across his chest had dissolved his fear, and when Conway's meandering musical inflections ended, her slow steps that led to her bedroom were impossible to resist.

CHAPTER 58

▼

LUCKY

The candles on the cherrywood nightstands were of varied size and scent and too many for Chris to count. Sarah lit them all. In the center of the tall wax soldiers on her dresser was a small wooden sculpture of a golden retriever.

"A friend of yours?" Chris said, pointing to the image.

"A long story. A gift from an old friend. Her name is Lady Lucky. And, if you play your cards right tonight, Mr. Inquisitive, some of her luck may rub off on you. Now, back to you and me."

She had decided to lend a little culture to the evening. She efficiently, as if rehearsed, pushed a few buttons on the small Pioneer receiver. With a little more digital dexterity, her new Sony cassette player came to life, joined by a set of Cerwin-Vega speakers placed in the two corners on either side of the queen-size bed. Sarah's music had wound its way around the heads of the machine many times over the years since she had compiled it. The sensual collection of classical music as always began with the overture of Richard Wagner's *Tristan und Isolde* and would move on to other luscious renditions, including selected segments of Tchaikovsky's *Romeo and Juliet.* Those were followed by the entire second scene of Ravel's *Daphnis and Cloe,* eventually climaxing with Toscanini's 1946 conducting of the love duets of Puccini's *La Boheme.* The sounds had been her friends and refuge for a long time. Tonight was the first time she had ever shared them. As Wagner's notes slid out of the speakers, she breathed deeply and wondered if she had the courage to slide her new friend out of his clothes and herself out of her own fear.

Chris surprised her when he made the first move. He took her by both hands and walked her over to the full-length mirror on the back of her closed bedroom door. He released her hands, and stepped behind her.

"Okay, Miss Prom Queen, do you have a plan here for this evening?"

"Yes, Your Majesty. Dinner's at ten—no chicken though. We'll be having steamed lobster tails with drawn butter and twice-baked potatoes with sharp cheddar and bacon bits. To insure you get your daily dose of veggies, we'll be having fresh corn on the cob, slithering in butter. All in all a very healthy fare. Don't you think?"

"I think you're gonna have to eat naked so you don't mess up those fancy gloves and dress."

"Oh, I forgot to mention. That was also part of the plan."

"Any other parts of your plan you left out?"

"Nope. That's as far as my planning skills could carry me."

"Well, it's almost eight o'clock. How long does it take you to get undressed?"

Now it was Sarah's turn to surprise. She had been stealthily undoing the nine buttons on the front of her dress from the bottom up, all the while holding the divided cloth together with the other hand. Chris's hands had never left her shoulders the whole time. His own trepidation held him in check. His eyes had been focusing on their differences above the neck. His straight, dark hair, parted easily on the left and neatly trimmed, sat in its appointed place. Sarah's blond swirls and curls were so dissimilar in color and shape. His face, a cultural mix and a tone different from hers. Their features strikingly contrasted; yet it was a match of differences that Chris enjoyed observing.

Chris's observation rapidly switched to the naked chest and torso that Sarah had revealed in one swift move. She had easily pushed Chris's hands off her shoulders and dropped the top of the calico dress so that it fell like a large, wind-blown leaf to the side of her hips and legs. She let him observe for a few minutes. His eyes roamed the mirror as his hands roamed the contours of her revealed skin. With patience, he moved his hands down her shoulders and arms. He joined his fingertips at the front of her waistline and moved up the subtle changes of her figuration. His hands stopped to massage the already-hardened nipples.

Sarah released herself and turned. In silence she slowly removed his hunter green Ralph Lauren polo. She took her time to return the favor of his earlier massage and kissed much of his tight chest. Chris interrupted to return the kissing favor. Things moved quickly after that. Clothes were jettisoned. They relived the joining of lips from the night before. This time, though, there was nothing between the two warming bodies but a bit of air and soon a bit of perspiration.

The stimulating sounds of opera coming from the speakers melded with the passionate whisperings and exclamations from the eagerly engaged twosome. Sarah broke away long enough to pull down the rose-flowered, blue-and-wine-colored Waverly comforter from atop the mattress of the New England four-poster. Chris had been drinking in every curved part of her body as she went about the deflowering of the bed clothing. He shamed himself for noting that, unlike the famous Meg Ryan, Miss Sarah was not all natural. Sarah spoke the first short sentence since they had discarded their apparel.

"Please, come here, Chris. This is the part where I have no plan and no history."

"Not yet, Sarah. *You come here.*"

She went to him and he repositioned their unclothed bodies in front of the mirror. This time, side by side. For Chris, the image was an inaugural moment of what he hoped might last a long time, maybe forever. It was also sexually mesmerizing. He wondered what it felt like for her as a salty tear made its way down her left cheek. Sarah did not tell him about the tear—did not tell him that she felt lucky with a capital L, and that was the origin of the transparent fluid that caused her mascara to run.

"Sarah, you led when we danced to Conway. Please lead us wherever *you* want."

She did. Chris had never known satin sheets and slipped a little when Sarah guided him down onto the bed. With the music as a background, the exploration moved slowly. They kissed in almost every way possible. Touched in ways neither had before. Laughed as each massaged and kissed the other's appendectomy scars illuminated by the flickering wicks embedded in wax. This was not the rise provided by the pages of Playboy or the cheap sex flicks Chris had enjoyed in the dorm room of Drew's classmates. These tastes, these smells, these sensations were all his, shared by no one else. Sarah's recollection of cinematic romance was replaced with scorching, climactic releases.

Dinner, along with a bottle of Bollinger Special Cuvée, was served almost on time. Neither spoke of the fact that they had entwined and joined in a myriad of intimate ways—but not the most intimate. Each had sensed from the other that it was too soon for that final act to be played on this stage, a stage that they had so quickly set. Wait they would, for now.

CHAPTER 59

▼

JOEY D.

There were a couple of things the lanky, smiling man called Joey D. didn't like. He hated when he was introduced as Joey D., and some smart-ass wanted to know where his Starliters were. He was always tempted to tell the inquiring fool that they were at the questioner's house, having sex with his significant other—sex that included sticking a peppermint twist into …

The second thing Joey hated was cold weather. This particular disinclination had caused him to take an early retirement from his management position with the phone company in 1984 and seek his fortune in the Sunshine State—or at least a warmer climate in which to make a living. So, before the next winter worked its way into Bridgewater, New Jersey, Joey and his beautiful wife packed it in and made their way to Jensen Beach on Florida's southeast shore. Within months the tall, lanky, ambitious, sandy-haired Joey had worked his way into two new businesses. Within a year, he dipped into his savings and bought both.

The tavern was just a block west of State Route 707, Jensen's Indian River Drive.

The motel and cottages were perched on the shores of the Intracoastal Waterway, here in Jensen called the Indian River. The rental complex was a mile north of the Jensen Beach Causeway that took you to Hutchinson Island and the Atlantic. The pink motel decorated with painted palms had two floors and thirty-two units. There were eight standalone clapboard cottages, all with one bedroom. Pink shutters, matching the hotel's color, dressed each of the three windows in each of the houses. A small wooden deck wrapped around one side and the front of each of the habitats. Sprinklings of grass grew out of the sandy soil surrounding the cottage area. Each had a kitchen, a living area, and a view of the waterway and Joey D.'s dock. The floors were oak planks and the walls were of old, rich pine paneling. The bedroom furniture in each cottage was a friendly set of solid, colonial maple; the rest of the furniture throughout the cozy, small structure was Early American eclectic.

Ironically, Joey D.'s tavern was named the Starliter Saloon. That had been its name for years, and Joey's wife, Deb, convinced him it was fate. Her hunch led to good times and better bottom lines for the Dannemanns. The house specialty cocktail was the peppermint twist martini. The starred menu item was Joey D.'s Lounge Lobster Tail. The flyers that made their way to the windshields of the cars in the local beach's parking lots read, "Joey D.'s Starliter Saloon—the best place for Good Times, Cold 'Tinis and Hot Tails."

The collection of rental facilities, whose land also housed Joey's three-bedroom beach home, was called the River Rest. Residents had access to Joey's dock and any of the three rowboats that rested on the sand next to it. All they had to do was ask, and the vessels' chains would be unlocked, and the seamen supplied with orange lifejackets. Joey and Deb already had the credit cards on file in case any voyage resulted in any damage or a lost oar.

Sarah had decided that the River Rest was where she would give herself fully to her new lover, her Mr. Christopher Sato Lee.

CHAPTER 60

▼

A LITTLE BIT OF HEAVEN—PARADISE FOUND

Fall was looming on the Lexington lovers' horizon. And, with it, Chris's return to New York. The plan to drop the curtain on the sweetlings' first summer was hatched on a late-July evening at the crest of the highest hill of the Lee estate.

That Sunday had brought a family worship at the church that Sarah had first noticed in the reflection on the front door of the Palms. The Presbyterian congregation had recently celebrated the 200th anniversary of its founding, and the Lees and Sarah sat and sang in happy unison a year later. The service was followed by brunch at the Southern Inn Restaurant on South Main, a short walk away. A special and private tour of the Stonewall Jackson house, another short stroll away, hosted by the Lees' neighbor Bobby Fletcher was next on the agenda. The city afternoon ended with a carriage ride that filled the passengers with more history than Sarah could absorb in a single ride. Dinner at the Lees' was a barbecue of juicy, onion-spiced burgers, Gin's famous potato salad, and grilled, freshly picked sweet corn.

The hint of sunset scattered the group to attend to their Sunday evening tasks. On the crest of the hill, site of Ed's homemade golf tee box, Sarah and Chris sat under the ripening pears.

"Wow, farm boy. Quite a day."

"Yep. How's your coffee, city chick?"

"Great, and laced, I believe, you sneak." A long sip was the only pause before Sarah threw down the gauntlet. "My turn, Lee-kun."

"What?"

"What? You don't know how we older women address you younger Japanese boys?"

"Okay, Jones-sensei, *what* is your turn?"

"I have years to take in Lexington. I'm Lex-ed out. I propose a road trip. Time for me to drive the bus, steer the boat, set the course, lead the way. Get it?"

"Got it. Lead on. Where are we going?"

"Harrisburg—meet the saints who raised me. Then New York—meet your crazy friends. And then you are gonna take me to the territory I own, where I will do all the tour guiding. If we can survive all of that, maybe we can survive a few months apart. If you can survive the Jensen Beach Sarah Jones, I think I might just keep you around."

The northern tour in Chris's Jeep took five days. Sarah's saviors, Jeff and his wife Lorraine, adopted Chris quickly. They entertained and fed him well. They wished luck to the happy twosome ready to make their way to the city that never sleeps. A special dinner at Aunt Ree Ree and Uncle Mike's with the rest of the Fearless Foursome was a hit. They all fell in love with Chris's girlfriend, and she with them. It was in the Irwin Avenue confines, after a few hits of after-dinner cordials, that Grady, Drew, and Jed cleverly initiated a chant of an unwelcome, teasing ditty. "Nobody doesn't like Sara Lee."

Chris left his car and the baker's slogan, which hinted at an impending marriage, in the Bronx with Drew. The late-afternoon flight to West Palm held no surprises. The same could not be said for the arrival area. It was late afternoon, and the air was still holding a penetrating heat. Sarah had told Chris that a friend was picking them up. The friend was sitting in his Chevy pickup with a maroon and silver Harley-Davidson Ultra Classic touring bike perched on its bed.

"Hey, Joey D. This is the Christopher Sato Lee I told you about. Are we ready?"

"Gassed up, gussied up, and awaiting."

Greetings were exchanged, luggage launched into the extended cab, and the Harley brought to ground. Sarah untethered the two helmets from the bike; handed one to Chris, and motioned for him to hop on the back. Chris was not a fan of two-wheel vehicles with large motors, but he was too embarrassed to speak his fears. It was an hour of summoning courage and serious appreciation for the bike's windshield and Sarah's skills.

Joey D. greeted them again at the River Rest, got them settled into their cozy cottage, and it was off to the Starliter Saloon. Almost every staff person in the establishment greeted Sarah with a major hello accompanied by a smile and a kiss. When they found a stool at the seventy-five-foot-long, dark, beech-hard-wood bar, a middle-aged barkeep introduced as Tall Paul Campbell lit up like a teenager on prom night. After a deep lean over the top of the bar, a long hug, and an introduction of Chris, he spoke. "Best damn, best-looking tapster, besides me, of course, that I ever met. It's a waste of talent, her going to law school, if you ask me." Drinks and a couple of tails were on the house. Sarah wouldn't let Chris leave until he tried one of the peppermint martinis.

Later that night, by the time Chris caught a few units of breath, the only thing he was longing for was a pillow with a mattress beneath it and some semblance of vestibular balance.

"This is where I *really* grew up to be such a charming beauty, Chris. How do you like it?'

"Great. Uh, exhausting, surprising. Good night."

"Get your rest, big boy. Tomorrow is a busy day."

Sarah had explained earlier some of her past in this paradise. How she worked her summers here, and how much she loved it and its people.

The queen-size bed and a warm, naked Sarah snuggling behind him were exactly what the medicine man ordered.

CHAPTER 61

▼

A NEW DANCE STEP

The next morning brought a simple breakfast from the breads, juice, and coffee that Joey D. had so kindly stocked. It also brought more questions from Chris and answers from Sarah.

"I worked every summer that I was in college. Joey D. is a good friend of Jeff and Lorraine's from high school. I met him when we all came down for vacation. I fell in love with the place and Joey and his wife. The deal was made. I worked five nights a week at the Starliter, helped with the rentals, and I got this cottage for the season. I phoned Joey—this man with a heart of gold and pockets full of green—after I almost ran you over. I told him I might need a long weekend in August in old Number 3, and here we are. What can I say? I'm prone to premonition."

Sarah went on to explain much more, including that these beach towns in the summer, her bar in particular, are all about macho, mammaries, and martinis. The male clientele bring the first, the girls the second, and the martinis just help mix it up. And she enjoyed the show.

Their day swooshed its way along from a trip across the causeway, to several lazy beach hours, to a lunch at the SL Saloon.

Back at Number 3, the showered couple sat and watched Freddie Couples and Wayne Grady battle it out at the 1990 PGA at the Shoal Creek Club in Birmingham. Chris quietly commented on the irony of someone named Grady being in the hunt. When the news came on, Sarah stood and planted her perky, inviting little body in front of the TV.

"I think I've got a bit of good news for you, Mr. Lee. If you're ready, I'm prepared to take our dance to its denouement. You know that word?"

"I hope so. Am I gonna get graded on this too, teacher?"

"I don't think it will be necessary if your previous performances are any indication of your skills in this particular pastime. Come on. Follow me into our luxurious accommodations, and then I'll let you lead."

Her blond hair hung and swung over the back of the Starliter T-shirt she wore. There was no impression of anything but her underneath the shirt. Chris watched her skimpy cutoffs sway into the bedroom. She turned on her bare feet to face Chris and repeated the puckish move that she had teased him with at the end of their first date. This time there was no bra to toss at him, just the finger between the lips and the shameful eyes, and at last an invitation to a dance Chris had been waiting and hoping for. He was ready.

And so, it was here, in a small beach cottage, with a Sony boom box playing Sarah's soothing classical collection, that Chris and Sarah, who had shared passion many times before, would do so in a way new to them. A way in which they had not yet been united. Sarah's wooden canine, packed for the trip, looked down on the lucky couple from her perch on the maple dresser.

When Chris finally entered Sarah, for both it felt like falling off a cliff into a sky of urgent desire, and, when spent, landing on a cloud of calm and complete fulfillment. Both knew that this act for many did not mean much of anything, but, for Chris and Sarah, it seemed to mean everything.

CHAPTER 62

▼

DANCE ON

There were three more August days for the newly initiated couple. One included a road trip to the town of Clewiston, known as America's Sweetest Town, on Lake Okeechobee—another Sarah surprise for the enamored boy. The town is on the southern shore of the 730-square-mile body of freshwater, the United States' second largest. The Clewiston area was home to sprawling sugar cane fields and one of the United States Sugar Corporation's mills. It's not difficult to connect the city's boastful sobriquet to its primary industry. Sarah had booked a suite at the Clewiston Inn.

The high-speed, eighty-mile, ninety-five-minute ride across State Route 76, down U.S. 441, and back up U.S. 27 was close to enjoyable for Sarah's clutching lover. It was a day of boating, fishing, and clear skies that easily explained Sarah's affection for the Sunshine State. They made slow, exploring love in the suite in the late afternoon. Dinner was appetizers and beers in the Everglades Lounge with its stunning wrap-around mural of the Everglades. Still leading this dance, Sarah's startling nighttime steps included a walk to the docks of Roland and Mary Ann Martin's Marina and a passionate stop at one of the small, local parks. After trying out the various playtime apparatus, they found a grassy spot near a couple of tire swings. Chris decided it was his turn to lead once more. And lead he did—his willing and eager Sarah.

Chapter 63

▼

Culex Nigripalpus

Sarah never felt the bite. Her focus was on the man on top of her nibbling on her vulnerable earlobe. Within seconds of their mutual release, with her fingernails gripping Chris's tanned back, Sarah became one of the 226 humans who were visited by an unwelcome, winged creature in the state of Florida in 1990.

The blood feeding of the female—the only gender that bites—is quick. The dangerous disease it sometimes leaves behind only takes a week or so to show itself.

On their last night in Jensen, the couple sat on the end of Joey's dock feeding to the waters below the petals of yesterday's yellow rose. Their only concern was their pending temporary separation. There was no awareness, and, hence, no fear, of the arthropod-borne viral disease that was invading and latching onto Sarah's central nervous system. The seismic shock of the St. Louis encephalitis, informally called SLE, delivered by the Okeechobee mosquito would come later, but not much later.

The next day, the smiling, joyous lovers, now united in the most intimate manner for man and woman, said tearful goodbyes to their paradise and its people. A sadder version took place at the Palm Beach airport, as Chris and Sarah parted ways. He back to New York; she onto the world of W&L Law in Lexington and unexpected pain.

Drew drove a shaken Chris back to Lexington and Stonewall Jackson Memorial Hospital—not far at all from the site of Chris and Sarah's first encounter. And, only blocks away from their first dinner date and the church with the impressive steeple, the one Sarah fancied might be where she and Chris would pledge "union till death." Chris spent every waking hour at the hospital. Since the disease, deadly only to a small number of the bitten, is not transmissible between humans, visitors were allowed—at least early on. In one of his most exhausted moments Chris's rambling mind tripped over the ugly similarity between what might have been Sarah's married initials and the virus—SL, SLE.

A fact that paled against the reality that there is no vaccine for the mosquito malady, and there is no cure—either for the mild cases or the fatal ones.

The doctors and the blood and spinal tests confirmed the worst. Sarah's own death spiral from fever and headache to seizure, paralysis, and coma ended the morning of September 4, 1990, after only twenty-three years, four months and three days of life.

CHAPTER 64

▼

LEE CHAPEL—SEPTEMBER 6, 1990

The Lee family, Edward, Gin, Chris, Katie and Meghan, tackled the well-known twists and turns of Jacktown Road for eight-tenths of a mile to U.S. Route 60 in Edward's new Lincoln Town Car. They traveled in silence in the white, 5.0 liter, V8 motor coach on the three-mile stretch of 60 that would take them to the campus of Washington and Lee University. Chris's father had called in a favor to ensure that Sarah's request to be memorialized in Lee Chapel was fulfilled. Katie tried to sneak looks at her brother, seated in the back to her right. She saw nothing in his eyes until the car rested at the serendipitous stoplight at Main and West Nelson and waited to make a left. She caught him trying to catch the onset of a tear. As they made the turn, she caught him pretending to scratch an itch in his eye, and she recalled the energy with which he shared his tale of near death at the hands of Sarah's big Ford truck. It would be only three-tenths of a mile from the street corner, which was witness to their first magical encounter, to Lee Chapel, where Sarah's remains lay.

After parking, the family made its way robotically down the long brick path to the Romanesque redbrick structure built under the supervision of Robert E. Lee when he was president of the university, shortly after the Civil War. Chris stared straight ahead at the steeple that dominated the front of the building. The large black clock with its white numbers told him it was a minute before eleven. The long windows below the clock and the two that stood guard on either side of the entrance picked up a little glow from the warm sun. Edward moved to the front to get the brass handle of the white door on the right of the entrance. The rounded arches at the top of the windows, including the one above the door, and the ornamental, crisscrossed wood behind the glass were details that Chris took pains to point out to Sarah when they first visited the chapel together. He had plucked a small sprig of the ivy that covered most of the front of the church's lower half. It was so meticulously trimmed that Sarah had scolded him for marring even a small piece of someone else's work of art. Today, Chris took no joy in this classic piece of history and artistry. He knew that inside there was only sadness to be dealt with.

At exactly 11:00 AM on Thursday, September 6, 1990, Chris Lee and his family left the sunshine of the day behind and traded it in for the somber environs of Lee Chapel. He had waited till the last possible minute to enter the current, temporary home of Sarah Jones. What was on the altar was *not* the energized body and spirited mind of his new lover—not even close. Harrison Funeral Home and Crematory, just down the road on Main Street, made sure of that.

Chris had requested that many of the lights in the chapel be left off. There were only a few left on that helped illuminate the front of the chapel. The pieces of the eleven-inch-long, seven-inch-wide, six-inch-high cherrywood box had been expertly routed and trimmed. The lone, well-polished adornment on the altar sat on a marble stand a few feet to the right of the centered lectern. The only flowers in the entire chapel were two dozen yellow roses in a simple pewter vase placed next to Sarah's ashes.

What was inside the beautiful box was approximately five pounds of white ash—the result of two hours of 1500-degree heat and flames ravaging the casket and body of Sarah Jones, age twenty-three.

On the lower level of the chapel, in the second of the center pews that were painted white with dark trim, Chris sat flanked on the left by his mother and on the right by the disconsolate Katie. After Chris and his family were seated, the organist droned out "The Lord is My Shepherd" on the modest-looking organ housed on the second tier of the chapel. Reverend Gregory Coffey, dressed in funeral vestments, made his way to the podium. Chris stared intently as the minister spoke, yet chose—as he had many times in Miss Carney's boring, seventh-grade geography class—not to absorb a single word. Katie had no use for looking at or listening to the minister. She was extremely pissed off at God and his damn mosquitoes at the moment. Her teary eyes had trouble focusing on her left hand that was entwined with her brother's right, lying limply at the end of his stiffened arm.

After the minister ended a very elegant and sensitive talk with lots of words speaking to tragedy and unexpected loss, the organist's fingers sprung back to morbid life to play another tenebrific selection. Coffey's homily was truly moving to most, but impotent when it came to soothing Chris's sorrow. Gin Sato, Chris's mother, rose from the second-row aisle seat and moved up to replace the Reverend Coffey.

Katie looked up for a moment and wondered how anyone could ever do what her mother was about to do without going to pieces. Her brother, still stiff, still staring straight ahead at the lectern, opened his mind and his ears. What he was about to hear, he knew, were Sarah's own words—her self-penned eulogy that she had created as soon as things started going south.

Gin cleared her throat, put on her reading glasses, and straightened out the front of the black jacket she wore over the quiet, gray, silk blouse. She first looked out at some of the faces already looking back at her. Her family, Chris's friends, the few friends that Sarah had made in the short time she had been in Lexington. She briefly scanned the others—Sarah's adoptive parents, Jeff and Lorraine, Drew's Aunt Ree Ree and Uncle Mike, some of Gin's own family's friends, and some faces she had never seen before. After taking in her audience, she turned her focus to the single, handwritten page in front of her. She had memorized most of it the night before. Now looking at it, she wasn't sure whose tears stained what words. She did know that the paper held some of Sarah's, and that she had contributed a number of her own when she first read it.

Gin began with her own words. "I have been given the privilege and honor of reading to you Sarah's last written words, a privilege and honor that pale in comparison to the experience of having known our devilish angel for such a short time."

Gin fiddled with the silver locket that hung from her neck. It was rectangular, somewhat book-like in shape, with a subtle "S" etched on the front. It was a locket that Sarah had Katie buy before she died. It was one of four. Gin, Katie, and Chris's youngest sister, Meghan, were each given one by Sarah. The small picture inside was one of Sarah and Chris sitting on the dock in Jensen Beach, the orange sun setting behind them spilling its radiance on the waters of the Indian River. Inside, the left page of the locket read, in tiny letters,

Another place
Another time

Gin "ahemed" one more time and began a journey she wished she did not have to take. One paved with Sarah's own thoughts courageously committed to the piece of paper Gin held.

"I had hoped to have these words delivered in my *own* voice to those of you who have been kind enough to say farewell today. They would have been recorded sounds, but still my own. But the wind that has carried my voice these twenty-some years is now but a wisp, barely audible, not particularly joyous.

"I burden the graciousness of Mrs. Lee, one of the new and precious souls whom I have been able to call friend. A favor asked one last time because she is a spirit who knows the depth of loving and can speak my words with true understanding.

"I've always loved the phrase 'blessed be the brief.' I shall be so.

"I have had one lifetime of sorrow, one lifetime of healing, and a final lifetime of treasures with Christopher, so pure, so precious, that it would be selfish of me to grieve for my own loss of the future.

"Thank you all who have been generous enough to share your love and friendship. To those who have the chance, please, please take care of my Christopher. Help him in any way you can to stay always Best in Class.

"My final request is to Christopher alone.

"Spread my ashes to the sea. Let them swim their way into the ocean and wash back to the sand and touch the tender foot of a child.

"Let a few come to rest on the footprints that you and I made together on the beach, and let the rest fill in the space in the 'sands of what might have been.'"

Gin paused and scanned her listeners. Then, with a hint of a smile, she went on with the last of Sarah's words.

"It's time to let y'all off the hook now. I'm betting that Jacktown Road has more food and spirits than you can handle. Go on and enjoy. Hopefully the sun is shining on the hills and waters.

"I hope I'm moving on to somewhere as peaceful, and so should you all."

Reverend Coffey walked Gin back to her pew, and closed the ceremony with more elegance. "Most funerals mourn the loss of a remembered past. Today we sorrowfully mourn the loss of a bright and promising future ..." The organist made a futile effort to give hope to the living with her rendition of "Amazing Grace." The Lees were the first to leave the chapel. As Chris left the building and its crypt that housed the bodies of Robert E. Lee and his family behind, he carried the smooth, cherrywood box with him.

The only request that Chris had made other than the dimmed lights inside the chapel was to lay the twenty-four yellow roses from the altar on the side of the chapel's brick path. A loose bundle of twenty-three at the path's beginning from the chapel door and a single at its end.

In charge, even facing death, Sarah had also written a short note to Chris, which he carried in his wallet. "I know you know exactly where to spread my ashes. Do it soon, my dear Christopher, and move on. Sorrow is for the sad. The best of you is in your joy. Share it. Thanks for 'The Dance.' Dance on."

That night, after the meal of plenty at the Lee home and all the condolences dispensed by family and friends between sips of bourbon, beer, and Bolla, Chris sat at the top of the hill on his father's land. He eyed a scattering of stars in the dark sky. He read Sarah's note for the tenth time and remembered the words of the Garth Brooks song—words he had not paid any attention to on the night of their second date, stinging words, yet words painfully true for him. He took a final, long drink from the still-cold can of Coors and stood up. He looked down at the note once more and softly whispered, "Sarah Jones, you are very welcome. The pleasure of our dance was all mine."

CHAPTER 65

▼

GOLDIE'S GRAVE

"Gentlemen, welcome to the final resting place of the Quisenberry Family. Old Harry here, a dentist, died in 1947, at the age of seventy. Wife Effa made it to eighty-five when she passed away nineteen years later. If you can read through the green mold on the gravestone with the angel on top, you'll see it shows that Goldie Elizabeth lived fewer than six years. The smaller tombstone next to it just says 'Infant' with only a single date. Probably stillborn.

"This is where I truly fell in love with Sarah. I think maybe before we sat here, I was in love with the idea of being in love. Sarah went on about the question of whose death must have been saddest for Harry and Effa. She voted for Goldie. It was the idea that watching her grow and dreaming of her future must have been such a joy for the parents. A joy ripped from them too soon. And, then, the still-born baby two years later bringing back the first tragedy.

"Sarah had been a lot of things. Funny, sexy, surprising, energetic, smart, pretty ... Here she showed me her soul. Her sorrow for Goldie and her parents was so genuine. She said she did not want to be an Effa. She wanted a flock of healthy kids running around the house, breaking things, and laughing. She was going to name the first girl Goldie. I was ready to ask her to marry me right then. I should have. I waited too long." Chris paused for a minute.

The Fearless Foursome was sitting in the Stonewall Jackson Memorial Cemetery the day after the funeral. They had replaced their Sunday-go-to-meeting outfits with jeans and polo shirts. Drew looked his beautiful self. Grady's hair needed mowing more than the grass they sat on. Jed and Chris looked the most somber. As Chris talked, the other three were silent, almost tearful. And Chris sensed it.

"Okay, cooler boy. It's five o'clock somewhere. Beers around please. And don't worry; I've cleared it with my friends in the department."

Grady pulled out four cans of Bud from the cooler that Drew, Jed, and Grady had brought into town from Drew's home. They had picked Chris up on the way. The trio was not sure what Chris had in mind when he asked that they come here the day after the funeral. But they came.

"Sarah and I toasted here to the souls of the unfortunate Quisenberrys. So now, we'll toast to Sarah."

After a long first sip of the afternoon, Chris went on.

"Okay. Now I am going to tell our story this once. Tell more than you probably need to know. Maybe I'm doing it for myself. I don't know. It just needs to be told. So, I would appreciate it if you, now my closest friends in the world, drink up and listen up."

Except for one short break to stretch legs, Chris spoke for an hour straight.

The boys knew some of the two lovers' history from Chris and Sarah's recent visit to New York. Chris's recitation was full of detail, both physical and emotional. All taken in together, very moving.

Chris gave a smile when he told of the "Ford Truck versus Chris" incident on the southwest corner of Nelson and Main—his introduction to lovely Sarah. He moved through their first date at the Palms, their first meal at Sarah's place across the street from where they were presently sitting, the trip to Jensen and ensuing Harley rides, and a lot of what transpired in between. The other three were a little surprised and a bit embarrassed when Chris recalled the particulars of Sarah and his intimate moments. There was no melancholy in his voice but a lifetime of feelings in his words.

"That's it, guys. After today, I am going to put on a protective shroud of denial. I do not want to spend my time reflecting on the fragility of life, mine included. I want to get on with what's in front of me. We should all do the same. It's much healthier. That's what Sarah Jones asked of me before she died. I don't plan to let her down.

"One other thing. No more me being best-in-class talk. Together we are the best. Together we are much stronger than any of us alone.

"Oh, sorry, one more last thing. Sarah taught me that a touch is worth a thousand words. So get up and give me a hug. I need it.

"Lunch at the Palms is on me."

The thunderstorms that never came a few months ago on the Pipestem golf course showed up with a drenching, driving force later that afternoon—washing over Goldie Quisenberry's gravestone.

CHAPTER 66

▼

"Ladies and gentlemen, we are beginning our descent into Washington Dulles Airport. Please make sure your tray tables are secured and your seats are in their upright position."

Jed recognized the voice of Daniela, his new angel of the airways and drinking buddy. She went on to thank everyone for flying with them. His last thoughts during the plane ride, which was helping him make his way to the 2005 episode of the Pipestem outing, were of that hour in Stonewall's cemetery. How he himself had thought of the most mournful moments of his own life, and how nothing he had yet to know had compared to Chris's loss.

He got a bit of an emotional lift as he deplaned.

"Thanks for flying us, Mr. Davies. I hope I see you again."

Jed stifled his instinctive, libidinal response that Daniela's words evoked and simply said, "My pleasure."

During his drive down Interstate 81, his thoughts were stuck on Chris. Not his tragedy, but the amazing post-tragedy success. How Chris returned to John Jay and continued acing his way through the final year. Chris's passion in taking on Washington and Lee Law School to get his law degree—maybe in honor of Sarah. And his rise through the ranks in the FBI. Jed mused that, based on Chris's phenomenal rebound, his 1990 request to cut the "Best in Class" chatter had hollowed. His dark haired, still-single-after-all-these-years buddy was still BIC.

As he guided the Avis Chevy Tahoe onto exit 188 in search of Route 60 and Lexington, he surprised himself by talking out loud. First about his Jesus H. problem and then on to better thoughts.

"Maybe Chris and the rest of the boys can lend me some insight into this mess. Shed a little light on the mystery of *who are these guys?* Yeah, like the *Justice League* heroes or maybe the *Four Musketeers.*

"Damn. Why couldn't these nuts crucify poor Jesus somewhere else, like Iowa or something?

"Oh, hell. Screw the crown of thorns. Bring on Pipestem.

"Ladies and gentlemen, we are making our final descent onto Jacktown Road. Please make sure your golf clubs are cleaned and ready. We hope you enjoy your stay."

Little did Jed know he was also descending into a deeper pool of problems.

PART III

▼

ONE IS THE LONELIEST NUMBER

"In violence we forget who we are."

~ Mary McCarthy

CHAPTER 67

▼

WAKE-UP CALL—JUNE 24, 2005

The yellow cab jounced east along 40th Street in the dark morning and took a right onto Fifth Avenue. The "Smallest Altar Boy," the large man's nickname, was at the wheel. Like the vehicle traveling in the black night, its driver was in the dark about the cargo in his cab's trunk. His instructions were simple. Just pull in front of the Mid-Manhattan Library at 4:00 AM. When a van pulls behind and blinks its headlights twice, pop the latch on the trunk. Wait for a double knock on the closed trunk and get the hell out.

The second driver was behind the wheel of a blue van that boasted the skills and 24-hour emergency service of Ryan's Electric Contractors on its side. He was guessing that the blood inside the "package" in the taxi's trunk had congealed by now. When the van stopped behind the cab, the man in the van's passenger's seat, dressed in dark blue overalls and an oversized cap, jumped out and started checking the front tire. The driver, identically clad, flashed his lights to signal for an open trunk and alighted from the van. With his two gloved hands, he retrieved the bloody package. It was already a humid 64 degrees and breezy under the Friday morning full moon. The knocks on the ass end of the yellow Ford Crown Vic sent Altar Boy on his way. The van's driver carefully stepped over the curb, crossed the empty sidewalk, and walked up the few steps to the landing behind a large stone statue of a lion—one of two guarding the entrance to the library. There he deposited the boxed prize. He double-checked to make sure no one was around in the darkness, sliced around the bottom edges of the box with his cutter, and removed the top and sides. Within seconds the van and the two workers had put the largest city public library in the U.S of A. and its ten million books in their rearview mirror.

The warm, shallow, and calm waters of Sarasota Bay had only a few vessels making waves at 3:30 AM on the same murky morning of the Altar Boy's delivery. The same full moon that lit up the New York night shone down from a clear sky on the 72-degree, pre-dawn scene. One of the bay's vessels carried a second special and bloody delivery. The three propellers of the thirty-four-foot Catalina yacht aided her two white sails in its early-morning adventure. The Daiwa fishing rods planted in holders at the back of the boat gave a false promise of imminent angling. The sleek ship cruised its way to the shores that washed the backside of the sixty-six acre Ringling estate. The grounds were home to the John and Mable Ringling Museum of Art, a separate circus museum and the Cà d'Zan mansion. The Venetian Gothic "House of John," first occupied by the circus man and his bride in 1926, was a 200-foot-long structure containing thirty-two rooms and fifteen baths. In 1946, seventeen years after the death of Mable and ten after John's, the Ringling estate was finally settled. That same year the donated landmark with all its art and furnishings that John had willed to the state was opened to visitors. It has since been one of Florida's most famous tourist stops.

Two divers in wetsuits made their way up to the cockpit of the Catalina and out into the bay waters at 3:45 AM. The ship's captain released the eight-foot-long Sevylor Fish Hunter from its ties to the Catalina. The divers joined the two Fortress anchors and the package—much like the one on Fifth Avenue—that had been loaded onto the raft. They quietly motored the pea green PVC boat to within five feet of the mansion's old stone dock.

The thirteen steps above the worn dock, where Ringling used to moor his yacht *Zalophus*, led to an eight-thousand-square-foot terrace of variegated marble. On a normal Friday, the gates that led to the grounds would be opened to welcome thousands of visitors. *This would not be a normal Friday.* And at 10:00 AM, disgruntled tourists would be informed that the attraction was closed until further notice. The sun that would glimmer down on the beautiful terrace and the colorful terra cotta exterior of the *Cà d'Zan* on this day would only warm a few mystified lawmen.

The men in wetsuits climbed out of the raft. Each took one anchor to either side of the boat. They planted the anchors deep enough in the bay's floor to secure the floating craft. The two then placed the package on the seat of the raft and removed the square, green cloth that had been covering it. The divers checked the two nylon ropes that were fastened to the package and secured them to the anchor lines. By the light of the moon, they could see their mother ship circling back to the drop point. The expert swimmers had no trouble navigating their way safely back to the Catalina.

Dawn would come in less than two hours for midtown Manhattan and Florida's west coast.

Shortly after sunrise, Karen Hill, a corporate attorney, was in the cool-down phase of her two-mile workout. Her route was methodically the same. It was only a few more blocks to her 39th Street condo when she noticed a glint of light bouncing off an object on the landing of the Mid-Manhattan Library. Curiosity pushed her up the steps. The reality she saw pushed a scream out from deep in her lungs. The previously peaceful, mid-city setting soon turned entropic.

At 6:00 AM, Johnny Harper, a handsome and rugged security guard at the Ringling estate, was the first to make the rounds of the *Cà d'Zan* mansion and its surroundings. The Sevylor Fish Hunter was lazily bobbing in the bay. A glint, similar to the one witnessed by Karen Hill in New York, caught his eye. The sight made him catch his breath. There would be no clowning around on the beautiful grounds of the famous circus man on this day.

Jesus Cruz was no longer the *lone* celebrity in the Broker's bloody doings.

CHAPTER 68

▼

PIPESTEM

Three days before the East Coast's two most populated states woke up to the gruesome "gifts" presented by the drivers and divers, the reunion with his three friends and a few beers had pushed any thoughts of Jesus H. out of Jed's mind. The challenges of Pipestem 2005 owned his consciousness at least for a few days. It was hard, but enjoyable, to believe that he and his three buddies had remained so close for the fourteen years since they had graduated.

The night of June 21, 2005, brought the usual exquisite repast and hospitality of the Edward and Gin Lee Lexington home. By the time dessert and the bourbon-spiked Cafe Royal were served, the talk had turned to golf. Ed and Gin excused themselves with kitchen duty as their convenient justification. And the game before the games was on.

The next two days at Pipestem were true to a forecast of warm and dry weather.

Not much had changed over the years. As the Fearless Foursome greeted each morning's dew, familiar happenings took place with predictable repetition. As usual, Grady was long and wrong. Jed managed to scramble to a respectable score, and Chris and Drew battled for best on course. The only testy golf course moment came on day one when Grady was lining up a four-foot putt on 18 for his only chance at par on the day. A putt that would give him a 114.

"Come on, for crying out loud, Gradster. Could you please hit the damn ball before Pam Anderson's tits are sagging down to her knees and we're all on Viagra?"

Chris's comment brought laughs from two of the three. Grady never lifted his head, *until* he stroked the ball. Very bad technique. Jed gave him the two-footer comeback for a bogey. Grady gave Chris the finger and his $100 Odyssey two-ball putter a nasty fling in Chris's direction. That night Grady had a little too much to drink. Not a good combination with the medication he was taking—a selective serotonin reuptake inhibitor, or SSRI.

He was mad at Chris and his trick, and he let him know it.

Grady's first nine the next morning rendered a few X's on his scorecard, but, thankfully for all, his back nine was almost respectable.

The second night took on a much different flavor than the first when Drew asked Jed about his Jesus H. case. Speculation ran rampant in Jed's three friends' dialogue, and only served to feed his own previous frustration. The other three were hungry for up-close-and-personal detail. Jed did not disappoint, but any hope he had had that his friends might lend valuable insight was dimmed. No *Justice League* miracle here. The evidence had the taste of bad, sugar-free candy. A satisfactory "case closed" did not seem to be in the offing.

Each of Jed's friends' bedtime ruminations were dominated by the gory image of the crucified Jesus Cruz—an occurrence all too familiar to the cop from Los Angeles.

Brainiac Drew Birdsall topped off the evening of horrific, homicidal discussion with, "The history of man is the history of crimes ..." The blond Adonis gave proper attribution for the quote to Simon Wiesenthal, a Nazi death camp survivor and the most famous of pursuers of the vicious criminals responsible for the Holocaust.

CHAPTER 69

▼

RISE AND SHINE

The third morning brought a sky painted with a few more clouds but the same pleasant temperatures. As was tradition on the third day, Jed and Drew prepared an early-morning breakfast of pan-fried sausage patties and scrambled eggs. Due to a lack of concern for starting the chicken's fruit with a clean pan, the eggs always emerged with a blackish-tan hue.

The two chefs were banging the dirty dishes around in the small sink when Chris finally gave the weather channel's looping reports a rest. Hoping to see "Imus in the Morning" on MSNBC, Chris was disappointed at first to see two talking newsheads on the screen. The screen had the incessant "BREAKING NEWS" banner near the bottom of the screen. His disappointment quickly morphed into curiosity as he read the crawler. He took the box off mute and jacked up the volume.

"Holy shit!"

The dishes ceased their banging, and Grady emerged from the bathroom as Chris blurted out his expletive.

The pretty brunette anchor introduced another pretty brunette standing outside the New York City Mid-Manhattan Library.

> "Shortly before 6:00 AM this morning, a New York City attorney discovered the decapitated head of an unknown male placed on the landing of the library, directly in back of the stone lion you see behind me. Before the police secured the scene, another early-morning jogger came upon this ghoulish scene and

captured a brief video on his cell phone. Mr. Robert Gillen, a Verizon employee, has given us permission to air his video. I have to warn our viewers that what you will see is extremely gruesome."

The video was a bit grainy but did not fail to portray the qualities the reporter had predicted. It was easy to make out the head, lying in a pool of drying blood, encased inside of a square, clear, glass or Lucite container. The head appeared to rest on some type of metal tray or platter. The bodiless man had very long, dark hair that was matted on his head and helped to mask any other distinct facial features.

The reporter went on for another four minutes about what the police had to say, or not to say, and turned it back to the anchor team.

"Isn't that your precinct, Grady?"

The frozen, speechless redhead just nodded in response to Drew's question. It was indeed Grady's territory, a prize precinct that included notable landmarks—Times Square, Madison Square Garden, the Theatre District, Penn and Grand Central Stations, the Empire State Building *and* the New York Public Library.

The Fearless Foursome watched for another ten minutes until repetition forced the question. "What do you want to do, Grady?" This time it was Chris asking the question. The darkening hue of Grady's visage was a close match to the red of his hair. His three friends were anticipating more fury, reminiscent of his Wednesday night blowup. Instead, what they got from the clearly pissed off New York City cop was a calm, simple, "Let's go play some golf. By the time I got back there today, there would be no room for me to join in the chaos."

The rest of the day brought more shocking surprises to the duffers. Grady quietly went about his game. Drew did not entertain the others with his incredible grasp of the world's minutia and beat Chris by two strokes. Jed, haunted and distracted by the nagging feeling that the head on the library step might somehow be related to his Jesus H., shot ten strokes over his handicap. When Grady rolled in a thirteen-footer on the 125-yard, number seventeen hole for a birdie two, they all realized even a double bogey on the 399-yard eighteenth would give him a ninety-nine. When Grady O'Connor tapped in a 10-incher for a five and a magical ninety-eight, the early-morning's shock and anger had seriously dissipated.

The celebration moved on from the eighteenth green to the back deck of Mulligans Sports Lounge in the clubhouse. On the wooden deck, the foursome looked down on the site of Grady's final and famous stroke and ordered sandwiches and lots of beer. Three of the four were reveling in Grady's good fortune. Chris was unusually quiet. Drew thought it might be because he had beaten him. It was not a common occurrence for Chris to lose.

Drew thought wrong. His mind was on sadder things.

Grady was more than put off by Chris's shunning of the celebration. The feat meant so much to Grady. And apparently so little to the man that had tainted his first shot at the under-100 club so many years ago.

It hurt, perhaps even more than what Chris had done to him before, when he thought it was *so damn funny* to move the flag on his first chance to break the magic mark.

CHAPTER 70

▼

BAPTISM OF SHOCK

After a few beers, Jed, grinning widely at Grady's breakthrough, made a trip to the men's room. On his way back, he decided to call his wife. He noticed that the phone had a message waiting. He had left the phone in his bag during the round and never heard the original call. He retrieved and listened, and paled.

"What the hell's wrong, Jed?" Drew, the first to see Jed's face upon return, asked.

"Everything. We gotta go."

On the way back to their cabin, Jed gave a brief fill-in on his wife's news.

A quick click of the remote took them back to MSNBC with a new pair of good-looking anchors, a parade of reporters, taped and live interviews—civilian and official—and the shocking news that had drained the blood from Jed's face.

> "The police have identified the man whose head was left on the steps of the New York City Public Library early this morning. His name is John Baptista, a resident of the South Bronx. Believed to be in his mid-thirties. Only known family is a younger brother named Alex. That's about all that has been released. They have sequestered the first witnesses on the scene."

The four sat silently on the main room's chairs and watched as they showed the video again and waited.

"We switch you now to our local NBC affiliate, WFLA in Tampa, Florida. Rhonda Wiggins is in Sarasota, the scene of today's brutal murder. Rhonda, can you hear us?"

Another pretty brunette filled the screen.

"Yes, I can, Kristin. Thank you. Well, it's been a most bizarre day here, matching the eerie scene on the steps of the New York City Public Library. The head of the victim down here was discovered around 6:00 AM by a security guard at the famous Ringling estate on the shore of Sarasota Bay. By ten this morning, the identity of the man was released by the police. A French passport sealed in some type of waterproof casing, with the name of Jean Baptiste and a picture of the dead man, was found in the small raft that carried the severed and bloody head. The clear containers that both heads were found in appear to be identical, and the few eyewitness accounts we have been able to get indicate that both heads were placed on some type of metal platter."

After Rhonda's wrap-up, things went back to the main desk of MSNBC in Secaucus, New Jersey, and Kristin Simonetti. She and her fellow anchor spent twenty minutes going through the day's timeline. They moved on to speculation that sounded more like conclusions, not yet confirmed by anyone in authority.

For the four golfers sitting in the West Virginia cabin glued to the TV—three of them, officers of the law and one, a lawyer not unfamiliar with the world of law and order—and for any other person with an IQ higher than today's temperature, there was no doubt. The two bloody displays and the acts that led to them were not just related but superglued together. The MSNBC newscasters moved on to ask the question about the possible connection of these murders to the famous Jesus H. crucifixion at the Hollywood sign only three weeks earlier. They implied no conclusion.

Jed stood up. "No doubt in my mind. None, zip, zero. Shit. Here we go again."

"None in mine either," Drew said. "Do you know whose feast day *this* is?"

No moaning this time from the three who normally bristled at the trivia that Drew frequently provided.

"Saint John the Baptist." Drew paused and watched faces. "Funny though, it's not the date of his death but his birth. Other than the Big J himself, only he and the Virgin Mary are celebrated on their birth dates. Catholic theologians believe John was cleansed of original sin in the womb and, therefore, along with Mary, earned sainthood without having to die."

The night led to more boob tube watching and a meal retrieved from the Bluestone Dining Room in Pipestem's McKeever Lodge. Theories and next possible steps were discussed. There would be no golf in the morning. Jed needed to get back to LA. Grady, now demonstrating his anger through strings of expletives, wanted in on the New York case. This was his ground, and someone had soiled it badly. Jed had the Tahoe, so, on the road in the morning it would be.

After they had had enough of the news stations and a variety of cocktails, they rose to search out their respective beds.

As he had done the night before, Drew had the last word.

"Gents, I failed to finish Simon Wiesenthal's brilliant observation last night."

They stared him down.

"The history of man is the history of crimes, *and history can repeat.* So information is a defence. Through this we can build, we must build, a defence against repetition."

Jed's painful lack of defense information and knowledge turned and tossed him through the night with the words, "Who are these damn people?" pounding continuously on and on.

CHAPTER 71

▼

THE RECRUITS—JUNE 2004 TO FEBRUARY 2005

Gilbert Osborne Dickerson had an impeccable history of depravity.

A colony of one of the 11,880 species of ants in the world had built their home in Gil's neighborhood. They were his first form of torturous entertainment. The first few he captured were treated to Gil pissing on them in a mayonnaise jar just to see if they could swim. The six-year-old demon moved on to dressing the Hellmann's container with a dose of diazanon, pilfered from Dad's tool shed, to see how long it took for the six-legged creatures to go belly up. His insect finale was a theatrical treat. He placed a large pack of his starved little buggers and a pile of ant corpses in a Tupperware container and watched the live eat their dead. Gilbert then placed the sated, still-caged, and still-kicking ants into an aluminum bucket filled with gasoline. A strike of a match brought on the mass, silent, and sticky cremation.

Gil, whose crack-addicted mother called him her "little GOD," using his initials to form the sobriquet, moved up the food chain to four-legged creatures. Cats and chlorine, canines and cuts, deep and wide, kept his interest for a number of years. He eventually reached his apex of agony when he planted the rusty axe from the family barn in the middle of his father's skull. Days later, when the nearest neighbor was concerned about the lack of activity at the Dickerson farm, the police found Gilbert still exploring the human anatomy—his father's. Mom was strung out in the bedroom.

The day Gilbert was finally released from the 210-bed, maximum-security Central New York Psychiatric Center located in Marcy, New York, a fit-looking woman wearing a gray habit with a large gold cross hanging from her neck greeted him at the gates. Together they would make the 240-mile trip down the New York State Thruway from Utica to Yonkers en route to a halfway house for Mrs. Dickerson's "little GOD." At the age of twenty-three Gilbert was a big and strong man, deemed to be socially viable. His looks might place that assessment into question. He was reputed to be as dumb as a bag of hammers but a superstar when it came to following very specific directions.

He had a large head and his puffy forehead protruded over the sockets of his eyes. His cheeks were oversized, and, matched with the forehead, gave the impression that his beady eyes had been hammered into his skull. His nose was snouty and wide in the nostrils. A small chin receded beneath the narrow lips that surrounded his smallish mouth. His hair was a scary red and army trimmed. Other than a sparse patch of pubic hair, the rest of his body was fuzz free.

Socially viable? Only time would tell.

Useful for the Broker's purposes? Absolutely.

Sable Turner, named by her mother for the expensive black fur her husband had given her when she announced her pregnancy, had a very different childhood than big Gilbert. The daughter of the two college-educated parents sailed through her first eighteen years like one of the Brady girls—bright, behaved, and beautiful. Her next four years started with a precipitous drop off of the pedestal that her parents had put her on. Her introduction to college life and its opportunities lit a fuse long repressed. The igniter came in the form of her first-year roommate, Eileen. Her roommate was well versed in all of the games that Sable had politely shunned out of fear. Within the first week of dorm life in a large southern university Eileen introduced her curious and willing roomie to the pleasurable distraction of liquor and recreational drugs. The grateful Sable did not take long to move onto the sex she had so long wondered about. First with one of the many horny college boys. And then sometimes with Eileen. Before the end of the first semester, sometimes with both.

Her unleashed passions led to an abbreviated college education, disownment by Mom and Dad, and eventually into the lucrative profession of escort. Her role as a highly paid attendant usually included all of the things she had chosen to major in at college. The Broker knew Sable and a number of the other women who pursued their careers under the tutelage of Miss Melissa, a New York City madam, with an impressive enterprise and an even more impressive clientele list. The Broker negotiated with Miss Melissa to contract Sable out to him for a few critical missions. Miss M. owed the Broker, and the tall, slim, irresistible, dark-haired Sable with the perky little tits and sparkling brown eyes was always up for new adventures.

The list of handpicked recruits ran into double digits.

There was "Trip." Born Bobby Blatney, he grew to be a large boy, a larger man, all muscle, with a touch of daring. His nickname had morphed from Big Bobby B, to Triple B to Trip. He had done some muscle work for the Broker in the past and was known to be reliable and tight-lipped.

There were a few more like him. One named the "Smallest Altar Boy," not because of his overall dimensions but for a lack of serious length and girth revealed in Saint Mark's grammar school gym showers. In high school he would grow up and out of the derisive hazing. More than a few who had christened him with the diminutive label suffered later at the hands of the growing, young, well-endowed Bobby Jones.

Completing the muscle brigade was Bubba Waugh. Strong and tall like the other two but with quite a bit more experience. He would take the lead on the heavy lifting parts of the Broker's blueprint for success.

Neither Trip nor Bubba could quite match Gilbert or the Altar Boy for brute strength, but both had the other two beat by a mile in the looks and brains departments.

There was one more of Sable's bent, only a little more educated. Her name was Patty. Juana, sans habit and gold cross, interviewed Patty for a specific role in the Broker's elaborate plan. The whore looked young by the standards Juana had adopted based on her habitual viewing of *NYPD Blue* and the *Law and Order* triumvirate. Unlike the trollops portrayed on television, she had none of the facial aging trying desperately to hide behind pounds of Revlon's finest. None of the drawn looks that usually accompanied the profession's dietary supplement of heavy drugs were on this young girl's face.

What did show on the lightly made-up, round face was a look of surprise. She had expected her client to have a dick that he would want her to service in some fashion, but in front of her stood a beautiful woman in her 30's. It would have been a first for the well-paid employee of Capital Massage Services. *What the hell? Money's the same*, she thought. And the money was good.

The "Have Table Will Travel" masseuse actually did hold a degree in massage therapy and was certified. She was also efficient when it came to her real mission. Once the door was closed, the courtesan took off her snow-dusted, tan New Zealand lambskin coat and draped it over one of the chairs in the hotel room. Then, with a single move, the short-skirted, silky dress fell to the floor. The descending of the shiny black garment revealed bare and ample breasts with perfect, salmon-colored nipples. The end of the descent showed a shapely, fit body, clothed only now in a deep purple thong. There was not a single hair to be seen on this beautiful specimen.

"My name is Patty. What can I do for you tonight, beautiful lady?"

It reminded Juana of the opening of FX's *Nip/Tuck,* another of Juana's guilty TV pleasures. The words of the obligatory, "So, tell us what you don't like about yourself" were different, but the practiced smile and the tone was the same.

Juana indulged in a real-time, guilty, yet new, pleasure. She took a minute to look at the beautiful shape in front of her. The pleasure part was interrupted by a stinging tinge of jealousy when she focused on the erect and splendid nipples of her hired Patty. For a lascivious second, Juana wondered what it would be like to be Patty—to be with Patty. But this was business, and the young, now impatient, girl with her whole womanhood intact, was staring straight at her when she spoke.

"It's chilly in here, honey, can I get under the covers?"

Juana took one visual last drink of the masseuse in front of her.

"Patty, please call me Juana. And, please, put your clothes back on."

"What? Juana? What kind of name is that, and what's going on here? If my boss gets a bad report, lady, I'm screwed. I need the money."

"Patty, relax. Get your clothes on and sit. Wine, beer, vodka?"

"Just water, please, and a goddamned explanation."

"How would you like to take six months off?"

"What? Well, do you know how much I ..."

"I know almost everything about you. Now, how about a massage while I explain a few things."

Along with these colorful recruits, there was an eclectic group of enlisted men and women with a wide range of talents and powerful connections. All specifically targeted to support the plan that the Broker had conceived. For nine months, the recruiting process moved stealthily on, and some of the upfront money that the Broker had funded changed hands.

Juana was the first of the Broker's recruits. She would become more than a soldier in the Broker's special forces. The Broker and the Latino beauty made a great pair when it came to assembling what would be needed to pull off their dangerous and costly game. The Broker had more contacts than Bausch and Lomb. Juana could persuade her way into heaven and wheedle her way out of hell. The master planner was confident that together they could solve Carmine's problem.

CHAPTER 72

▼

BEGINNINGS IN BALTIMORE—JUNE 2004

Before Jesus H.—Before the Johns

"The place is really coming along, Rick."

"Yeah, Carm. My contractor, Stan Lewicki, has done a great job. This is the last of six. I'm liking it so much I just might not flip it like the others. I've customized the place for our upcoming work. Maybe I'll just keep it and join Baltimore Country Club. Can never belong to too many clubs, huh?

"Hang on, Carm. Grab a drink."

The Broker spoke into his cell phone, "Yeah, that's right. Stay on 95 to exit 53. Then jump on 395 for about a mile. You'll pass the Ravens' stadium and then Camden Yards. Stay right onto Conway. Right onto Sharp. Left onto Barre, and Hanover will be on your right. Good. There's a space for you in the back alley behind my building. Remember how to get in there? Good. See you in thirty minutes or so."

Carmine Antobelli asked, "Juana?"

"Yeah."

Location, location, location. The Broker's place was just east of Camden Yards, a little northeast of the football stadium and a tad southwest of Harborplace, Charm City's premier shopping, dining, and entertainment center.

For tonight's meeting—the first of the Pelham 1-2-3—another popular Baltimore landmark, a block east and a few south, would be providing the sushi, crab cakes, and steamed shrimp. Sometimes the Broker thought the Cross Street Market and its banquet of vendors, all with fresh eats, might be enough reason to keep his newly renovated rowhouse. Rick's place, one of many undergoing reclamation and transformation in this area of Baltimore, was one of a long row of brick structures. The steps were new brick; the rest was the original deal, needing special care and treatment to bring it along for the ride to a stylish rebirth. Inside, the entire right side wall was of the old brick. New sheet rock hung on the rest of the aged wood framing. The basement had been excavated to add several feet of height. Enough for an average man to walk through, and, in Rick's case, provide a home for some of the electronics he was so fond of—all connected through the home by a maze of wires hidden behind the new drywall.

The first of three levels above ground was taken up by a large kitchen, a half bath, and one large sitting room. The walls were painted a quiet shade of tan. The floors were a dark hardwood throughout. New, cherrywood bookshelves lined one wall with a 37-inch HD Sony in the center. Leather lounge chairs and cherrywood end tables populated the rest of the room.

The second floor was sleeping quarters. Two large bedrooms, each with its own full bath, shared a wide hallway. The hall and bedroom one were painted in a pleasing light-rose color. Bedroom two, the Broker's, was walled with more cherrywood bookshelves throughout. The plush Karastan that ran throughout the second floor had a slight rose tint to it. The walls were decorated with various small pictures of flowers and landscapes.

The third floor seemed a bit schizophrenic. Half the floor was a comfortable, tan-carpeted den setup with a La-Z-Boy couch splitting the room and a large Sony HD between the two windows on the front wall. The floor on the other side of the room was dark hardwood. The back wall had a 40-inch Samsung LCD monitor mounted on it. There was a long, narrow, cherrywood table and four comfortable leather chairs on one side of the table. Those seated would be looking directly up at the Samsung or down at a Dell keyboard and a 17-inch, flat-panel screen.

The right wall in the den area had a large, framed print of a golfer in plus fours. The border of the print had a repetitive pattern of a mortar and pestle. Just above the bottom border were the words, "Golf, life's best prescription." Below the print was a set of the Broker's Calloways.

In the left, back corner was a narrow winding staircase that led to the rooftop and a spectacular view of the city.

It was in this gentrified rowhouse that all three would be together for the first time.

Carm and the Broker had met alone twice before concerning the Little Don and his intimidating May visit to Carm's Disney condo. Carm had met with Juana only once before this June night to discuss his predicament. Carm had reached out to these two who owed and loved him deeply, and now they would plot a way out of Frankie Noto's threats.

They were here in Baltimore for two reasons. Well, three actually. First, the Broker wanted to meet away from the New York City area. Another reason was that the Yankees were in town for a midweek, three-game series against the Orioles. The core reason was to devise a way to save the lives of those whose life insurance policies Frankie Noto had thrown on the small kitchen table in Orlando only a month before.

The sins of Carmine's son Alberto were being visited upon him, the father, and his family. Even without a plan yet in place, both men knew that to save blood would mean letting blood—to protect their loved ones from brutal violence would mean just that.

Tonight, shortly after Juana had parked her car behind the house on Hanover and rang the Broker's bell, she would come to know it too. She was no stranger to blood and brutality, and she owed the man requesting her commitment. On this night, the Broker talked of needing people who can handle blood and death; people dedicated to the mission either for money, fear, or love; recruits who can color outside the lines. As he spoke, Juana just nodded and took a long sip of the Picpoul de Pinet that the Broker had uncorked. The light white wine with its floral and citric fruit aromas was in stark contrast to the heavy, unpleasant tasks being spoken of.

There would be no talk of Carm's rescue of the Broker as a younger man. The two men were bound by Carm's friendship with Rick's father, Carm's intervention with one of New York City's men in blue to keep Rick out of the system, and the disposal of one of Rick Huse's murder victims. A man named Fran "the Man" Dramus, a man who had put one of Rick's running buddies in intensive care for no good reason, now rested in the cement foundation of a Bronx foot-bridge. The Broker would answer Carm's call for help, no questions asked.

Juana had much different reasons for the same kind of response to her aging savior's request for aid. Even though she knew that to do what he was asking meant she would have to make a phone call she never wanted to make; to set up a meeting for a heart-breaking discussion she hoped never to have. And jump back into a world of violence and blood she thought she had left far behind.

CHAPTER 73

▼

MARCIA NUZIALE

Juana took what remained in the bottle of Picpoul de Pinet to the bedroom the Broker had made up for her. She also took the copy of the *Italian Tribune* article Carmine had given both of them. The article was dated June 4, 1995, a Sunday, and was a translation of a piece that originally appeared in the *Corriere della Sera*, a paper the Italians consider their *New York Times*. The *Italian Tribune*, a weekly, had been published on June 8, 1995, a Thursday. The article detailed a massacre that took place on Saturday, June 3, during the wedding of a young couple from Naples, Italy. The groom was the owner of a local restaurant. The bride, the daughter of a reputed member of the Provenzano crime family in charge of the Rome franchise of the mob family's business. The newspaper article hinted at the possibility that the father of the bride, Tito Rizzo, was skimming from his Sicilian crime boss, Bernardo Provenzano, and that the gruesome murders were payback from the man they call the Tractor.

"They call him the Tractor because of the way he mows down his enemies," Carm had explained. "Even as a fugitive from the law, Provenzano has wielded his brutal power over there for years and years. In this case, according to my sources, Provenzano's men waltzed in as the band was playing the tarantella. Two of them walked through the galloping and glissading crowd to the head table and shot the bride, Donanta, three times in the face. Before her father or any others who might be carrying could respond, a second tier of the Tractor's men opened up with their Beretta sub-machine guns and mowed down the crowd. Body count was fifty, including twenty women and ten children. Only a handful escaped to tell the details of the slaughter. The dead included Tito, his wife, and second daughter, as well as the groom.

"If Frankie Noto is telling the truth to me about Alberto and the Little Don's own deal and debt involving his Sicilian connections, these are the kind of people we need to fear. Women and children get no pardons when it comes to their threats and revenge. Oh, did you read in the article about how they burned down the reception hall when they were finished? As if the killings weren't enough of a goddamned message. Jesus."

As Juana sipped her wine and reread the short article, the frightened and desperate look on Carm's face, as he told the story to them, haunted her mind. Sleep came with difficulty. Her dreams of piles of dead bodies in festive outfits made her wish it had not come at all.

"Marcia nuziale," Carm had whispered as he shook his head. "Some wedding song. The sound of bullets flying to the dying notes of the band and the lively Italian dance."

Carm was spending the night just up the road at the Renaissance Harborplace Hotel on Pratt Street. Juana wondered what kind of sleep and what kind of dreams this night would bring to her friend.

CHAPTER 74

▼

PELHAM 1-2-3-4

A week before the demise of Jesus H. Cruz, the Broker, an avid golfer, assembled a very different kind of foursome. This group was gathered around a round game table in the basement of a Pelham, New York, home—not standing on the first tee at Rick's New Rochelle Country Club.

The town of Pelham was part of a larger purchase from the Siwanoy Indians by Thomas Pell on June 27, 1654. It is the oldest town in New York's Westchester County and is named *not* after Pell but after Pell's tutor Pelham Burton. It was also the site of the Battle of Pelham fought on October 18, 1776. A bloody battle in which a few hundred patriots fought four thousand British and German troops and saved General George Washington's army as it withdrew to White Plains. The four in the basement were planning their own bit of sanguinary history.

Pelham to New York City's Grand Central Station was a thirty-minute train ride on the New Haven line of the Metropolitan Transit Authority. That was one of the big reasons the redheaded owner of the large, Mediterranean-style, light brick home had chosen this upscale, quiet town. He liked the quiet, but he also liked to be close to the action, and his action was in the city.

However, today's early-morning action was here in Pelham, and about a different kind of battle and a different kind of taking than the New York City subway train hijacking in the 1974 movie. The only thing this foursome would borrow from the *Taking of Pelham 1-2-3* would be the use of code names—a precaution that was also somewhat entertaining for the four. But, instead of using colors for code names as the movie did, they simply used the numbers 1, 2, 3, 4.

The group was eclectic, for sure. What was even more so was the collection of movies that filled the custom shelving that surrounded the 65-inch Panasonic plasma TV. They took up the length of the 20-foot wall. Divided by VHS and DVD format and then placed in alphabetical order, the trove contained everything from *This Gun for Hire*, the 1942 hit starring Veronica Lake, Robert Preston, and Alan Ladd, to a bootleg copy of *Sin City*, starring Bruce Willis, that would not be released on DVD for the rest of the world to see for a few months. The Broker found comfort in his movies. He also spent quiet hours in his upstairs library browsing through an extensive collection of books, ranging from the works of Plato to the latest James Patterson thriller.

On this spring morning, the owner of the home was flanked by his two, seventy-pound, twenty-seven-inch-tall Doberman pinschers. The dark-eyed, black-and-tan male canines, named Jaws and Jaws II, were rarely away from their master's side. They were in attendance this morning, not because he did not trust his visitors, but because in this business he just did not trust *anyone*—period—ever. The expertly trained canines, named after Herr Louis Dobermann, were descendants of the man's mid-nineteenth-century, crossbred creations in southern Germany. These two scions of the breed had been quite feisty and vocal when the visitors arrived. Their owner used one word to calm down his troops, "Yankees." He told his guests that they did not want to be around when he yelled, "Red Sox."

Their owner was known in many circles simply as "The Broker." To say that the Broker was connected to many important people in the New York metropolitan area and elsewhere was like saying Tiger Woods had a modest trophy collection and a reticent fan following.

Like Mr. Eldrick Woods, the Broker, christened Richard A. Huse, had a passion for the game of golf. He belonged to two country clubs; one was the 6,702-yard, par-72 Wykagyl Country Club, just ten minutes up the road on North Avenue in New Rochelle, New York. The other was quite a ways down the road in Fairfax, Virginia. Rick, as most called him in person, had found his business caused him to spend a lot of time inside the Washington Beltway—and for Rick, spending a lot of time anywhere meant at least some time spent pounding the little white Titleist. When down south, Rick lived in a modest, single-family, brick ranch in a quiet Fairfax neighborhood, just off Rugby Road—a short five-minute ride to Route 50 and International Country Club. The twenty-five-mile drive to our nation's capital was often another matter altogether, time wise.

Today, there would be no golf, only business. The Broker, the son of a New York City cop named Al, was a maker and breaker of financial and political successes and failures. He was also a conduit for large, serpentine business transactions where money was added and taken away along the way. But on this day, he was unhappily back in the kind of game he had thought he had given up years ago, but back in he was. He had told his main client, Carmine Antobelli, that this kind of business would have to be bloody and expensive.

His next move, the first public step, was critical, and today, the perfection and timing it required needed to be drilled into the three in the room. As was his way, he waited until the last practical hours to share all the details of the plan with his three partners.

There would be a lot of independent actions—each blind to the others—that were needed for success. Things were already in motion. Rick, the Broker, just needed to wrap up the final threads with these three and be sure the necessary finishing touches were taken care of.

Three of the conspirators who had gathered in the Broker's Baltimore, Hanover Street rowhouse only months ago had agreed that not Sam Walton, but the government of the U.S. of A. had the most money in the world. Now it was time to go get some of it to keep Frankie Noto, the Little Don, from killing Carmine Antobelli's family.

Carm had thrown down envelopes with six photos in each, faces that matched up with the names on the insurance policies that the Little Don had slapped on the kitchen table in Orlando. The photos, better than any documents, were to be reminders for his partners of the stakes involved in their efforts. There was one photo that they all paused over a little longer than the others. They prayed their efforts would keep these photos from becoming posted in the *New York Times* obituary column.

Carm's mention of Frankie Noto's own pain and suffering at the hands of the serious and nasty Sicilians, to whom the Little Don owed the money, had made the reality of the threats stick in their collective throats. The people with whom the Little Don was involved would kill without conscience. The Broker's team needed to pull off their plan to make sure that killing stayed far away from the potential victims listed by the Little Don. This business was as serious as the Broker's disposal of his taunting, childhood nemesis, as bloody as Juana's violent solutions to gain her childhood freedom, and as brutal as Carmine Antobelli's making his bones many years ago.

CHAPTER 75

▼

THE MANOR AT PELHAM

At lunchtime, the second white van of the day pulled up in front of the Broker's house. The driver carefully backed his vehicle into the driveway. The tail end of the van eased just inside the opened, carriage-house-style garage door. The morning van had had Percopo Landscaping painted on both sides, joined by an enticing rendition of a garden scene that did not look much different from Rick's front yard. In addition to the usual tools of his trade, Joey Percopo had transported the three people now inside Rick's home. Any clever law-enforcement agent who might be watching the comings and goings would only see the vans and not their cargo.

The driver of the lunchtime van was deli owner and caterer Danny Magnotta. An hour earlier, Rick Huse had keyed a contact entry in his cell phone and reached Danny. They exchanged the usual pleasantries and Danny finished with one question. "How many?"

"Four, and your two buddies, and can you stop at the Pelham Bakery and pick up some Napoleons?"

"Sure. That's the newer one on Fifth?"

"Yeah."

"Hey, Danny, how's your golf game?"

"Pretty much the same. An adventure accompanied by a few beers. But when I get the chance to get out, it stills beats the shit out of working."

"Well, you give me your schedule, and I'll match it up to mine, and we'll make a date. You know how much I enjoy taking your money."

"Of course. And you know how much I love playing and drinking and eating on your tab over in New Rochelle. I'll give you my calendar."

Rick was there to greet Danny. He had gone out to the driveway to ingest a number of the hundreds of nasty ingredients wrapped in the once-innocuous-looking white paper with a tan filter tip. The Marlboro smoke was welcomed and the nicotine soothing. *Hell, I'm down to only five a day. Well, if I don't count the cigars at night with the gin and tonic.* Rick was finishing the last puff of one of Philip Morris's finest when Danny and his white van pulled up. Danny was about Rick's height of five-ten. Both wore their fifty-something body weight fairly well, and both were long past fretting over the gray hairs that were taking up residence in place of Danny's black and Rick's striking red. Danny wore no facial hair. Rick's well-groomed mustache and beard gave him the look of a weathered fisherman. Today, both shared smiles in the foreground of the Huse hacienda, meticulously landscaped and groomed. A spread of lush, green Kentucky fescue was dotted with islands of mixed foliage; the holly bushes, hostas, boxwoods and emerald green arborvitae stood staunchly, colorfully accented by combinations of the deep red and white flowers of the planted begonias and impatiens.

"Hey, Rick. Here you go. Napoleons are in the little bag. My calendar's inside of that."

"You didn't have to come yourself, Danny."

"Ah. It's always fun to get out from behind the counter, and I haven't seen you in a while. Johnny Gambelli can manage without me for an hour or so."

Rick had Danny put the cardboard, food-laden tray on the workbench in the garage—his movements concealed by the carriage door. Rick the Broker reached into the bag where he had correctly guessed Danny had included two six-packs of cold Bud cans; popped two. He led Danny out to the backyard and took the precious time to talk to one of his favorite people. No bill had been included in the bags or handed to Rick. As they shook hands to say their farewells with a promise of a golf game in the near future, the hundred-dollar bill easily passed from Rick's to Danny's palm.

The opening of Danny's bags unleashed a cornucopia of delights. Meats and salads on various types of rolls and breads were laid out on the kitchen table. The meal would be upstairs in the kitchen and would be void of any business discussion. Rick, the gracious host, allowed Pelham 2, 3, and 4 to load up first. The pastrami and corned beef with a side of hot beans and cold macaroni salad seemed to be the first grabbed. Rick settled on one of the hot veal parmigiana wedges and a second cold Budweiser. The four cooked bratwursts wrapped in white butcher's paper lasted less than thirty seconds with the Jaws twins after Rick tossed them into the middle of the backyard.

The Pelham 1-2-3-4 discussed everything from the Yankees' lack of pitching to the stock market's volatility. It was Buds around to go with the sandwiches. Lunch, concluding with the light pastry layers filled with a sweet vanilla cream and melted semi-sweet chocolate and a heavy touch of powdered sugar, ended within the hour. Pelham 2, 3, and 4 were allowed a brief respite in the back of the house under the cover of Rick's screened-in porch. The warmth of the May sun and its natural light was a welcome relief from the confines of Rick's underground, morning conclave. After a few private phone calls, Rick retrieved his guests, and they made their way down to the basement.

The lunch and the break were meant to relax his team before they bit into the final details of the high-wire acts they were about to attempt.

CHAPTER 76

▼

FIREWALLS BEFORE FIRE ONE

When the accord between the Broker and his main client, Pelham 2, had been struck, Rick assured his old friend that their discussions and future communications were secure. If he wanted to know the details, Rick would be glad to give them. But his client waved him off. "You know I trust you with my life, Ricky boy." Ricky smiled at the bold truth of that statement. Pelham 2's life and the lives of quite a few others hung in the balance.

The main room in the basement, home of Pelham 1-2-3-4's planning, looked like an elaborate home theater and a small computer center, all in one. Off the big room was an unfinished work area with a concrete floor painted the color of a putting green. This room housed three workbenches, walls of pegboard adorned with hand tools, and shelves of power tools. The most important tools, however, were locked in a light gray, fireproof model S5149 Sentry Safe with a combination lock. Just shy of twenty-four inches high and nineteen inches deep and wide, the mini fortress held the special tools that unlocked the maze of servers and network machines housed in a third room—lead lined and sealed off from the other two. The small safe also housed key hardware backup components, copies of the Broker's custom software and one hundred and fifty thousand dollars in Benjamins and Jacksons.

When it came to telecommunications and Internet security, the Broker's houses in Baltimore, Pelham, and Fairfax—especially the basements—could serve as models for a number of well-to-do governments. What the Broker's "toys" were connected to, what they could spy on and listen in on was incredible. With the flip of a few digital switches or the tapping of a few keystrokes, the data intercepted from the "protected" network of others was impressive—not to mention highly illegal. The Broker always enjoyed finding a bargain in many of his business transactions, but when it came to communications, and privacy and protection, he only went with the very best.

The very best for him meant two names—nicknames actually—Maximum Al and The X-man.

Al Plempel was an ex-military spook with a myriad of skills that provided privacy among those who needed to communicate without fear of exposure.

Kenny O'Brien, the X-man, an ex-telecom executive, was so named for his in-depth knowledge of the binary ones and zeroes, the lone digits together forming the number 10. An X in Roman numerals. Those two little numbers that drove everything from a lifeless keyboard to the high-speed modems and routers that Rick was so fond of.

Just for kicks the Broker had the two magicians change out the key hardware and software in his homes every six months and then challenged each to try and break the other's firewalls, encryptions, and whatever other wizardry they had installed. The reward for any successful breach was one hundred thousand in cash. To date, much like the elusive Publisher's Clearing House big fat check, Rick's one hundred grand had not made it to either's front step.

Unbeknownst to his two wizards was Rick's use of a third master of the keystrokes, Corey Young. While Rick trusted in Maximum Al and the X-man, he always liked an outside auditor to give him that extra level of confidence. When the Broker needed to be the hacker into others' networks, Corey was his man. When the Broker wanted to insure he would not be the hackee, Corey was also his man. To date, Maximum and X and their workings had not succumbed to any of Corey's sophisticated, nefarious attempts at invasion.

It was under this veil of secrecy and security that the four plotters were now meeting. The Broker had spent a great deal of money, not only on his systems and networks, but also on his quarters. There would be no listening in to any of the Broker's meeting rooms. Rooms that had been frequented by high-powered politicians, well-heeled corporate executives, as well as the occasionally required streetwise journeymen of varying skills. The rooms were frequently swept for any bugs and had anti-listening devices to keep out unwelcome eavesdroppers. He had also spent a considerable sum of money on the particulars of his current, bloody plot. The Broker and all his players, as well as the victim, were all in place for the next move.

The meeting ended at four o'clock. The visitors said their good-byes to the Broker and Jaws and Jaws II and made their way into the back of the van owned by Vito's Expert Plumbing.

Pelham 1-2-3-4 were ready for Tinsel Town.

Well, almost. The Broker needed a break, and tonight's break would come in the form of Isabella, the sultry waitress from Graziella's in White Plains. Rick and little Richard had anticipated a hot night, and Isabella did not disappoint. Cognac and cigars followed.

CHAPTER 77

▼

SUCCESS, ALMOST

Fire One had gone splendidly. Gilbert, Big Bobby Blatney, aka Trip, and Bubba performed their heavy lifting flawlessly. Their cleanup work and little cigarette butt DNA diversion done to perfection. Juana's convincing payoffs to the Broker's friends in the right security establishments went as smoothly and crisply as the cash that changed hands. The publicity was much more than fifteen minutes of infamy, but the DOJ remained silent. No money. No Maria.

Stupid bastards.

Fire Two—New York Public Library and Sarasota Bay—masterpieces.

Little Altar Boy and the other New York drivers delivered on time.

The sail to Mr. Ringling's mansion was smooth and dramatic. Boat captain and divers pulled off the special splash in the bay.

Decapitations had done the deed. Thank you, Gilbert and friends.

Now the work of the Broker and of his boys and girls was being splashed across the media canvasses with twice the force. The tie between the Jesus event and the beheadings of the Johns was beginning to get serious play. Bloody chum to the news sharks.

Let's see if the DOJ has the onions to stay silent now.

CHAPTER 78

▼

WAKE UP, DOJ

Hell has been on fire for one hell of a long time. On June 24, in the year of 2005, feast day of St. John the Baptist, it broke loose in the office of fifty-year-old Jerry Whalen, a member of the executive staff of the United States Attorney's Office for the Southern District of New York. The guy who strongly recommended against responding to the terrorists after the Jesus H. affair.

Shit storm number two—the Broker's Fire Two—fiercely whooshed its way in when the lovely Lea greeted the severely hungover Mr. Whalen with, "Boss, have you heard or seen the news?" It would be a long day at One St. Andrew's Place in lower Manhattan.

The first FedEx package arrived at 10:00 AM. It was from a Staten Island location.

The package did not contain a blood vial like the Jesus H. delivery back in May. But it did have a four-gigabyte Memorex thumb drive in a protective-plastic carrying case. The digital device was packed inside bubble wrap in the top of the box.

Jerry Whalen was in one of his standard issue dark gray suits and white shirts with a red power tie. His helper Lea was mildly advertising her smashing figure in her Nine West, black-and-white print, V-Neck top, with a hint of cleavage, accompanied by a tight Michael Kors pencil skirt. The nattily dressed pair assumed the size of the first box meant more party gifts inside than just the drive.

With caution and held breath, Whalen worked his way through more packaging until he reached a dark, rectangular, wooden case. The case was about twenty inches long, eight inches wide and six inches high. A simple clasp and a pair of hinges held the top in place.

"Jesus Christ Almighty," Lea whispered when Jerry opened the box.

"No. I believe in this case it's probably John the Dead Baptist."

The dark blood was caked on the nine-and-a-half-inch, mirror-polished, stainless-steel blade of the Case 1224 Alamo Bowie knife. The finish on the Central American cocobolo-hardwood handle had a dark orange tint to it.

"Shit. Are you kidding me, Jerry?"

"I wish to hell I was." He left the box right where it was, walked over to his desk, and found the aspirin bottle. Took three and offered the bottle to his assistant. The DOJ lawyer decided to crack open whatever files were on the thumb drive before he made any decisions. He and Lea watched the MPEG twice. For the encore viewing, each laced their second cup of morning coffee with the Jack Daniels Jerry kept in the bottom drawer of his desk.

"Hang on," was Jerry's response to the 11:00 AM knock on his office door.

"Okay, I'm coming."

Another FedEx. The second, all the way from an office near Sarasota on Florida's Tamiami Trail, had made its way to Whalen's office. Another thumb drive. Another bloody Bowie knife.

Lea could not bring herself to watch the second video. She plugged it in and set it up for Jerry's viewing. When the same music as the first started on the second, she simply left.

She had watched the first, horridly frozen to her chair. Lea had actually recognized the wordless opening with a chorus of bongos and screeching birds that led into a mellow, melodious, satanic Mick Jagger challenging the listener to guess his name.

When the Rolling Stones "Sympathy for the Devil" moved into the chorus of "Ooo, who?" the blank screen on the first video jumped to a dim and deadly scene.

Jerry and Lea assumed they were looking at the back of the New York John the Baptist tied to an open-back chair. The lighting was minimal and the video choppy, making it even more gruesome than a professional camera shoot. With each gunshot, the naked man in the chair flailed, more with some of the shots, less with others. Jerry rewound and counted. There were ten in all—all in the shirtless back.

What looked like, and was, a gas-operated, short-recoil assault rifle, originally designed by Mikhail T. Kalashnikov in the late 1940s, was tossed onto the floor on the right side of the bulleted victim. The AK 47 made of metal and hardwood bounced twice, slid a foot in the blood-drenched floor, and came to rest. Ballistics would later reveal that the rounds were .223 caliber projectiles—and that in fact Jerry's count was correct.

What came next was the catalyst for the retrieval of the bottle of bourbon. One man held John's long hair in his hand and pulled it up over the victim's head. With the way cleared, a second man, masked, as was the first, proceeded to separate poor John's head from his bullet-ridden torso. It appeared to be no easy task, but the sicko with the long blade finished the job. The first view of John's face came when the holder of the head turned it around to face the camera.

The first video went blank and silent for a few seconds, and then the demands came—similar to the Jesus event's demands, but for more money. The music behind this series of frames was an old Jim Reeves rendition of "Please Release Me." Jerry and Lea just looked at each other in silence. Jerry replayed the prose images three times.

Mr. U.S. Attorney, our demands are simple.
Free Maria Calabrese, now.
You will pay us <u>EIGHT</u> MILLION DOLLARS to make up for your mistakes.

If you agree to these terms, post a new link on your Web page,
(just to the left of that pretty picture of your smiling face)
http://www.usdoj.gov/usao/nys/

Title the new link "Conviction Review #2."

Password protect it for my eyes only.
Use the letters "DamneeuQ". Case sensitive, please.

Place only two lines on the page.

"Site Still Under Construction.
Try again soon."

If you follow these instructions, I will present you with the compliance process by which we, together, can satisfy our demands.

If you don't believe we are serious, ask Jesus
and his buddies John I and II.
Oh, sorry. That's right, they're dead.

If you fail to respond as requested, more Innocents will perish.

RSVP no later than June 30, 2005—or else!

Eight, not five million. Link name has the #2 added to the original. Password significantly changed. Got Jesus and two Johns now—all dead. Deadline only six days away, not nine like the first time.

The video of the Florida John was identical except for one thing. No bullets were used. Just ten stab wounds with the Bowie knife in the bare back of Florida John before severing the flesh and bones and blood vessels that connected the victim's head to his body.

The solitary Jerry wasted no time in dumping the remains of his coffee cup and refilling it with Lynchburg, Kentucky's, fine Old No. 7 Brand, Mr. J.D. himself.

CHAPTER 79

▼

JERRY AND LEA AND FRIENDS

"Four more Guinnesses, please."

After several reviews of the Broker's "Fire Two," Jerry Whalen decided there was no easy way to bury this one like the last.

Jesus H. was one thing. The two JBs made the situation a whole other can of those long, thin, soft-bodied, backboneless creatures that live in the dirt. He had called on two more attorneys in the office to watch what FedEx had so promptly delivered this morning.

"It's not just a package, it's your business," and "When it absolutely, positively has to be there overnight," two of the FedEx familiar slogans, had popped into Jerry's brain just before he made the calls. *Shit. Couldn't they have sent them in the U.S. Mail?*

Now, at one o'clock in the afternoon, Jerry, Lea, and the two others were seated in the back of Slainti's on Bowery Street.

"And bring a couple of orders of cheese fries, please," a hungry Jerry added. His morning breakfast was long since lost in the men's room at the DOJ building.

"Gentlemen, Lea, what in God's name—no pun intended—do we do now?"

Lawyer number one, who was wearing a conservative black suit with a plaid bowtie answered first. "Well, we need to get the boss involved before we do much of anything."

Jerry answered Bowtie Barrister, "No shit, Sherlock. I already tried, but he is out of pocket till later today. He's on a plane to Reagan National."

Lawyer number two, with the large handlebar mustache, righteously piped up. "Well, under no circumstances can you give in to these terrorist maniacs. You've got what? Six days? Need to find a way to get to them. Maybe forensics will give you something this time."

Jerry and Lea both noticed the pronoun that distanced Mr. Mustache from the problem and conveniently left it in Jerry's lap.

The Guinnesses and discussion continued on for several hours with talk of containing the evidence and managing the press and the pressure that would come from above. The afternoon ended with at least one firm conclusion—not unfamiliar to the U.S. government or corporate America: "Task force!"

CHAPTER 80

▼

TASK FORCE ASSEMBLED

"How do you feel about New York City, Chris?"

"Well, I am quite fond of it. Spent my college years there. Still have good fiends there."

"Oh yeah. Forgot you graduated from John Jay. Well, that's great. They're calling. Actually, they want you in White Plains, a bit north of the city, at the DOJ office there for a task force assignment. Apparently, someone in the DOJ thinks you're a pretty good profiler, not to mention proficient at having solved numerous crimes based on your help to local FBI offices. And, quite frankly, they are in the deep end of the septic tank on these Jesus and John killings. The heat is on, and they want the best, and when I asked who that might be, your name came out on the top of their list. Apparently, your reputation is quite widespread. And, of course, I confirmed that *you* were the best we had. So, what do you say to a little road trip up north?"

Earlier, Chris wasn't sure what was up when the head of the FBI's Counter Terrorism Division summoned him to his office. He knew he was one of his boss's favorite employees, and, even by his own recognition, one of the best ex-profilers who had supported the National Center for the Analysis of Violent Crime (NCAVC) of the Critical Incident Response Group (CIRG). The people who provide operational assistance to FBI field offices and law enforcement agencies. He had been an instructor at the Behavioral Sciences Unit in Quantico. In his last few years with the FBI, working in CTD at the J. Edgar Hoover location in D.C., Chris had gained unpublicized, national prominence for his work in uncovering U.S.-based terrorist cells. In one case, he had gone under deep cover to penetrate an Asian terrorist group trafficking in heavy-duty arms to any mad-man with enough money to buy the product.

Now Chris was being summoned back to New York for a special assignment, and he was not surprised that the whole Jesus and John thing was the reason.

A similar conversation had taken place the day before at 150 North Los Ange-les Street in LA, home of the Parker Center, LAPD headquarters. Jed Davies caught the 3:25 PM Continental flight out of LAX, passed over some of New Jer-sey's finest fuel-storage tanks and landed at Newark Airport's C terminal at 11:52 PM. The Department of Justice folks had arranged for a National rental car for Jed to pick up at the Emerald Aisle with no wait. Although midnight in New Jer-sey, Jed's body was wide awake enough to easily make the trip up the turnpike to the Palisades Parkway, across the Tappan Zee Bridge, and into White Plains. A short ride down North Broadway, and a shorter one down Barker Avenue, took him to Cottage Place and the Marriott Residence Inn. He parked in front and ignored the ornate and finely decorated lobby as he walked through it and made his way to the check-in desk. A porter helped him to his room on the twelfth of the hotel's sixteen floors, one of the 134 suites available at this Marriott.

Jed retrieved his laptop and placed it on the desk just off the kitchen-din-ing-room area and tested the high-speed Internet access. By the time he was logged in to his e-mail, the TV had warmed up enough to display the latest MSNBC "Breaking News." Jesus H. was back on the airwaves, and Jed Davies was back in New York. A very grateful Jed retrieved a cold can of Coors Light from the fridge—the DOJ man who had given him the details of his itinerary had promised the brew and had delivered. Impressed with his quarters and delighting in the cold beverage that was quenching his thirst, he toasted, "To the good old U.S. of A. Thank you, Uncle Sam, for springing for the digs. Tomor-row, we start Jesus H. all over again. Lord, pray for me."

He checked in with his wife in LA, and all was well. He moved on to a pack-age of information that was left on the desk labeled for Detective Davies. He browsed through the directions to the United States District Court Building, which housed the local DOJ office over on Quarropas Street. It looked like a short walk or drive; simple enough. There were instructions: if driving, park in back and go inside and ask for Lea at a certain extension when he arrived at the courthouse.

MSNBC was now looping back again to the Jesus H. and double John details and their own speculation. Jed had shed his travel clothes, laid out tomorrow's more formal garb on the couch in the living area, slipped on his well-worn John Jay sweats, and grabbed a second Coors when the phone rang.

"Hello?"

"Jed?"

"Yeah, who … Christ, is that you, Chris?"

"The one and only, packing for an early-morning trip to White Plains, old buddy."

CHAPTER 81

▼

THE HUNT FOR "THESE GUYS"

By noon the next day, Sunday, June 26, 2005, the task force had assembled in the U.S. District Courthouse on Quarropas Street—the same one in which Alberto and Maria heard the definitive bangs of a judge's gavel and the piercing word, "guilty." The interesting-looking building with white stone arches reaching up two stories from street level, topped with floors of red brick and more of white stone, was home to four district judges and three U.S. Magistrate judges. It also housed the bankruptcy court, Pretrial Services, U.S. Probation, Federal Defenders, and an office of the U.S. Attorney. On this day, and for a number of weeks to come, it would be home to the DOJ task force, joked about as and quickly renamed the DO3J's task force, referring to the victims and crimes they were focused on.

If you look at the organization chart for the U.S. Department of Justice, you will see the title of Attorney General at the very top and forty-one more boxes below him. The boxes included all sorts of familiar legal and law enforcement titles of the federal government. The two who had successfully hijacked one of the large jury rooms for their task force were the boxes that said United States Attorneys and Federal Bureau of Investigation.

At noon the games would begin; the hunt was on.

"Ladies and Gentlemen, my name is Jerry Whalen. I am a member of the executive staff of the United States Attorney's office for the Southern District of New York and the appointed head of this crisis team."

Jerry introduced the members of the task force whom he and the powers that be had recruited for this DO3J effort and described the strategy and various tasks assigned to each. His rhetoric drifted between calm, cold, calculated direction and Hollywood-like histrionics.

His opening speech ended with the latter.

"I want to know everything there is to know about the following people: Maria Calabrese, Alberto Antobelli, Jesus Cruz, John Baptista, Jean Baptiste. Everything. And everything about their families, their friends, their boyfriends, their girlfriends, their goddamned grade-school teachers, their doctors and dentists, their buying habits, their financial history down to the second decimal place.

"We are not giving in to these goddamned terrorists or whatever the hell they are. These guys are not going to get away with trying to hold the U.S. government hostage. We are going to find them, and they will be begging for their own crucifixions or beheadings before we are done with them. I want this to outdo anything seen on "Law and Order" or "CS bleeping I." I want to see my name on the front page of the *New York Times* and on CNN, thanking all of you for putting these animals in the cages they belong in."

Jerry pointed to the enlarged posters taped to the walls of the jury room. They showed the scenes of the crimes. Gory, brutal death jumped off the paper.

"What kind of human beings could do this to another? We need to stop them now. We need to do whatever it takes. Get to it, folks. I need your best on this."

The rant ended and most moved onto their tasks. Jed Davies and Chris Lee made the mistake of approaching the distressed lawyer.

"Mr. Whalen?"

"Please, Jed, call me Jerry, and thanks for coming all the way across the country."

"No problem, sir, uh, Jerry."

"What can I do for you?"

"Well, Chris and I have a college friend who works in Manhattan South, and we thought, since we know him, he might be a good fit for the task force. Maybe work with me or Chris."

"Really. What's his name?"

"Grady O'Connor."

The shift was as sudden as Jerry's rhetoric had jumped before. He went from calm to not so. "Gentlemen, let me say this once and only once. I have a bit of history with your friend. He completely screwed up a federal investigation we had going. We were on the verge of nailing a group of high-end drug lords who worked out of his territory. Under no, and I mean *no*, circumstances do I want that man near this case. As far as I am concerned, your friend is a first-class, bleeping idiot. Right up there with the best of them. No, maybe he is the best of them, period. And he's an asshole to boot. No Grady. Got it?"

Both men nodded and moved on. Jerry went back to his temporary desk in the White Plains DOJ office and retrieved Lea.

"Let's go. You can drive."

Lea led him to her 2003 silver Hyundai Sonata, started the engine and air and asked, "Where to?"

He pointed their way through a couple of rights, one left and then a final right onto Lake Street. Told her to stop on the opposite side of the street from a small deli. Jerry returned within minutes with two steak and cheese subs and four 16-ounce cans of Budweiser. After one more finger point and a right, Lea found a spot in the parking lot of Delfino Park. She was silent as she watched her boss select an aged picnic table near the softball field. He unwrapped the sandwiches from the white deli paper and popped the tops of two of the beers. It was already into the 80s by noon. Another hot, humid, and hazy New York summer day. Jerry did not seem to notice or mind. Lea's perfect hair was suffering under the heat, but she did not complain. After ten minutes of shared silence and numerous bites of the warm meat and cheddar on the soft roll, Jerry finally spoke.

"Lea, I want you to know one thing. No matter how ugly things get with this DO3J mess, no matter how bad things get for me, if we don't get this pile of crap scraped off the sidewalk, I will make sure you land on your feet clean. I owe you that much, and I will make sure I pay that debt if worse comes to worst."

Lea choked back some emotion and asked a bland question. "How do you know about this place, Jerry?"

"Play softball here for the DOJ team once in a while when they need a sub and I'm available.

"I meant what I said, Lea. There is no shallow end to this pool we are in, but, even if I fail to float when this is over, I'll make sure you end up back on the deck."

All of Jerry's words spoken to his assistant had been mouthed into the heavy air in front of him. After this last rescue metaphor, Lea moved closer to Jerry on the rigid bench. He was surprised when she wrapped her arm inside his. The softness of her breast that pressed into his bicep was like a flash of lightning, striking and waking up his repressed libidinal desire for the young woman. In what seemed like a frozen moment, Lea gently placed her hand on his thigh, and with her other hand rotated his neck so that he was facing her directly—no more speaking into the wind. Her kiss, darting tongue, and touch almost made the lawyer forget where he was or why he was where he was.

Lea and her voice were trembling slightly when she said, "Thank you, Jerry. I do worry about you."

A few beers and a few tears later, the duo returned to the latest location of their hell-on-earth, Quarropas Street, White Plains, New York. A pretty city, thirty miles north of "The City." One of three cities that would have their attention for a number of days to come.

So far, business wise, the only good news was that Jerry's boss agreed to White Plains as the location for Task Force Central. It was close to Jerry's and Lea's homes and much cheaper than housing task force personnel in the city. His boss and his boss's boss had secured the brightest and best for this effort. Time would tell. His team, which was located at the Marriott, seemed pleased with their quarters—how much time they would have to spend there remained to be seen.

June 30, "the deliver-or-else day," four days from now. Ticktock, ticktock, a metronomic sound, like the one that echoed from the stomach of Captain Hook's alligator. The imagined tone repeating in Jerry's head. Ticktock, ticktock.

CHAPTER 82

▼

END OF DAY ONE

Jed and Chris's first night in the county seat of prestigious Westchester ended with one drink, shared in Jed's suite at the Marriott. During their brief dinner break the two college friends had made their way over to Mamaroneck Avenue and Carhart's liquor store to purchase some essentials. Chris thanked Jed for the Grey Goose on the rocks. It had been a long day of catching up for both. Chris was new to all of the real details that the various law enforcement departments possessed concerning the cases. Jed found out a number of things about *his* Jesus H. case that the damn DOJ had held back from him and the LAPD. Both John Jay graduates were exhausted.

Chris made it back to his own suite two floors down. He toyed with a major decision. He hung up his suit and filed his dirty laundry in one of the bags in the closet. He barefooted his way across the green carpet of the living area, flipped on ESPN, looked over the oak dining table to the oak cabinets in the kitchen. The decision was made quickly. He walked across the tiled kitchen floor, rescued a tall glass from a kitchen cabinet, loaded it with ice, and invited his own bottle of Grey Goose from the freezer to join in the swim.

Things had happened too fast in the last two days. He needed a mental trip down memory lane, to a better time, to slow down his jacked-up anxiety. Jed had said before that he was going to call home in LA to talk to his wife and kids.

Chris just looked at his silent Sprint cell phone and envied Jed's connection, his devotion. With one of the talking heads on ESPN's "SportsCenter" droning on about the New York Yankees, Chris Lee muted the sound and closed his eyes. It was not the first time that he had replayed this mysterious series of emotional events from the past in his mind. The Goose would help make the excursion a smoother trip, he reasoned.

CHAPTER 83

▼

BETTER TIMES

Chris always tried to make the annual trip to Jensen Beach close to the date on which he had spread Sarah's ashes. His first trip alone to Joey D.'s place was on September 9, 1990, three days after Sarah's funeral. This year, 2002, that date meant a Monday.

Labor Day had come and gone a week before. The kid beach brigade was already back in school. And tropical storm Gustav was nowhere near his destination.

Chris flew in Sunday night, had dinner with Joey D. and settled in to the cottage next door to the one in which Sarah and he had made their promises. He had just gotten off a tough kidnapping case and decided to take the whole week.

At 6:00 AM the next morning, the sun was washing the calm beach with a pleasant peach glow. Chris sat on the dock so full of memories. Through his black-rimmed Ray-Ban Highstreet sunglasses—very FBI-looking—he watched the water lap the shore and the hull of the small boat. He pondered where the twelve-year-old ashes might have found their way. The memories came in free form. No structure. No sequence. They never did, and he liked it that way. It reminded him of Sarah, the surprise queen. And so, he let them come over him like the shifting breeze that blew off the waterfront.

It was only when he had run out of tears that he felt the presence of another behind him. He got up and turned to see a woman who looked to be in her thirties, dressed in a black bikini top and a white towel wrapped around her hips.

Her hair was wet, and beads of water clung sensually to her chest and her tight, defined abdominal muscles—a six-pack that would challenge the look of Chris's own fitness. She stood on a pair of legs that said dancer or runner, strong and sleek. He was so busy taking in all of this that he failed to notice the locket that hung around her neck, nestled in just above her semi-exposed cleavage. His eyes moved from the overlooked locket to her sculptured face and smooth skin. A pair of gold-rimmed shades with pink lenses guarded her eyes. Her olive tone suggested either a sun worshipper or a heritage given. Chris thought he might have seen her around here before. He had, but never this close.

She smiled. "Hi. I'm Juana. I brought you a small present."

The long-stemmed, yellow rose she had produced from the hand that was behind her back left Chris speechless and open-mouthed.

He finally moved closer and took the rose. "Uh, well. Thank you very much. What did I do to deserve this? Oh, by the way, I'm Chris."

Another smile, this one a bit slyer. "I know."

From the large straw beach bag that stood at her feet she retrieved a tattered photo and sat down next to Chris on the wood dock. It was a slightly faded photo of a handsome woman and two young girls on a large Circle Line cruise boat. New York City's twin towers gleamed in the bright sun behind the three females. Juana let Chris soak in the scene and then turned the photo over.

"My two little angles, Juana (8) and Sarah (5), 1972, New York Harbor," was scripted on the back in Elena Romano's smoothly flowing handwriting. The classic photo having been taken by her husband, Big Tommy Romano—long deceased by 2002. The younger girl was noticeably lighter in all ways than the older one and the mother.

Chris flipped the photo over and back a few times, never letting his eyes leave the serene scene. When he did look up at his surprise guest, she had a locket in her hand. Chris was always teased about his steel-trap memory, and he had no problem recognizing the shape of the precious metal as being identical to the ones Sarah had given to his mother and sisters just before she died. Juana handed it to him. It was rectangular, somewhat book like in shape, with a subtle "S" etched on the front.

"Go ahead, Chris. Open it."

The left side on the inside read, "But she that dare not grasp the thorn."

The opposite page read, "should never crave the rose."

It was a slight variation of the words of Anne Brontë, the last of six Brontë children, born in 1820, with "she" substituted for "he."

"You were, are, Sarah's sister?"

"All my strange life, yes."

"She never mentioned you. Why have you stayed away? Wait—you were at the funeral in the back of the church."

Juana nodded, chin down against her chest. She let her face focus on the ebbing gentle waters of the river.

"I have stayed away, I guess, because I did not want to bring any more hurt into your life. Sarah never talked about me to anyone because it hurt too much. It was a thorn she felt was better left untouched. But, my God, with you, she told me she had finally dared to crave the rose. And, well, I guess, she captured her rose. And then she left us."

Like a slow slideshow with flowing transitions from frame to frame, the images danced across Chris's mind's eye. The yellow rose Sarah had brought him on their first date at the Palms in downtown Lexington. The calico dress with a pattern of light yellow roses on a white background on their second date and the fiery slow dance to Conway Twitty's "The Rose." The rose-flowered comforter on Sarah's bed in her Lexington flat. The petals of the day-old, yellow rose that they, together, had plucked and fed to the river's current running by the dock on the Indian River. The same dock that he and Sarah's sister sat on at this very moment. *Jesus, Sarah's sister.*

They went from the dock to Joey D.'s for a lunch of beer, wine, and grazing food of all kinds, and finally to Chris's cottage. Juana told him all she could remember of her life and other parts that her mother, Elena, had recalled for her eldest child.

From the early, dreamy days of Big Tommy Romano's romancing of Elena to his unlikely, drug-laden demise at the hands of his young daughter. To a new home in western Virginia and new hopes with a new man, Conrad. And, well, old Conrad's head running into Sarah's Slugger. The bizarre tales generated sadness and laughter, often within the same minute. Juana walked Chris through the ordeal of separation when the authorities stepped in and decided Elena, their mother, was unfit to raise the two girls. And then the separation of the young girls, sent to two different places, two different foster homes. Sarah's success, after some daunting challenges. Juana's own struggles until rescued by a kind man and his family.

A chilled bottle of Cavit pinot grigio, two glasses, and two tired beach people made their way to the dock as the stars dotted the clear skies above Jensen Beach. For some more sadness and a touch of sweet remembrance.

"What was it like for you and Sarah in Shenandoah, Virginia, with Conrad the Pervert? If you don't mind telling."

"He didn't always violently rape us, Chris. Oh sure, it was statutory, but he was an artist at work. He would drug us, stroke our hair, and play us like a fiddle. Shit, what did we really know at that age? A few glasses of wine and whatever was in them put us in another place. And then he liked us to play with his *thing* and kiss it. And then he would use different lubricants to minimize the physical difficulty. And when he was ready, he would gently put himself inside us, over and over. But then there were times when he would drink way past his limit. Those times he raped us. Raped us in every way possible. He made sure our mother was on one of her overnight adventures with her girlfriends. That way the bleeding from the tears inside of us would stop before she got home. First, it was me alone who was his victim. Later on, when I got a little too old for him—twelve, goddamned twelve years old—he moved on to your Sarah."

A few minutes of silence interrupted only by the occasional car making its way home up the Indian River Drive and a glass of white wine later, Chris spoke. "Juana, where do you think they have settled? Her ashes."

"Don't know, but I know there was no vessel short of God's waters that was large enough to house my sister's spirit."

"Juana, she, Sarah, gave me more love in a few months than I had ever known before or have known since. And her touch was such magic. My God, I always knew a peck on the cheek from my sister was meant to have no romance and it never did. My kissing days in high school and college were not bad. I enjoyed it and it played its part. But with Sarah, her lips on my cheek, her hand touching mine, were always deep touches. And her lips on mine and our tongues touching. I feel like she invented soul kissing. Because that's what it was. All of her touches captured my soul and woke it up. She never hid her heart from me for one second. At least that's how it felt then. It took a lot of time and words to understand her, but not for one second did I feel she was not completely open to me. Maybe she was just the best at compartmentalizing. There was nothing false in her love for me. I'll never believe that."

"Chris, don't. She hid a few parts of her heart for so long that she probably treated them as deceased. She told me you were her rose.

"We've all, through no fault of our own, just seemed to have earned a black belt in bad luck. Maybe things will change."

It was midnight by the time Juana gave Chris a goodnight peck on the cheek and crashed on the small couch in his cottage. An overwhelmed Chris shuffled his way to his bed and without changing his clothes or pulling the bed covers down just flopped down and faded into a deep sleep.

CHAPTER 84

▼

MIRROR, MIRROR

Chris Lee, in his White Plains digs, turned off the TV, put his empty vodka glass in the sink, and made his way down the hallway to the plush queen-size bed. He put his 2005 weary head down on a comfortable pillow and, with closed eyes, went back to the better times.

The long day of revelations in September of 2002 shared between Chris and Juana turned into a week filled with more shared memories, good and bad. Jensen Beach's Joey Dannemann, their landlord—now that Juana had moved into one of his motel rooms—ever the sweet talker, had grown fond of Juana. One of the evenings meant dinner on Joey D. at the Starliter Saloon with the owner himself. More shared memories from the friendly proprietor, all good. Juana had explained that her sister Sarah had legally changed her name to Jones as a gesture of putting the past behind her.

Juana, at this point in her crazy life, knew that she could not change the past, but the future was a different story. And hers had to start sometime. She felt this was the time. This was the place. This was the man. *Maybe, just maybe, Juana, your life doesn't have to be so mad after all.*

The goodnights moved from a peck to a kiss on the lips, until one night Juana explored Chris's willing tongue with her own, wet and soft, and hungry. Chris was having feelings he thought had long since been buried. Juana was reaching for the man who was once her sister's rose, thorns and all. And, with it, a chance to fill the emptiness housed in her soul for too many years.

"Tomorrow night I will make you dinner at your place and for dessert we can take up where we just left off. If that's okay with you, Chris."

"White wine or red?"

"White. Lots of it, please, pretty boy."

The next night's dinner was red snapper, poached in white wine and lemon, served on rice with a caper-onion glaze and a tossed green salad. The dessert Chris could not take his mind off of since last night's promise was delayed by a serving of coffee, dressed up with a shot of Grand Marnier. The splendid, sweetened zest of the key lime pie and its whipped-cream topping were almost enough to make Chris forget for a second about the other dessert.

Juana told Chris to leave the dishes and bring drinks out to the front porch. Chris brought out two glasses of the orange-flavored liqueur on the rocks. Coffee time was over. They drank in silence, with Chris's arm draped over Juana's left shoulder, and watched the moon try to peek out from the clouds and light up the water. Within a few minutes the drinks had run out along with the patience of the two who had grown so close. Chris led Sarah's older sister into the cottage.

It was to be a night of measured moments, tender trepidation, and passionate hunger. A sudden Florida rain seemed to have cleansed the air of its sultry humidity. A lucent band of moonlight cut its way through the small window on the east side of the cottage. Chris had put his compilation of country love songs in the dated Sony tape player that also served as the room's clock radio. The music from the small machine seemed to be carried through the room by the evening's breeze that drifted through the small window. Colin Raye's "In This Life" was followed by Garth's "The Dance." Since Sarah's death, Chris had grown to listen to the words and live the emotions. The uncertainty of life and fate were melded with heartfelt cheers for the love that comes along the way. As he danced and held onto Juana, he prayed for another chance. Juana prayed for her first.

She had told Chris of her gruesome physical damage, and tonight, she thought to herself, as Elvis had said, "It's Now or Never." Tonight she would show him and invite him to have the scars and all the rest of her. She had showered after their day at the beach and now shuffled on the "dance floor" in her brown sandals, dressed in a simple pair of white shorts and her blue Derek Jeter T-shirt. Chris had chosen his favorite black flip-flops, a pair of old, cutoff Levi's and an unbuttoned, black Nike polo. Juana had groomed her long black hair to sensual, enticing perfection. Chris's still-damp, ebony locks hung just over his collar.

The silent, unhurried dances in the dimly lit room spoke of a shared desire for the ultimate intimacy. Juana was surprised to hear the small tape machine push out the King's request to be loved tenderly. So, it was to be now—a now that she prayed would lead to way longer than never. She stopped Chris in their fifth deep kiss of the night. Juana easily worked the polo off Chris's body and gently kissed him on his perfect nipples. The hardness in his Levi's signaled what his body wanted so badly.

The look in Juana's eyes was suggesting another storyline, a revealing, telling preamble to Chris's and her heated desires—a challenge she needed to offer. A challenge, maybe a dare, which Chris would have to deal with *now*. Chris knew what she was asking, knew what she feared. He also knew exactly what he was going to do.

The crisp, tan bamboo window shade came down easily for Chris. The light from outside died quickly in the room. Only the small candle on the kitchen counter glowed. Chris strolled over to the counter and extinguished the last remaining light in the cottage.

Juana's chest tightened and disappointment shattered her resolve and hope. *He can't bear to look at my damaged body in the light.*

Chris came over to her, and, with just a splinter of moonlight leaking in, led her to the open bedroom door. He felt her faint resistance but moved on. They both could now only barely make out Tim McGraw singing "Not a Moment Too Soon." In darkness, Chris led her to the large mirror hanging on the back of the closet door. He pulled back soft strands of her hair and let his lips and tongue play on her neck.

"Don't move, Juana, not an inch."

She was startled and surprised when the two bulbs housed in the old, smoked-glass covering that hung in the middle of the ceiling came to life. She turned her head.

"What's the matter, Chris?"

"Just one simple thing, and I am gonna take care of that now."

He turned her shoulders so that she was facing her own reflection, something she had done many times before—sometimes for pleasure, sometimes to relieve the pain. But she had always been alone.

Chris stood behind her and gently took the hem of the T-shirt and began to lift. He knew from the dances that, except for the locket, she was naked underneath.

"Sorry, Mr. Jeter. This lady belongs to me tonight."

The T-shirt hit the floor. Chris's lips brushed her shoulder. His mirrored eyes bore into hers. She watched them in the reflection as they slid down to the decades-old scars. Juana watched his smiling gaze and then felt his hands move up from her waist to gather in and embrace her breasts. Her view moved down to the heat of his hands on her breasts. The way his fingers traced her scars reminded Juana of a perverse game of tic-tac-toe, but she knew this was no game, just the sweetest of tenderness from a tender man.

The feathery touch was pleasing and newly erotic. Chris turned her away from the mirror and toward him. He took her hand and led her to the old, wooden chest that sat at the foot of his bed. In one move he placed her on top of the chest and knelt in front of his naked-chested guest. His touches, his lips, his tongue, his movements that brought her own fingers to touch her breasts lit a fire in Juana. It was a fire of long-awaited passion and a flame of hope.

The rest was easy for both. The light stayed on the entire time, shining down on the discarded clothing, the probing tongues and hands, a damaged twosome reveling in repair. The low, rhythmic hum and thump of the ceiling fan kept time with the movement of the two lovers as Chris glided on top of Juana and pushed himself again and again deep into his new soul mate. The waves of air pushing down from the bamboo blades of the weathered fan cooled their heated, joined bodies; dried the tears that had found Juana's cheeks.

Their prurient passion calmed into a set of tangled bed clothing. And after a few deep breaths, came an honest-to-goodness, out-loud, communal laughter. And on this night, perhaps, two hearts and souls had bonded even more powerfully than their bodies. Juana felt none of the emptiness that always followed her own lonely ritual that began in front of her mirror. The looking glass in Chris's small bedroom had been the beginning of a new ritual, one of fulfillment. She no longer had to envy the perfect teats of Salma Hayek from *Desperado*. She now felt, knew, that she could now have what she thought her scarred breasts would forever deny her.

"Wanna beer, beautiful lady?"

"Hell yeah. But, hey, can you bring in the candle and kill that spotlight? It's killing my sensitive eyes, and my mascara must look like hell.

The cold beers, a welcome full-bodied lager from the Irish master brewer George Killian, were delivered, candle lit, and light slapped off. They sat up on the cream-colored, combed-cotton bed sheet with knees pulled up to their chests and sipped their beers.

"Nice locket, beautiful lady."

"Thanks. Got it from a special friend a long time ago. Nice pup you got on that dresser."

"Sure is. Got it from a special friend a long time ago. The pup's name is Lady Lucky." Chris paused. "And, if you behave yourself tonight, some of her luck just might rub off on you later when I catch my second wind."

Juana buried a laugh. *She* was the friend who had given Sarah the carving long ago.

Their laughter settled into quietude. The two spent, first-time lovers had shared the life force that had been Sarah. Both bled pain over her unfair exit from this earth. But on this night, the aura of her memory and its remnants, in the form of the candlelit Lady Lucky and the silver locket, did not dampen their passion, did not dim their hopes. For both, it felt like Sarah's memory, along with their physical act of passion, had created some kind of extraordinary trinitarian union.

"Think there's a God, Chris?"

"Oh yeah. That water out there and the wonderful ocean did not come from the South Florida Water Management team. And then there's you, one of Mama's two little angels.

"I just think maybe he was taking a day off when that son-of-a-bitching mosquito landed on our Sarah."

With his hand gently tracing the ripples of her naked spine, Juana knew that although she still owned the physical cicatrizations, the ones worn on her marred breasts, on this night, those images would not haunt her search for sleep.

CHAPTER 85

▼

CHILLY NIGHT

They both knew that the convenient bliss of that week in September of 2002 would have to end. Work and duty called.

For Juana, back to Northern Virginia and her thriving real estate business. For Chris, back to Quantico for at least two months to finish his current assignment, but now with hope for a transfer to the FBI's Counter Terrorism Division in Washington, D.C.—a bit closer to Juana's home. He would have to trade in the fresh country setting in Prince William County for concrete and asphalt, but what counted now was to be near his new lover. The Director of the CTD had asked for Chris, but his current boss had put him off for a while. Now with Juana in his life, Chris would look for the chance to move closer to Juana's Waterford, Virginia, home.

Chris got his wish, and the two new lovers found every opportunity to get together. On the weekends they preferred her early-1900s home set on a hill and three acres of idyllic property. The home was a renovated barn; the original structure was mostly cobblestone with a slate roof. On opposite sides of the original building, two sections had been added on. The exterior for the new extensions was simple clapboard painted light tan to blend in with the stone. The inside was a combination of century-old, wide pine planks for flooring, walls of plaster, antique tables and chairs, and the latest in stainless-steel kitchen appliances, and polished granite to top the old, wooden cabinets. Juana's bedroom, one of three, was massive and as eclectic as the rest of the house, with an old, cherrywood poster bed and dresser, joined in the window-filled room by a 50-inch Sony high-definition TV and matching DVD player, and a full home-theater audio system, of course. Concerned about his cherished, lazy, early-morning TV watching, he was happy to see the night shades on each of the windows that looked out onto the peaceful property with a myriad of trees and sections of cultured flower beds.

Chris's place, by contrast, was a relatively new town home in Clarendon Park, in the city of Arlington, Virginia. It was near the Clarendon Metro and just across the Potomac River from Washington, D.C. A short commute to the J. Edgar Hoover Building on Pennsylvania Avenue, in the heart of our nation's capital.

The two homes were only about fifty miles apart. But the traveling time between both could be hours. So, the two lovers picked and chose their times. If Juana had appointments in Fairfax, she would find a way to spend the night with Chris. On the weekends the traffic was bearable, and Chris would find his way out Route 66 to the Dulles highways and finally to Routes 7 and 9 to "the country."

For almost two years, they reveled in the ease and passion of their newfound relationship. After weeks of looking forward to their return to Jensen Beach and Joey D.'s place in September of 2003, Mother Nature, aka Hurricane Isabel, altered their plans as it smashed its way up the east coast. They were going to drive down in mid-September—work schedules made that timeframe the best. Isabel had other ideas.

It would be nine months later when a much more damaging force battered the handsome FBI man from Lexington, Virginia. For those months and for a year before that, the striking couple had "tripped the light fantastic"—words borrowed from John Milton's poem *L'Allegro*. The intriguing phrase had morphed over time into words that conveyed dancing on air. And dance the two lovers did.

It was a chilly, Friday night. It was June 11, 2004, and Juana and Chris had decided to walk the two miles from Chris's home to the original Bob and Edith's Diner over on Columbia Pike. Mr. & Mrs. Bolton's establishment had been an Arlington fixture since 1969. Since moving to the area, Chris had favored a late-evening dinner of their four-ounce rib eye, with two country fresh eggs and home fries, and toast and jelly. All for under nine dollars. Juana, this night, had the Delmonico steak, hold the fries and toast; just a salad, please. They each ordered a soft drink and chowed down. Chris noticed he was chowing more than Juana.

On the walk home, the temperature hung in the high fifties with a slight breeze, chilly for this time of year. Chris imagined that there was more than the brisk air that was chilling his lover, but she remained silent until they reached Clarendon Park. Earlier in the week, when Chris had suggested her home for the weekend, Juana said she wanted to try a weekend in the city.

The liquor-free diner had obviously left Juana wanting. Within seconds of entering Chris's town home, she pulled the bottle of Grey Goose out of the freezer, retrieved some ice, and poured herself a double shot into the Tervis Tumbler with the Redskins helmet planted between the layers of plastic.

"Can I get you something to drink?"

Chris nodded and said, "I guess I'll have what you're having, but with a splash of tonic."

"Sit down, Christopher. I want to snuggle."

"Works for me. Anything wrong?"

"Not at the moment."

Snuggle they did, and Chris was surprised, yet enthralled, with what happened next. Juana stood up from Chris's leather lounge chair and stripped off every piece of her clothing. She went back to the kitchen and refilled her glass with more vodka. She snapped on his Bose Wave System and grabbed one of Chris's CDs. She pushed a few buttons and Conway Twitty came back to life with his classic rendition of "The Rose."

"Do you mind if I dance, Christopher, Christopher Lee?"

Chris struggled to find his voice while his brain seemed to be otherwise occupied with the blood rushing to his eager friend trapped in the crotch of his Levi's.

"Not at all."

Her dance was slow. It was sensual and sexy. There were intermittent moves over to Chris, stiffly sitting in his chair. She teased his lips with hers. She washed the lobes of each ear with her moist tongue.

"I love you, Christopher Lee, in every way possible. Let me show you one."

Juana downed the last of the Goose and walked to the chair. Her mission was simple and quickly accomplished. Chris was naked within seconds. She kissed him deeply, their tongues sharing the smooth, lingering, subtle taste of the vodka. Chris made a move to get up, but Juana would have no part of that. Her lips circled his nipples, first the right, then the left. She moved down and gave him a friendly bite just inside his left thigh. Juana looked at the still-half-full drink that the closed-eye Chris had left on the oak table next to his chair. She sipped down the mixture in deliberate fashion, held some of the liquid in her mouth, warmed it with her own saliva, and smiled.

She teased him with her hands and then took him in her mouth until he shivered. Chris invoked his deity to never let this end, and, finally, face smiling, eyes rolled up in his head, he relaxed every muscle in his body—well, almost every muscle.

One hour later, in Chris's bed, under the covers and protected from the June chill, Juana let Chris return the favor, and the finale for the night was a passionate, soulful joining, like their first night in Jensen Beach.

The next morning the temperatures crept into the seventies. It did not much matter to Chris by the time Juana walked out the door. His home was as cold as it had ever been.

The afternoon before their glorious Friday night of passion, Juana had made the phone call she never wanted to make, to set up this meeting, an early-morning good-bye. To have the heart-breaking discussion she never hoped to have. The meeting in Baltimore with Carmine and the Broker, only weeks before, had made her exit from her lover's life inevitable. Maybe even permanent. Saturday came and so did the chilling heartbreak.

"Chris, I have to leave you for a while. And I can't tell you why or for how long. If you love me, try and trust me."

Juana's stabbing words lingered in his mind. His body felt a familiar, unwelcome, and unexpected ache. He made his way through the next few days in a stunned, funereal-like trance.

These were the last memories that Chris managed through before his eyes and brain shut down for the night—exactly one year later in the White Plains Marriott.

The five hours of sleep were deep until Chris's cell phone belted out an obnoxious ring on his night table. The bitterness of his last, dreamy thoughts of Juana's leaving still lingered as he sat up in bed.

"Wake up, Chris Lee-san. There's trouble down the road."

CHAPTER 86

▼

CLOSE TO HOME

"What the hell's going on, Jed?"

"I'm already at the office. I just got a call. Somebody turned Whalen's new Chrysler Crossfire convertible into a very large firecracker and, subsequently, a fireball right there in his driveway. But no one was hurt. Thank God."

"What? That black beauty his rich wife just bought him?"

"You got it."

"Where?"

"I told you; his driveway in Scarsdale. It's got one of those really fancy car alarms with a remote starter and a bunch of other stuff. Whalen apparently likes his car at the exact preferred temperature before he leaves for work. Well, when he pushed one of those magic buttons his gas tank lit up like the Fourth of July. Luckily, or maybe unluckily, because it gave someone easy access, he had parked it outside last night. Didn't want to wake the wife and kid when he got home late. Well, the whole neighborhood is awake now. If he had turned the key himself in the car, Mr. Jerry Whalen would be among the charred shards and pieces that make up the smithereens strewn around his property. He just finished screaming into the phone I picked up in the office. I think we should go down there and see how the other half lives in the one and only Scarsdale, New York."

Jed and Chris made the short trip down Route 22. South Broadway turned into Post Road, and, with a left on Drake Road and only a few turns, they made their way to Jerry Whalen's busy driveway. The home was set back from the street and was a Tudor, showing brick, stucco, and wood that all merged into an impressive and welcoming frontage—well, except for the shiny red-and-white fire trucks and the gray police cars with their lights flashing red, white, and blue that had screamed their way from their brick headquarters at 50 Tompkins Road that morning.

There was not much for Jed or Chris to do except try to calm Jerry down. His wife was overseas on another of her all-important, international legal negotiations for the latest merger or acquisition. His seventeen-year-old son, Timmy, had already left for school.

"Well, Chris, I never really knew the origin of the word smithereens, but I guess it's kind of like pornography. You know it when you see it."

The Village of Scarsdale's Police Investigations Section was running the scene. One of the forty-five full-time officers, a section commander, a handsome Dave Foster, was barking out orders to the other men and women at the scene. A "Law and Order" or "CSI Miami" kind of scene, calling for his men to secure the crime scene, to canvas the neighborhood for any witnesses, to properly collect any pertinent evidence—mostly smithereens at this point—and to get hold of the police chief. When he ran out of things to bark, he simply wiped his furrowed brow and quietly said, "Shit. Of all days to have a tee time at Westchester." He would have to remember to call his rich father-in-law who had been a long-time member. *Shit, damn, son of a bitch.*

Because of the nature of the crime and its target being the head of the DO3J task force, the FBI agents from Federal Plaza down in the city would be involved real soon.

"What the hell is this?"

It was now 10:00 AM and Jerry, Chris, and Jed had made their way back to the White Plains DOJ office building on Quarropas. The forensics were already in. The bomb was C4, to those in the know, cyclotrimethylene trinitramine. The explosive itself is usually coated with a plastic binder, to keep it safe and stable, to make it easy to mold—like in a shape that would snugly fit under a back fender near the gas tank of a Chrysler sports car. The required partner to tear apart Jerry's car was believed to be an electrical detonator. Only a brief electrical charge is required to set off the small amount of explosive material in the detonator, like a wire run from Jerry's ignition to the detonator. Its likely makeup was a 12-inch waterproof fuse, a spent .223 cartridge, smokeless gunpowder from a pistol cartridge, mercury fulminate powder, sulphur, and potassium chlorate powder. A simple, deadly combination that delivers a powerful shock that triggers the C4 explosive material. And renders the kind of smithereens that lay in and about Jerry Whalen's scorched driveway. A frightening and fiery image.

The only fiery image that hung more fiercely in Jed's mind later that night was the smithereens that once had been Jerry Whalen's cool. The C4 event and one other happening had blown the top off of the DOJ attorney.

The answer to Jerry's, "What the hell is this?" from one of the FBI agents was, "I hate to tell you this, boss, but it's a box with a Verizon cell phone in it."

"So?"

"Well, the big so is that your son, along with the assistant dean of students, brought it over here early this morning. A woman in a police uniform had intercepted Junior on his way into Cardinal Stepinac and said that you wanted him to have it."

The fifty-seven-year-old, redbrick Catholic high school over on Mamaroneck and its pristine grounds were only minutes away from the DOJ office.

"When Junior turned the cell phone on, it buzzed and rang an alert to a message already left. He assumed the message on the unexpected phone was from you. But …"

"But what, for Christ's sake?"

"Well, it's best if you listen. I think."

The tiny machine was primed for playback and the lovely Lea, with latex gloves on, put the phone on speaker and pushed the right buttons.

"Can you hear me now?" Louder, slower, and with much more sting, "CAN YOU HEAR ME NOW?"

"Maria. Free her now. Money. Get it now. Get your Web site working. Your time is running out, Mr. Whalen. Ticktock." And then a pause.

More bizarre visions of Captain Hook, Mr. Smee, and the fleet-footed croc snuck briefly into Jerry's head.

"More innocents will die unless you act. Sorry about the Crossfire, but you've been ignoring my calls. Can you hear us now?"

The voice and words on the sleek phone and the intrusion into Jerry's family were all the detonators needed to unleash a Whalen tsunami.

CHAPTER 87

▼

SAFE HOME

No matter how much Jerry or anyone else yelled and screamed, or how touching the pleas for citizens to come forth with any clues were during the FBI press conference, the DO3J task force was still staring at piles of data scratched on a flock of whiteboards and layered in deep, eleven-by-fourteen boxes—without a clue.

Chris had highlighted the obvious change in pronoun between "I" and "we" in the messages from the bad guys. There was no profile in his mind or any book that fit these guys and their acts or possible motives. The FBI's best in class was in the dunce's corner.

The metal platters that held the heads of the two Johns turned out to be silver-plated pieces manufactured by Reed & Barton. It is one of the oldest and most renowned manufacturers of sterling and silver-plated products. Their factory and factory store are located in Taunton, Massachusetts. You can buy this particular plate there, at any number of department stores across the country, or over the Internet. Over 500 such pieces were ordered in just the last twelve months. Good luck trying to tie these nineteen-inch-long, twelve-inch-wide plates that retail for $300 to anyone tied to bloody noggins from New York and Sarasota. The etching on the back was similar to the tattoos on Jesus Cruz's back. "John was innocent. So was Alberto. Free Maria." The font, again, was Caesar, and the words were bordered this time, not by crosses, but by swords etched onto the back of the plates.

Roxie Amato had flown in from LA to present the task force all of the evidence gathered in the Jesus H. case. The Manhattan South and Sarasota boys and girls in uniform had done the same—sans any Grady O'Connor. The facts about the lives of the two Johns were on whiteboards and easels. Investigations into Carmine Antobelli, his son Alberto, and his wife Maria Calabrese were like the streets with the yellow, diamond-shaped sign, with those two definitive black words painted on them—DEAD END. There was nothing to be found either on the search for any meaningful connections to the mob uncle of Maria's unfortunate lover, Frankie Noto. Mysteries abounded. Clues and evidence were elusive.

When Chris tried to explain to Jerry that these guys knew what they were doing, Mr. Whalen's anger and frustration displayed in front of his task force looked pre-coronary. He wasn't ready to deal with the fact that New York City sidewalks don't hold footprints and the calm waters of the Sarasota Bay are even more reluctant depositories of useful evidence. And the FedEx surveillance tapes and packing slips yielded nothing but unidentifiable faces and phony names and addresses.

The one clue that had excited the task force on the morning of its second day had only further driven home the fact that these guys, Jed's guys, these bad guys, were clever, deceptive, nasty, and well funded.

"Semen. Semen in the mouths of both Johns. It took the medical examiners a while to make sure that's what they had." The excited forensic analyst was yelling as he entered the jury, now task force, room.

Unfortunately, the semen from the Florida John and its DNA had been traced back to a shortstop who played for a double-A baseball team in Florida. And who happened to go three for four the day of the Sarasota John killing. It was an away game against the Chattanooga Lookouts.

One of the techs on the task force explained. "His DNA was on the FBI's Combined DNA Index System, CODIS. Apparently Mr. Ellison was falsely arrested in an FBI sting on some kind of insider stock trading deal. Never convicted, but they kept his genetic deoxyribonucleic acid on file anyway"

"Get the son-of-a-bitch in here anyway. Now! I want to know how his sperm ended up in one of our Johns," Jerry demanded.

Only hours later, a confused and nervous Wade Ellison was staring at an angry crowd. He would miss his next game against the Montgomery Biscuits.

"And when was this, again?"

"Sometime last week."

"What time last week?"

"A week ago Saturday. We were still in Jacksonville. I got kind of loaded that night at the Ragtime Tavern in Atlantic Beach. I met this chick. I think her name was Patty. She said she was in town visiting her brother Greg, who worked an off shift at some hospital. Said she had ventured out looking for friendly conversation. Well, to make things short here, I followed her down the A1A to her brother's place, and one thing led to another."

"Hate to barge into your personal life here, Wade, but how exactly do you think your semen ended up in the mouth of the poor man who was decapitated and left on the steps of the Ringling Mansion in Sarasota?"

"I have no idea."

"Well, okay, how exactly might have this Patty collected a deposit of our evidence? Can you remember that?"

Wade almost smiled, almost laughed, and then caught himself. "Well, Mr. Whalen, sir, there were several ways that I left my semen behind that night. It was quite a long night, and Patty was quite serious about having friendly conversations, so to speak. So, I made sure to give her my best effort. Played like shit the next day though. Exhausted."

"Can you describe her?"

"You mean her face?"

"Yeah, that too."

"I didn't see much of her face, but I can try."

Another yellow sign with black letters.

Later that afternoon, after a bit of a haggle with the U.S. Coast Guard, the task force had invited the second semen donor into the White Plains jury room. DNA was received from his branch of the service, after the haggle was concluded. This semen depositor just happened to be a *seaman*. Coast Guard Seaman Apprentice Jay Snyder stationed in Fort Hamilton, not far from Bay Ridge, Brooklyn. A different woman, different vague description, same plot. Bar, booze, lots of positions, lots of deposits. Another DEAD END.

Both were entertaining stories that yielded only confirmation that these guys had resources, all kinds. The simple guess was that the sperm was retained in some fashion by the two enticing women and then frozen, transported, and inserted into the mouths of the two unfortunate Johns—clever, expensive, deceptive. The amorous ball player and seaman had taken their shots in the dark, and Jed and Chris and the rest had just wasted precious time.

It was late by the time Jed and Chris left the office on the night of Monday, June 27, 2005. But not too late to stop for a drink and a snack at the Vintage Bar and Restaurant on Main, across from the Galleria—highly recommended by the locals. Beer-battered shrimp and two glasses of Grey Goose on the rocks were just what the doctor ordered for the tired lawmen. The car bombing, the Verizon inquisition, Jerry's ranting with the sperm donors, and the DEAD ENDs had almost worn them out. But not quite. Tonight it would be two drinks, not one. They sat on the wooden bar stools devouring the crusty and tasty shellfish, savoring each sip of the vodka. After two drinks, they decided to take the short walk up Grove Street back to the Marriott. There was nothing in their cars that they needed tonight. The contents of the two cars tonight were about as useless as all the non-evidence sitting in the courthouse.

It had been a hazy day, and the partly cloudy night hid most of the sky's half moon. Streetlights were the White Plains walkers' guide on the night of June 27, 2005.

The report and flash from the twenty-five-inch, steel-grade barrel of the custom-made Decision Maker, 308 Winchester rifle shattered the silence of the quiet, late-night street in downtown White Plains.

Jed recognized the noise. It sounded like it was coming from the rooftop across the street from the Vintage Bar. Within an instant the .308 Winchester, 165-grain Triple Shock X-Bullet, traveling at twenty-seven hundred feet per second, a product of Federal Premium Ammunition, slammed into Chris Lee's chest and dropped him to the ground like a bag of rocks.

For some reason, Jerry Whalen's last words of the day echoed in Jed's mind. "Safe home, now, boys. We got a lot of work to do tomorrow. Safe home."

CHAPTER 88

▼

PLEASURE BEFORE BUSINESS

"Good morning, Mr. Huse. How are you today?"

"Doing just fine, Linda. It's always a good day when one can put golf first and business second. And seeing you makes it even finer."

The Broker moved on from the reception desk and stopped in the office and said hello to the rest of the administrative staff at International Country Club, and, as with Linda, he dropped off a handful of Hershey kisses at the desk of each of the ladies. The men got one of the Broker's signature Sancho Panza Caballero cigars, a mellow Honduran blend of tobaccos. As he headed to the men's locker room, he mused that the application for a position in that office must include bright, pleasant, and good-looking—at least for the female positions.

The Broker strode down to the pro shop and said his hellos to Aaron, John, and Joe, the assistant professionals. Erika, the female teaching pro, was on the putting green with her junior students. Rick said a quick hello to the pretty lady and made his way over to the starter.

"Hey, Lionel. I'm expecting three guests today. Treat them nice, like you always do, and let them know I am at the practice range."

"You got it, Mister H."

For his promised work the Broker slipped a ten-dollar bill into his hand.

The man who loved this game, this feeling of walking onto the crisply cut grass that ached for golf, in a place full of friendly faces, was all decked out in his Ashworth, double-pleated, twill slacks, colored in a fashionable stone shade, and a black Cutter and Buck polo with the ICC logo in white resting on the left side of his chest. With a lighter flaming his own Sancho Panza and a tip of his off-white Masters golf cap, he was off to begin his routine on this hazy, hot June 30, 2005, day.

As the Broker smiled and exhaled his first puff of the flavored smoke, the DO3J task force members were all holding their breath on this deadline day. The stance had been immovable, "We will not give in to these terrorists, ever."

After a brief test of speed on the putting green, he and his guests, Corey Young, Maximum Al, and the X-man, Ken O'Brien—his computer-security brain trust—turned to watch the match of the day.

It was a match that had become an annual challenge. Derek Pinner, a member of the Fauquier Country Club, and his friend Patti Ansel faced off against Tall Tom, the head Pro at ICC, and Allan Mason, also a friend of Derek's from the Middleburg area of Virginia. The first match between the two teams had taken place in 2002. Derek, a low handicapper, and his partner, all five foot four and 100 pounds of her, whooped up on a much larger Allan and much taller head pro. The match in 2002 had no following in any way. But after two more years of the larger team handing over money to the smaller but winning team, it had gained some notoriety. And today was the day. They were ready to tee off in front of the Broker and his boys. The assistant pros had come out of the shop to watch the start, and the upstairs patio was crowded with onlookers. For this one day, at least, the club in Fairfax, Virginia, took on a feel of Vegas. Bets had been placed on almost every aspect of the match.

There was no serious rumbling when the foursome all hit safely into the middle of the first fairway, but the game was on.

When all was clear, Mr. Rick Huse ripped a Calloway three metal just to the edge of the pond on the left. Through the waft of the cigarillo's smoke he smelled birdie. Unfortunately, the trap on the right had other thoughts. His first birdie was not found until the long, 3-par fourth hole.

As he stood on the fifth tee, he let the other three, Corey, Max, and Kenny, tee off first. He was interested in the foursome in front of his, and their fourth annual battle. They had just teed off on number six. He watched a group of members he recognized, Mary Lou and Larry Haines, Chris Fox and his wife

Reggie, on the sixth green. They must have been playing some kind of alter-
nate-shot match play, because when Reggie sunk a six-footer for par Chris
clapped and cheered and they moved on. Rick waved hello to the foursome and
then proceeded to smash his Titleist Pro V1 with a five iron, high and straight,
safely away from the ponds on the left. The Broker had time to hang back and
watch the other foursome hit their second shots on six because the X-man had
whacked his ball into the trees on the right.

Things got interesting when Rick saw Allan's ball struggling to clear the pond
in front of the sixth green. He didn't hear Allan articulate, "Piss, damn,
son-of-a-Nike-bitch, piece-of-shit ball." But he did witness the orb with the swish
career off the wall of wood that separated the water from safety. He *did* hear that
"whack" sound followed by the sickening sound of the ball hitting water. He
watched the depressing ring of ripples spelling out the end of life for Allan's ball.
He didn't need to watch anymore when Allan, after re-clubbing and fishing a
new Nike out of his bag, drove his second attempt into the trees behind the
green, behind the cart path. He noticed Patti and Derek standing on the top of
the hill in the familiar one-leg-crossed-behind-the-other, leaning-on-the putter
stance—subtly letting the infuriated Allan know that they were waiting for him
because their shots had found friendly territory. He waved to Allan who returned
the favor with a one-finger salute. The Broker had a good feeling about his
one-thousand-dollar bet with the handsome black man who just lost hole number six. The crossover house after number seven meant a four-finger wave to José,
which was followed by the serving up of four of the world's best hot dogs and
four cold Yuenglings.

When Mr. Huse's group finished their round, white-whiskered Jack was on
duty.

"Have your boys clean the clubs up good for me will you, Jack. Appreciate it."

Another ten exchanged hands and Rick and his group headed upstairs.

The Broker and his pals caught up with the combatants in the match of the
day in the grillroom. Derek and Patti were smiling and sipping a cold draft. Allan
and Tom were handing over one hundred dollars—the cost of losing by two
points in their low and aggregate 18-hole match.

Valinda, the charming hostess, had Mr. Huse's table ready. A different Erika,
pretty as well, had already poured his Grey Goose on the rocks, and Gerard carried it over to the smiling redhead. When dinner was over, Rick made sure Gerard had put the other foursome's tab on his account—always the gracious
winner. On the way out, the Broker said his goodbyes to his security crew and

316 Best In Class

met up with Allan in the men's room. The defeated bettor tried to hand over ten crisp hundred-dollar bills to his friend.

"Keep it. Allan, I need your help."

"Legal or illegal?"

"Guess."

"Shit."

"Don't worry. You'll personally be far away from the nasty stuff. I just need a passive action taken care of, and I need layers of insulation between it and me. And there's nobody better at that than you, you ex-Army spook."

Like so many others, Allan owed the Broker in a way that did not allow one to just say no.

CHAPTER 89

▼

ALMOST SHOWTIME

While Rick Huse was showering down at the country club, Juana was relaxing in his air-conditioned sun room off the back of his Fairfax home.

She had had a long day beginning with a predawn trip from her Waterford home down to Irvington, on Virginia's Northern Neck. She had taken the back way down Routes 15, 17 and 3. Juana hated traffic, and Northern Virginia was the poster region for traffic. Her date with James Acerno, another of the Broker's minions, was not until noon at Rose's Crab House & Raw Bar, but she had other business down at the Tides Inn in Irvington. This would profitably occupy her time until savoring Rose's fried oyster plate and a cold glass of draft beer, and taking care of the other business with Ace.

Now, after a nice lunch at Rose's and her two-and-a-half-hour drive back to Fairfax, she was savoring the last few pages of the book the Broker had lent her, *Black Vortex* by Dennis O'Connell, along with a cold glass of Picpoul de Benet. Juana, in a way, related to the main character in the novel, Julie O'Connor. A woman first, an officer of the law second, with a violent past that included the gruesome carving of COP on her stomach. A scarred woman, who, in the end, danced on the other side of the law to find some peace. Juana swilled the rich white wine and thought, *Hell, he was playing golf all day. I can take time out, too. You go, Julie girl.*

When Huse made it home around six, he arrived with a box of Buon Appetito's almost-as-good-as-the-Bronx pizza, sausage, and mushrooms—just like Juana likes it—and a large Greek salad. It was bottles of Yuengling around and dinner was on and then over.

"Time to get to work, Juana. Let's go."

There were no whiteboards or easels in Rick's Fairfax basement, just computers and other electronics—eerily similar to his place in Pelham. They soon got Carmine Antobelli on the secure phone. They discussed the lack of a DOJ response and their planned strategy to move forward.

"It's almost showtime, folks. Everything seems to be in order. I have spoken to Allan Mason, and Juana, Miss Pelham 3, has been in contact with Ace."

The phone call participants agreed that things were indeed in order for their next move, assuming midnight would come and go with no response from Mr. Whalen and crew.

"Are you sure about this, Rick?" Juana asked haltingly.

"Juana." Rick interrupted himself. "Carm, can you hear?"

"Loud and clear, One." The Broker brushed back his red hair with one hand and planted his eyes directly on Juana's. "Juana, I know we all thought in our own way that this kind of thing was behind us years ago and that we could move on to a more normal existence."

Juana thought of the two fathers she had killed and the reasons for doing it.

Carm envisioned the way he made his bones back in Yonkers long ago. At his father Sal's bidding, he executed a man who had made threats to Sal concerning his daughter. The reason for the killing masking its brutality.

"Think of the six insurance policies Noto gave to Carmine in Florida, and then let's get this done. Then we can move on for good. I hate to get philosophical on you two, but, as Aristotle said, 'We make war that we may live in peace.'"

Silence delivered consent.

"Oh, and, Carm. I need to ask you. How much?"

"How much what, Rick?"

"How much do you need for the other Florida thing?"

"I think we all agreed one million would do it."

"Okay. Got it."

As Juana went to leave that night, she was filled with fear and anticipation, and the Broker sensed it.

"Hey, Juana. Remember what the great Roman author Virgil wrote in his *Aeneid*, 'Fortune favors the bold.' Things should go well. You have done a great job. Safe home."

CHAPTER 90

▼

YOU LIGHT UP MY LIFE

The days were going better than planned for Geordie Williams—swimmingly in fact. He and his honey, Mary Brennan, had taken off the Friday before and the Tuesday after the July Fourth weekend to make it a five-dayer. At 4:00 AM on the morning of July 1, 2005, alarms went off. By five, the Sonata was packed. They blew through the usually traffic-clogged Dulles Toll Road, laughed as the Beltway felt like an empty racetrack, gave a Bronx cheer to invisible drivers on Route 50, and even smiled when their E-ZPass rang up the $2.50 toll to cross the Bay Bridge. A combination of Tim McGraw and Rascal Flatts got them through the last hour of the two-lane roads of Slower Lower Delaware. It was a little after 8:00 AM when Gary LeVox, Joe Don Rooney, and Jay DeMarcus started "Praying for Daylight." In an answer to their prayers and the travelers', the Fenwick Island skies gave passage to the sun's struggling rays. Friday was a day of beach, bocce, and beers. Saturday's clouds and off-and-on rain kept the young couple sequestered inside of or on the protected deck of the Bunting Avenue home they were borrowing from good friends. After the early-morning haze, the stingy sun became more generous and Sunday earned its title, and therefore more beach time was in order. The post-beach, outdoor showers were followed by a sumptuous meal of grilled filet, roasted potatoes, and fresh white corn. When the second bottle of Hess Select cabernet went dry, Geordie suggested a walk on the beach to be rewarded by a one-block walk up East Essex Street to the Dairy Queen. On the beach, the moon was nowhere to be found, but the stars joined the sky in abundance.

This was it. This was the moment. The Atlantic was making that special sound the ocean makes at night on a deserted beach; the rhythmic, enticing lapping that the tides orchestrate on the sandy shore. Like the mighty sea was resting from a long day's work.

The nervous, curly haired thirty-year-old stopped their walk and knelt in the damp, warm sand in front of his longhaired beauty. He managed to forage the intricate, lacey, white gold ring from the pocket of his black Nike Dri-Fit shorts. He held it up to Mary, level with her folded hands resting on the hem of her Georgetown hoodie. The nervous boy managed to squeak out his petition. Mary Catherine Brennan looked up to the sky, Geordie's eyes, now opened wide, burned into her chin.

"Well, Mr. Williams. I had always planned to confer with the man in the moon on this decision, but he appears to have taken the night off. So, let's check his backup, the North Star. Ah, Mr. Star just gave two winks. So, I guess it's yes."

The plan from here was to celebrate with a couple of hot fudge sundaes, get some sleep, and on the following day head back for the Fourth in our nation's capital.

On the way west the next morning, Mary had wrestled command of the Sirius radio from Geordie and found a Maryland oldies station. Halfway to D.C., Debbie Boone melodically poured out the sweet words from her 1970's hit, "You Light Up My Life." Mary slid her hand on top of her driver's and commented, "Appropriate, don't you think? July Fourth and all."

The died-in-the-wool country zealot grunted and said, "LeAnn Rimes did a better job, but you still light up my life."

Hours later, as the fireworks began from the Lincoln Memorial reflecting pool, Mary squeezed Geordie's hand and thanked him for the extravagant celebration of their engagement.

"Well, I guess since all these people here know, we ought to call our parents tomorrow and let them know, huh?"

They were watching with others from the roof of Mary's company's office building just across the Potomac River in Arlington, Virginia. When the festivities ended, the couple went for a late-night supper at the Carlyle on South 28th Street in Arlington. After devouring the Tex Mex egg rolls and a dinner of mango chicken, the newly engaged twosome found room for deep-dish apple pie with vanilla ice cream on the side.

"One more surprise tonight, Mary. You game?"

"Sure. Does it include walking any of this off?"

"You bet."

It was a short ride up Route 395 into D.C. The crowds were gone and parking was easy. They walked the area around the Vietnam Vets and Lincoln Memorials—the backdrop of their first date. A few trucks were rolling in the streets carrying the dismantled infrastructure of the day's ceremonies and celebrations. They and a large thermos filled with coffee laced with amaretto found their way to a wooden bench not far from the Korean War Memorial.

"Well, Geordie Williams, you sure know how to charm a girl and throw a party."

"Well, you know it's always all about you, babe. That's what I'm here for. Just thought it would be special to return to where it all started—the scene of the crime, so to speak."

They chatted for hours about what was, and what was to come. Their dreams were simple ones of warmth and happiness and family.

"Come on. I'll take you home. We have a big day tomorrow."

"Oh yeah, that's right. Let's see. You're making pancakes and sausage at noon. This will be followed by a feeble attempt to tackle the rest of the Sunday Post crossword, a subsequent bloody Mary and a long nap. Have I got that right?"

Geordie was ready to respond to Mary's words and the soft massage she had going on his neck when he heard and saw a large white truck make its way south on Henry Bacon Drive up to the circle by the Lincoln Memorial and stop. In tall blue letters the word "ZAMBELLI" was spelled out on the side of the truck. Underneath was the word "FIREWORKS" in smaller red letters and below that the word "INTERNATIONALE." There were blue and red bursts of sparks of different sizes, all together making up the logo of the best in class in the pyrotechnics business. It was an enterprise founded by Antonio Zambelli in 1893. The Italian immigrant settled in the small town of New Castle, Pennsylvania, and built a company that is still considered worldwide as the one that sets the industry standard in design and technology.

The couple was surprised when four men got out of the truck wearing ski masks and black jackets with "MATTHEW 13:42-43" written on the back. Three men went around the back of the truck and unloaded three man-size tanks and took them to the curbside of the truck. The fourth carried out what looked like three black hoses and disappeared behind the side of the truck. Geordie and Mary's surprise went to shock when the side of the truck facing them fell to the street with a loud clang. Shock went to disbelief when they saw three people standing on a platform mounted on the flooring of the truck. They appeared to be women bound to three large stakes, lined up in a row. The platform was several feet above the trailer's floor. There were three pyres of twigs and larger pieces of wood in three teepee shapes—one piled around each of the women. One of the men came up to the front of the truck's cab. He had grabbed another hose from the back of the truck's bed, this one clear. He opened the cap on the fuel tank and stuck in the hose. He took a large, rubber, bulb-shaped object and stuck it on the end of the hose. With only a few pumps, the truck's fuel began spilling out onto Lincoln Memorial Circle. That done the man jumped up onto the edge of the truck bed and turned a large flow valve spewing a heavy liquid onto the floor of the truck bed, which was rimmed on all sides by a two-foot, solid metal rail.

A black van sped past the truck, made a U-turn, and pulled up to the curb fifty feet past the back of the semi. The siphoner made his way to the van and opened one of the back doors.

With an incredible whoosh, a fire, brighter than any Fourth of July fireworks, jumped up from the bottom of the platform on the truck's bed. The holocaust was fueled through the openings in the crisscrossed, iron beams that made up the platform, and engulfed the three bound females. The flames did not lick at the wood and the enclosed victims. They burned with inferno-like intensity. Ferocious and torrid.

The three others in black, with the handles to the propane tanks' shutoff valves in their hands, jumped into the back of the van and all sped away.

Geordie and Mary would not get any sleep or sausage and pancakes that morning. The only puzzle they would be trying to solve had to do with the mysterious happenings they witnessed. They, along with two other witnesses, one, a sanitation worker on his way into work, the other, a homeless woman who had been sleeping on a bench near the Korean Memorial, would first be the guests of both the United States Park Police and the Metropolitan Police Department, and after that the FBI for most of the day. The hardened veterans of the law enforcement agencies winced with the recollections of the fiery pain provided by the witnesses. Both the bag lady and the sanitation worker became teary eyed when recounting the screams they heard from the infernal platform parked in front of the Lincoln Memorial.

By that night, via local and national news programs, most of Mary and Geordie's relatives had learned that the couple who witnessed the event was engaged. Excitement over the news of the betrothment and the unfortunate celebrity of the twosome kept the phone lines burning and their home answering machines loaded.

CHAPTER 91

▼

"Nice shot, Mr. Huse."

"Thanks, Mr. Steve."

Steve Dowd, a bank executive from Pleasantville, was the Broker's guest for the day—and quite a credible alibi, if it ever came to that. Rick Huse's second shot on the ninth hole, a 500-yard par five, had landed just past the flagstick and spun back to within three feet. A few people on the putting green and others on the back patio of the majestic, brick clubhouse gave the Broker a short round of polite golf applause. He tipped his cap down to his black Footjoys and smiled.

"Man, you are burning it up today, Rick."

If you only knew, thought Rick.

Inside the Wykagyl clubhouse a few members were snacking on Danish and bagels and hot cups of coffee—almost as hot as the news they were watching on CNN the day after Independence Day.

> "Another stunning and ghastly set of executions took place early this morning. This one in our nation's capital, in front of the Lincoln Memorial. I have to warn you that the footage you are about to see is gruesome."

"Nice eagle, Rick. I believe that gives you a ..."

"Don't tell me, Steve. It's bad luck to know. I'll just take my three and move on; thanks."

At the same time CNN was showing the violent flames from D.C., Rick Huse lit up one of his Sancho Panza Caballeros.

"One of the victims has been tentatively identified as Joan Hornsby of Amity, Arkansas, a small town twenty-eight miles south of Hot Springs, where she worked as a waitress. Our sources did hear from one of the firefighters on the scene that apparently the bottom of the truck bed was somehow housing many gallons of oil that ignited when the propane jets were lit. When the firefighters first arrived and tried to put the fire out with water, a second explosion of flames engulfed the victims. A female firefighter told our reporter that with the top and two sides of the truck in place, it looked like a large crematorium. The police are keeping a tight reign on information but our reporter on the scene was able to pick up this exclusive …"

It was 10:00 AM and the Broker had just dropped his eagle putt. The lead CNN story was the same one it had been since early in the morning. And the shit was hitting the proverbial fan once more in the task force room on Quarropas Street in White Plains, New York.

"What do we know? Anything? What the hell do we know?"

"Only what's on the news, Mr. Whalen."

"Agent Chris Lee and Detective Jed Davies caught a private jet out of Westchester this morning. They got clearance to land at Reagan, so, we should be hearing from them soon."

"That's it?"

"Oh, sorry. That and United States Park Police CCTV shots from the Lincoln Memorial from this morning were transmitted up here. We got a few glimpses of the perps, but, with the jackets and masks, we did not get much. Just the lettering on the back of the jackets. License plates were stolen."

"And, Lieutenant?"

"Well, we looked up the passages from Matthew's gospel. I have it printed out over here. I got it from the Web."

Lieutenant Kenny Riordan, a handsome thirty-year veteran of the NYPD, with the gray hair to prove his seniority, handed over the sheet of paper. Jerry Whalen mouthed the words of Jesus.

"Matthew 13:42: '… and shall cast them into the furnace of fire: there shall be weeping and gnashing of teeth.'

Matthew 13:43: '… then shall the just shine as the sun, in the kingdom of their Father. He that hath ears to hear, let him hear.'"

The lieutenant spoke, "It was part of a parable. Jesus was in a boat talking to his followers on shore. This part is about the harvesting of the fruit of the good seeds and the bad seeds at the end of the world and their separation. You know, the bad guys get to burn in hell and gnash their teeth. The good guys go to heaven and hang out with the Big Guy."

"Yeah, yeah, yeah, Ken. These guys are messing with our heads again. Jesus." The DOJ executive gave the paper back to Riordan, put his head in his hands, and muttered, "Oh shit. Here we go again."

Riordan guessed that the lack of any threatening thumb drives arriving in the morning's delivery had caused Jerry to hold out some sliver of hope that this morning's executions were the act of some group of nutcases—different from the group that had been making his life miserable and putting his career in serious jeopardy. Now that hope went up in flames as consuming as those on Lincoln Memorial Circle. The task force's relief, when the June 30 deadline came and went without further violence, went with those virtual flames.

CHAPTER 92

▼

THUMBS UP, THUMBS DOWN

"Well, Mr. Lee, it looks like we don't know much more than before we spent this lovely day in D.C."

"Yeah, we do. We know they are not going to stop until either we pay them or catch them. We'll have to wait till the crime scene crew does their thing to know much more."

"Unbelievable. Three propane tanks loaded to the gills. There wasn't much of anything left to see. The heat was so intense everything was beyond charred, all ashes."

"Well, let's see what they find in that mess. What are the odds that Joan Hornsby of Arkansas, our Joan of Arc, was joined by two other Joans of Arkansas in that truck bed inferno?"

"My bet is on 'No doubt'. Well, at least *you're* still among the living."

"Yep. Best damn decision Whalen has made so far, I guess." Chris's thumb was pointing upward toward the ceiling of the early-morning jet that was taking them back to Westchester Airport.

It had been seven days since the rifle shot from the Galleria rooftop had slammed into Chris Lee's chest. Jerry Whalen had insisted that, after the car bombing in his driveway, anyone involved in the task force wear the expensive

PointBlank body armor. The black ballistic vest had caught the bullet and saved Chris's life. Of course the shooter left no clues behind, just a feeling of fear and desperation.

On the morning of July 6, 2005, at 9:00 AM, Chris and Jed briefed the task force on their interviews with the witnesses, their surveillance of the crime scene, and the fear that there may be more dead ends ahead.

At 10:00 AM, it was thumbs-down time for any hope that the ashes that were the aftermath of yesterday's dramatic torching would not end up in Jerry Whalen's lap.

Mr. U.S. Attorney, you have 24 hours to do as you have been instructed.
The demand is now for 11 million dollars.
And, as from the start,
Free Maria Calabrese, now.

Title our Web link "Conviction Overturned."

Password protect it for my eyes only.
Use the letters "BAOWMABYS". All caps please.

Place only two lines on the page.

"Site under Construction.
Try again soon."

If you follow these instructions, I will present you with the compliance process by which we, together, can satisfy our demands.

If you don't believe we are serious, ask *Jesus* and the *Johns*
and now the *Joans*.
Oh, sorry, that's right, they're dead.

If you fail to respond as requested, more Innocents will perish.

24 hours! You know, just like Jack Bauer.

The words moved on, and a graphic of dollar signs and green bills floated across the screen followed by a stark picture of Maria Calabrese in her prison garb.

This time Lea had set up to play the Memorex drive for the whole task force to view in the jury room. Jerry asked for silence until the show was over. There was no music in the beginning this time, but when the words finished scrolling off the large screen they had set up, it was Rolling Stones time again. "Gimme Shelter." The pictures that started to accompany the lead track from the Stones' 1969 *Let It Bleed* album were led off with a shot of Chris on Main Street in White Plains, just before the bullet hit him. The photo was not the least bit grainy. As Mick Jagger's words warning that war was just a shot away played on, pictures of each of the task force members transitioned onto, and then off, the screen. Images of all twenty-five who were in the room and thirty more that were either off duty or out in the field chasing down ethereal leads appeared. When Mick was winding up, and the words "shot away" had morphed into "kiss away," a set of photos of Jerry Whalen's wife kissing their son good-bye outside their home—a custom she did not give up as he got older—plastered the digital screen.

Whalen's team held its breath as a new song started up and the pictures became another series of sentences. The song was the oldie from 1965, words from the Book of Ecclesiastes, music by Pete Seeger, sung by the Byrds. "Turn! Turn! Turn!" The pressing harmony of the vocals led by Roger McGuinn, the chime-like stinging of his 12-string Rickenbacker, the rhythmic drums, and the dichotomous lyrics gave the words on the screen an ominous feel.

You have ignored and angered me.
If you do not comply and render a time of peace,
the war will go on and we shall repay your insults twentyfold.
The remnants of your automobile are a shrine to our power.

Watch and C4 what we can do!

As the Byrds sang on about times for love, hate, war, and peace, a strange view hit the screen. It was a backhoe on a lonely plot of dirt. There one instant, shattered and in flames the next. The noise and brightness of the explosion made those watching blink and take a step back as if the heat would consume them.

"Stop the video." Chris Lee shouted. Whalen gave him a scowl. "See that, there in the far background? That's one of the air traffic control towers at Dulles Airport. The one right at the main terminal." Chris's voice came close to a whisper. "Holy shit on a Popsicle stick."

"There's been construction at that airport for years and years and it's still going on big time. How the hell did they get explosives onto that site?" one of the FBI guys said.

"Just like they've been doing everything else, cleverly and convincingly. Crazy bastards!" Jerry Whalen said. "Now, start it up again, please, Lea."

The remains of the backhoe smoldered for only seconds, and the scene shifted to a beach scene with a lighthouse in the background. The bottom half of the lighthouse was painted white; the top half of the tower was red and loomed to a height of 165 feet above sea level. The non-working light sat atop the conical structure. The early-morning sand on the north end of New Jersey's Long Beach Island, with the lighthouse for a backdrop, took a washing from the Atlantic. Seconds later, a section of beach blew apart in a shower of sand, shells, and sea, scattering the gulls.

No one recognized the structure as the Barnegat Lighthouse, the second tallest in the United States. Nor did they know it was only a short walk away from one of the U.S. Coast Guard's stations. They only knew the message was terrifying. Some kind of remote control landmine on the shore of a beach. A beach that could be loaded with people almost any time of the day this time of year.

The Byrds' "Turn! Turn! Turn!" looped back to the beginning of the lyrics telling the audience about a time for every purpose under God's home—heaven. A slow, zooming shot of a small, wooden structure with a cross at the peak of its A-frame roof came into view. Below the view of the tiny church the words simply said, "Number One of 24." Then the picture disappeared, and the strange and frightening digital dialogue began again.

The clock starts at noon today.
You have 24 hours to comply.
If you fail, I will take down one church every hour after that, until you do comply.
If you are still stupid enough to refuse our wishes, we will move on to even more public places, like beaches, for example, or maybe tunnels and bridges.
By now, you should know we are not amateurs nor are we kidding around.
24 hours before the twenty-four churches start coming down.

All that these churchgoers treasure and hold dear will be flattened,
their aisles awash in blood.
Blood you made us shed.
America will not be happy.

The time is now.
Don't wallow in the mire.

Jed caught the paraphrase of the *new* tune eerily pumping through the computer's Altec Lansing speakers. The music had changed when the scene of the church appeared. Jim Morrison and the Doors were pounding out their lengthy 1967 hit, "Light My Fire."

CHAPTER 93

▼

THE FIDDLER

"Have you even tried to negotiate with the crazy bastards?"

"Well, no, sir. I thought we agreed that we would stay staunch in our stand not to negotiate with these terrorists."

"*We? We?* This has been your show from the beginning, superstar. Now we have the press slamming us all over the place with adjectives that usually precede the end of a once-promising career. Unemployment-like phrases and headlines, like, 'Our Leaders at a Loss?' or, let's see, 'DOJ Body Count Now Six', and then there's, 'Clueless about the Six J's.' Or, how about this one, 'Crucify, Behead, Burn—what's next from the elusive J Killers?' And don't think for one second that the Attorney General down in D.C. is going to lend any help here. He will claim he doesn't even know your name. As far as he is concerned, the buck stops at your desk."

Jerry Whalen's boss had veins popping and blood rushing through his carotid arteries at an unhealthy rate. Jerry's own pulse was dangerously high as he thought to himself, *What happened to* your *desk, boss? I guess the buck doesn't make it to yours either. You knew what was happening. You didn't come up with any great GD ideas.*

During the ride down in the limo from White Plains to One St. Andrew's Place in lower Manhattan at three that afternoon—before his boss blew his

334 Best In Class

cork—Jerry Whalen and Lea were trying to organize the forensic data from the latest attack in D.C.

"Let's start with the three Joans and their IDs. We'll need to explain that one of them was named Jeanne, but that Joan of Arc was also known as Jeanne d'Arc.

Now, let's see. We got one ID from the wedding ring inscription, the other from dental records, and the last from what? What?"

"They told us; remember? The crime-scene technicians' reports. Here. There was an iron plate below the burners on the floor of the truck bed. 'This Joan of Arkansas, Miss Kendall, was innocent, just like Maria Calabrese.' It was etched into the plate in the same Caesar font they used before. But this time, the words were not bordered with a cross like the images tattooed on our Jesus on the Hollywood hill, or the swords etched into the two silver souvenirs from the John killings. These words were bordered by an upward pointing triangle, which is the alchemical symbol for fire. We only found fifteen Joan Kendalls in the records, fourteen accounted for, the one from Greenwood missing for three days. She was a secretary who worked at a car dealership."

On the hour's ride down, they sifted through lots of data. The scene at the Hollywood sign had yielded nothing of consequence. They rehashed the foolish idea of footprints on a Manhattan sidewalk or on the waters of Sarasota, two sets of stolen plates, fire wiping out almost any hope of clues in D.C., and demonstrations of what these crazy people were ready to do next. The scouring of too many surveillance tapes from the possible FedEx offices from which the dreaded thumb drives might have come showed them nothing useable. The escalation pattern was clear and powerful. The devastating Fourth of July fire burned right in the backyard of the United States government's home. The same government these guys were trying to extort millions of dollars from.

All of the man-hours spent looking at Maria Calabrese, a convicted killer and wife of the dead crook, Alberto, stabbed in prison; Carmine Antobelli and associates; the Little Don; and exploring all the possible angles, gave them stale air— nothing new, nothing to hold on to and run with. There were no significant financial transactions to be traced anywhere. No physical movements of the trailed, mob-connected Italians that told any story other than normal stuff.

"Six people dead at the hands of these sacrilegious sickos. No clues. Jesus Cruz gets up to go to work in the morning and ends up a major hit in Hollywood the next night. Nobody saw him in between. He just vanished and ended up in Los Angeles crucified. Two freaking Johns, bodies missing, heads making headlines in New York and Florida. One, a bad boy from the South Bronx; and we all know that, almost always, nobody ever sees anything in the South Bronx when it's the cops asking questions. The other, a Frenchman on vacation ends up with his head floating in Sarasota Bay. Nobody missed him either. Then, we got three women from Arkansas whom apparently nobody seemed to miss either. Jesus, these guys had this planned down to a gnat's asshole." Jerry ended his litany of lament with a loud string of expletives, so loud the limo driver jumped and Lea cowered in the back seat.

Lea knew that the more sifting they did, the more depressing was the realization that they were still nowhere—except on their way to what surely would be a less-than-pleasant encounter.

At five that evening, after Jerry's boss had exploded, Jerry and Lea gratefully accepted the coffee that was brought in by the secretary assigned to them. One was also supplied to the Webmaster who was crafting the opening Web salvo to try and contact these guys, these possessed pricks. Jerry excused himself for a minute, feigning Mother Nature's demands, and made his way back to the brown liquor in his New York office drawer. He took a long swig of the strong bourbon and topped his half-full coffee cup with two more shots of courage.

The link on the DOJ Web site named "Conviction Overturned" was established. The password as instructed was BAOWMABYS—easily deciphered earlier as BOMBSAWAY by one of the FBI geniuses, the same guy who had deciphered ESORWOLLEY as YELLOWROSE, and DamneeuQ as possibly being Mad Queen. More useless information to add to the heap.

But instead of displaying "Site Under Construction, Try Again Later" in response to the password, Jerry, as instructed by his boss, had the Web guy put in the gentle phrase. "We hear you now. We would like to end the violence. Can we discuss a truce? Can we negotiate? Please respond to jwhalen@usdoj.gov."

The Broker's boys, Maximum Al and the X-man, had set up a program that would constantly work its way through the DOJ Web site searching for the "Conviction Overturned" link. When found—and Rick Huse was not sure how these geniuses did all this—the machine in his Pelham basement would text message his cell phone. A simple alert tone interrupted the Broker's quiet dinner at home with his Isabella. He excused himself and went downstairs. He signed in and received Jerry Whalen's pathetic plea. He picked up his secure phone and made two calls.

Jerry and Lea sat in Jerry's office. They managed to get sandwiches from a local deli, and Lea had snuck out for and back in with a new bottle of Jack

Daniels to spice up their Cokes. Other than a call every ten minutes from the boss, things were quiet. Jerry drank and muttered about his career going down the shitter. Lea tried to console him. She had decided she might just love this poor, persecuted soul. She had a weakness for the misfortunate. But even her neck and shoulder massages and gentle brushes of her firm breasts against the back of his head did little to ease the DOJ executive's tension—waiting for the annoying mail alert that he had turned on.

She sensed that and tried harder. She pushed her full front into his head. She knew he could feel her breasts, and her heat pour into him.

"Remember the first time, baby. God it was fabulous. I did not know if you would cross the line, but I'm glad you did. Remember? The Crowne Plaza in White Plains. All those pillows. The white bedspread. The white sheets."

Jerry did remember, would never forget. The beautiful, lithe body that he had imagined naked a million times, finally was. Her beautiful, small, white breasts that she had teased him with when wearing the low-cut blouses and their surprising dark areolae moved only slightly when she rode him to paradise.

Lea continued to run as much of her body as she could into his back. Her hands skirted and then squeezed Jerry's own nipples.

"It was the night that poor Chris was shot. You had to rush back up there and you called me in, and well, you got a room. And I asked if I could get one too. Baby, your smile was my ticket to a heavenly night. You were so good. My whole body was on …"

Lea never got the word "fire" out. The message alert shook them both out of their sensual reverie and sent Jerry's physical rising in a southern direction.

Jerry could not see that the sender, *freemaria@justice.net*, also blind copied his boss. Hours later, the best the government had would conclude that the e-mail address was untraceable. Right now Jerry concluded that they were probably at the end—the end of this mess, the end of his personal aspirations, the end of maybe a lot of things.

Subject: Bad Decision; New Clock
Your ignorance has caused us to begin our 24-hour clock as of one hour ago.
See attachments.

The first attachment in the e-mail was a repeated view of the small church in the last-delivered thumb drive. The second was a picture of the same place of worship reduced to a pile of rubble. The only thing that resembled the first image was the sign out front—the one with the missing block letters.

THE IRST BA TIST C RCH OF   OMAC

Try as they might, none of the bright people assigned to this failing task force had been able to come up with an algorithmic answer to solving the *Wheel of Fortune*-like puzzle. There were lots of Baptist churches with Baptist and Potomac in their titles, but none looked like this diminutive structure, now leveled by the devilish bad guys.

It would be hours from now when the report of an explosion at a small church on Virginia's Eastern Shore, not too far from the town of Birdsnest, would reach the boys and girls in White Plains. Confirming that indeed *it* was the Church of the Missing Letters—Pastor James Johnson, unharmed. More J's.

The next attachment was a collage of churches. The pictures, unless enlarged, were too hard to recognize or track down. The only obvious thing was that, as you looked down and associated the imbedded numbers 2 through 24 to the small photos, the structures became larger as the numbers progressed, and they all had crosses on them.

Jerry's boss did not bother to phone. He had seen the e-mail at the same time as Jerry Whalen and his pretty assistant had, and decided it was time—maybe way past time. He simply made his stormy way down to Jerry's office and told Lea to get out.

"Jerry, you've been dancing with these guys, and you are, by your own pathetic admission, nowhere. They have played you and your high-powered crew like a fiddle. Time to pay the fiddler. You will stay on but in the background. I am giving the operation over to the FBI. Special Agent Colette Zacharias. Do what she says, *if* she needs you at all. We will pay them their damn blood money and free the bitch, Maria Calabrese, from wherever she is and follow their directions. Colette will interface with the bastards and whoever else needs to get involved. You are going to take the heat for all of this. Do you understand? If you do it well, I'll let you keep a job somewhere on my staff. You will have to lie and cover this mess up with words like, 'Negotiated an acceptable compromise to bring the end to this terror, the details of which I am not at liberty to disclose. We do not give in to terrorism, but we strive to work our way out of it in the most peaceful, life-preserving way'. Got it. C-O-V-E-R I-T U-P. Make it go away."

A little more than one year after the Broker, Juana, and Carmine met in Baltimore to start the planning of the bloody trail that took their mission to Hollywood, New York, Florida, and finally, Washington, D.C., and thirty-five days after the first sacrifice in the heart of Tinsel Town to save five members of Carmine Antobelli's family, the DOJ gave in.

The Broker and Carmine and Juana and the others had won. Carmine had dodged a bullet much larger than the one that nearly killed him on the streets of the Bronx in 1998. The Broker was right, just like Willie Sutton. When the infamous bank robber was asked "Why?", he answered simply, "That's where the money is." And so, like Willie, the Broker had correctly chosen the right spot to go after millions of dollars—the people who print the damn things.

They had won enough money to get the vicious Little Don, Frankie Noto, and his thugs off the executioner's stand, and cover expenses, and a few extras. As was planned, Carmine had sent the Little Don's wife a dozen yellow roses to let the man know that the money was now available for his own use, to get himself out of hot water with the Sicilians.

And then, along with the money, there was the little matter of Maria.

CHAPTER 94

▼

PAY DAY—JULY 6, 2005

A handsome, well-built, blond man sat in the office of the bank manager at one of the Vienna branches of the Bank Austria Creditanstalt, one of 400 branches in the country. In his leather satchel he had an Euberbringer account passbook. All of the Austrian Sparbuch accounts, savings book accounts, had the same account name. The once easy-to-get, untraceable accounts were now difficult to come by. As of November 2000, the establishment of new Sparbuch accounts was prohibited by two powerful organizations. One was the G7, a forum for the finance ministers of the seven largest developed economies—Canada, France, Germany, Italy, Japan, the United Kingdom and the United States. The second was the AFAT, America's Financial Action Task Force on money laundering set up in 1989. The precious accounts could still be had with the right maneuvers and the right amount of money. However, for this casually dressed man with the long, curly, blond hair, that had not been necessary.

The Broker had secured three of these accounts years ago on the advice of Maximum Al, a man who seemed to know a lot about the more delicate parts of securing one's personal data. And on July 6, 2005, 2:00 PM Austrian time, 8:00 AM Washington, D.C., time, eleven million dollars American had been successfully wired to the Vienna bank.

The blond, the holder of the totally random set of ten digits and letters that made up the secret account code word, retrieved a manila folder from his satchel and handed it to the bank manager. All but two million of the dollars made their way out of the Austrian bank account many times faster than the takeoff of the four-passenger Gulfstream that had taken Maria Calabrese to freedom a few hours before. The two million that stayed in the country was transferred to one of the Broker's other Starbuch accounts in the same bank. The rest found its way first to eleven different accounts in eleven different countries. Then twenty-two. Then the money bounced like lottery ping-pong balls across the world until it was in places that worked for the Broker and the Little Don. Frankie Noto would get his six million; the five that was left had other places to go, including the enormous expense incurred by Pelham 1-2-3-4 in their plot to keep Carmine's innocents safe.

Mission accomplished, the blond collected his paper work from the bank manager and hailed a taxi to take him to the airport. The Lufthansa flight would connect in Frankfurt, Germany, and have him in Paris in time for a late dinner in the intimate and beautiful, 145-year-old Brasserie Flo. The food would be secondary to meeting up with his gorgeous bride and a taste of some well-earned French wine.

By the time the longed-for repast was initiated with a glass of red and a long, wet kiss in the restaurant with Alsatian rich woods and stained glass, Maria Calabrese, wife of the deceased Alberto, would be in a different setting an ocean away.

CHAPTER 95

▼

FREE MARIA CALABRESE

An hour after the monies flew in and out of the Austrian bank, Jerry Whalen held a nightmare of a press conference on the steps of the White Plains federal courthouse. The onetime golden boy of the DOJ spewed out a cover-up, PYA speak about having negotiated an equitable truce that has released the American people from any future threats from the perpetrators of the recent violence. "And yes, after reviewing the facts of the Maria Calabrese case, it was deemed appropriate to release her with time served as a proper settlement to the unfortunate incident."

Maria Calabrese, born August 27, 1971, was now just shy of thirty-four years old when she was escorted out of the Tallahassee Federal Corrections Institute prison. The most alive part of this petite, dark-haired woman was her curiosity. She had no clue as to what was going on other than that she was leaving this place. Prison had at first broken her. She had lost weight, her face sunken and sad. But after a short time in her new surroundings, she had regained her tough resolve and made better of a bad situation. She had worked her body back into shape and pushed some swagger back into her tiny frame. The move from Danbury to Tallahassee had been a positive one for her. She liked the change. It was kind of a strange physical and emotional wake-up call for the once-spirited nymph.

Now, three years and seven months after the devastating shots were fired in the Yonkers hotel room—Maria and Rob Speck's playground turned into a death scene—she was walking out of the redbrick prison to an unknown, unexplained future. Per the Broker's directives to the DOJ Web site, Colette arranged for three men and one woman in uniform to be dispatched from Tallahassee Police Headquarters. Two of the men walked Maria from the prison doors to the car. The woman helped her into the back of the unmarked sedan and got in next to her. One of the walkers slid into the other side of the back and closed the door. The other into the front passenger's seat. And the cop at the wheel took off.

Maria had been dressed, as ordered, in what looked like blue hospital scrubs. The car sped away with its precious cargo, previously one of the 1,100 inmates of the Florida jail. Within five minutes of departing from 301 Capital Circle, N.E., and traveling on the Tallahassee beltway, the police radio came to life.

"Officer Quain, this is command."

"Yes, Chief. We're on the Capital Circle Freeway. What do you want us to do?"

"Frank, they want you to drive the package to the Budget Rental Car place just off the airport grounds. Someone will be there to meet you. They will be wearing dark red Florida State University caps. Just do what they ask. We knew the airport was in play. We have some men there along with some Feds. It's their show, for the most part. Just get your package there and get out. Got it, Frank?"

"Yes, sir." Officer Quain turned to the driver of the sedan and said, "You heard the chief, Timmy. Step on it."

Within another five minutes the package was being dropped on the southwest side of the city at the rental car parking lot and handed over to a tall man with the FSU cap pulled over his forehead. He stood twenty feet away from the officers and was loaded with dark facial hair, making an ID difficult. After Maria walked to the man, the sedan pulled away, and the man led the woman toward a sea of black Ford Escapes. There were ten SUVs in all, no easy feat in this small facility, but money—cash, and a functional corporate credit card for a company that did not really exist—can work wonders. Five of the ten vehicles pulled away from the rental facility and made the short trip to the general aviation area of Tallahassee Regional. There were over 100 planes, corporate and privately owned, housed in this area of the facility. Today's story was only about five of them.

The SUVs cleared security, thanks to Special Agent Colette Zacharias's intervention. In her FBI heart, Colette wanted a shot at trailing these bastards and bringing somebody down, but she had orders.

The Ford Escapes spread out, and each quickly approached one of the five Cessna Skyhawks positioned on the tarmac. In a bizarre, synchronized fashion, a woman of Maria's size, dressed in light blue scrubs, emerged from each of the

SUVs, five in all. They were quickly escorted by five large men, all in FSU hats, to leather seats in the back of the single engine planes. The Feds and local police who were assigned to observe this event were not sure what they were supposed to do in the first place, but when the five Cessnas taxied out to the shorter of the two runways and began taking off as if in some aeronautical ballet, they knew exactly what to do—nothing.

These guys could climb the Hollywood Hills with a crucifix undetected, had the bravado to leave two bloody heads in public places, and toast the hell of out of old Abe Lincoln's toes. Flight plans meant nothing to these guys, and there would be an override on any tracking devices in the sleek, white, one-million-dollar-plus fleet that just left Tallahassee Regional. At 140 mph and with a range of 700 miles, they had their pick of out-of-the-way places to drop off their equipment and their packages.

CHAPTER 96

▼

LOS ROQUES—JULY 6, 2005

Maria had done a lot of things in her thirty-four years. Screwed half of the boys in her high school in Yonkers, and a few of the girls. Got married, cheated on her husband, shot an FBI guy, did time and things even she never imagined in two different prisons, but she had never sat in a leather seat of a four-passenger single engine plane—with her hands handcuffed in front of her by two heavy-duty, plastic straps. Things were beyond strange, surely incongruous. She was a captive, yet now, after takeoff, a captive being offered the finest of fruits and cheeses on the small plane. When the man in the FSU cap reached into the empty seat by the lone pilot and retrieved a loosely corked bottle of Moët & Chandon Grand Vintage 2000 and a flute from a cooler, her mouth watered. Her mind froze with anticipation and with no room for trying to figure this adventure out. Even with her hands bound Maria ate and drank with a vengeance.

Before the pilot of the Cessna, with the real Maria in it, put down on a private airstrip in Nassau, capital city of the Commonwealth of the Bahamas, Maria had been given a change of clothes. With her hands temporarily released, she, in the confining space of the aircraft, had Houdinied her way out of the scrubs into a sleeveless blouse and a pair of khaki cargo shorts. After the 600-mile flight, she was whisked out of the plane into a limousine.

The limo trip from the small landing strip to Nassau International would be less than twenty minutes. On the way, Maria begged for a pit stop to facilitate urgent, bladder relief. Her escort obliged on the way by stopping at a gas station. He put his cap on her head, covered her wrists with a flowered beach jacket, and led her to the restroom. The small .380 Glock in her back, which he had picked up in the limo, was enough incentive to keep his friend under control. Easing her bladder meant this stranger's hands being involved in the process. Once in the restroom, Maria struggled to free herself from the cargo shorts. The man in the FSU cap silently unzipped her shorts and pulled them and the prison-issued panties down to Maria's feet, and watched and listened, gun in hand. The same man who had supplied her tasty delicacies on the plane was now cruelly and stoically acting as her partner in this very personal act. But the demands of her organ overrode any shame she was suffering at her audience's view of her micturition.

Maria, relieved and happy to feel terra firma under her feet, was not happy when she, wrists covered again with the beach jacket, was soon led to another aircraft at NSI. At least this one was significantly larger than the expensive puddle jumper she had exited a short while ago. Still, not a single word had been spoken to her since her drop-off at Tallahassee Regional Airport, just nudging and shoving to direct her moves. All questions were met with silence—unrecognized inquiries.

The new, gleaming white Gulfstream G150 in all of its sleekness and luxury fled Nassau International. The twin-engine plane soon was traveling 0.85 Mach at 41,000 feet. Several hours, and still no dialogue later, the jet was wheels down in Caracas, Venezuela. The exchange from this aircraft to the next took some time, but the Broker had made all the necessary moves to make it go smoothly. American money tends to speak a universal language.

Another Gulfstream, this time a twin prop Turbo Commander AC690, took the weary Maria on a short hop to the northern coast of South America. The man in the FSU cap was now long gone. Frankie Noto, the Little Don, and a tan Venezuelan had replaced Maria's previous attendants at Caracas Maiquetia International Airport. The one-hundred-mile, due-north, final leg of her journey would be swift. The tired woman, who had been flying for way too long on three different planes, was still bound at the wrists. Maria was seated next to a small window. She was amazed at the crystalline waters below. The hues ranged from turquoise to dark blue. They were the same magnificent Caribbean waters that she and Alberto had enjoyed on their Aruba honeymoon. Her wrists and her thin tail end were both sore. She could only see the back of the pilot's head. The black leather seat next to her was empty. She turned her head quickly and saw her two captors, one much older than the other, seated and silent behind her. She did not fail to notice the well-developed musculature of the younger man's arms and upper torso. Even with all that had happened to her today, she was pleased to feel the automatic, warm response her body had to the well-built, strikingly handsome, tan male. Her tired mind toyed for a few seconds with the kind of concupiscent thoughts that had been an integral part of her life, but her anger and need to figure out what all these circumstances meant caused her to refocus.

The new pilot and his three passengers—Maria, one older man who looked vaguely familiar, and a younger sexy man she did not know—took a tourist-like flyover of some of the 350 islands, islets, and coral cays that make up Venezuela's Los Roques archipelago. The treasured and scattered islands surrounded by inviting waters had been declared a national park in 1972 by the Venezuelan government. The archipelago spanned an area of over 850 square miles.

Maria enjoyed the view but lost her patience.

"Jesus, now, can you bastards tell me what the hell is going on?"

The older one responded, "You need to keep your mouth shut until I say so. It will only be a little while longer. Trust me; you don't want to piss me off. So, turn around and shut up. We will land shortly. Then we will head to your final destination. Shut up and behave, Maria, and you won't be harmed. Your current options are extremely limited. The one I am offering in return for your cooperation is significantly better than the others."

Maria's mouth sighed a "shit," and she turned back around in her seat. Her brain and body longed for land—for more than a few minutes—in order to restore her equilibrium to a tolerable level. On her first plane ride of the day, she had filled the cabin with her words, including those that highlighted her serious dislike for air travel. They began as a litany of polite questions that received no response. When her polite mode failed, she regressed to her more common vernacular of well-strung-together malisons. That approach—Yonkers accent and all—still yielded no answers. Now, a frustrated, still-curious Maria did as she was told and anxiously awaited the feel of Mother Earth under her feet.

The pilot eventually made his way to a small airport. The landing strip sat on the biggest island in the archipelago named El Gran Roque.

The true author of this convoluted series of airplane rides knew that El Gran Roque meant The Great Rock. He guessed the island was named such because it was the largest of the landmasses, but he did not particularly care. He just knew this beautiful and peaceful part of the world provided what he needed. He had first seen it several years before Maria's big mistake in the Yonkers hotel room.

His wife had begged him to take her to this special spot on the Caribbean for their wedding anniversary. He fell in love with the place and siphoned off a nice pot of his ill-gotten income to purchase a place on the Great Rock—*better this one than the one with the steel bars in San Francisco Bay*, Noto thought at the time. And now it was perfect for his current needs.

The airport was located by the sea, just a few meters from the beach. The three travelers and their baggage made their way through the national park authority gates and paid the entrance fee. As in Nassau, Maria's ID was handled by one of her captors. The handsome Venezuelan national only had to pay the fee of five thousand bolivars. Because the other two were not nationals, the charge was double and was ten thousand bolivars for each, along with an airport tax of two thousand bolivars. The sum total of their park fees was about the equivalent of the price of a bottle of Hess Estate cabernet sauvignon. The man in charge of this voyage, the man who had bluntly threatened Carmine Antobelli, the man who had given the Broker directions for certain pieces of the past few months' events, favored the grape. He had had a case of his favorite shipped to his island residence. He was anxious to finally *welcome* Maria to her new home and toast to her future, thousands of miles away from Yonkers, New York. A Venezuelan paradise—for most visitors.

CHAPTER 97

▼

CLASS DISMISSED—JULY 6, 2005

By the time Maria and the Little Don and friend landed in paradise on that Wednesday, Jerry Whalen had long fled the White Plains courthouse. He had taken his pretty Lea with him, and together they wallowed in the tastes and smells of each other's bodies. This time the surroundings were a little less glamorous than the first. But the lovemaking was more furious in the Hampton Inn over in Elmsford, a short ride from the scene of Jerry's political demise.

Jed was still in the task force area of the courthouse, saying goodbyes and packing up whatever he needed to take back to LA. The LAPD administrative people had made arrangements for his flight back the next day. All he had to do was pull the e-ticket from the computer and catch a ride to the airport. Finally some down time.

Chris spent his time on the phone with his boss back in Washington, filling him in and asking for a week's leave.

Juana had called him on his cell phone for the first time since she took her mysterious leave on June 12, 2004. Her call came from Joey D.'s place in Jensen Beach. She had asked if he could get time off. She wanted to see him as soon as possible, in Jensen, if that worked for him. Chris ached for her company, her smile, her smell, her touch. Her pleading voice melted away any reason to resist her request. The chance at seeing her again and maybe taking up where they left off jolted his heart rate and inspired his imagination and hope.

Juana, having left behind Pelham 1-2-3-4's own version of killing fields, looked forward to Jensen Beach and her Christopher Lee.

Chris called his folks in Lexington and said he would be stopping by there the next day. His plan was to spend the night with Jed in White Plains, head out early to D.C., check in at the office, and get out to Lexington in time for dinner. Chris's father had recently had some troubling medical issues, and he wanted to touch base, in person, to make sure, as his mom swore, things were under control and Dad was just fine.

And the following day he would head down to Jensen Beach to meet Juana.

"How drunk do you want to get tonight, Jed?"

"Well, let's see, Mr. Best in Class. Somewhere between shitfaced and rip roaring. Can you handle that?"

"You bet. But let's start out with some good food for a change. I'll call Morton's and make a reservation for seven. And let's take cabs tonight. I don't feel like getting shot at again standing on the streets of Laredo here."

The two lawmen finished packing up their goods at the courthouse and drove their cars back to the hotel and got organized for the next day's departure.

Their road to inebriation was paved with oysters on the half shell and Maine lobster cocktail as shared appetizers, followed by rib eye steak for Jed and a porterhouse for Chris. Both indulged in jumbo, baked Idaho potatoes. The first liquid step of the night's long journey was a double shot of Grey Goose on the rocks. They laughed as they recalled their friend Drew's reaction to his first shot of naked Goose. With the tumbler in his hand, pinkie finger extended, Drew waxed poetically. "The initial soft and silky touch and hint of vanilla on the palette wakes up to a pleasantly stinging satisfaction. Finally touching the stomach with a welcomed warmth."

The middle part of Jed and Chris's last meal in White Plains was refreshed with a bottle of Syrah.

"What do you say we make our dessert a liquid one? Ingredients will include any and all of the leftover libations left in our rooms."

Jed responded to Chris's suggestion. "Brilliant! I'll call us a cab."

The two left Morton's home, a four-story shopping center built only last year on the site of what was a Saks Fifth Avenue. A cab from Broadway Taxi took them from Maple Avenue to the Cottage Place entrance for the Residence Inn in less than five minutes. Chris took care of the fare and tip, the same as he had done at the fancy steak house. Jed objected but Chris reminded him that he had no dependents and Jed did. Besides, the FBI would pick up part of the tab.

"Dessert is here," Chris said as he entered the open door to Jed's twelfth floor suite.

"Glasses and ice are on the table."

Chris did most of the pouring; Jed did most of the talking.

"They outdid us, Chris. Me. You, the Best in Class. The whole damn U.S. of A. Justice Department. They left no clues except a few misleads that wasted our time and embarrassed some semi-pro shortstop and a young, horny Coast Guard seaman, whose semen somehow ended up on two of our victims." Jed lamented the same way Jerry Whalen had on his way down to DOJ Headquarters in New York. Except in Jed's case, on some level, the failure of this hotshot task force did somewhat vindicate his own failure in LA, the case of the infamous Jesus H.

At midnight, both men with two too-bloodshot eyes, some of the effect from a few tears, most from dessert in a bottle, decided they needed some sleep before tomorrow's traveling.

"I'm going to keep going over what evidence I have in my spare time, Chris. Maybe there's something in here we're missing. Maybe a clue to unravel this damn mess. These guys have been messing with my head without mercy. I'm a little more than pissed."

"Hey, just get home safely. Say hi to the wife and kids, and get some rest. Being home will seem like paradise to you compared to your time here in White Plains. Love ya, Buddy. Fairways and greens. Keep your head down and your spirits up. See you next year in Pipestem. But for now, enjoy your LA paradise." With those final words, Chris made his way to his room and pillow.

CHAPTER 98

▼

CHRIS'S PARADISE
SURPRISE—JULY 8, 2005

The two legs of the Friday US Airways flight—Roanoke to Charlotte and Charlotte to Palm Beach International Airport—went smoothly for Chris. After the fifty-seat Canadair regional jet set down in the North Carolina hub for the airline once known as Allegheny Airlines, Chris had a one-hour layover—time for a quick beer, a chaser for last night's overindulgence. He hustled down to the Budweiser Brewhouse in concourse D, only a few gates away from his flight to PBI. He thought about all the things that were finally over and mused about what was to come. The hunt for the group martyring the pseudo Lord and his saints was in the cold case files—for now. The unknown perps' proven ability to plant high-powered explosives undetected, and their threat to blow up twenty-four churches and then maybe some bridges throughout the country—and perhaps the U.S. economy at the same time—put the "bad guys" in the winner's circle. The good guys had been forced to give in. The risks, especially to some of their political reputations, were too high.

Money and Maria in hand, they seemed to have just vanished. Chris was glad that the whole business was finished and it was time to move on. The long hours of fruitless work, the personal tension, and the pressure that filled the task force room, and his lonely nights without Juana, had taken their toll on the FBI expert.

As for what was to come, he felt mildly apprehensive predicting the very near future, as in the next five days. He did not get through envisioning all the details of the upcoming evening before it became time to head back down concourse D and catch his flight. Those visions included a quick pick up of a Chevy Trailblazer from National's Emerald Aisle, a speedy drive up I-95 North, and a few twists and turns. And then the sight of the well-remembered, green-posted, cat-faced sign announcing the town of Historic Rio, "A Little Bit of Heaven on 707." The tannish-colored sign with the green lettering was a landmark burned into Chris's soul, and only minutes from the *other* cottage on Jensen Beach. These many years later, it would not be Sarah, but the beautiful Juana, standing at the cottage door with a perfectly chilled bottle of Hess Select chardonnay, two glasses, and not much else, except some lascivious thoughts and plans. He had missed Juana horribly since her shattering announcement and subsequent hiatus from their torrid love affair.

The next five days were to be a lot of R & R for the overworked agent and perhaps a prelude to making his relationship with Juana a permanent thing—something only a year ago he thought not possible.

Sarah had never left his consciousness, but he had followed her orders and was finally moving on and letting the joy in. As he hit the little town of Rio and smiled at the sign, it hit him that fifteen years had passed since he and Sarah were here, finally joined, comfortable and resolute. A comfort and resolution so easily crushed by her awful and early death. While this place, this road, these buildings, the cottage, and the beaches brought Sarah's memory to a brilliant life, he was happy to know that there was still enough room in him to absorb and delight in Juana's brilliance.

Chris had made good time and was pulling off of Indian River Drive into the parking lot just before 5:00 PM. It was still a hot-as-a-pistol summer day, and things just got hotter. The grin he had on his face as he approached Joey Dannemann's riverside resort and fishing camp, good old River Rest, vanished when he was hit with a familiar, unwelcome type of brilliance.

"Jesus. Juana?"

When he jumped out of the red Trailblazer, he was staring at as many cop cars and police motorcycles as the Martin County Sheriff's Office could fit in the tiny parking lot. The lights were flashing on the two white Ford Crown Vics. An elongated, yellow stripe sat on top of a slightly longer green stripe on the doors, from the top of the back door to the bottom of the front. Their look screamed cops. The scary word SHERIFF sliced through the middle of the slanting triangle in big, bold, matching green letters. The two new police Toyota Prius models were sans light show. There were no sirens except for those screaming in Chris's head. The eight Uniform Division deputies from Martin County East Coast Operations and their three-to-eleven watch commander stood erect in their dark green uniforms. The American flag was sewn into the right chest material of their shirts, the Martin County Sheriff's badge image on the left. Except for the two motorcycle officers with the crash helmets on, the others all donned their trooper-style hats. There was not an ounce of friendly in any of the faces of the three women and eight men.

There were only a few residents in Joey D.'s low-rise motel, but now they were all outside or on the second floor balcony watching the show. Joey D. himself was standing just outside the side door of the pink building trimmed in Caribbean blue. His thin frame almost blended in to the palm trees painted on either side of the motel's glass door. The three people that had been in the pool were gawking from the pool's edge. Four residents from two of the rented cottages were standing just off the edge of their small patches of lawn. Most of the cops were standing outside of the cream-colored cottage—one of the eight that Joey D. owned—with shutters painted almost the same color as the motel. This was the cottage in which Chris had expected a sexy Juana to be ready to greet him with a smile. The unsmiling scene that he saw had Chris in shock.

"Juana. Is Juana all right?"

The watch commander strode over to Chris with a little bit of a John Wayne-like saunter and tipped his hat.

"She's fine. Name's Buddy Snyder. Can I ask you to turn around and put your hands on the railing, please."

"What? What the hell is going on here?"

Commander Snyder did not answer. He just gently turned Chris around to the railing, which ran from the ground up a few steps to the front porch. He nudged Chris's arms up in such a way that his palms landed on top of the pressure-treated wood that capped the balusters.

"Just relax, Mr. Lee."

Chris did not utter the obscenities that flew into his consciousness as the cop frisked him.

"He's clean. Let's take him in."

A female officer walked up to join the commander and introduced herself as Tracy O'Connell. They flanked Chris and walked him up the decking to the front door. Tracy knocked on the door, and a familiar voice replied in a somber tone, "Come in." The commander opened the door to the cottage that was much older than he was, but well kept. In the center of the oak-planked main room that housed the living and kitchen areas stood Grady O'Connor. His red hair was still misbehaving, but his visage was stern and locked in place. He was dressed in his detective garb of a bargain-priced, gray suit from Sears, white shirt, drab blue tie, and scuffed, bus-driver-like, black shoes. Juana, in jeans and her Derek Jeter T-shirt, sat with a bowed head in one of the four pine kitchen chairs—looking like a hostage.

CHAPTER 99

▼

CAUGHT IN PARADISE

"Jesus, what the hell is going on here?" Chris made a move toward Juana. Grady stepped in his way.

"No touching, big shot, not until we talk." Grady nodded at the Florida cops and they did a Snagglepuss, "Exit, stage left," and closed the door behind them.

"Sit," one of New York's thirty-five thousand finest said as he pulled out a second chair and placed it three feet away from Juana.

"Hell no, you idiot. Not until I hear why you're here."

Grady pulled out what looked to Chris like a Schweizerische Industrie Gesellschaft, SIG P-229, forty-caliber pistol. "Borrowed it from a friend down here. Too much trouble to fly with one. Now, Juana, get the handcuffs off the table and put Chris's hands behind the chair back, put the cuff's chain through the spokes, and leash him up." She did as told. "Okay, now, I'm gonna talk and you two are gonna listen.

"You always thought you were the best in class, Chris, and I was the loser. Thought my mother should have named me Goofy instead of Grady, right? The only time *I* ever got the really *pretty* girl in college, she turned out to be a lesbian in need of a beard. Par for the course for poor old Grady, huh? All these years I've been playing just another one of your obsequious admirers. I have detested that role for too long now."

"Grady, I had no idea. I didn't realize. But, what …"

"Shut the hell up. I'm talking now.

"No idea, Chris? You didn't realize? No idea that I had to watch the great Christopher Lee get the best grades in school, get the prettiest girls fawning all over the macho, half-ninja, half-Virginian land baron? Watch you hit the winning jump shot; score the winning goal; tap in for another goddamned birdie, like it was just another day at the office. Even when life throws Mr. Perfect a hell of a curve ball, what does he do? He buries the poor, young, beautiful girlfriend, and, without a beat, moves on to finish school at the top of the class, become a famous FBI big shot. Still standing tall. Still looking down on little old Grady. *Me*, struggling to make it through John Jay. *Me*, the one who still hits a good golf shot as often as George Bush admits he's wrong or pronounces nuclear right. All those late nights talking in West Virginia like you were my best friend. Did you think I did not know those words were just another version of a mercy hump?

"Well, this time *I* have outdone Mr. Number One. *I* have bested the best in class. Yeah, that's right, *me*. The cop who didn't get invited to join your serial saint-killer task force, even though it happened right near the front door of my precinct. Chris, your crown has been taken away. You have just been topped by poor old Grady. It'll be *my* name that they'll be talking about on the news, not yours. You and your girlfriend here will be the stars of a little photo session real soon. You know, those front- and side-shot photos that are never flattering? Maybe it's the police station backdrop that makes them look so drab. The game is over, Chris. Go to the back of the classroom and sit in the dunce's corner.

"Maybe you and your pretty Little Miss Sunshine here will have an opportunity to be the best in class at, let's see, Folsom for you. You could compete with Erik Menendez to be the best. Or, maybe Attica; you and Mark David Chapman could go head to head. And, for the lovely lady, wouldn't it be fun in a cell up at Bedford Hills? She could battle old Pamela Smart from New Hampshire. You remember her, Juana, don't you? Back in 1990 or so she was twenty-two and screwing some fifteen-year-old high school kid. And she had the kid kill her hubby for her. Not too bright. I bet you could best her, Juana."

Juana, now with her head up, looked to Chris like she was doing her best to damn up a burst of tears. Grady paused and paced for thirty seconds.

"You made a deal with the devil, Mr. FBI, and soon I'm gonna welcome you to your own personal hell on earth. Shit, you're gonna have to turn in your Superman cape for some horns and a pitchfork.

"You probably don't feel this way right now, but you're lucky *I'm* here. I could have had this played out on a much bigger and more embarrassing screen. This way, I'll just take you in quietly, at least for today. Besides, I wanted some time to savor the moment of winning, besting the best. Sorry, I'm repeating myself.

"I'm thirsty and we're gonna be here a while. Do you have anything to drink, Juana?"

"In the fridge," she squeaked.

When Grady opened it, Chris saw the bottle of the Hess Select he had had his taste buds set on and a scattering of Pilsner Urquell. Chris also saw two bottles of Bollinger Brut to the left of the wine. His mouth was desert dry with fear.

Grady selected one of the twelve, cold, green bottles with the name spelled out in green letters on a white background, topped with a red medallion. The red circle was showing off the brand's 1842 birth date. The world's first pilsner beer, developed by Josef Groll in Plzen, Bohemia, was Chris's absolute favorite. Drew had introduced it to him and its history, of course.

"I really shouldn't be having a beer while on duty—especially your favorite, considering your predicament. But, hey, I guess you're in no position to complain. Now, where was I? Oh yeah, prisons and your future competition."

"Grady, you crazy bastard, what are you doing? What do you want?"

"I want Kim Delaney. You know, the hot brunette who used to be on NYPD Blue? I want her in the backseat of one of those cop cars, naked and begging for it. That's what I want. But for now, I'll settle for this."

"Put the damn gun away before you hurt yourself or one of us." Chris's plea was ignored. Grady, with the beer in his hand and a searing stare in his eyes, moved on. His mordant behavior had Chris wondering if Grady was off his meds and seriously scared Chris.

"Why did you do it, Juana? You hung poor Jesus up on that cross. Dropped a couple of Juans—excuse me, only their noggins—in New York and Florida. One of them right in my damn precinct. That's what really pissed me off. Then, let's see, three Joans, a car bomb, a church bombing. Very versatile, I must say. But also very, very illegal.

"And *I*, poor old, stupid Grady, figured it out and here I am." Grady took a long swig of the bottom-fermented beer and smiled at its heavy, ale-like taste pleasantly assaulting his dry taste buds. After swallowing, still smiling, he pushed the air in his lungs forcibly out between his lips. "Ah, great brew. And the wine and champagne? I guess Juana was planning a special weekend for you two criminal lovebirds. Were you thinking about creating your own little version of Paradise here in Jensen? Well, maybe I'll let you each have one drink of choice. It might just be your last chance for a long, long time. Barbarous business, this killing. Very frowned upon by our legal system.

"And you, Christopher, Mr. FBI superstar, why did you get yourself wrapped up in all of the murders? You see, I have you both tied to all the killing, all the planning, all the crimes along the way."

"What the hell are you talking about?" Chris said, trying to be convincing but losing the battle to a resignation that both Juana and he had been found out.

Grady grabbed another of the kitchen chairs, turned it around, straddled it, and faced his two captives, gun in hand, now resting at his side. "You're not the burning bush in this class anymore, Chris, or should I say Judas? You bastards seem to be fond of names that start with J.

"I know all about Pelham 1-2-3-4. What number were you, Juana? Three, I believe. Well, lucky for you, Chris, I am giving you first chance to flip. You know, based on our previous friendship. I have not yet taken the Broker and Carmine Antobelli into custody. If you would like to help my case against *those* two criminals, I might be able to buy some consideration with the various D.A.'s that will be trying to nail your ass. Same goes for you, Juana."

Chris, pretty much giving up, had only one word that he could manage to say. "How?"

"It was all too coincidental for me, Chris. You see I am not all *that much* of a loser. First, Jesus bites the dust in Jed's precinct. Then, some poor Juan loses his head and it ends up in my place. Then, big time FBI profiler gets called in on the DOJ task force and it's you. Strange triangle, don't you think?

You, the best-in-class fox in the henhouse. Very clever. Keeping your eye on the game; making sure the good guys remained clueless; steering them away from your Broker. And your Latin lover here, right in the middle of it. I got curious about the case and then I got suspicious. I know the tale of the Broker. I know his sordid history. I guessed he might be involved. In my heart, I always believed that Antobelli was in the middle of this. The other cops never found anything, but I kept my own vigil. Tracking their travels, their credit cards, and they led me to you, Juana. Mr. Rick Huse slipped when he paid for your plane ticket to LA. Then I started tracking your E-ZPass charges. Did you have a nice trip to Baltimore, Juana? The same weekend that the Broker and Carmine made their way down the turnpike? You see, I sensed a lot of coincidence, but I didn't have enough, until now. You guys were good, but not invincible. You see, the hotshit Feds called my bosses to let them know about their decision to wimp out and pay up. They agreed to let *me* try and follow the money, and your buddies made one slip up. Nobody else saw it but me, and that's what brought me here. Funny how facts can turn coincidence into convincing evidence.

"And now, for every one of the greedy masterminds behind or involved in this thing that you give up, I believe I can buy you a small piece of justice's mercy." Grady paced the floor and then turned, physically and emotionally.

"Damn it, Chris. Who did you think you were dealing with here? These guys aren't the Mickey Mouse Club. They are the federal government of the United Freaking States. When I lay this out for them, they are gonna want big-time, never-get-out-of-jail-free sentences.

"And *I*, I do not drive around the Bronx in Car 54 with my head up my ass. I am a detective in New York's Manhattan South. I am one of three thousand detectives in the largest police force in the whole damn United States of America.

"And your other friends. Did you think your *I*-talian associates were seminarians?

"You *didn't realize?* You had no clue how I felt all these years? You arrogant son of a bitch." Grady, red rage in his face, stood up. "And don't say you're sorry, cause you're not *sorry*. You are goddamned pathetic." The green bottle took a speedy flight toward and out the cottage's side window, bounding off the deck. Buddy Snyder and Tracy O'Connell, the only two cop friends of Grady who still remained at Joey D.'s, rushed in the front door.

"It's okay, guys; it was just a beer bottle. It slipped. Sorry." Grady nodded his friends back out the door and got himself a replacement pilsner.

He took a long swig of beer, as if he was trying to calm the burning fire in his mind and body. He took a heavy breath and gave a wave of the SIG first toward Juana and then at Chris.

"You two are gonna get an all-expense-paid trip back to my precinct for your first booking, and then, I think, *your* boys in D.C., Chris, want to take a few shots at making sure the bunch of you grow old at the government's expense. Let's see. Then, there's Florida; they want a piece of you, too. Ah, not to mention the United States Park Police and the Metropolitan Police Department of our nation's capital. Maybe you ought to have that last drink now, as you consider your unenviable future."

Grady opened the fridge, and asked his ex-college friend, his ex-golf buddy what he wanted.

"Oh, sorry, you can't drink without a straw. I'll get you a beer, and I'll let Juana help you gulp it down. Juana, you?"

She just shook her head no.

Chris was still wondering if maybe Grady had gone off whatever drugs he might need to be on. And Chris was boiling hot and beyond pissed off. He decided it was time to speak and stood up with the chair attached to his back. "Listen, Serpico, or Kojak, or Mr. NYPD Dickhead Blue …"

A shaken, but resolute, Juana stood and, with her hands in the air, palms out, cut Chris off. "I need to tell you why, Grady. Please listen."

She badly wanted out of this hell Grady had put them in. She had spent so much of her life in other hells, and now she wanted it to be over, to be different.

Given Grady's condition, whatever high or low he was on, Chris doubted that "the why" and even "the how" would bring any relief to the redhead, but Juana was determined.

CHAPTER 100

▼

WHY?

"It is easy to go down into Hell; night and day, the gates of dark Death stand
wide;
but to climb back again, to retrace one's steps to the upper air—there's the rub,
the task."

~ Virgil, *The Aeneid*

"You are as wrong as acid rain on this one, Grady."

"Oh yeah, sweetheart? How is that?"

Juana took a minute to think to herself. *Okay, Joanne Romano, daughter of the late Tommy Romano, stepdaughter of Conrad Jameson, also deceased, eldest daughter of the beloved and beleaguered Elena, sister of Sarah Jones, God rest her beautiful soul, get your shit together and get this situation under control.*

"Grady, let us tell you why. I'm sure you'll understand why we had to do what we did."

He held the beer up in the air. "Hang on a sec. Let me get my phone."

"What the hell for?"

"So you can call the Make-A-Wish Foundation. You'll need their help to make that happen."

Grady's mistake was actually making the move to get his phone out of his suit jacket to play out his charade. He never saw the legs of the chair that was hanging off Chris's back coming. The wooden chair was attached to Chris by the cuffs entwined in the spokes of the chair's back support. And it came at Grady hard.

Chris's aim was perfect, and the gun flew out of Grady's hand and across the floor to Juana's feet. She grabbed the gun and pointed it at the stunned New York City detective who was trying to shake away the sting in his right hand.

"Now, *you* sit!" She pointed him to the kitchen chair she had just vacated. "And don't think I don't know how to use this thing. I've been taught by the best. So sit."

Grady did as he was told.

"Give me the keys to the cuffs."

"They're in my pocket."

"Well, get them the hell out, now."

Gun pointed at Grady's nose, Juana retrieved the keys and went over to Chris. The SIG never wavered as she undid the manacles. Chris was kind enough to restrain his erstwhile assailant with the same cuffs in the front. And then Juana handed Chris the pistol.

"Now tell your posse out there that they can go home. Tell them you'll call them back, if you need them. Tell them you need to be here for a while and thank them for their assistance. *Do it!*"

The 3.9 inches of the gun barrel was pressed against Grady's cheek, and he yelled out to Buddy Snyder as he was told.

"You sure, Grady?"

"Yeah, man. This is gonna take a while. Appreciate all your help, but I got this situation under control, and you guys got other things to take care of. Thanks, Buddy."

Chris heard the police vehicles pull away. Joey D. had wandered over with questions for the cops earlier and had gotten no answers. Now with the cops gone, he wandered back to the cottage. Through a half-opened door Chris told him it was a misunderstanding that he was now taking care of.

Juana went to the refrigerator and retrieved three beers. She didn't know if the beer would help soothe and calm the wound-up redhead or stir his boiling pot worse. She bet on the former as she uncapped the green bottle using the Baltimore Orioles steel opener fastened to the kitchen wall, a touch of fashionable décor supplied at no extra cost by the owner, Joey D. She placed one bottle between Grady's cuffed hands and handed one to Chris, who almost downed the whole bottle in one long gulp. With the SIG pointed in the air, Chris depressed the magazine catch and dropped the cartridge into his hand. There were eleven of the twelve rounds still in it.

"Safe," he said to Juana, who took the cartridge and disappeared into the bedroom to secure the deadly projectiles in the small Sentry Fire-Safe combination safe, home to Chris's collection of Florida firearms. Chris recycled the ejector, and the live round in the chamber flew out onto the floor. He picked it up and put it in his pocket. "Dangerous things, these forty caliber guns. Need to be more careful, Grady."

Juana returned to the kitchen with a briefcase that she had been taking with her wherever she traveled. She opened it on the table next to Grady and pulled out an old copy of an Italian newspaper. The yellowed *Italian Tribune* article, the same one Carmine Antobelli had given her at the beginning of this adventure, was dated June 4, 1995. It was a translation of a piece that originally appeared in the *Corriere della Sera*, a paper the Italians consider their *New York Times*. She placed the article on the table for Grady to see. It detailed a massacre that took place on Saturday, June 3, during the wedding of a young couple from Naples, Italy. The groom was the owner of a local restaurant. The bride, the daughter of a reputed member of the Provenzano crime family in charge of the Rome franchise of the mob family's business. The newspaper article hinted at the possibility that the father of the bride, Tito Rizzo, was skimming from his Sicilian crime boss, Bernardo Provenzano, and that the gruesome murders were payback from the man they call the Tractor.

"I know whose these people are. Why do you give a shit about some crazy Ginzos over in Sicily, Juana?"

"Because these people and others like them have threatened to kill people I hold dear, if we did not deliver what they demanded. And when it comes to saving those people from slaughter, there's not much I would not do. You were right, Grady. These guys, the *I*-talians, are not seminarians. They are at the head of a worldwide, powerful, criminal organization. Twenty thousand "made" killers with another two hundred thousand associates, probably itching to become made. Well, desperate times and all that shit.

"Carmine Antobelli saved my life. I owe him. I owe Sarah.

"I was a wretch of a sixteen-year-old girl in 1980. One step away from prostitution as a means to feed myself." Juana pointed to the paper. "And these people, these monsters had threatened him and others. I had no choice."

"No choice but to hang a man in Hollywood and all the bloody rest of your violence?" Grady, slightly high, belched out after a drink of his beer.

"No. No choice. Now, just listen." Juana went on with a steady, soft voice.

"I am the product of two abusive fathers, both dead at my own hands. My mother was taken away from me *and* my sister. I was twelve. My sister was nine. We were all separated. My sister and I bounced from foster home to foster home for four years. She suffered through her own series of places; mine was a different chain of rat holes. Lost in the system.

"I was one of the 10 percent or so who go from a foster home to the streets to join the ranks of the homeless. Luckily I did not follow the familiar pattern all the way into the criminal justice system. My last foster home was in New York, and I escaped and took to the streets. On my first outing, I solicited the wrong man. Well, actually the right man. His name was Del, Anthony Dellacamera. Instead of taking me to some alley or some hotel, he took me home—home to his wife. They had a daughter my age, and they decided to play savior to the teenage wanna-be whore. And they did.

"Carmine Antobelli, Del's boss in a way, heard my story from Del. He told Del to arrange for my education, private schools, nothing less. Perhaps Carm was trying to buy God's good graces back for all the bad he had done in the past. I don't know.

"After I received my college degree, I went to work for his real estate company. He gave me a new life when I thought I had nothing much to live for. Back then, he also put wheels in motion to try and locate my mother and sister. I had told Del my miserable life story, including my separation from my mother and sister.

"Del and his family, Carmine and his—it was like divine intervention halting my trip to the deeper depths of hell. My mother was in the wind. My sister, the girl born Sarah Romano, was nowhere to be found. It turned out that, at the age of thirteen, she ended up in Pennsylvania. She had been taken in by a carbon copy of our second father. The bastard and his bitch wife collected the fees for Sarah's foster care at the same time he was drugging and raping her. My feisty, little Sarah never lost her touch with a Louisville slugger—her solution to our raping stepfather years earlier—and managed to hurt her foster father one time, enough to escape. She made her way to a shelter in Harrisburg.

"She was a pregnant teen—that's right, pregnant by the pig of a foster father—now renamed Sarah Jones. She was attempting to escape a horrid past and finally got lucky. One of the counselors at the shelter politely pushed the pregnant girl for a detailed history. She recorded it all in the girl's file. Even got her real last name, Romano, placed in her profile.

"The people at the shelter placed my sister with a wonderful family in Camp Hill, Pennsylvania, the Flemings. They helped her in ways too many to count.

"The most divine of interventions came when, at my begging, Del asked Carmine and his wife, Sophia, to retry the search for my mother and sister. It had been six months since the first try, a try that had Carmine using his connections and his wife working through her church. The original search came up empty.

"Shelters, like the one Sarah had found refuge in, get hundreds of requests to check for missing children. The milk-carton pleas and the posters in stores and government buildings across the country sometimes come through. Most often they do not. There are hundreds of thousands of kids who go missing each year." As she now paced the floor, Juana's voice was still deliberate, but more intense and a bit louder.

"We got lucky on the second try. A new and eager volunteer at the shelter went on a personal mission when Del's new inquiry came in. This inquiry was different. It came with a copy of a faded Polaroid of a mother and two daughters and an offer of a reward of ten thousand dollars."

Juana paused long enough to retrieve a nine-by-twelve envelope from the briefcase and fished out a copy of the faded picture. "Look. My mother, my sister, and me. Three innocent females looking for happiness, finding only heartbreak, and worse. The volunteer's exhaustive search of shelter records found my sister. She connected the first name to the age and caught the Romano/Jones notation in the file. To match the picture that Carmine had sent the shelter to the one the shelter had taken years later had taken a leap of faith. But the name match generated a phone call.

"I would not know all this until years later. The report on Sarah's situation when given to Carmine and Sophia led to a set of decisions. Leave her where she was—happy, protected, secure. The baby on the way, my little sister's baby, was to be put up for adoption. Sophia, missing the spirit of a young child in the home, coaxed her Carmine into adopting the child. It was a girl. They named her Carlotta.

"She is now in her mid-twenties with a baby of her own. Carlotta, my blood niece, the daughter of my dead little sister, is happily married with a little boy named Sal Boccardi—Carmine and Sophia's baby grandchild by adoption, my grandnephew."

Chris had seen the photo before when Juana first told him the saga of Sarah and herself. He had remarked on the fact that even the faded picture showed one fair-skinned daughter and one with more of a Latin look. Juana simply explained that she had gotten her mother's looks and Sarah had gotten the lighter Sicilian pigment from her dead father.

Grady had finished his beer by the time Juana had finished this part of her tale. She got him another. She had barely sipped her own, but she had made the right bet. The beers seemed to have cooled down the redhead, who listened with docility and attentiveness.

"Juana, that's a cute little story, but what does this have to do with you and your friends terrorizing half the population? And what the hell is up with freeing the whoring, murderess bitch, Maria?"

It had been fifteen years since Sarah Jones had been eulogized in Lexington's Lee Chapel and Chris had spread her ashes into the shores of Jensen Beach. The name did not appear to resonate with Grady. Juana decided to drive that part of her "why" home before going on.

"Sarah Jones. My sister. The mother of Carlotta and grandmother of little Sal. Remember her?" She moved closer to Grady and bent down to his face and pointed at Chris. "Chris was gonna marry her. Remember? Remember meeting her? Remember what she meant to Chris? Remember that she died in her early twenties? These people, the ones we were trying to save from being killed, were her legacy, hell, my legacy, my mother's legacy."

She moved back and picked up the envelope again, and one by one, she laid out the six pictures. Each picture matched one of the six insurance policies that Frankie Noto had dramatically laid out in front of Carmine in the kitchen of the Disney World condo. Carmine had given pictures of the people whom Pelham 1-2-3-4 were trying to save from violent deaths, one set for each of his three conspirators. The Broker, Juana, and Chris.

"Carmine's sister, the first to be killed. His wife Sophia. His son Vinnie and *his* wife, Mary Kate." Juana was slapping down the pictures on the table in front of Grady in a deliberate and pounding fashion. "Carlotta, Sarah's daughter. And little Sal, her son. All waiting, innocent targets for the most violent people in the world." Juana explained the Little Don's insurance scam that would yield him the money he needed to save his own hide—once these members of Carmine's family were killed. Juana had laid out the same details of Sarah's sad journey and the threats to Carmine and his family to Chris months before. He had hounded her until she broke and let him know why she had to stay away. That's when he demanded in. He would help and he knew how. They would still have to stay apart and stay out of touch in any fashion, except for the one Pelham Manor meet before the events started. But he was in, for better or worse. A conspiratorial vow to protect the family of his first love.

Juana continued on. "Carmine Antobelli, his family and friends saved my life. Even after college, they continued to help me with a position in their real estate company. A great career, in Virginia. They gave me a chance at a normal life and I am more than grateful and forever indebted to their kindness."

After a pause, Juana's voice found an emotional urgency and a louder, higher pitch. "They gave me a life without abuse, a way to hold my head up high without …" Juana made a move that neither Grady nor Chris ever expected as she resumed her story. "Without believing that *these* were the only things my life was about." She tore the Derek Jeter T-shirt off her body, exposing her braless and tortured chest. Juana held the limp shirt in her right hand and puffed out her chest and moved close to Grady.

After a few long moments, silent moments, Juana turned around and put on the blue shirt with the big number 2 on the back.

Juana took a deep breath, turned back to Grady and moved on. "Carmine and his family rescued me and my sister's baby. And we, yes, Pelham 1-2-3-4, saved his … our family. We paid off the six million in blood-saving money that the stupid Alberto Antobelli owed to the biggest of the big, bad *I*-talians."

Juana took another deep breath and then the time to explain how Alberto had gotten in way over his head, and repeated how Frankie Noto, the Little Don, planned to get the Mafia's money back.

"I got Chris into this. The Broker vetted my life before he got me involved. Carmine had told him that I probably would help, because of the debt I owed him and the threatened price Noto was promising to extract. There was no question that I was in. When he learned of my relationship with Chris, he thought he might be a key asset. Someone who would know how this sort of thing might work. Someone who could help plan a way to get the money from the richest bank in the world, the United States government. Damn, Grady, they spend that much on a bag of hammers. Rick Huse wanted someone who could find a way to get inside and watch. And he did it in spades. At first, I refused to get Chris involved. Then when Chris pushed me, I gave in and told the Broker and Carmine that he was in."

Juana had to take a break. She took the time to quench her dry mouth with the pilsner. The pause inspired Chris to stand up and take over. Before he spoke, Grady had something to say.

"You still killed innocent people, and where'd the other five mil go, Chris?"

Chris moved between the entrance to the cottage and the center of the living area with a disciplined, pendular precision—five steps to the door, pivot, five steps back—while he talked. He only paused to take a swig of his beer.

"Grady, like she said, Juana wanted to keep me out of this. But when she left, I could not let it go. I needed to know why the sister of my first love, now my new love, needed to walk out like she did. It made no sense. I pursued her and then convinced her to let me in.

"You've heard the why, and now, if you would like another beer, I can get you one. And then I will tell you *how* we did what we did. And I'll explain Maria."

CHAPTER 101

▼

THE GREAT ROCK

The only inhabited island of Los Roques, the Venezuelan archipelago in the Caribbean, was a piece of volcanic rock. A place of spectacular sunrises and sunsets, pristine beaches, and a friendly population of about fifteen hundred. This island, El Gran Roque, was now also the new home of Maria Calabrese.

The Gulfstream Turbo Commander, its pilot, Frankie Noto, his South American friend, and Maria had made a safe and smooth landing at the El Gran Roque airport. A landing strip where the control tower is nothing but a tiny, square, windowed room, painted on the outside in red and white checks, and hoisted by a scissor lift on the flatbed of a truck. It is a small facility whose landing strip looks more like a local road. A place where not a single runway light can be found.

In almost every way, except for the combination of sand and water, the Great Rock was the anti-Caracas. Planes could only land in daylight, and once the passengers alighted, there were no nearby high-rise hotels, no bustling city, and no rental car counters—no cars on the island, period, not even a motorcycle. Wherever you wanted to go, it was either on foot or by boat. There were only three sandy streets that wound their way between the island's homes and small businesses.

What the small rock did have was a Plaza Bolivar, the center of town, the gathering place for relaxed locals and tourists alike—no bustling, just dancing, drinking, and doing as one chose. The island was home to ninety-two species of birds feeding off the teeming waters. The fishing, especially the bonefish catch, was good enough to attract the likes of George Bush 41. The lobster is considered some of the best in the world.

Visitors would make their way from the airport on foot to one of the sixty posadas on the island. The inns ranged from low-rise, upscale luxury to the most simple of accommodations, some with hot water, some not, some with air conditioning, some not. It was one of the small posadas that the Little Don, Frankie Noto, had purchased back in the late-nineties. His wife had the whole place redone, including the addition of heated water and air-cooling machines. The stone walls were painted a pleasant peach, and the terrace was redone with new, white tiles that led to the small beach. The former inn had a sizeable kitchen and dining room. There was a cozy central room and four bedrooms, large for this island. Most rooms were done in a pale salmon color. It was here that the threesome was headed to from the airport. All three were dressed appropriately in shorts and short-sleeved shirts. With their sneakers on, they were the exception to the largely barefoot population. They had no luggage, so, the walk from the airport, past the edge of the laguna, to the house was not taxing. Maria, hands now free, had been directed not to talk but walk and smile. Frankie Noto's home was on the left side of Calle Marao, the village's main street. You could see the Plaza Bolivar just up the road.

Frankie Noto opened the entrance door and waved Maria in. He motioned to the kitchen area just off the foyer. "In here, Maria. Wanna beer?"

A saturnine Maria answered, "Several, please. Can I speak now?"

"You have to listen first. Let me introduce you to your guardian, Benedicto Delgado. Benedicto means blessed, but we just call him Benny. Now let me tell you about ole Benny here. We met almost seven years ago when I first visited this paradise. His mother, God rest her soul, was our housekeeper during our stays. Back then he owned a single boat and took tourists to the other islands for a day of private pleasures. Now my friend here owns, along with me, a fleet of boats and has a crew of ten men who work for him. He knows everyone in this town. And all his friends knew that you were coming to stay. And they have been instructed and paid to be courteous and friendly, but in no way will they help you if you get the notion to flee. In other words, forget about trying to get off this island without my permission. Benny lives here and so shall you. Now let me get a few beers and I will continue."

Maria was somewhere between mystified and pissed beyond control, but she held her temper and her tongue in check. She even stood to shake hands with the handsome Venezuelan. If prison had taught her anything, it was acquiescence to those in authority.

"Now, let me continue. Don't think I haven't caught you eyeing up my boy here. Forget about it, as they say. Mr. Delgado does not have any sexual interest in women. Never has. Never will. So, put those thoughts out of your head. But he *is* very skilled at home care. He has a degree in practical nursing, and comforted his mother in her final years in a most heroic way."

Benny smiled, and Maria downed half of the Brahma Malta, the popular Brazilian brew Frankie had served her.

"Refreshing, isn't it? Maria, you will be well treated here. I know you know who I am, and, perhaps, you fear me and you should. But you are here for a purpose and, as long as you fulfill that purpose, I can promise you a much more pleasant environment than Danbury or Tallahassee could ever offer. Now, bring your beer, and I will show you to your quarters."

Maria was somewhat shocked when she was shown to a large bedroom with a private bath. The small closet and dark wood dresser were filled with new clothing, the correct size and beach fashionable.

"Benedicto will make sure you have everything you need in the way of food, shelter, clothing, etc. I will be checking in every month or so to see how you are doing. Now let me explain your role here."

"Please do." Maria put the empty beer can down on the doily that was on the dresser, and without request, Benedicto immediately retrieved a refill.

The shock at the comfort of her quarters was a dull pinprick compared to the next thing she saw. Maria was glad to have the second cold drink in her hand.

She had half suspected that the Little Don might be a little kinky and that the room he was pointing her to would be filled with chains and shackles, and maybe a few whips and doggie collars with spikes. And that her mission here was to serve his perverse predilections.

Maria's suspicions were dead wrong.

"In here," Noto said as he gestured to another bedroom door. Maria had heard a steady hum when she had passed this door on the way to her room and assumed it was the air conditioning—it wasn't.

In the only colorful room of the former posada, with walls of bright pinks and yellows and sea blue scenes, was a hospital bed.

Older, thinner and silent, but still easily recognizable, its occupant was her former lover, her downfall in a sense, Rob Speck.

Maria walked, transfixed on his pale, drawn visage. Thin, clear, oxygen tubes hanging from his motionless face. Rob Speck was alive. She moved toward the head of the bed, ignored the tubes from various parts of the still bed and whispered, "Rob, oh my God. Sweet Rob."

CHAPTER 102

▼

How?

The scene was a bit bizarre in the small Jensen cottage. A handsome, Japanese-featured American man; a beautiful, tanned Latino; and the redheaded Irishman sitting on a chair in handcuffs. And now, the subdued Grady was firing up his scolding, holier-than-thou dialogue. "How? Why do I care about the how? You need to pay for *what* you did. Both of you. You both have killed people, haven't you? Haven't you?"

"Yes, we have, Grady, but, please, be patient here. I need to explain. I need to get you on the same page as Juana and I."

"Same page! We're not even in the same book, not standing in the same damn library. Chris, you're gonna pay."

"Shut up, Grady, and listen."

The "how" was the kind of story that deserved a "once upon a time" beginning. Chris did not give in to the temptation to do so.

"Once I convinced Juana to let me in, I met with the Broker in White Plains. It was a small park on Lake Street. Not far from where the task force would end up. We sat there, like two strangers sharing a park bench, eating our deli lunches. He filled me in on his basic thoughts of how in the world one comes up with the kind of money they needed to get the Little Don off their backs. I finished my lunch before he did and he instructed me to walk over to Magnotta's Deli and ask for Mr. Huse's *New York Times*. Inside was an envelope full of details.

"I asked him for two weeks to think through a plan. He agreed, under one condition. One of his men would have to participate." The man Rick Huse had chosen was known to most as Maximum Al.

"His man and I met in the Broker's Virginia home, the next night, sans Broker. We shared takeout from a local Italian joint and a little wine. Two days and more takeout later, we had an outline and a list of options to consider. Three days later, a week ahead of my promise to the Broker, we had a detailed plan for all that came after."

"You mean all the goddamned *blood* that came later."

"Grady, please. This is gonna take a while. Just frigging listen. Yes, the phrase 'blood in the streets' was one of the Broker's basic tenets, and we had signed up to follow it."

The cuffed redhead looked from Chris to Juana and back. "Jesus."

"I'll get to that now." Chris briefly explained that they had recruited and paid a number of people to pull it off. Those who helped with the act. And those paid to look the other way, like the security people in Griffith Park. Grady shook his head in disbelief and with disgust as Chris began his story.

"Now, let's talk about Jesus Heraldo Cruz. Better known by the media as Jesus H.

"Our Jesus is *alive and well* on a beach in Puerto Rico. The name of the man on the cross was actually Alejandro Santiago Perez—killed the night before in a knife fight in East Los Angeles, the largest Hispanic community in the U.S."

"How?"

"Take it easy, Grady. That's what I'm trying to tell you."

"Part of the plan included contacts with specific friends in the mortuary business and appropriate compensation." Chris left out the detail that Rich "Tank" Tomasello, a very clever man, working with his Uncle Frankie, a very connected funeral parlor owner, knowing the targeted LA location, made critical connections in order to secure an already dead Hispanic.

"You see, Grady, there are over three hundred homicides a year in LA. We were patient and lucky. Our Jesus did have a resemblance to the real Jesus H. Cruz."

"But I heard his mother identified him."

"Quiet, please. I have had a long day. As I said, her lovely son is enjoying a six-month stay on the beach. He will return as a cousin of Jesus, looking a bit different, with a full set of papers and needing a place to stay. And the generously compensated mother of our Jesus H. was happy to make the identification in exchange for more money than she had ever seen at one time. Done deal.

"It was another man, poor Alejandro Santiago Perez, already killed and well preserved, until the crucifixion, who ended up on the cross. A kind of unique version of the Broker's "blood on the streets" theme. Don't you think? Sure got the nation's attention. And the fingerprint switch in the FBI database was no big deal. Access to that ability was key and always part of the plan. We needed to have, well, connections in the Bureau."

Chris seemed to be enjoying himself, and Grady seemed not to be enjoying Chris's glee.

"Beer, Grady? I'll try and finish this quickly."

Chris went on for thirty more minutes.

The New York John the Baptist found himself, the day before the library drop, on the wrong end of a gun. When we got him, he was already hours dead by the bullet of a South Bronx enemy. We borrowed his head for the event on the steps of the New York City Library. Our undertaker friend appreciated our taking the dead body off his hands, with the appropriate funeral costs being covered by the Broker. And, it was not hard to get a fake ID and make a few more payoffs to secure confirmation that one John Baptista had indeed lost his head. Let's just say New York City has a number of untracked, often unmissed residents. His real identity is not important now.

"The Sarasota John was pure luck. His name actually was Jean Baptiste. A visiting Frenchman in the wrong part of southern Florida trying to rip off the wrong people on a drug deal. It's amazing what you can find out on these new digital police scanners, as long as you know where to listen and have the people to do it. We had to keep this John's head on ice for a few days until we had our New York corpse available. More unfortunate blood on the streets. But blood by someone else's doing. Not ours. The semen *was* our doing. A couple of willing gentlemen just doing what boys like to do. This time it was with two of our female recruits. Very pretty girls, very clever and efficient in the art of coaxing the sperm from our ballplayer and sailor, *and* capturing it as well. The cigarette with Jesus and the semen with the Johns were something to distract, confuse, and frustrate the authorities.

"What we did was get the attention of the people with the purse strings. You don't get that kind of money at the racetrack. Once we targeted the government, we knew the plan had to be dramatic and terrorizing. Something that would make it better for them to pay up rather than get their public image slammed all over the front page. And I know from past dead-end investigations that the politicos want a way to close down the bad press. In this case, that meant money and some bullshit cover-up of the give-in. Oh, and Maria.

"It's over, Grady. I, we, knew that the breaking point would come when it did with the church bombing."

Chris paused to look at Juana, who just nodded. Grady was silent.

"You see, Grady, we did not kill anyone. Sure, we broke a number of laws and caused a lot of trouble. But, in the end, we saved the lives of six innocent people."

A less indignant Grady, asked, "What about the Joans?"

"Before I go *there*. You see, what we did when we laid out the plan was try and think like those guys on the other side of our demands. Try and predict a breaking point. Try and raise the stakes until we were positioned to get enough money to cover all the expenses and the payoff to Noto.

"Now, the Joans. Interesting logistics with the propane setup. It took us a while to nail down the engineering, but I'll tell you that Maximum Al is one smart dude. Even smart enough to keep himself just far enough away from the actual deeds. But, boy, could he put a plan together. Of course, I had a bit to do with it."

Chris realized he had given up a name, even if it was a nickname, and needed to be more guarded in his telling.

"The Joans. Surely, the most spectacular. Another very dramatic location. But perhaps the easiest, as far as the victims were concerned. There was only one real body involved—a drug O.D. before we picked her up in Southeast D.C. The other figures were wooden mannequins with some simple enhancements to provide the screaming and flailing—all dust by the time the DCFD put the flames out. Before the fire, we had collected enough remains of cremations from our mortuary connections to scatter on the truck bed to add to the illusion. And a cremation usually takes two to three hours at 1400 to 1800 degrees. So, in addition to the propane, which we jacked up to a slightly higher temperature, but not enough to melt the metals, we had the oil in the bottom of the truck bed. When the firefighters started pouring their water on the oil fire, things only got worse for them. But it bought more time for the process to finish. We planted the evidence with metal that would not melt. The words etched in the metal were enough to lead the authorities to the identities of the three Joans, well, actually, two Joans and a Jeanne. And, we knew that, between the mess we left behind and the metal leading to the Joans' ID's, the investigators would be confused as hell. The real Joans were all down-on-their-luck souls from Arkansas, now much happier with well-endowed annuities and new identities and a new place to live, and, well, a new life. See, we not only saved lives with all of this, we gave others better lives. When the Broker told us this would be bloody, he was very right. But the blood that we shed was that of already dead people."

"Christ Almighty, you're all crazy. Wait. Wait. What about you getting shot?"

"Oh, almost forgot. A hired marksman to insure no one on the task force or anyone like you might think I was on the wrong team. A bit risky, but, until you came along, it sure kept me above any suspicion. Hurt like a bitch, but it was part of the plan."

"Jed?"

"Jed knew nothing. He is completely innocent of any of this."

"Damn. Go back. The church bombing. That *building* was not already dead. How does your warped mind try and justify that? Damn it, Chris."

"Let's just say that Reverend James Johnson of the First Baptist Church of Accomac, Virginia, will be holding services in a nearby place of worship until a very large, anonymous endowment is made in a couple of months. The tiny, very run-down church will be replaced with a sparkling new and larger facility in the very near future. All part of the plan."

There was so much more detail to reveal.

The complex, covert communications schemes.

The identities of all the recruits.

The amazing response of Chris's college roommate, another of the Fearless Foursome. The Adonis, known as Drew Birdsall. The trivia king jumped into what he considered an adventure like a starving man into a box of Krispy Kremes. Chris knew they needed help with moving the money at the end. He assured the Broker that Drew was the right man. Drew looked forward to the trip to Vienna and executing all the transactions to put eleven million dollars on their way.

His wife Karen, the straightest of New York district attorneys, was in as soon as she heard about the threats against Sarah's child and grandchild. Straight went by the wayside when the family of the girl whom Chris loved and lost was on the line. She volunteered to keep an eye from her vantage point on what the law enforcement crowd was knowing and not knowing.

And then there was Uncle Mikey Reardon. An all-expenses-paid week in Sarasota, sailing, scouting things out, and, finally, with two other recruits, dropping off the head of the dead French drug dealer on the silver platter in the bay. Chris did not have to ask Uncle Mikey twice, and Aunt Ree Ree had her string bikini packed and ready to go weeks ahead of time.

The Broker was nervous about the risk of getting some of these folks involved, but Chris managed to convince him that they would be committed and smart about it.

And then, there were the two witnesses to the D.C. inferno, both arranged for and taken care of by Allan Mason, Rick Huse's buddy from International Country Club. The unexpected couple of Geordie Williams and Mary Brennan as witnesses was just a lucky break.

Without having revealed any of these details, Chris concluded his story.

"End of story, Grady. Yeah, Juana and I have both killed people, but not in this case. Juana did it before to save herself and her family from destruction. I did it once in the line of duty. *These* deaths, the six J's, were all a charade meant to preserve life, not to destroy it."

Grady did not have a word to say. Chris had noted two things as he told his story. One was the bulge in the left leg bottom of Grady's suit pants and the other was an obvious question that Grady, Mr. NYC policeman, should have asked and did not. He waited a minute to see what his captive would do next. And then he moved on.

"What would you have done, Grady? We did what we had to do. Now, I guess we're asking that maybe you can forgive us and understand."

After a long silence, Grady finally spoke up. "I do—*both*."

CHAPTER 103

▼

ROB

"He's alive," Maria said as she turned from the bedridden blond to face his uncle Frankie Noto. "I never knew. Things happened so fast. My lawyer knew nothing. He just assumed with the federal charges I was gone for life and the state wouldn't bother with the expense of another trial." She looked back to the man she had fallen so madly in lust, and perhaps love, with and whispered, "Jesus."

"Yes, Jesus," Noto said, pointing to the crucifix on the wall. "One of your duties, per my wife's instructions, is that you will pray with him every day. Morning, noon, and night. My wife will also be checking in on both of you from time to time. There is a small church on the island, and when a priest or minister comes to the island, you will be expected to attend services and pray for Rob, my nephew. Perhaps, besides being a sinner, you are also a non-believer, but I'm sure your lovely mother taught you how to pray. And if you have forgotten, Benedicto can help you relearn.

For the next hour, Frankie Noto explained a lot of things to Maria.

Benedicto had been Rob Speck's nurse for the past three years.

The bullet meant for Rob's groin had entered his jaw when he tried to jump up from the adulterous hotel bed. It hit and passed to the top of the spinal column, specifically the atlas, the first of the seven cervical vertebrae. It left him in a coma and motionless. After several failed surgeries, the New York hospitals and doctors had given Rob a lifetime sentence of this. They even talked about pulling the plug.

"We decided to bring him here. And, now, with you and Benny as his caregivers, we want to take one last shot at making a better life for Rob. My wife believes in her heart that his brain is in there and working on some level. She swears that he has had moments of hand movement in this bed in response to her touch. That maybe he can enjoy the sounds and smells of the ocean. That maybe a constant dose of the voice of the woman he may have loved, at least enjoyed, would trigger some kind of spark. That maybe a familiar touch may wake up a single nerve.

"And that is your new sentence, a sentence of works of mercy for the man you and your desires have reduced to *this* horrible sentence. None of it will be easy. Benny will teach you all the issues of caring for a bedridden man, many of them strenuous, and some distasteful. A neurologist will be in next week to explain as much as he knows about Rob's condition and the best things to be done to try and induce any reaction or perception.

"Comas are difficult things to deal with, to predict. In Rob's case there is not much hope, since he has been in this state for a while, but we won't give up. And neither shall you, or the consequences will not be pleasant, not even close to pleasant, and not the kind doled out by any American justice system. That's it for me. We have all had a long day. Your new work starts first thing in the morning. Dinner will be brought to us in a few hours. Any more questions?"

Maria, with her eyes still locked on the beautiful, once-so-alive, blond man, had missed half the words Noto was saying, but she sure got the gist of the recitation. She turned to her new captor and his pretty friend and said, "No. I will do as you say, Mr. Noto. He deserves every … any chance. You're right. It is my fault he is like this." Maria remembered the last time she cried—her first night in prison. She was now shedding tears on the first night in her new prison. A sincere-sounding thank-you was pushed out through a filtering series of sobs. "Thank you."

CHAPTER 104

▼

I Do

Grady surprised both of his captors with his, "I do—both" response. Neither Chris nor Juana expected the quick answer. Both were suspicious, and Chris was now pretty sure that the bulge at Grady's ankle was a small weapon.

"Can you uncuff me? And then, it's my turn to talk."

"Not with that pistol strapped to your ankle."

"It's not loaded, but please, go ahead and take it. The Sig you took before is loaded with dummies, so, you need not worry too much about that piece either."

Chris carefully lifted the pant leg and took the holster off Grady's ankle and removed the pistol to check it. It was a Walther P22, all of fifteen ounces and only about six inches long. He grabbed the soft, black-polymer-finished handle. He ejected the cartridge that would normally have ten .22 caliber rounds in it. It was empty. He checked the chamber, empty also. Chris reloaded the cartridge and handed the gun to Juana. She took it to the safe. When she came back, she released Grady's hands. Grady rubbed his wrists and stood up.

"Great beer," he said to both. He walked over to the table with the pictures Juana had played like an angry poker player and sorted through them. He chose the one of Carmine's sister and held it up.

"My wife's mother."

He put the picture back on the table and took a long swig of the pilsner beer.

"I was the first call Carmine Antobelli, Uncle Carm, made after the Little Don threatened our families. The first snippets of the plan he shared with you were a product of my initial meetings with him. He wanted my advice. Should he go to the authorities? Knowing Frankie Noto and what he had threatened did not make that a very desirable option. So, the plan, the conspiracy, began with him and *me*. Him and *me*. How about that, Chris?"

The question that Grady did not ask before now made more sense to one really angry and surprised Chris. Juana was relieved that their peril was over and ready to ask the same question Chris half-screamed out.

"Why the hell did you put me, put us, through all of this, Grady? It's your damn turn to give up the why. You redheaded son-of-a-bitch. Shit, Grady. Are you off your meds again? Are you nuts? Why? *Jesus!* I'm ready to beat the ever-loving crap out of you. Right here. Right now."

"Easy, hotshot. You deserved every minute of it. Maybe not Juana, but, hey, she was in the wrong place at the wrong time. I needed to do it here, but I'll explain that later. Grab another beer and relax. At least I'm not gonna send you both to the jail time you deserve."

Grady moved around the room and then closer to Chris and spoke.

"Now, the 'why' is a pretty sad story. You remember the first time I was about to break 100 and you moved the flag three feet to the left on my uphill approach putt and I three putted for 100? This was payback, Mr. Best in Class. I thought I had put it behind me with all of my other crazy, depression-based notions; but, when you did not even join in the celebration of my ninety-eight at Pipestem this year, it all came back." Grady reached in his suit coat pocket and pulled out the tattered scorecard from 1990, from the round where, in Grady's mind, Chris had betrayed him. And threw it at Chris.

"My first chance to ever have that feeling that was always so easy for *you* to come by. And you took it away. I believe that if I had done it that day, things would have been different for me going forward. But, thanks to you, I had to wait fifteen more years to reach that goal.

"Today was my one chance in life to best you. To take something precious away from you. To move the flag of *your* hopes and dreams three feet to the left and let you know what it feels like to almost fulfill an elusive, haunting dream, only to have it ripped away. Your dream, your new life with Juana here, was where you were headed free and clear, or so you thought. And I had the power to destroy it, and, if only for a little while, to make you feel the despair."

Grady was trying to make Chris and Juana see the logic in his actions, and maybe, just maybe, was trying to convince himself that what he had done to them was justified. The logic of his plan had seemed so much clearer on his way down to Jensen Beach.

"I had so looked up to you. I counted myself a better person because of our friendship. What you did, for whatever reason, shattered an already fragile soul—mine. It was the final straw, as they say, on an already strained back of emotions. None of you knew at the time what I was going through. Nobody did. I was in a horrible world of depression. Golf was the one thing that I thought might be a release. Yours and Jed's and Drew's friendship were three good things in my life; reasons to think maybe life ain't so bad after all. And then the real chance to break the magical 100 for the first time, to join a kind of club that the three of you and millions of others belonged to, was there for me. I know it sounds foolish, but it was important to me. It meant a lot at a time when not much else did. I decided that there was only one way to put that hurt behind me, behind us. And that was to let you know what it's like. And I think *now* you might.

"And to answer one of your questions. Yes, I am on my meds. Much milder than they used to be. It has been a horrible climb out of the hell I have been in. A hell that no doctor could explain to any satisfaction. But I'm pretty much out. For some reason I just had to get this hate out of my heart for what you did. I know it sounds silly, but to me it has never been silly. I carried that moment around with me all these years. Even in my most suicidal times, that insult, your insult, that betrayal, your betrayal, loomed large in my psyche. Your moving the flag became a symbol of how I thought you three really thought of poor old Grady.

"And today. What I did today. I saw this as maybe a chance to purge a burden I've carried too long. I thought I might be able to erase the pain by getting this revenge.

"I had to make you feel it like I felt it, just for a little while—the crushed dream. Not for the fifteen years like I've been dragging mine around with me. Depression is a very tangled nest of emotions. If you've never been in the hell it brings, it's hard to understand the pain of the fires and the real reasons the fires are stoked so violently.

"And now, maybe, we can put it all behind us. If *you* can't put today behind us, I will understand. Trust me. I will understand. I'm sorry. I never wanted to be the Best in Class. Just wanted so badly to belong and feel like I fit in. It's been a constant, searing pain.

"I wanted you, the Best in Class, to know that I was not the unworthy, witless human being you always thought I was. Crazy maybe. Paranoid maybe. But, those of us who suffer from this wicked disease have been known to do the strangest things. This was mine, my turn to shake a devil from my soul. I so desperately wanted, no, want, your respect. I had gotten past everything except you, Mr. Perfect.

"I guess today was just another case of Grady being Grady the Loser."

CHAPTER 105

▼

Christopher Lee did something he had never done before in his life. He knelt before another man, his friend Grady, and wordlessly cried like a baby.

Juana was locked into her chair with mild shock, but more by the sadness of Chris's redheaded friend. She understood perfectly what it meant to be in hell. For her, a different kind than Grady's, but a hell nonetheless. His scars were inexplicable scars of the mind. Hers were of the body. Visible scars that seeped into her mind and emotions. Reminders of the hells with her father Tommy, her stepfather Conrad, and the other loser foster parents who abused her in their own ways. With the help of Chris's love, she had been able to put the past scars of her own mind behind her. She wiped the tears from her own eyes and walked toward Grady and Chris. She looked Grady straight in the eyes.

"Grady, I'll speak for myself. If you can put today and that day fifteen years ago behind you, I would very much like for *us* to be good friends. I will put today behind me. I understand. No need to apologize to me." Juana, who as a child had killed her two fathers to get the devils off her back, grabbed a beer and walked out to the dock. She thought it best to leave the two men alone. One half of the Fearless Foursome, in a place they never would have predicted they would be.

Chris knew what he had to do. He got up from his knees and came to Grady. He hugged him, his tears staining the shoulder of the redhead's suit jacket. After a few seconds, Grady put his arms around Chris and returned the strong caress. He shed a little of his own water on his friend's shoulder.

"Let's sit, Grady. Let me tell you a story. A story I have told no one else."

Chris talked and Grady listened for thirty minutes. He talked of the shield he had put up to the world after Sarah's death. The false front of strength and tough guy. The reality was that he had come to know the depths of depression like the back of his hand, like millions of other people in the world. He told of how, as he had just done in front of Grady, he knelt in the Lee Chapel and asked God why. How his asking turned into a desire to tear the church down, tear a hundred churches down, to pay God back for his personal cruelty to Christopher Sato Lee. Grady nodded as Chris spoke of the images that involuntarily invaded his mind. Images of memories, good and bad. Chris was not sure which ones made him sadder. The good with Sarah that should have lasted a lifetime or the bad of her withering body at the end. And those last breaths that came with pain and labor. Now, when the memories came, he retreated into a shelter made up of his awe at what was Sarah's spirit, after all she had been through. And her words, telling him to get on with life. To go for the good it offers and leave the sorrow behind.

"I finally came to realize, with my mother's help and some therapy, that maybe none of this was God's fault. That my anger, paranoia, and depression were a natural part of the grief. I forgave God. Grady, I hope you can forgive me."

On that crazy day in Jensen Beach, Grady and Chris shared something much more important and vital than being in the under-100 club. They unsheathed the daggers of depression that each had hidden for so long from each other.

CHAPTER 106

▼

THE LAST THUMB DRIVE

It was the end of July, and Jerry Whalen was breathing easier at his desk in New York City. He wasn't sure if his career path had been severely impeded with curves and bumps, but he was just glad to have the DO3J, DO6J, whatever, task force weeks behind him.

When the lovely Lea came into his office with another FedEx box, his breathing went on hold for a few seconds.

"Should I open it, Jerry?"

"Yeah. Let's hope it is not another one of those stupid computer things."

It was. Lea closed the door and set it in the USB port on Jerry's computer.

When it started up with a screen full of big red letters on a black background, spelling out, "This is what you must do or you die," Lea gasped. It was a Power-Point file with an arrow at the bottom right of the screen. The first screen with its message was signed "The Piper."

"Jesus," Jerry muttered. He thought he had already paid the Piper with his actions.

"Ah, it's a joke, Lea, from a friend in the Washington office who knew about all the fun we had with the previous FedEx deliveries. You can go back to your desk."

"You sure?"

"Yes, I'm sure," he lied. What he was sure about was that this was very bad news. He recalled the first time he had met the Piper, and, months after that, the irony of his boss telling him he needed to "pay the fiddler."

The memory of the whole event from months before was both vivid and haunting. Jerry and his wife had gone out for their usual Saturday night dinner at a Mount Kisco, New York, restaurant. They made it a standing date, at least when his wife was not in some foreign country making another huge deal and a pile of money. They always ate in the smaller, cozy upstairs dining room. That night the waiter had told the frequent customers that the evening's dessert special was on the owner in appreciation for their patronage. It was a raspberry cheese-cake with swirls of the red preserves laced through the heavenly mixture of cream cheese and sweetened, heavy milk, topped with fresh berries and whipped cream. After a meal of veal parmigiana and spaghetti, the cool cheesecake tasted like the perfect finish. It turned out to be the beginning of a long, horrible night.

The delicious dessert was also laced with a syrupy dose of an emetic derived from the dried rhizome and roots of the ipecacuanha plant. The emetine in the drug ipecac takes about twenty minutes to work on the stomach and the vomit-ing center of the brain. Jerry's episode was a violent one. The meal and its Italian red sauce and the cheesecake, a separate one just for Jerry, which the chef had loaded up with red food coloring, made its way from Jerry's stomach to the toilet in the men's room of his favorite eatery. It was over a second cup of coffee, spiked with a shot of Kahlua, when the rumbling started. When the purge became almost liquid only, it was the color of blood, lots of blood.

Another visitor to the men's room had called 911. The ambulance arrived within minutes. They put the scared attorney on the gurney and sped away. The siren was turned off after only a three-minute ride, and Jerry was breathing better assuming the hospital was where they were. He was wrong. The driver had pulled into a darkened church parking lot. One of the emergency medical technicians who had been holding his arm spoke.

"Don't worry, Mr. Whalen, you are not gonna die. All the red you're seeing is just a combination of the red gravy and a heavy dose of red food coloring. The liquid is just a combination of the martini and three beers and coffee that you had with dinner. The ipecac that we arranged to be put in the cheesecake you ate is what is causing your problem. They won't even have to pump your stomach."

"Who the hell are you?" Jerry spit out between wretches.

"Just call me the Piper. And it's time to pay the Piper, or else."

He was a tall, well-built man with thinning blond hair. He was Richard "Tank" Tomasello, Carmine Antobelli's right-hand man. Jerry never got a good look at him because of the flashlight being shined in his eyes and would never know him by any name other than the Piper.

That night, he told Jerry Whalen that just because Alberto Antobelli was dead did not mean he was off the hook for the one million he owed in gambling debts.

In Orlando, when Frankie Noto told Carmine of the man who was into Alberto's bookie business for a cool million, Carm filed that piece of information away, thinking it may be used to help with the weight of Noto's demands and threats. It turned out to be true.

And, in the back of an ambulance, weary and sore from the violent heaving, Jerry Whalen agreed to join the conspiracy that would become the Jesus, John, and Joan show. He did not want any part of what the "or else" might be.

This part of Chris and Maximum Al's plan had made the Broker and Carmine laugh out loud. A DOJ man, all their own, on the inside, making sure things were steered as needed. Playing the fall guy for the DOJ's inability to crack the cases; getting Chris on the inside with him. A perfect and vulnerable target for their scheme. Someone to make sure Grady did not get tangled up in the investigation. For Grady, it was too personal, and he did not have the same level of cool that Chris had to manage inside the task force environment.

The tall man in the ambulance had lied that night. Doing everything that he was told to do to pull off the plan did not unburden Jerry of his one-million-dollar debt. They were back for more.

In his office he worked the mouse with a trembling hand walking through the message the Piper had sent. His work on behalf of Pelham 1-2-3-4 had only paid off half of his debt. The Piper wanted the other five hundred grand paid off in an annuity, over five-years time. *Well, at least that's some relief*, thought Jerry. But Jerry was still angry. He had done all they asked. He had reacted to the thumb drives and the Hollywood, New York, Sarasota, and D.C. incidents as instructed. He steered the whole thing perfectly. He even let them blow up his damn car to make it look like he was a target and not a conspirator. They had gotten their money's worth with his stellar acting performance. Damn. Now they wanted more from him.

The fifth slide of the PowerPoint show had a thumbnail picture of a man and a woman in bed, naked. The woman was on top. The man had his eyes closed and his hands gripping the backend of his partner. Under the thumbnail were the words, "Click here to see the whole show."

Jerry not only recognized himself and Lea, but he recognized the décor in the Crowne Plaza hotel in White Plains. The index finger of his right hand slowly pushed down on the mouse's left button.

The video went on for a full three minutes until they climaxed. And then, the PowerPoint presentation climaxed with a final page.

We're sure you can steal the money from your rich wife, like you did when you first dabbled in the dangerous art of gambling.
I'm positive it will be less painful for all involved to do that, instead of sharing with your wife and boss this marvelous and enjoyable movie clip of your tryst.
I'm sure you know by now that it is not a good idea to screw with us.
Bye, for now.
Oh, by the way, Lea, you look even better with no clothes on.

The Piper

The man from Dunkirk, born on his aunt's kitchen floor in Hamburg, New York, knew how to pilfer his wife's millions, and that is what he would do.

The last thumb drive, crafted by Corey Young, one of the Broker's tech whizzes, as they all had been, had done its job.

The Broker's crew of many had indeed all done their jobs.

Epilogue—One Year Later

On the horizon, the sun was retreating into the dark sea. Its fiery red tint made Maria Calabrese think that it just might sizzle the Caribbean's waters when it began to disappear. She was sitting on the hilltop that was home to the old, crumbling, Dutch lighthouse constructed of coral, conch shells, and stone built in 1862. The red and orange twilight hues of the sky made for a spectacular ending to a miraculous day. It was a year since Frankie Noto had flown her to the island of El Grand Roque. She had done as he said. Things she had never done before. She surprised herself. Maria's years in prison had hardened her on the outside but saddened and softened her on the inside. It was as if all the sorrow she had brought on herself had seeped into her soul and cleansed some of the physical greed that had driven so much of her life. Today's miracle was a small one on the scale of divine phenomena, but to her it was a marvel unexpected.

Rob Speck had opened his eyes. She was bathing him as she did every other day. She was wiping his hands when she felt movement. The tips of his fingers pressured hers, and when she looked up, Rob's eyes were open, looking at her. She swore she saw recognition in them, the first light in the darkness of the last year.

✳ ✳ ✳ ✳

"Hey, I got myself a bream. He must be eight pounds. Heat up the frying pan. Dinner's on its way."

The crowds, one in the gazebo, the others gathered on the large back deck just waved to Uncle Mikey. The proud fisherman walked down the hill in the Lees' Lexington yard with his thermos of coffee in one hand and his gear in the other. The slimy, narrow fish would live to see another day. The merciful angler had returned his trophy to the Lee pond. *Hell, it's July Fourth. A perfect day for liberation and freedom.*

Uncle Mikey noticed that the party had gotten louder and filled with more laughter since he left it an hour ago. He guessed all the empty wine and beer bottles might have something to do with it.

The wedding took place in the same place of worship that Sarah Jones had seen in the reflection of the Palms restaurant door back in 1990 on her first date with Chris. Juana and Chris said their "I do's" in front of Deacon Anthony Weaver of the Lexington Presbyterian Church, a jovial fellow with a sincere and rich way with words.

Grady was the best man and Karen Birdsall was the matron of honor. The groomsmen, Drew and Jed, were accompanied by Chris's two sisters. The ceremony was brief and beautiful.

Juana and Chris, Pelham 3 and 4, danced their first with grace on the floor of the gazebo to Conway Twitty's "The Rose." The mellow voice and piercing words echoed in the yard from the garden speakers. The crowd applauded loudly at the finish. And now the party was on at the Lee home. The newlyweds would spend their first night as man and wife in the guestroom on the first floor in the back of Edward and Gin Lee's spacious home. Far away from the cluster of bedrooms upstairs.

At noon the next day, a stretch limousine arrived to whisk the married couple to a quiet stay at the Tides Inn, three-and-a-half hours to the east on Virginia's Northern Neck. A place of beauty and luxury bordered by the Chesapeake on the east, the Potomac on the north, and the Rappahannock on the south.

Juana had made all the arrangements when she went to the area a year before to meet with Ace Acerno, the ex-FBI agent whose partner was killed in the Yonkers hotel by Alberto Antobelli. The same Ace whose bullet expertly flew from the roof of the White Plains building into the center of Chris Lee's protected chest. The same Ace who, with a little help from his friend Mike Sheehan, a willing fellow conspirator, had seen to the destruction of the church not far from his hometown of Birdsnest, Virginia.

Carmine Antobelli, Pelham 2, had insisted on paying for the honeymoon—out of his personal account, not from any of the government money.

He wanted to, but did not, attend the wedding. As he had done from the beginning, he followed his belief in separation as a safeguard. With all the people involved in the complex conspiracy and saving acts, Carmine kept as many degrees of separation as possible between the normally unconnected players.

*   *   *   *

There was no separation from his family and close friends for Carmine on the same day that Chris and Juana wed. A year after the deal was done, he threw a huge July Fourth celebration at his Yorktown Heights home. He had gathered family and friends and reveled in his return to normalcy—a much healthier one since his real estate deals were finally beginning to pay off. With a glass of red wine in one hand and Carlotta's gorgeous, six-month-old baby girl, Sarah Joan Boccardi, in the other, he sat on his deck and watched.

His sister, Grady's mother-in-law, now feeling better, was having a three-way catch with Carlotta and her son, little Sal. Carm's wife Sophia waved at him from the kitchen where she was working her magic for the evening's meal. His son Vinnie and his wife sat across from him, and, with an innocent smile, lifted their own glasses of wine in a friendly salute. The six people whom Frankie Noto had promised to murder, if Carm could not deliver, were safe—alive and breathing today's fresh air. *Worth every minute of his efforts,* Carm thought. The Broker, Pelham 1, would be finishing up his round at the Red, White, and Blue tournament at Wykagyl Country Club, and he and his Isabella would join the party at dinnertime. From the authorities' point of view, Carm and Rick getting together was not out of the ordinary. Carm looked forward to raising his glass to Mr. Rick Huse on this Independence Day.

*   *   *   *

After a glorious week at the Tides Inn, the honeymooners returned to the scene of the nuptial crime. After a simple dinner and a good night's rest at the Lees' home, Chris and Juana took a short walk hand in hand along Jacktown Road and then up a dirt road that led to a quiet hilltop to catch the sunrise's final moments.

Later that morning Ed and Gin Lee served up a decadent breakfast of fresh fruit and sweet crepes filled with strawberry jam with a touch of melted chocolate. To drink, there was fresh-squeezed orange juice and a pitcher of chilled mimosas. Anthony Weaver and his wife, Dian, had joined the Lee family. The newlyweds said their goodbyes. They had two stops to make, and then they were on their way to Jensen Beach to take care of some business.

The business had been incorporated as the Sarah Jones Foundation for Hope. The cottages that had been available to rent at Joey Dannemann's River Rest facility were now permanently booked by the foundation for abused women and children. The funds, the trusts, to make this happen were seeded by that million dollars the Broker had asked Carmine about just days before they lit up the streets of Washington D.C. Additional annual funding to the tune of one hundred thousand dollars would be coming for the next five years from one Mr. Jerry Whalen.

The four travelers drove into town, then up Route 11, past the Virginia Military Institute campus to the Jefferson Garden and Florist. Juana and her new husband picked out a dozen yellow roses and drove his new Jeep back toward town. Chris crossed over Nelson Street, after stopping at the red light, just across the street from the one that Sarah so serendipitously failed to notice a long time ago. He made the short trip down South Main to the Stonewall Jackson Memorial Cemetery. Chris parked across the street from the red house where he and Sarah had fallen in love.

Juana and Chris's new companion, Lady Lucky, Lady for short, a one-year-old golden retriever, was happy to be out of the car. The animal with the feathered golden coat was a wedding gift from Chris's sisters, Katie and Meghan.

The fourth traveler, who had been a ward of the Lees while the honeymooners were away, had become good friends with the larger Lady. The spunky little Maltese with the bad leg, Juana's Jeter, fought for release from Juana's arms to join the retriever.

The foursome made their way through the black metal gates, down the path to the small monument of Goldie Elizabeth Quisenberry, the child who never made it to her sixth birthday. Chris had told Juana every detail of Sarah's words when Sarah and he had sat on the same bench they were sitting on now. How the twenty-three-year-old lamented out loud for a life extinguished before having a chance to know the joys of love. Juana and Chris now sat silently.

When he had shed enough tears, Chris got up and walked to the century-old, stone tombstone of Gloria Elizabeth Quisenberry and took one of the dozen yellow roses and placed it on the shelf of the four-foot, rectangular base that held the carving of a stone, angelic child.

The sun was now high enough to shine through the branches of the tall oak that rose behind the bench. Chris took Juana's right hand. The left was softly caressing the silver locket that Sarah had given her. The precious metal with an "S" etched on the outside gave the older sister comfort. Juana recalled Anne Brontë's poetic message that Sarah had etched on the inside. "But she that dare not grasp the thorn should never crave the rose." She smiled and gave Chris's hand a squeeze. Together they walked the four steps it took to stand over the two-foot-square, bronze marker that rested in the ground beneath the oak.

He passed a handful of yellow roses to his new bride and together they spread them around the edges of the words on the marker. Words that were separated by a single rose etched into the bronze.

In Memory of Sarah Jones.
The Best in Class, ever, on Earth and now in Heaven.

The End

Final Acknowledgement

These are the final words I will scribe in this book, my second novel.

As I type them, I look down at the gold ring with its hematite stone on my right hand. Incised in the blackish stone is an intaglio of a facial profile of a Roman soldier. The ring was my father's ring. Given to him by my loving mother many years ago. It has always been part of my image of him, for he wore it every day—a true and courageous soldier in his own life.

Dad passed away last year on June 14, 2007, after eighty-six long and happy years of life on this earth. I wear the ring with pride, and sometimes tears. I watched the man who saw my first breaths take his last.

I look up to the picture on the top of the hutch that sits atop my desk, a picture of my granddaughter, my little Magpie, not quite a year old in the photo. And I think of the cycle of life and all the beautiful souls my father and mother have sprinkled on this earth, and there flows a different kind of tear.

For every word in this book, every page that you have turned, every chapter that starts and ends, I have a reason to acknowledge *my* real-world "Best in Class," George Louis Hess.

My next novel that has already been residing in my head and on lots of little notes around the house for over a year will be dedicated solely to him.

It will be a very different kind of story for this writer, a story about the wonderful game of golf, courage, friendship and a special kind of love. All of which were an integral part of my Dad's life.

Dad, we miss you.

978-0-595-45756-4
0-595-45756-8

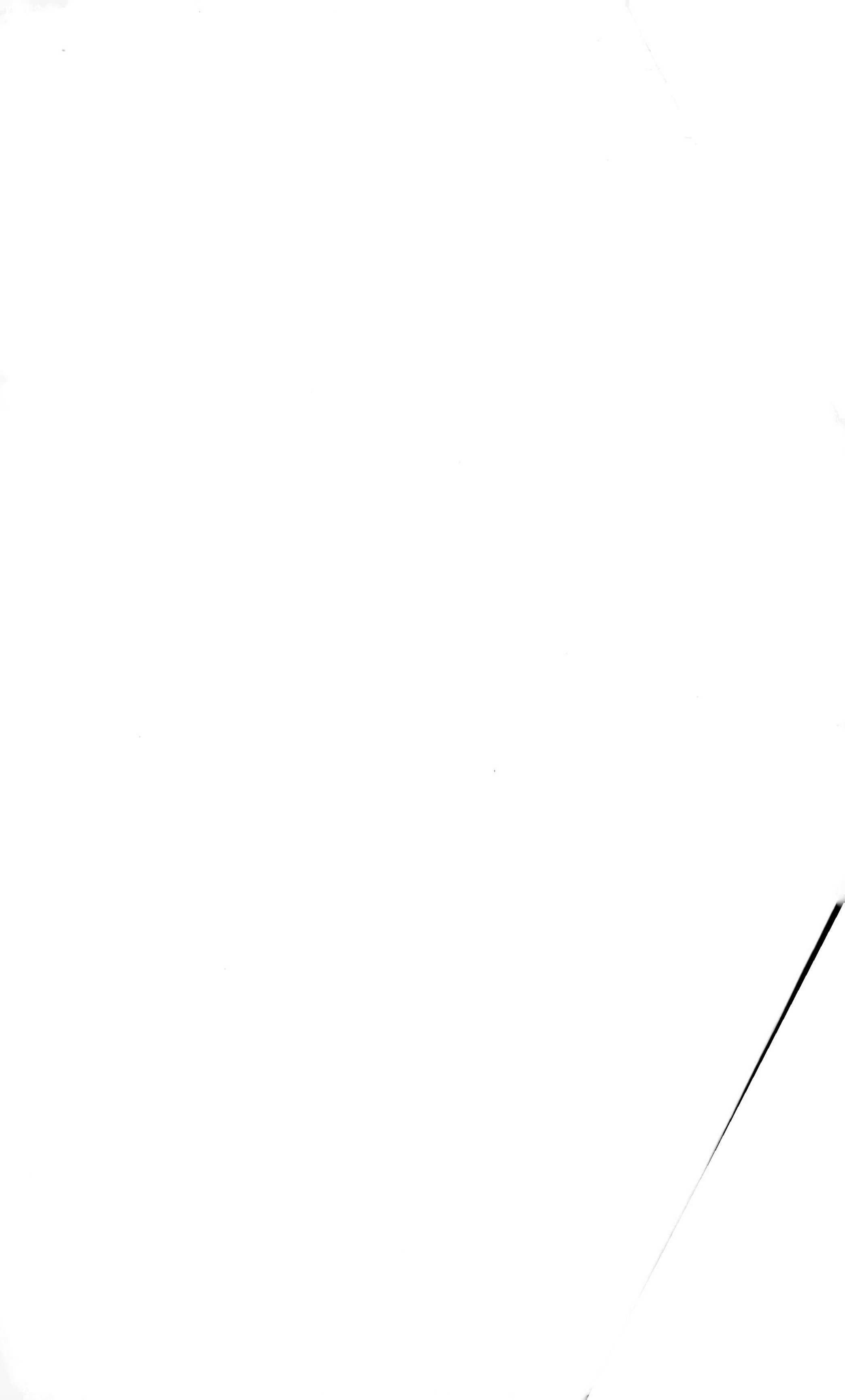

9 780595 457564